KU-497-442

Julia O'Faolain

No Country For Young Men

Penguin Books
in association with Allen Lane

Penguin Books Ltd, Harmondsworth, Middlesex, England
Penguin Books, 625 Madison Avenue, New York, New York 10022, U.S.A.
Penguin Books Australia Ltd, Ringwood, Victoria, Australia
Penguin Books Canada Ltd, 2801 John Street, Markham, Ontario, Canada L3R 1B4
Penguin Books (N.Z.) Ltd, 182-190 Wairau Road, Auckland 10, New Zealand

First published by Allen Lane 1980
Published by Penguin Books in association with Allen Lane 1980
Copyright © Julia O'Faolain, 1980

Made and printed in Great Britain by
Richard Clay (The Chaucer Press) Ltd, Bungay, Suffolk
Set in Monotype Times

1

In late March 1922, the following item appeared in the columns of the *Gaelic American*, a journal published in New York City, price 5 cents:

AMERICAN CITIZEN
LATEST MARTYR TO IRISH CAUSE

Word has been received by relatives in New York and by The Friends of Irish Freedom of the death of one of their delegates to the Old Land. John Chrysostom Spartacus (Sparky) Driscoll was killed while performing his mission which was to observe the fighting being fomented in Ulster by agents of the Crown. The time-honoured tactic, 'divide and rule', has set Irishman against Irishman in a last-ditch try by the old usurper to strangle the new Free State at birth. This act of perfidy strikes at John Bull's oft-aired claim to 'justice and fair play'.

Do the tyrant-masters think such acts will stop Irish men and women from taking part in the onward march for the regeneration of their country? Do they believe that the sight of young Driscoll's corpse going through the streets of Dublin will make Irish people more loyal to the English connection? What fools they are! What fools they must remain so long as they believe so!

The sympathy of a wide circle of friends and business acquaintances in New York, Massachusetts and other parts of the United States will go to the parents and relatives of this new martyr to an old cause. Sparky Driscoll could have lived a life of ease and comfort if he had so wished. Instead, he felt that the Old Land needed him and hearkened to her call. Deliberately, he chose the road of the Patriot and it led him, as it has led many, to a tragic end.

His father, Mr Aloysius Driscoll, has always been prominent in the Republican movement in New York as has Sparky's mother, Mrs Mary Driscoll, whose children have not forgotten the lessons in Irish Nationalism received at her knee. All have remained identified with the IRB Veterans' Association, the Gaelic League, the Clan na Gael and other similar organizations working for Irish freedom.

At the last meeting of the Robert Emmet Club a resolution was passed sympathizing with the family in their irreparable loss.

Beannacht De le h-anam.

1979

They didn't call it 'Children's Hour' any more but the ingredients were the same: two children, a dog, some mystery – what? Sister Judith was galvanized in her chair, her mind jerking from the screen before her to one whose picture curdled as though she had failed to adjust the setting. There was tension in her stomach and in the back of her neck.

Something was wrong.

She must – what must she do? Oh God, she begged, let me remember before it's too late. Please, Jesus, I know it's important. Remember, Oh Most Gracious Virgin – something appalling was about to happen. A knifing? There was a gap in her brain: a hole, and meanwhile . . . A hole?

Terror ebbed. Like water from a basin. Like blood. There had been a redness before her eyes but now it was all right. She was sitting here watching television and the well-spoken children were laughing with their dog. It was 'Children's Hour' and she must have dropped off, got confused. The dog was the link.

Hers had been called Bran. A red setter. Dog? Digging? That was it. A hole. She closed her eyes and the image steadied. Bran's bright body rippled like a feather boa,

8

doubled, laboured. His chocolate nose was down, his feathered feet digging in the backyard of their house long ago. The soil flew. It was suspect, too soft, recently tampered with. Oh Jesus, Bran, stop! Judith was seventeen and the country in a perilous state. She hauled at the dog's collar, screamed. She was seventy-five and wanted to see what happened next but the image had gone jumpy and her seventeen-year-old self pulled the dog from the hole. She was sweating. Both Judiths were clammy and terrified inside their clothes.

She had been found wandering the corridors and once – though that was years ago – naked at the convent gate. In the moment between sleep and waking, she had felt her night-dress – flannel – muffling the doors to her soul and had twitched it off. You could hardly explain such a thing by daylight, though could you? Especially to unflappable nuns! So she'd let them think she'd done it in her sleep.

Her fear was that they'd make her undergo more electro-shock.

'Look,' a doctor had told her. 'I accept what you say. You've lost or nearly lost a memory. Well, why not let it go? Just relinquish it?'

Cheerily smiling at her, he might have been proposing to remove an old tooth. 'Poison your system to hold on to it,' he might say, 'not so pretty any more either. Why don't we get you a nice false set, h'm?'

Old tooth? Old heart? Your memory was you.

'You think someone might fear your testimony?'

He was humouring her. Did he think her senile? The next thing she said sounded it. 'The past can kill,' she told him. 'There's an urgency,' she said, 'about this anxiety. I feel it.'

'Ah, that's nerves,' he told her. 'Tension. The urgency is in yourself. I won't say "relax" because I've found that that only makes people tense up. Worrying about worry, ha ha, has half the population on pills. I'll let you have some if you like, mind, but what I tell my patients is "a little worry keeps off worse".' Laughing. Pleased with himself. *Did* she want pills, he asked.

No, she did not. What about her dreams now, he wondered.

'Do you think you see Christ?'

She was astonished. 'I'm not mad.'

No, no, but she'd *said*, hadn't she, that she dreamed of a man who held his guts in his hand. 'Now, that would remind you of the statue of Christ showing his sacred heart, h'm?' After all, he must be thinking, she was a nun and who else would nuns dream of?

She refused to see any more doctors and Reverend Mother said all right. That had been years ago. The side door to the building was kept locked so that she couldn't get out in her sleep even if she had wanted to.

'We'll have to pray that there's never a fire,' said Reverend Mother.

Sister Judith told Sister Gilchrist that she would no more think of going to confession to that new pipsqueak of a chaplain than she'd fly. 'With all respect, Sister,' she'd said, 'it's what he is. How old is he? A teenager?'

'He's an ordained priest, Sister.'

'Well, they must be badly off for priests.'

'They are.'

Sister Gilchrist made an effort to explain, although, with Sister Judith you never knew whether it was worth while. 'There aren't enough to go round the religious houses,' she told her, 'so we share him with the Dublin Juvenile Prison. It must be hard for him to change his style when he comes to us, and style,' said Sister Gilchrist, speaking against her convictions, 'is but a superficial thing.'

'Poor Father Merryman, God rest him,' said Sister Judith, 'was helping me with my therapy before he died. He became very involved in helping me to track down my buried trauma.'

'He had great patience,' said Sister Gilchrist absently.

'He was fascinated,' Sister Judith corrected her. 'He thought that it might turn out to be of National Importance if only I could remember it. It was a setback to me when he died. Recently, however, I've made some advance. I'm back on the track, thanks to television.'

'I see you've been watching it a lot.'

'I watch the murders,' said Sister Judith. 'I get a fizzle in my extremities whenever I watch an axe or sword murder. Ha!' she cried in a muted shout and shook her fingers at Sister Gilchrist. 'A tremor in the tips,' she said, 'like in a diviner's rod. What do you say to that, Sister? I watched *The Seven Samurai* again last night and afterwards my dream was several degrees clearer. Almost understandable.'

'How do you know the television didn't cause the dream in the first place?'

'I've been having my dream for fifty-five years, Sister Gilchrist, as you know right well, and for how long have we been allowed to watch television? Tell me that? I told you that they gave me shock treatments years ago to destroy my memory.' Sister Judith managed to nod her head and at the same time roll her eyes. 'What do you say to that?' she insisted. 'Was there a plot or was there not? I see blood,' she added, 'in all my dreams. Gushing in a jet, Sister Gilchrist. Red.'

Sister Gilchrist had other things on her mind. Poor Sister Judith was in her manic mood, as she had been before, but more important things were going on in the convent. 'Maybe,' she said repressively, 'you're remembering a visit to a butcher's shop? Or you might have lived on a farm? People slaughtered their own animals in your young day.'

'And the guilt?' Sister Judith demanded. 'What about the guilt?'

'Were you ever a vegetarian?'

Sister Judith would not dignify this by a reply. She continued to flap her fingers and nod.

Sister Gilchrist sighed. Something would have to be done about her. 'Are you coming to the meeting?' She hoped Sister Judith wasn't.

'I may. Depends what's on "Children's Hour".'

Reverend Mother had decided a year or so back that Sister Judith might as well spend her days in the television room as getting in everyone's way. There was merit to the argument, though things had perhaps gone too far, for the poor thing was becoming detached from reality. But what could one do? The old mechanical tasks like lace-making and pea-shelling had been abandoned and she was too old for heavy work. Best leave her to her hobbies.

Unfortunately, recent developments in the Order as a whole were threatening such individual arrangements. A new Savonarola had arisen and instead of being burnt at the stake was being allowed to disrupt a great number of lives.

Sister Judith's life had been disrupted before. Her lost memory was disruptive and the ones which did come to mind were of being bundled from pillar to post without having much say in the matter. Her mother had died when she was small and Judith had been boarded out early. Between the ages of five and seventeen, she had attended a school with the ugly name of Mucklea. It was run by nuns and housed in a sharp-angled, Gothic structure built of Victorian brick. Her clearest, least-troubled memories went back to the time spent there where not much had happened. The grounds were kept in rigorous trim. Topiaried trees and slices of lawn contrasted with the surrounding landscape which was a bog. This region was as active as a compost heap and here the millennial process of matter recycling itself was as disturbing as decay in a carcass. Phosphorescent glowings, said to come from the chemical residue of bones, exhaled from its depths. 'Bog' was the Gaelic word for 'soft' and this one had places into which a sheep or a man could be sucked without trace.

The bog was pagan and the nuns saw in it an image of fallen nature. It signified mortality, they said, and the sadness of the flesh, for it had once been the hunting ground of pre-Christian warriors, a forest which had fallen, become fossilized and was now dug for fuel.

Sometimes, in later life, Judith would say 'my memory is a bog', referring as much to its power of suction as to its unfathomable layers.

The dog's nails scratched on metal and Judith's first thought was: guns. A truce with England had been signed in July and there were caches of arms all over the country. Her brother and her sister's *fiancé* would certainly not tell *her* what they'd got hidden in the backyard. The best strategy was ignorance if a house was raided and – suddenly it came back to her – the reason nobody had noticed the fresh softness of the soil before this was because she herself had taken a flagstone from on top of it two days ago to make a tombstone for her pets' graveyard. There had been nobody to notice or stop her because Seamus was off drilling men in the hills, their elder brother, Eamonn, had been killed two years before and Kathleen's fellow, Owen, was in prison. Probably Kathleen didn't know.

Cover it then? Yes. Quickly. Her throat contracted painfully at the danger, for a neighbour could burst in, someone who'd been drinking in her father's pub, a spy, someone pretending to need the privy and be lost. At the same time – she recognized Eve's and Pandora's evil curiosity in herself – she knew she'd never sleep peacefully in the house again if she hadn't satisfied herself as to what was there. It was twilight, misty, as good a time as any to be digging here among the crazy pavement. Why should anyone see? Bran would alert her if they came.

'Who's there, Bran? Get him, boy,' she whispered, while her Pandora fingers scrabbled in wormy soil. Better get a spade. The dog's ears pricked. He moaned questingly, ran round in a foolish little circle, then came back to the hole.

The metal was part of a tea chest. Inside was a fisherman's bag lined with rubber and inside that were wads of green notes. American dollars. Twenty-, fifty- and hundred-dollar bills. Big wads of them. How many? There must be thousands there. Terrified, as though she were handling sin – guns would somehow have been better after all – she stuffed them back into the bag, the bag into the box and the box into the hole. Then she got her spade and spread the soil over it, tamped it down and covered it up again with the flagstone. She threw withered leaves over the edges of it, then made a quick survey of the points of access to the yard to make sure she had not been seen. After that, she went into the kitchen and collapsed in a chair. Her grimy fingers on the arm-rest were beating a wild tattoo. That kind of money – there must be thousands – frightened her. Had she misread the figures? So much! Why here? How? And whose?

After a while, she began to see the thing differently and to upbraid herself for being a silly convent girl. Of *course* the lads would have to have large sums of money if they were to get guns and run a revolution. Money was power. Not guilt. Not temptation, not something from which you learned to turn away your eyes because it was above your station. Nothing was. Nothing would be. Not now. It was the slave mind the English had bred in us that thought that way. *They* didn't think money was crass or dirty, you may be sure. Oh, not they. We'd have to take a leaf out of their book. Get fierce, and greedy for the goods of this world.

That night, though, she had a nightmare that she was digging in the hole and gold coins had stuck to her skin so that she couldn't remove them. They blinded her eyes. They choked her mouth, and spies whom she couldn't see came from behind and drew a bag over her head.

JAMES

The bump of wheels on the runway set off a corresponding bounce in James Duffy's spirits. A capriole. A positive gambolling. He was alone, free and in search of a neglected aspect of his youth.

Dublin. Duv linn. Having just filled out his landing card, he remembered that his name shared a syllable with the city and that 'duv' meant black.

They taxied in. Time pleated like a fan. The city was a mnemonic. Something was said about seat-belts. This was Molly Malone's city – she of the cockles and mussels and hot-blooded fever from which none could relieve her. It was Molly Bloom's city too and the second city of Bostonian Molly Osgood whose husband had been shot by an Irish Free State firing squad and whose son lived to become the State's president. James had been boning up on the history of this island to which, in his wife's view, he had no call to have come. Crossing the Atlantic from West to East struck Therese as a regressive act. Her own people had come from Poland.

'You don't think I'd go there?' she had challenged. 'What for? To chase up old memories? Furs?' she derided. 'Vodka bottles with grass in them? Knick-knacks made from straw?

Rotting dinner-jackets? It's easy to feel good where your dollars put you at an advantage.'

Her family got begging letters from cousins in Cracow and her mother sometimes sent money but Therese wouldn't.

'They're not my people,' she said. 'I want no part of them. Yours are unlikely to be better.'

'I've got a job to do there, Therese.'

'In films!' She dismissed it. 'Stay here and I'll stake you until you get another academic post.'

'Later,' he bargained. 'This is a chance to travel a bit. See something of the world. Live.'

'Live it up, you mean? What about me?'

'Come with me.'

But Therese had a job and jobs were scarce. 'I belong to a pension scheme.' Overwhelmed, Therese began to cry. 'We can't both be grasshoppers!' she sobbed. 'Besides, why Dublin?' She had heard that Irishmen were all priests or homosexuals or both and their women driven to the ruthless entrapment of foreign men. 'My body's gone off, hasn't it?' she'd said at one point. There had been several replays of the conversation. Once she pulled up her skirt and asked whether he didn't think her thighs were getting lumpy. James felt aggrieved. It seemed unfair that only the husbands of women with lumpless thighs should feel free to travel.

'Do you deny me the right to go where my job takes me?'

'James, it's not a job. It's not serious. You've been given a chance by a guy who happened to be on the same football team with you at college. OK. Great. But if you can't do it you'll be out on your ass.'

'And now where am I?' He had a job at the University but his contract had not been renewed.

'Are you too proud to let a woman keep you? I'd hate to think you were, because *machismo* of that sort . . .'

The word made him roar. His roar made her cry. Later she informed him soberly that, according to Erik Erikson, every woman's basic motivating emotion was the fear of being abandoned.

He had stared at her in wonder. He didn't for a moment

believe she was as vulnerable as she was pretending. They had been married seven years.

The plane stopped; a few passengers clapped. The stewardess announced that anyone who had had contact with farm animals should report this to the agricultural official now coming on board.

James's suspicion was that Therese while trying to work on his sympathies had frightened herself. She had been his professor. He had sown the most old-fashioned wild oats and they had come up tame. Convenience-packaged. She had been the older woman: knowledgeable about wines and how to order in a restaurant. He had left decisions to her and she had got him to bed, to the registry office and through his Ph.D. She had failed to get him tenure but not for want of trying. Like a protective playground Mom, she made him look puny. He had to get away. For a while anyway.

'For both our sakes,' he had pleaded. 'A moratorium.'

He had got away. Dublin, as he walked down the gangway, had a taste of guilt in its air. Imported? Native? He had always heard that it was an indigenous product. He was here on parole: free and less than free like the place itself, capital of four-fifths of an island in economic thrall to the old oppressor still. He had given himself a crash course in Irish history but it was unsorted in his mind and his vision was like that of a man wearing prismatic lenses. Images made shifty rainbows. Wet air fizzed under his nose as though emerging from an aged soda siphon. A conman could probably have sold him O'Connell Bridge.

Customs and Baggage-Claim areas were one and the same: a dinky place which reminded James Duffy of airports in country resorts. Groups holding children in their arms waved from behind the exit door and added to the holiday air. He handed over his passport and answered questions about his financial resources. He was here to work on a film. Historical. No, he wasn't a famous director or actor.

'I'm nobody you'll have heard of,' he told the official, and smiled.

'What's the film about?' The man flipped through James's US passport. 'Anything to declare?'

The film was a promotional one about the IRA. But James was not about to mention this.

'Oh,' he remembered, 'someone gave me some cigars.'

Cuban cigars had recently become available again and O'Toole, the father of James's employer, had pressed a box on James when he'd stopped by the old guy's office on his way to LA airport. James didn't smoke but hadn't liked to say so.

The Customs official opened the lid of the box and a sheet of paper fell out. It was covered with handwriting and had a letterhead in Celtic script. The man began to read it and to look less amiable.

'Is this your property, sir?'

'First I've seen of it. I guess the friend who gave me the cigars must have put it there.'

'Well,' said the man, 'maybe you'd as well read it. I'm going to have to confiscate it as a subversive document.'

'You're kidding?'

'No.'

James, his laugh unfinished and unreciprocated, took the letter. Old idiot, he was thinking of O'Toole, goddamned maniac. But it was his own fault. He'd been warned that the old man was bananas, and he should have been alert for this sort of senile trick. The official was now doing a thorough search of James's suitcase.

God bless Banned Aid for giving so unstintingly to
the Irish Republican Cause . . .

Shit, he knew what this must be. O'Toole had mentioned some letter he'd got from a 'source' in Queens, New York, which he'd wanted James to see. The Customs man was pinching the interlining in James's overcoat with the air of a man whose mind was running on ripping things apart. Might he make James strip? Unbelievable? No, believable. Better see what else is in this letter.

From the earliest days Republican sympathizers here
in the US have given more than dollars for the Repub-

lican Cause, although the Irish in Ireland have not always appreciated this. Who now remembers Sparky Driscoll?

The writing was crabbed, scarcely legible.

A nod is as good as a wink to a blind horse and there is reason to believe that research . . .

James groaned.

'It's garbage,' he told the Customs man. 'You can't take it seriously?'

The man looked snotty. He pulled the insole out of one of James's shoes.

James went back to the letter.

. . . research might show that this gallant American Irishman was stabbed in the . . . gaff on their own sinister machinations . . .

'It's a joke,' said James. 'Deadpan humour – you know? Like Woody Allen?'

'Banned Aid is a very real organization, Mr Duffy. There's nothing humorous about them that people here can see.'

The next bit of the letter was in caps:

THE DE FACTO AUTHORITIES IN IRELAND TODAY MIGHT BE DISTURBED BY THE THREAT OF SEEING SUCH DIRTY LINEN DRAGGED FROM THE CLOSET OF HISTORY AND THEREBY DISSUADED FROM HAMPERING BANNED AID'S CURRENT EFFORTS TO HELP THE ONGOING STRUGGLE AGAINST AN IMPERIALISM . . .

The official plucked the letter from James's hand.

'At best,' he warned, 'it's Republican propaganda. It may be evidence of conspiracy.'

'Look, it was put in that box by a man of seventy-seven. He's gaga,' said James. 'Nobody takes him seriously. I have introductions to prominent citizens of this country . . .'

But the official claimed that this was no matter for him to decide. Would James care to step into a nearby room? James followed him to where another, apparently more senior, official was shown the letter. James thought of offering him the cigars, then thought better of it. Outside the window a rabbit – or perhaps a hare? – skipped along the grassy edge of the runway. How ridiculous if he were to be shipped right back on the plane. Seeing a hare was either good luck or bad. Idly, he wondered which. Definitely don't offer the cigars.

To his surprise he heard the second official apologize for inconveniencing him. He was older and fatter than his colleague and his uniform had the slight mutinous untidiness of fat men's uniforms.

'It's probably innocent enough,' he told James and handed him back the letter. 'Seventy-seven, you say? There's great fight in some of those old geezers, isn't there? The wife's father is the very same: a fire-eater. All cod, mind. God help us, we've a population here that's totally unbalanced as to age: all old men and teenagers. The working population emigrates, though they say that'll be falling off now with the Common Market. Yes, well, old men and young men dream, eh, Mr Duffy? Fellows like yourself and myself have to bring home the bacon. I don't think you'd have carried a dangerous document as openly as that. Sorry you were troubled. You'll appreciate that we have to take precautions.' The date on the letter, the fat official then pointed out, was several years old. 'If there's a time bomb there, ha ha, it's a bit slow. Can I get you a porter?'

By the age of seventeen Judith had been head girl of Mucklea school for over a year. The prospect of leaving depressed her.

'But child,' said the Mistress of Studies, 'if you feel that way, then our whole effort with you has been a failure. Education is a preparation for the World. You must use your gifts in the secular sphere.'

'Why, Mother, why must I?'

'It would be selfish not to. You have a father and a brother. When your sister gets married they will need you to look after them. Then there is the fighting going on . . .' The nun crossed herself. The frame of her coif gave her a look of one cut off from time. A blue shadow fell through it and lay on her skin like bloom on a plum. 'Each station in life,' she said, 'imposes duties. Women's role in our troubled times . . .' With a practised crackle, the nun flicked back the goffered coif and applied a papery cheek to Judith's. 'Safe home,' she said.

The train home rocked along a monorail above a sequence of cliffs. Lights were not supplied and by the time the bog vegetation had given way to the milky surface of the sea it was too dark to read and Judith delivered to her thoughts. Like cards fanned in a hand, these were from different suits: school and home. Home was male territory. Judith's sister, Kathleen, struggled without hope. Maids, she complained, were breakers and wreckers. Moujiks. Mohawks. They destroyed and did not belong. Country girls, gross, good-natured and alive with parasites, they had the clumsy vigour of outdoor creatures and went back to their distant farms when they got the chance. Not understanding comfort, they provided none. The house was full of men's boots, smells of unemptied chamber-pots, a clutter of unassigned hats and macintoshes. Closets held clothes which nobody had thought to throw out: Judith's mother's dresses, jackets belonging to an uncle who had fought with Kitchener and died. Drawers were stuffed with British army medals, broken rosary beads, spats, curling tongs and a device for curling moustaches. There was clutter and there were lacks: nowhere to tidy things. Fishing rods and walking-sticks stood in a deep jar. On the chimney-piece there had once been china figures but the maids had done for them. Their mother's collection of Waterford glass had gone the same way.

What bound the family together was their Republicanism. In the yard, behind the family pub, a coal pile and stacked porter barrels provided a ladder for quickly scaling the back wall in time of need. Unknown young men came and went unquestioned, sleeping on the kitchen settle or in the guest bedroom. Kathleen's *fiancé*, Owen, was active. Eamonn, their elder brother, had been killed when Judith was fifteen. Seamus too was with the lads. Only their father held back. A disappointed, mildly alcoholic man, he twitted the fighting men on the uselessness of their activity. What difference was it going to make if and when they got their Republic? he asked. Where was the money to come from to make good the promises they'd made the people who sheltered them and who had been pressured into buying bonds for the national loan? Would they ever see the colour of their money again, heh? A widower who had returned from America with less than the fortune he had hoped to make, the Da's dreams had withered and left him unsympathetic to other people's. But he was over-ruled in his own house.

Judith's memory of the train journey was like a fossil containing within itself the essential shape of twelve years of such train journeys. For two of these years there had been fighting and ambushes were a thing to be counted with. On journeys homeward she thought of the two forces which set up strains in her family. These were the war and – though she would not have called it this – sex. Sitting on the wooden seat, she remembered once – she must have been just seventeen – putting her hand to her hair. It was bright when she washed it and foamed around her head like a dandelion cloud making rainbows in the corner of her eye when the sunlight broke on its fuzz. Three or four days after washing, it began to tighten and grow dull, shrivelling into knots the colour of dried glue. It was reddish hair and in school she was obliged to wear it dragged tightly back. Judith never reached the stage of being vain since she never discovered whether she was plain or pretty. She had a suspicion that she might be about to blossom, but put off the moment by slouching and wearing unbecoming clothes. She could dance, though, and did, for the nuns had brought in a dancing teacher and, girls dancing with girls, wet Sunday afternoons were waltzed away, feet tracing spirals on the gymnasium floor. Sister Murphy played. When everyone was breathless, they leaned against the piano and talked about dances. The nun had been to two before she entered and the girls to none, but, last May, Kathleen had attended one which Judith could describe at length: a secret, sanguinary dance.

It had been organized in the ballroom of a great house whose owners were away in England. The caretaker was an IRA supporter and some wild fellows had decided that, damn it, here they were fighting and on the run, while the old cods of owners, Protestants and loyalists, were off toasting their toes in their Pall Mall clubs, and why shouldn't the lads commandeer the place for one night and have a decent dance for once, after curfew, in a proper ballroom with all the comforts, instead of behind lowered blinds by day in small parish halls? Was theirs a social revolution or was it not?

The nuns shook their heads at such talk but listened anyway. Those brave lads! Wild, wild but forgivable because at any moment they might die. The prospect purified them. They might drink and swear. They'd surely never sin against the sixth commandment. The fifth, God help us, was negotiable in time of war.

'Go on, Judith. So then what happened?'

'Well the girls, the Cumann na mBan, took charge of refreshments and decorations. Miles of bunting they made. All in green. Kathleen says it was very tasteful. They took the bags off the chandeliers and brought ferns and wove the letters IRA in fern with white carnations, and wound ivy up the bannisters, so the place looked like an indoor garden.'

Sister Murphy was reminded of the Lady chapel on Holy Thursday. Lights. Foreboding. Flowers.

'They made themselves ball dresses. Romantic, silky things. Kathleen says it was lovely.'

Images pulsed in her head. How much had she invented? Maybe her imaginings fell short? 'They put French chalk on the floor and spent an afternoon sliding on it to make it slick. Then they had the dance. They thought they were safe because the place is in the heart of a big estate full of thick trees and, besides, there was curfew. Nobody should have come.'

But someone had. A neighbour, an Anglo-Irish landowner himself, had, for some reason, dropped by, seen lights, heard music and, knowing the owners were away, gone down to the local barracks and reported. Or it could have been a poacher or an informer among the lads themselves. These things happened.

'God help us, yes.' The nuns fingered their fat beads for comfort. These were wooden, half as big as conkers and worn round their waists. They sighed for secular unreliability.

In the small hours, said Judith, two lorry-loads of Tans had roared up the drive. The scouts were taken unawares and the place surrounded. The Tans came in shooting.

It was like a Last Judgement.

A man had been killed on the spot and two girls wounded. A few managed to skip out the back and into the undergrowth but the bulk of the boys were rounded up and taken away. At the barracks, 'spotters' with bags over their heads and slits for their eyes identified known activists. A bloody night. As a result of it, several were gaoled and two lads shot – a favourite trick of the Tans – 'while trying to escape'. The story ended in depression and anyway it was time for prayers. In chapel, Judith leaned her mouth on the polished pew and tasted its bitter, resinous flavour.

'Let us *pray* for the *souls* of the *faithful* departed and of all those killed in the present conflicts.' The priest gave out the litany in a lilting drone and was answered the same way.

'*Eternal* light shine upon them and may they rest in peace.' Some priests refused absolution to the fighting men. Bishops too.

People were living on their nerves.

Kathleen's *fiancé*, Owen, had been in gaol since the night of the dance and one small, unpromising outcome of this was Kathleen's discovery that she didn't miss him at all. After a three-year engagement, though, there was no backing out.

It had been a long-distance engagement from the first, for Owen had spent three months in America in 1920, making speeches to sympathizers there and helping raise money for the cause. Then, when he came back, it wasn't long before he was on the run. Now, he was gaoled. At least he was safe inside, thought Judith, though she knew Owen himself would despise the consideration. Some windy fellows, from what you heard, couldn't wait to get behind bars.

One dream she gets – message? memory? – starts with the creaking of cart-wheels. The noise is convincingly real and guarantees that she is awake and not dreaming. There is some urgent job to be done, something she has neglected and must now see to swiftly or consequences will be dire. The exact matter at stake eludes her but there is no time to puzzle about this. The wagon is pulled by a donkey with an angular rump. Bones jut so sharply under his hide that the creak seems to be coming from them, but no, it's from the wheels. Or could it be her window? Often she gets out of bed and goes to it, flinging open the casement and even climbing on the sill, so that now the nuns have decreed that she must sleep on the ground-floor. She has put the heart across them once too often.

The wagon load is covered by a tarpaulin. Blood oozes from under it and trickles down the wheels. What's under there? Illicit salmon? A dead deer, perhaps, poached on some estate? Or butchered meat?

'Where's it going?' she asks the driver.

'North,' he tells her. 'Up to the bloody Orangemen. We'll get it on the night train. Yer man can travel in the guard's van. A butty of ours is making the arrangements.'

So Sister Judith had decided to attend the meeting after all! Well, she'd have to learn the worst sometime, decided Sister Gilchrist, and sat next to the poor thing so as to give her moral support. They were in a pew reserved for elderly nuns, many of whom were bravely smiling and trying to put the best face on things. On the podium stood a nun aged thirty who had had her hair dressed professionally and was wearing a tailored suit. Sister Mary Quinn's 'dynamic commitment' to change had the archbishop's blessing and the *nihil obstat* of the Mother House. Today, she was giving her victory speech.

'The Church,' she said, 'is a living organism. An organism which fails to adjust to change risks being fossilized and ultimately exterminated.'

A tremor was perceptible in the 'oldies' pew'. Sister Mary Quinn called it that. Sister Gilchrist had heard her do so. The oldies did not look well. They wore black. Their clothes were odd, wistful and, in most cases, graceless approximations of the habit which they had worn all their lives, until six months ago, when it had been abandoned.

'Some,' said Quinn, 'may be disconcerted.'

Undisconcertable herself, she had slipped into an old and populous convent, as a guerrilla-fighter might slip into a city or a mite into cheese, and had managed, in the course of a few years, to hollow it out. This was to be the last time the nuns would assemble in this room. Tomorrow they would begin to disperse. The building would be sold. From now on, nuns were to live in small apartments in the poorer parts of the city.

'We shall be going to the people,' triumphed Sister Mary Quinn, 'living in manageable units and acting as the shock troops of the Lord.'

Sister Gilchrist sighed. Stability had gone the way of the Latin mass. So had trust in the efficacy of prayer and with it the older nuns' sense of their usefulness. *They* could hardly be shock troops or join Sister Quinn, who was planning to live and work with tinkers and alcoholics. Quinn set great store on scoring points in the here and now. Politics and social work attracted her. To Sister Gilchrist's mind, if religion was the opium of the people, politics was the people's benzedrine.

'Future shock . . .' Quinn was crying. 'Inability to adapt . . . Old wood . . .'

Sister Gilchrist tried to find it in her heart to forgive her. Looking along her own pew, she counted five nuns in tears. She gave them a rallying smile. Beside her, Sister Judith Clancy was making a cat's cradle with her rosary and seemed to have taken nothing in. She gave Sister Gilchrist a lunatic beam of non-recognition. One small, precise charge for which Sister Quinn would have to answer on the Last Day was that she had turned this gentle madwoman loose in an alien world after fifty-five years in the convent. Here Sister Judith had been looked after and who could say that her prayers had not been as valuable as anyone's, rising clear of terrestrial folly to swell the ghostly bank of grace on which all must draw, even the most active, even Sister Mary Quinn? Sister Judith might not always recognize her sisters in religion but she did know Christ. Indeed, she worried that she personally had hurt and wounded him, and pushed this belief, not in itself unorthodox, to extremes which, though they might have been welcome in a twelfth-century religious community, were harder to accommodate today. They would fit even less well in the secular world. Sister Gilchrist had made this point to Reverend Mother but, since her defeat by the forces of Quinn, Reverend

Mother – her new title was 'the coordinator' – was a bruised reed.

'Arrangements are being made,' she had told Sister Gilchrist, 'for younger nuns to look after those who may be more of a hindrance than a help in the society to which we are returning. In Sister Clancy's case, however . . .'

'Yes?'

'A special one, don't you think?' Reverend Mother tapped her forehead. 'Now that we are going public, it would jeopardize the impact of our overall effort if . . .'

Sister Gilchrist recognized the Quinn vocabulary. She sighed.

Reverend Mother looked guilty. 'We shall,' she recited in a singsong, 'be mingling with the people. There will be little or no supervision. Can you imagine Sister Judith Clancy who, as we all know, regrettably – well, she's seventy-five and a *bad* seventy-five and there are things distressing to consider which must be considered nonetheless. She takes her clothes off, for goodness sake, Sister, in public, as you know right well. Besides, my predecessor warned me . . . You do know that her delusions are not all religious? Her mind – well.' Reverend Mother raised her eyes to heaven. 'I must ask you to trust me in this,' she appealed, invoking a loyalty which she had done nothing to deserve. 'There is a nephew,' she remarked. 'He is not best pleased at our sending her back to him but, after all, the convent has done the family a favour for fifty-five years. Perhaps, later, we might manage to have her in one of the new mini-communities. But in the first weeks there will be media coverage. Sister Quinn, you see . . .'

Sister Gilchrist saw. Reverend Mother, a latterday Pope Celestine, had thrown in the towel. Useless to expect anything from her and anyway Sister Judith's was no cause on which to make a stand.

'Isn't it great news, Sister Judith, that you'll be going home?'

'Home?' Judith thought of heaven – Christ clasping her to his bleeding bosom – and of her childhood. 'What home?'

'To your grandniece and -nephew's place. They're married to each other. Cousins. They must have got a dispensation for that, I'd say. It'll mean you'll be with all blood relatives. Isn't that grand?'

'I want to stay here,' said Judith. 'I don't want to go where I'll be a burden. Do I *have* to go?' she asked the falsely smiling hussy in front of her. She didn't know who the hussy was but knew a false simper when she saw one. She braced herself. 'Do I?'

'Yes,' said the hussy, showing her true colours and switching off the smile. 'This place is closing down and we're all going back to live in the world.'

'Oh law,' said Judith, 'did they have a revolution then? Like in France? Are they closing down the convents?' she asked.

'We're closing them ourselves. We're giving up our own spiritual comfort so as to put ourselves at the service of the people. To do corporal works of mercy. We feel the times are ripe for it. There's no use making heavy weather of this, Sister Judith. The decision has been taken collectively by the community. You'll just have to make the best of it.'

Sister Judith closed her eyes and told herself, 'Live, horse, and you'll get grass.' When the powers-that-be took a decision all you could do was bow your head and live inside it.

2

The bus for the city terminal – *An Lar* – was cream-coloured and streamlined as a butter pat. While waiting for it to move off, James read the local paper. A headline ran: GARDAI URGE RETENTION OF DEATH PENALTY. The Gardai were the Irish police and the penalty aimed at members of the IRA who might be planning to kill them. Republican police *v.* Republican army might sound like a football game but James had done his homework and knew that the republics did not coincide. One was a place of the mind. He had received briefing on the matter from his employer, Larry O'Toole.

'Language over there,' Larry had warned, 'is highly charged. Better avoid the word "republic" completely. Don't say "free state" either. That's obsolete. The best bet is to say "the twenty-six counties". That shows your sympathies. The ideal republic, you see, would have thirty-two.'

Larry's main directive was 'don't make waves'. Though the incident at Customs had surely been no more than a ripple, Larry would not have liked it. He was nervous about this film and about his irresponsible old father who was putting up the money for it and had to be kept sweet. The Irish authorities, as Larry had impressed on James, also had to be kept sweet.

James had run into Larry at a radio chat-show on the Irish situation. James had been standing in for a sick colleague.

'You go,' the colleague had begged James. 'You have an Irish name; you're articulate. That's all they want: someone to hold the ring and keep the two sides from disembowelling each other.'

The radio station was in a kind of shack in North Hollywood run mainly by volunteers and James had been surprised to find Larry there. He'd known him years earlier, when they were both on the same college football team, and the two felt an exaggerated sense of kinship on recognizing each other in that bunch of amateurs who looked as though they'd never got anything quite right in their lives.

There was an Orangeman from Belfast in a pair of bright new cowboy boots, a local priest whose gold cuff-links were slightly bigger than quarters, and a fierce, butch-looking girl from Ireland who turned out to have a remarkable knack for scoring debating points and keeping physical control of the mike. She spoke with the fluency of a mimeographed flyer, and reminded James of the years when he'd been a student, and a confetti of mimeos were forever proclaiming the need to sit in or stand up, ban some product or put your body on the line. That game was no longer played on campuses where kids now were busy grooming themselves to snatch the jobs as yet uneroded by the West's decline. On reflection, though, this girl wasn't like the Sixties radicals at all. She was tough, a tough cookie.

James felt a lurch of depression which he couldn't place right away then attached to the word 'job'. Of course: he'd lost his. He hadn't liked it but now he'd lost it and his wife might have to go on keeping him indefinitely. Therese too was a tough cookie. She had been college-age in the Fifties, as this girl had in the Seventies, and both were tough compared to James, a child of the siren decade in between.

After the discussion, Larry invited the group back to his father's house in the Hollywood Hills.

'The old man will be wild to meet you,' he told James. 'He used to travel out to see all the games when I was at college. He still talks about you as the greatest quarterback ever.'

To James, having that sort of success behind you was like having been an infant prodigy: it made you a has-been for the rest of your life. He managed not to say this though, for he didn't want to snub Larry's old man, who turned out to be an amiably leonine figure. O'Toole had obviously once been a bigger man, and a contracting spine had left him with a top-heavy lope. His eyelids were moulting and the lashless eyes themselves had an air of startled excitement. It was impossible to dodge his eagerness and James found himself surrendering to the limpid memories and smile. It was true that O'Toole could talk endlessly about games in which he'd seen James score.

'A quarterback's got to have brains,' said the old man. 'That's where you were ahead, son. You had the grey matter.' Orthodontia and lashlessness had given O'Toole a saintly expression. When he made a point, he looked James deep in the eye as though eager to trade commitment. 'I told Larry, "that boy'll go far. He has what it takes here."' Tapping his own forehead. He laughed: 'Fantastic his meeting you like this. They wouldn't let me come on the show, you know!' The big, winning smile. 'I'm too excitable.'

On the other side of some potted jade plants, the Irish girl was arguing with the priest. Both supported the Irish Republican movement, but it was turning out that their conceptions of what this meant differed.

'Democracy . . .' the girl was saying.

'There's no such thing. People's minds are manipulated,' the priest told her. 'Always have been. Always will be. What we've got to ensure is that they're manipulated to a good end.'

'I remember a field goal you scored in '67,' O'Toole reminisced, 'in a game against Penn State, was it?'

'But you're an elitist!' The girl sounded shocked.

'It tipped the balance,' said O'Toole. 'Brought the team from behind. You'd covered three yards in three downs and time was running out. Then you decided to go for a field goal. The wind was against you but you managed it. Great judgement. Cool execution.' The old fan's eyes watered. His tones were religious. 'I always told Larry: that kid'll go far.'

James braced himself for the admission he was going to have to make sooner or later, which was that he hadn't gone anywhere. Not even out of school. All he'd done was change campuses and take a job as assistant professor. Even that seemed inconclusive, as people around the campus were constantly taking him for a student. He looked that young and half the time thought he was – *had* thought so until a month ago when the sword fell and the Drama Department decided not to renew his contract. James couldn't get used to it: failure. Expulsion from the garden of youth.

'Can you believe,' he asked the old man, 'that I haven't been out of school since I was four? My mother sent me to kindergarten early and I guess I got addicted. I've been in school in one way or another since.'

'We're all elitists,' the priest was saying.

'Not me,' the Irish girl argued. 'No, Mister. I represent the ordinary people,' She was deliberately denying the priest his title. But she spoke indolently. They were off the air and she was saving her breath.

'Exactly,' said the priest. 'You decide for them, speak for them. Unless,' he spoke slyly, 'you represent God? Leaders believed that once.'

'I'm not a leader.'

'What does Larry do these days?' James asked.

'He's in films,' said Larry's father, 'and real estate. Real and unreal, ha ha! Did you say you were in the *Drama* Department at UC?'

'Was,' said James with unnecessary truthfulness. 'I've been let go.'

'Being an elitist,' the priest was saying, 'is nothing to be ashamed of. Small groups have always taken the lead. Did you know that the Irish War of Independence was planned by a clandestine organization, the IRB? They moved in secrecy,' cried the priest, 'used men who never knew of the hidden hand manipulating them.'

'You love that word,' said the girl disgustedly.

'Read your history,' the priest told her. 'The "people" as you call them,' he hammered at her, 'never decide anything. Neither do abstract forces.'

'Who did the fighting then?'

'Wrong question. Ask who paid for the gun. American greenbacks did. He who pays the piper . . .'

O'Toole was listening with amusement. 'Father Casey,' he whispered to James, 'has a theory that the Irish back in Ireland have less claim to Irishness than men like himself. Something to do with accidents, essences, and being born in a stable not necessarily making you a horse. A man with your training would grasp it at once.'

'Socialism,' Father Casey was telling the tired or indifferent girl, 'eliminated God then man. For you history is like a weather report: ridges of pressure move; confrontations occur. Can't you *see* that that's not how things happen. Somewhere,' said the priest passionately, 'an individual *has* to make a decision, exert will-power . . .'

O'Toole nudged James. 'Every game needs a quarterback, eh? Listen.' Gleaming and grinning, he contemplated James. 'I've got a dilly of an idea. Come and talk to Larry – no.' Slyness seeped up the expanse of old face. O'Toole tapped James on the shoulder. 'I'm retired,' he confessed. 'Larry likes to make his own decisions. Father Casey says I have to learn to work like Lucifer: be the power *behind* the throne.' Again that swell of zest. The old man, James saw, milked every eventuality. Obstacles were challenges, boredom a time for plotting. 'Don't go.' O'Toole gave James another squeeze. 'Got to plant an impulse. Wait for me.' Another theatrical wink and James was alone.

Amused, he got himself a drink and ate some of the cold food scattered around. The house was standard Los Angeles upper-crust taste: full of natural materials and a pretence at casualness. A tree grew through a hallway and appeared to hold up the roof. The old man, he remembered, had made a killing in real estate. Now Larry ran the firm, having eased his father out of it and into what the two described jocosely as the 'unreal estate' of propaganda for the Irish cause. O'Toole and his side-kick, Father Casey, were the mainstays of the West Coast Chapter of the Honourable Heirs of Hibernia and their fund-raising organization, Banned Aid.

'It keeps him busy,' Larry had confided to James on the drive over. 'For a while there I thought I'd never get him out of the business. You know how old guys get? He'd lost touch and in five years he'd have destroyed it.'

Now it looked as if the old man wanted Larry to offer James a job. Excited, James poured himself some more whiskey and, coming back from the bar, tripped over a girl lying on a rug. People were sprawled around the place like

shepherds in a frieze. Surprised, he heard himself confide to
her about the humiliations of having a wife in the same pro-
fession as oneself but more successful. The responses he
elicited struck him as only slightly more articulate than
those he might have got if he'd pressed the stomach of a
teddybear. 'Not *more* successful,' he corrected himself,
'successful, period. She made it. I didn't. She has tenure.' But
he cared less than he had supposed. The tenured were tethered
and he wanted to roam. Leaving the girl, he found a couch
where he stretched out to wait for his hosts. Were the other
unconvivial loungers lying about like knights of the Round
Table also waiting for tasks and assignments?

'The old man,' said Larry, 'has been dropping hints of the
delicacy of sledgehammers. He wants me to ask you to work
on a propaganda film we're making: *Four Green Fields*. It's to
raise funds for the Irish Republican cause. Before you say a
thing,' Larry lifted his palm, 'let me say that I can't think of
anyone I'd rather work with. Point number one. Number two –
I'd better spit it out right from the start – is that this is *my* film
and not my father's. The Honourable Heirs – and for practical
purposes that means my father and Father Casey – are backing
it but I'm the director. I say this because the old man's like a
kid: crafty, tries to have things his way. He'll go behind my
back to you. I know. It's ridiculous but I've got to say it. We
couldn't work together if I thought your loyalty wasn't with
me.'
    'I'm interested,' said James. 'I'm also embarrassed.'
    'You'll have to live with that.'
    Larry had probably toned down and created himself in
opposition to his exuberant, charming, over-ripe old Dad. He
explained that the film would be made in Ireland and that
therefore James and he would have to work with the Irish
authorities. No point antagonizing them, right? The old man,
he explained, was unable to see this. He had a hundred mad
ideas a day which James must promise to ignore.
    James grinned: 'OK. You're the quarterback. You call the
plays.'

                                    *

In the autumn of 1921 Judith went back to Mucklea for a final term. She was going on to be a teacher and, since experience never comes amiss, helped now with classes like map-drawing. Juniors learned from a coloured globe.

'England's cruel red,' said the geography nun, and spun it to show the colour visible at every turn. She came from a Sinn Féin family. 'They'll have to make new maps,' said she. 'Ireland, the first land conquered, will be the first to go.'

History pupils were reminded that it was an Irishwoman's frail morals which led to the English first coming here in 1169. Women bore inherited guilt.

The chaplain prayed that all should be cleansed in the blood of the Lamb.

Blood was invoked for secular purposes too, though there was debate about this. Padraig Pearse had gone too far when he wrote that 'the old earth of the battlefields is thirsty for the wine of our blood'. The allusion could be blasphemous and nuns from Loyalist families – most were – found it out of keeping with the taste and refinement which this convent had always sought to inculcate.

The chaplain's view was that the mystic sacrifice of the mass was one thing and sending young fellows out to die for no practical purpose was another and one with which he, personally, didn't hold. To seek death was next door to suicide and though nobody, to be sure, could look into Pearse's heart, they could look into his writings and what they'd find was unhealthy. All that about the wine of the battlefields was one of two things: heresy or blather. His view, as their spiritual pastor, was that it was blather. The Irish weren't heathens, thank God. They didn't go in for Voodoo and the like.

The chaplain had a loud voice. Discussion died while he was talking. Later it took up again. Politics was not a matter of faith and morals. To be sure, we weren't Africans, but accepting English ways was slavish.

'What sort of civilization is the English anyway? By their deeds shall ye know them. The Tans caught four fellows from our townland and cut the nose off of one, the tongue off another, the . . .'

'*Girls*! Please! Manners!'

Judith guessed that someone had reminded the others of her dead brother, for the subject was swiftly changed.

Travelling homewards on the rickety train, she thanked her stars that the truce was on. Last year, the lads had jumped this train more than once to rescue prisoners or shoot English soldiers travelling on it.

Kathleen came to the station to meet her with the pony and trap and wrapped rugs around the pair of them, for it was a cold old night. The pony trotted along fast and Judith sat on her hands to warm them. Everyone was grand, said Kathleen. There had been an anniversary mass said for their brother, Eamonn.

'How did the Da take it?'

'Cried,' Kathleen told her, 'drank. Got over it.'

'Have you seen the Yank?'

'He drops round. Why?'

'No reason.'

'Ha,' said Kathleen, teasing as an engaged girl will, safe in her own allegiance. 'You like him. That's why.'

'He likes you,' Judith retorted. 'I've watched him watching you.'

Sitting quietly on the edges of gatherings, she had noticed the American, Sparky Driscoll, smile and throw quick glances towards Kathleen.

'Not me,' said Kathleen. 'He's starry-eyed about Holy Ireland. Caitlín Ni Houlihan, not Kathleen Clancy, has yer man's interest. There's two of them over here now. Observing us. They send reports back to sympathizers in America.'

'What kind of reports?'

'You don't imagine he tells me?'

'When are you getting married?'

Kathleen didn't answer. She went quiet the way a marine creature will when it hides in shallows, imagining that it can fool or tire you into leaving it alone. It wasn't Judith who was harrying Kathleen. It was the question. Suddenly, Kathleen answered it, and threw the reins forward, shaking them urgently over the pony's neck.

'If the peace holds and Owen gets out of gaol,' she said, 'then right away. I'm sick of waiting.'

'So why did you wait before?'

'Owen doesn't want me left with a string of kids if anything should go wrong.'

The pony kept up its panicked trot between windy hedges and Kathleen's profile flashed in and out of starlight as loose branches strained and swung. Judith had a feeling that Kathleen herself was panicky: eager to marry and get it over with. Terrified of being told about this, she began to sing a snatch of a mocking song about matrimony, then stopped, for the thing wasn't funny.

Owen got nightmares. Judith had heard him one night last year when he'd hidden in their house. A bed had been made up for him in the kitchen and she had been asleep upstairs in her room when something woke her. The war had been at its worst at the time and she had lain rigid, wondering was it a raid, waiting for the noise of lorries pulling up and the shots and shouts. She imagined these so clearly that it took her some moments to realize that she had not heard them. Normal sounds came to her: a creaking pine-branch, wind, the distant sea, a fog-horn. None of these would have woken her though. She reached for the matches, struck one, lit a candle and padded to the door of her room. The noise was below. Putting her candle on the floor so that her own shadow leaped, she opened the door and stood on the landing outside it looking down into the kitchen. Owen was out of bed. She could make out his shape in the glow from the range. He was wearing a shirt and waving his arms, whingeing like a small child. 'Don't,' he pleaded in the child's voice. 'Don't do it. I don't know a thing, Mister. I swear to Jesus. Don't . . . Oh, how can I prove it? Please, please, Mister, don't, for the love of God, Mister.' And all the time that child's whinge as though he were fending something off while the voice broke and wavered.

'Owen!' she called down the stairs. 'Wake up!'

'Wha-at?' His grunt was strangely deep after the little voice of his dream. Nervous still but in a different way, he jumped aggressively. 'Who's that?'

'You were talking in your sleep.'

'I? Ugh? What did I say?'

'Nothing. Just noise. I thought I'd better wake you.'

'Oh, well, thanks, Judith. I suppose I was dreaming.'

'Yes.'

'Sorry I woke you then.'

The next day he asked again if he had said anything intelligible and she told him no. But another time when he was staying she had again heard the sound rising thinly and unevenly through her door. This time she let him go on dreaming, horrified at the memory of his crushed, reedy voice and at the picture which came to mind of what his face must be like. She hadn't seen it at all, for he had been turned away from her facing into the red glimmer in the range. This time she had a notion that he was not crying but bellowing. After a while she covered her head with a pillow and managed to get to sleep.

She mentioned the nightmares to Kathleen who did not sound worried.

'Sure we all have nightmares,' she said, 'all the fellows do. They say if you didn't have them you'd go mad.'

But Kathleen had not heard that shrill, pleading voice.

Judith wondered what the nightmare meant. It could be a memory of childhood: an old, childish fear which had got mixed up with Owen's present one of what the Tans might do to him if he was caught. Or – and this was the solution she liked least but thought likeliest – it might be a memory of some child Owen himself had tortured to get information. She didn't want to know and could see that Kathleen wouldn't.

Now there was the new anxiety: the money in the backyard. Dollars. Could Owen have hidden it there before he was gaoled? But if he had, why leave it so long? Wouldn't the lads need it? Surely he could have got a message out? It was true the truce was on but from all you heard one of the reasons our side had signed it was because of the lack of funds. Maybe the money was Sparky's? Did Kathleen know? Judith couldn't ask. But neither could she forget the thing or accept that there wasn't something unsavoury and wrong about the matter. It was on the edge of her mind like a speck at the corner of your eye or fluff in your nostril. Silly, she told herself, pull yourself together. But she was feeling sick. It was the motion of the trap. Kathleen was nervous and had been urging Rosie on.

'Gwan,' she shouted now to the already speeding pony. 'Getoutathat!' She shook the reins and Rosie tried responsively to gallop so that the trap shook and bumped into her rump. Kathleen checked her a little then gave her her head to trot at top trotting speed down the dark, narrow lanes.

The bus had left the rural land around the airport and was in a built-up district. From its top storey, James could see over tall garden walls to where Edwardian façades crumbled and monkey-puzzles died from below. A tuft clung to the tip of each moulting branch so that the effect was of lions' tails massed for a ringmaster's display. Lawns were mangy and windows inflamed in the sunset. Behind them, he imagined frugal lives of the sort portrayed in *Dubliners*. Repressed, genteel. Though maybe not? Things must have changed, after all, grown better since Independence and Ireland's entry into the Common Market?

'Worse,' Therese had prophesied.

On hearing of Larry's offer, her patience had melted like snow before a blow-torch. She got the notion that the thing had been fixed up behind her back.

'Hey James,' Larry had telephoned the day after his offer of a job. 'I was serious last night. Were you? Well, we'd better get our asses in gear and line the thing up. When can you leave? What do you mean you didn't know? Sure, you'll have to travel. To Ireland. Where else? Listen, I've got to know whether you meant what you said or not?'

Therese, who had herself been expecting a call, had picked up the extension.

'You *said*,' she heard Larry say, 'that you'd had it with academic life: guys sitting on their butts hatching out irrelevant monographs to earn tenure, right? And your wife breathing down your neck . . .'

James had no memory of having said such a thing, but she hung up in the midst of his denial.

'Go to hell,' she had yelled during their subsequent row. 'Go to Ireland. Have your Junior Year Abroad.'

And here he was. Riding through the city like a man in a tank. A silver drizzle had started up. Umbrellas, down below, jostled on the principle of dodgem cars, nuzzling out space for faceless walkers underneath. A grey, eighteenth-century building pleased by its visual echo of Yeats. Small shops merged into domestic architecture: B. Grady, Boot repair; Newsagents and fancy goods; Clothiers of distinction. He noted the muted mode of harangue. Even the occasional neon sign was discreet in its claims: Seafresh fish; Tony's wedding bouquets; riskily, Fryer Tuck's. He liked the decorum. But where was the myth and swagger envisaged by Larry? Did Romantic Ireland die cyclically?

'The Celts,' Larry had mused on their second meeting, 'are on an eight-hundred-year losing streak and touchy, so play it cool over there and don't let my old man foul anything up.'

Making this film in Ireland, he explained, was a delicate operation. 'It's geared to helping raise funds *here*, right? So it's got to appeal to an American audience and it's got to be hard-hitting. Our subject is American intervention in the fight for Irish freedom. Historically, it was big and we aim to show *how* big. Financial mainly. There's a parallel with Israel today. The difference is that in the Irish case the help always had to be clandestine. Was in the past and is now. In the Sixties this might have appealed to donors here. You know: conspire to help a beleaguered minority in Northern Ireland that's had WASP oligarchs sitting on their necks since the seventeenth century, denying them civil rights, etcetera. Somehow all that's less appealing now. The climate has changed. We're less hot for justice. But that's only half the story. The real trouble is that the fat cats in Southern Ireland are ass-hole buddies with London. The Dublin government is scared shitless that a successful revolution up North would topple their own regime. They do counter-propaganda which really dries up the sources of donations to Banned Aid.'

The Irish Minister for External Affairs – 'Lovely title,' said Larry. 'Don't tell me those guys are verbally sensitive?' – had been over here bad-mouthing Banned Aid and had stepped heavily on the Heirs' corns. Apparently the dude went to some banquet and at the end of it stood up to denounce the IRA as zealots and murderers.

'This really hurt the Heirs in their idealism: a sensitive part of their make-up.' Larry gave his little laugh. The word 'Mafia' had been used, he explained, and they'd been made to look bad in their own backyard. 'My father would have lynched him on the spot. But there's a strategic way to play every game, eh, James? If you can't out-physical the opposition, for the moment you use finesse.'

Larry was counting on James to moderate his father's zeal.

'Tell him you're doing whatever he wants. Then don't do it. You see, we've got to film in Ireland and need the locals to cooperate. Ergo, don't let them see we're not on their side.' This was not as difficult as James might think. The Dublin government paid lip-service to the ideal of an All-Ireland Republic which would include the North. However, as England was their major client, lip-service was as far as they dared go. 'Now we,' said Larry, 'must let them think it's also as far as *we* want to go and that we're just making a nice nostalgic movie about the Great Old Fight. That way there'll be no problem. OK? And don't breathe the word "Banned Aid". Just mention my film company. No need for the tie-up to be known.'

The film, said Larry, was in fact going to focus on old sell-outs and by implication rub today's pols' noses in the analogy. The hero was an American fund-raiser with whom the sponsors could identify. He'd gone to Ireland in '22 and got himself killed by Orangemen in the North. This linked up neatly with today's troubles.

'His name was Sparky Driscoll,' said Larry. 'He's the human interest on which we hang our history.'

James's first job would be to interview survivors of the Twenties, and to get them on tape before they died off. 'Let them reminisce. We don't want leaders. Just ordinary Joe O'Does.'

There followed some directives about camera and other equipment which Larry would be sending to Ireland and which James was to pilot through Customs and store in a place already hired for the purpose. Larry had contacts who would help in case of a hitch. James was to keep their phone numbers handy at all times. O K? And the less Larry's father knew about any aspect of things the better. The same went for Father Casey.

'Hey, do you know what that pair remind me of? Ever hear of the prehistoric rulers of Ireland and how they fought their wars? The Tuatha De Danaan? They wrapped themselves in a cloud and withdrew into the hills. Not a bad move: proto-guerrilla tactics. Unfortunately, they never came out. They lost the key to reality and turned into fairies.' Larry laughed. 'The Reverend Casey may be one, for all I know. Not my old man. He had an eye for girls in his day. But they're both great, misty plotters. Seriously, though, James,' Larry's voice grew urgent, 'I'm trying to rescue *you* from a world of faded things: campus life. That's another instance of people wrapping themselves in a cloud. A film like this is something else. It acts on people. It's live stuff. Ireland may not be the hub of the universe but you can sure get involved there and . . .'

Larry had talked lengthily about this and other matters. James listened happily. Only a businessman could have ideas so unfreighted by footnotes, suspicion or fact – off his own financial terrain, of course. He was grateful to Larry for giving him a chance to travel. In the end, he had reason to be grateful too to Therese, who gave in gracefully when she saw that she had no choice. She was a person who felt the force of moral arguments and, since she did not believe that people should be possessive of other people or ask them to sacrifice their careers, she had been obliged by her own principles to accept James's decision to go.

Reverend Mother was speaking into the telephone. 'I feel,' she said, 'that it would be misleading to describe her as *disturbed*. With us she fitted in, had her little habits, friends . . .' She tried to remember what friends Sister Judith had had. In the old days – which had been Sister Judith's days – particular friendships between nuns had been frowned on. Sad. Yes. Well. 'It might be better for you to decide, yourself, as next-of-kin, what sort of institution would suit her,' she told the grandnephew. 'We will provide fees up to a reasonable rate.'

When the grandnephew arrived, Sister Judith was watching television. Reverend Mother gave him tea in the parlour and talked reassuringly about his grandaunt. 'Surprisingly hale and hearty,' she told him. 'She has great stamina. But, to be sure, you come from a noteworthy family. Your grandfather was one of the great men of his day. I believe he used to visit her here, but that was before my time. She too, they tell me, was active before she entered. But you'll know more about that than I. Women's role was more of a back-up one, wasn't it, in the old Republican movement? With a few shining exceptions, to be sure. Sister Judith,' said Reverend Mother in a little rush, keeping her eyes away from the grandnephew's which had a disconcertingly frantic glare, 'seems sometimes to think we're living back then. In the Twenties. It's not clear whether this might be her little joke. Solitary people develop an eccentric sort of humour, don't they?'

'Solitary?' queried the grandnephew. 'Didn't you say she had friends? I was going to ask you for their addresses in case she might want to keep in touch.'

'Oh, she'll know about that herself,' said Reverend Mother. Oddity must run in the family she thought with a twinge of disappointment for, after all, the O'Malleys were distinguished. The grandnephew's hand shook and that glare was not the best balanced. To think that his grandfather . . . Well, it showed the truth of the old saw: *Great wits are sure to madness near allied*. Pope, *Essay on Man*, was it? She'd have known that in her teaching years but her memory wasn't what it had been. Oh, she'd end up on the scrap-heap soon enough herself. The hungry generations tread us down. Let's hope and pray that this fellow will treat poor old Sister Judith with a bit of humanity. An elder nephew had refused to have anything to do with her. 'Shall we go and meet her?' she asked, and led the way to the television room.

It was dark and Sister Judith was sitting alone, leaning, witch-like, over flickering shadows. It had been explained to her that her grandnephew would be coming but she might not have taken this in. If she was presently convinced that the year was 1921 – as she had been when Reverend Mother had tried reasoning with her – then the grandnephew's existence was, of course, inexplicable. She had taken her shoes off, Reverend Mother saw with vexation, and her feet flopped like a pair of pale, flat fish against the rail of her chair.

'This is your grandnephew, Sister Judith,' said Reverend Mother carefully, 'Mr O'Malley.'

'Ah!' Sister Judith shoved the guilty feet into her shoes. 'The new Principal Man, is it?'

She took her leave of the nuns with worldly aplomb and chattered pleasantly to her grandnephew as he drove her across Dublin from the suburb in which the convent was to the one where he lived.

'Dublin must look strange to you?' he suggested, and thought of old newsreels he had seen of the city in the years she had known it: men with bowler hats, horse-drawn cabs, open-topped trams – had they too been horse-drawn? – and, oh yes, the tram-wires threaded above the streets like a web darning the sky. Lamp-lighters, thought the grandnephew sentimentally, chestnut-roasters. 'It's changed a lot since your day I'll bet,' he said.

Great-aunt Judith looked about her. 'It's very old-fashioned,' she remarked, craning her neck. 'I was expecting something like the cities you see on films: Los Angeles, San Francisco. To be sure, the climate is against us, but is that any reason for not putting on a slap of paint?'

'Who are you?' she asked after a mile or so, and turned to scrutinize the chap into whose care she seemed to have fallen. He looked, she thought at first glance, like a good-looking goat.

'I'm Michael,' said Michael. 'I'm your sister Kathleen's grandson.'

'How's Kathleen?'

'She died,' he told her, 'they must have told you that. Fifteen years ago.'

'Kathleen did not die,' she argued stubbornly. 'Our brother, Eamonn, was killed in 1919 and the Yank in '22 and Kathleen's fellow, Owen, went queer in the head after the Troubles. Kathleen was all right.'

'My grandfather was not queer in the head. He was in the Cabinet for decades. He was a great man,' said Michael

O'Malley with annoyance. 'Though a bit hard to take from close up,' he added. Michael had lived his life under the shadow of the patriarch. Someone's calling the old bastard 'queer in the head' made this seem avoidable and therefore worse. 'He was brilliant,' he told his grandaunt with bullying emphasis, 'internationally acclaimed.'

'Who was?'

'The old man. Owen O'Malley.'

'Great?'

'Great,' said her grandnephew, who had suffered from a literal and crushing belief in this when he was a boy. Humour had eventually alleviated his discomfort and, by the age of eighteen, he was clowning in pubs about the difficulties of being the grandson of a patriot hero and the son of a maker of underpants. 'How do you follow that act?' he used to demand in mock mockery and was astounded to find himself with a reputation for high spirits. How *did* you honour a grandfather who, having helped forge change through violence, ended his days guarding the outcome from any further change? Wild songs and tame realities had been the fare of Michael's youth: puzzling stuff for a young fellow to swallow. In the hall of his monastic boarding-school, a fresco of the guerrilla leaders of the Twenties – Granddad to the fore – had faced an effeminate image of Christ the King. The aunt, to be sure, had given her vote to the second.

'Owen,' he told her, 'went to the League of Nations.'

'Oh?'

He wondered if she'd heard of the organization.

'My wife, Grainne, is your grandniece,' he told her. 'We're cousins.'

'You got a dispensation?'

He quipped: 'We live under hers.'

It was a joke from the days when Grainne, then a schoolgirl with a determined crush on Michael, had managed to chase him to Rome where he'd been having his voice trained. He, like the aunt, had tried to opt out of the world he knew. His singing-master had supported him and his father been relieved to acquiesce. To O'Malley senior, thrift and industry were the major virtues. He lived for his woollen mills and retail outlets and genuinely feared that prospective customers who saw the O'Malley scion in low dance halls or getting drunk in pubs might be the less eager to buy the firm's broadcloth, darning wool, and other sundries from off the sheep's back. 'Stick to what comes off my back and you'll be on his,' ran one of the firm's ads from those years, featuring a ram and a pig. Both animals had strong, thrusting torsos and a look of old O'Malley. Michael had often wondered whether the artist had been conscious of this.

'Did you know my father at all?' he asked the aunt. 'Maybe my grandmother brought her children to visit you?'

'No,' said the aunt shortly, 'never.'

She wouldn't have. He remembered now: the aunt had been 'odd' and oddities were not tolerated in the Granddad's day. Into convents with them: to God or the Devil. Dynastic families must be above reproach. Mind, that sort of treatment made the odd odder. You lived down to expectations and Michael himself, the wool-merchant's black-sheep son, had played his rake-hell role as faithfully as if his father had mapped it for him. When Grainne reached Rome – she'd got herself sent to finishing school there – Michael had been living for two years with a girl of Edwardian unsuitability. Outrageous in a period way, Theo was English and on the make – which meant that she too would have liked to have been saved – and was strategically unfaithful to Michael who, though feverishly aroused by her, jibbed at marriage. Theo, supposing her sexual hold over him to be a trump card, played her hand the wrong way. She could not know that Michael's thrashings about in her bed were half intended as aversion therapy. He saw her as Circe and one does not marry Circe. Looking back, he saw a comic pathos in her efforts to provoke him into marriage. She used to dangle herself before his friends, bestowing herself like a good-conduct prize on the soberest and going home with whoever that happened to be after a night's drinking in the bars along the Via Babbuino. Poor Theo. She became as snugly familiar as his own armpit but he had never, for a moment, been jealous about her.

Then Grainne had turned up at a concert where he was singing. He remembered that: she was pale, in a mantilla and all excited reverence for what she supposed him to be. He was to her, he saw instantly, what Theo had been to himself: freedom, a spreader of colour, something like a stained-glass window when the sun refracts through it. Seeing the family face in hers worshipping him, he had been unable to resist.

Naturally, cracks had been made when news of their engagement got out. One was: 'the fellow couldn't marry his hero grandfather so he did the next best thing'.

There might be some of the same motive in his taking the aunt home. A mistake? Too late to worry. In the pause before a traffic light, he inspected her. The family face? On the grandma's side this time? Too true. My own past and maybe my future if I swaddle my lean chin in a triple band of fat. Front-face she was shapeless like poorly impressed sealing-wax. Half buried in half-dead flesh. How old? Eighty? No, seventy-five if the Reverend Mum wasn't lying. Had the familiar profile still: lean lines among the slack, like drawings on sand. Well, here we have her then: the last of the great generation. Michael's parents – not great, pigmy in fact – had died in a car-crash some years back but he'd seen little of them for the previous decade at least. The old man had never forgiven Michael his disinterest in the business and left it in the end to Michael's uncle, Owen Roe, a go-getter, who paid Michael a not too generous stipend and had procured him an un-demanding job to keep his family fed and clad. It was in the Heraldry Commission: a joke. Let the blot on our escutcheon occupy itself with escutcheons, ha ha. Or so Michael read it: blots to blots.

'If you can't keep sober,' Owen Roe had said, 'I will not be responsible for putting you in a position where you can bring the family name into disrepute.' Then up he'd come with this sinecure: *sine cura*, worry-free. But Michael would have relished a challenge.

They came to Mount Street Bridge. He pointed out the canal.

'Looks dirty,' said the fastidious aunt.

'Polluted,' Michael agreed. Like memory's stream – was he stark, raving irresponsible to be bringing this old thing home?

He'd agreed to do so when other members of the family had refused, for – oh, a tangle of motives. Pity. Curiosity. About her. About the past. The grandfather. Himself in whose veins that exuberant generation's blood had thinned. Funny that she should say the Granddad had been queer in the head. Must have heard someone say it of herself and shifted the smear. Or maybe the whole family *were* a touch highly strung? Like race horses. Grainne was certainly not the cart-horse breed. Bad at pulling burdens, she'd slipped her harness five months back and left for London with their son, Cormac, leaving Michael to dry out alone – that was the hope. Go on the water-wagon. Kick the habit.

The move was punitive. In another era Grainne might have gone on a pilgrimage or prayed for his soul. What she'd done instead was to take a job with an old schoolmate who ran a Halfway House for Battered Wives. Michael, who could read metaphor as well as the next man, got her drift.

Needless to say, so did their friends. Some assumed she was an inmate and Michael a wife-batterer. Others pretended to for the sake of raising a laugh. Dozens of times he'd been on the point of going after her – or perhaps not quite on the point. He tended to be tipsy when this looked viable and by the time he sobered up, it no longer did.

Grainne, having fallen in love with a prince, had woken up married to an amphibian: a soak who croaked where his former self had sung. Michael, having lost his singing voice through an accident of his own devising, had, ever since, been seeking the pithy glories of grand opera through the bottom of his next glass of whiskey: her version. Home she would not come – she'd sworn – before getting a good report of him. From whom? Spies. Busybodies. Possibly the maid? He'd sacked *her* forthwith. But drank the more. How go off the liquor in a lonely house?

'Come home,' he'd bargained, 'and then I will.'

She wouldn't.

A bitch – but you could end up loving the faults you'd bred in someone. They were signs of their adjustment to you: tokens of loyalty, like a seeing-eye dog's gait. He needed her and need had bred cunning, hoho and alleluia! He was about to get her back. Now. Pronto and with no more ado. The aunt was bait. Heel, Grainne! I have you foxed.

Yesterday he'd written again:

Dear G,
     You'll appreciate that I can't hold the fort here alone
while our joint great-aunt is in residence. Between us, she
and I could burn the place down.

No sentiment. No emotion. He'd laid his trap coolly and
if he knew her it would bring her belting back.

Christ, though, why did it have to be like this?

Why was because he'd got stuck in a pattern which might
not be ideal or fulfilling or – never mind what it *wasn't*, the
important thing was that it was his. His habitat. His rhythm.
He needed it if he was going to get on with a secretly nourished
project: writing the life of his grandfather, source of weal and
woe. This had to be kept dark. People would split their sides
if word got out. Ancestor-worship, they might quip. God help
us, think of that lush, that unvoiced eejit thinking up such a
plan at his time of life. Him that never did a day's honest
work. Come here to me – the chorus clacked conspiratorially
in his head – didjez ever hear the story of how Michael lost his
voice? What? The bottle? What else? And what's open to
him now but to drown his dreams in further bottles of
Powers' Gold Label, Paddy, Jameson and Tullamore Dew.
He's a prop to the National Industry. You have to give him
his dew, ha ha.

Oh the cynicism would stymie him before he got going at all,
if they knew. So know they wouldn't. Let their first intimation
be a title on a publisher's list. Then they could laugh out of the
other sides of their mouths. They were success-worshippers,
as materialistic as the inhabitants of any other city. More so,
claimed Uncle Owen Roe who said the Church had no power
in the country any more. He should know for he was forever
sniffing the changing wind. New materialists, he stated, were,
like the new rich, always crasser than the old.

'How come so,' Michael had asked, 'that there's no divorce
here and we're one of only four countries in Western Europe
that has no legal abortion? Want to bet we'll be the last to
bring it in?'

'That's not the Church,' said Owen Roe. 'The Catholic laymen who run the country don't want it.'

'Do you?' Owen Roe was a T D.

'I have objectives closer to my heart,' said the uncle. 'I can't afford to alienate voters by backing controversial issues.'

Helping the I R A tear the country apart was the objective close to Owen Roe's heart. In the hope that he, personally, might profit from the ensuing breakdown. One reason Michael wanted to write his grandfather's biography was because that generation had left such a mucked-up heritage. When had the pure become impure? Or was purity a theatrical simplification? Was Michael, an ex-would-be singer, seeing life in operatic terms? A would-be historian now, he wanted to understand the Grandda, Prime Mover in his own and the country's life.

Until Grainne came back, though, he couldn't put pen to paper.

'Here we are,' he told the aunt. 'This is the house.'

'You live on a canal,' she said with delight. 'How pretty.'

'Yes,' he saw with surprise, 'isn't it?'

Sun was gilding the water. The grass had a deceptively clean look and bicycling children wheeled like swallows through luminous, lemon-coloured air.

3

James was remembering his last session with O'Toole Senior.

'Larry's warned you against me, hasn't he?'

James had tried to look amazed.

'I know,' the old man said quickly, 'it's not fair to ask. You're in a delicate situation.' Childish eyes held James's at embarrassing length. Old fox, thought James, this is how he made his fortune, smiling at people, being patient and open like a trap. They were in the office from which O'Toole and Father Casey conducted the business of Banned Aid. The glass in the windows was tinted brown to screen out the California sun and beyond it lay a land like old coffee grounds, sepia snaps, a world visited by blight. The blight wasn't here though, O'Toole explained, but in Northern Ireland where . . . He listed its woes. Other men his age were living in Sun City, James reflected, or they raised funds for boys' towns, research on spina bifida, their church. Larry, like a rich kid's father, had got his child-father into something too tricky for unsupervised play.

'Larry doesn't come clean, you know,' Larry's father complained. 'Never has. I doubt if he has with you, so why would I interrogate you? That's not why I asked you here.' The pale globules of his eyes were too transparent for truth. Still as frogspawn, they were hatching something.

The old man started talking about the 'real' Sparky Driscoll, some information which had come his way from an old guy he'd met at a Banned Aid rally. 'We could use it,' he told James. 'Apply pressure to the authorities over there if they give you any trouble, see what I mean? If what this man told me was true they wouldn't want it coming out. A lot of facts never come to light. Refugees living right here in America could rewrite the histories of the Russian, Irish, Chilean and God knows what revolutions for you. Losers have their own truth,' said O'Toole who, in his heyday, must have had as much time for losers as a Jansenist for souls impervious to God's grace.

Then he gave James the cigars. 'Take them. Don't lose the box. Someone will appreciate it if you don't.'

'Listen,' he said, before letting James go. He had another small favour to ask, an errand. Would James mind? It was to commission a rendering of the O'Toole armorial bearings to be painted and gilded by a professional scribe and heraldic artist. O'Toole showed some shyness about revealing such a taste. 'A present for Larry,' he winked, turning the hick request into a joke. 'The O'Toole armorial bearings are very militaristic – pikes, battle-axes – and Larry used to be a peacenik. We had some run-ins.' Well, that was behind them now. Larry might have changed. O'Toole had not. He was an unrepentant hawk. America had a mission laid on her by history . . . The soporific phrases made James's mind wander. He was on his way to the airport, and he glanced at his watch. Unfortunately, he had plenty of time and the old man knew he had. Even on the Irish question, he heard O'Toole claim, his concern was as an American. 'Listen, you might think we had no vital interests to protect there?' The slow smile exuded the triumph of a man about to confound all polemic. 'It's in our zone, though.' Seductive, not to be gainsaid, he asked James, 'What about our image? Do you know that Ireland is crawling with pressmen from Marxist countries? The West,' cried O'Toole the umpire, 'has to clean up its act.' All means were fair, he assured James, when a task was so Herculean and money was a sacred trust. What politicians couldn't do, the lone, well-heeled man of goodwill could perhaps achieve.

'But Larry, I don't know. Larry's pussyfooting. Maybe he doesn't trust me? I hope *you* do, James, I hope you'd come to me if you needed help over there? Mm? I'm not asking you to break confidence. Maybe he's up to nothing? Maybe he's just making a film? Propaganda?' O'Toole looked shrewdly at James. 'Maybe he hasn't told you yet?' Pause. The old man seemed to drowse, staring out of his tinted windows whose darkness invaded the room. Indoor gleams, domesticated like dim haloes in the murk of old religious paintings, played on chrome and Perspex and converged about his capped teeth, white hair, enfevered eyes whose shine, James now saw, was due to the old man's wearing contact lenses.

'Listen, listen,' he said, 'you've heard of young men in a hurry. That makes sense. But an old man in a hurry makes more. Time's nipping at his – my – heels. I'd like to leave my mark. Making money isn't enough. You want to use it. Put it to use. I've got a friend, my age, rings me up asking me to help on his favourite project: campaign to promote the humane slaughter of cows. *Cows*, I ask you, when the world's in the state it is. The world's given me a lot.' The old eyes swam in what might be sincerity, though they had lost the gift of projecting this effectively. In the past O'Toole had probably persuaded when insincere and now the after-image of his deceit imprisoned him. 'I want to give something back,' he pleaded. 'Through Larry – but he doesn't confide in me – or you. Don't dismiss the rumours about Driscoll's death. They were suppressed. What can that mean but that pillars of the state you're going to are afraid? Maybe, like Samson, you'll want to knock them down? More things are possible than you might think if you think big. Anyway, follow up the lead. It might take you places and what can you lose?' More pleading grins. O'Toole lit up one of his own cigars. Sweet smoke eddied in tinted sunlight. No glow: a sun-smothered smouldering.

Did James know, he asked, that in the sixteenth century one of the Cecils, chief minister to Queen Elizabeth, had been in the pay of her country's enemy, the King of Spain? 'Harder to infiltrate on that level now,' O'Toole admitted. 'In this country the Senate Inquiry and journalistic tripwire catch up. In Ireland maybe not? They have a muzzled press. "Mafia" they called us,' he growled, still smarting at the slight to the Honourable Heirs. 'Maybe it's what *they* are: a mafia? You'll never know what you can get away with till you try, eh James? Listen, I won't hold you. You've got that plane to catch. Keep in touch, eh? Oh, and I want the motto and war cries of the O'Tooles on that Coat of Arms. Know what they were? *Fianna Abu* or "victory to the fighting men" and *Semper et ubique Fidelis*. Don't forget your cigars.'

The new maid, Mary, had a voice for calling cattle home across three fields. 'We have her nicely installed now, Mr O'Malley,' she yodelled down the well of the stairs to Michael.

He'd been having a quick one in the drawing room. There were peppermints in the drinks cabinet. Popping one in his mouth, he laboured upstairs to the nun's room. Mary was a treasure all right. A niffy treasure. He'd have to drop a hint about washing, now Grainne would be coming back. On the bedside table, the nun's possessions were all laid out: a missal with beaded ribbons, a sewing kit, a silver crucifix and a framed photograph of two girls and a young man. All three wore hats pulled low over their foreheads. Michael recognized one as his grandmother. The younger girl would be Judith. Christ, Grainne had a look of her now – when would *she* turn up, he wondered. The man had a look of James Cagney.

'That's Sparky Driscoll,' said the nun. 'Did you know him?'

Waiting for chat, he saw, lonely, hopeful. What the hell sort of a chat could you have with someone who thought you might have known a man who was killed sixteen years before you were born? She was bonkers all right. Grainne would be as sour as vinegar when she saw what he'd landed her with. And here was the poor old thing desperate for company, her vowels lengthening in wistful refinement. 'Did you kneugh him?' she'd asked.

'No,' said Michael, whose impulse was to cut and run for the pub. Thank God for Mary – he'd got her from an agency after sacking Grainne's spy – whatever her shortcomings, she had country warmth to her. She was teasing the old thing now, asking had Sparky been her boyfriend or what.

The nun ignored this robust note and began to admire the room they'd given her. 'It's in lovely taste,' she gushed. 'I've always liked pink.' Her false teeth slid when she smiled.

'Glad you like it.'

'Oh yes.'

'If there's anything you . . .'

'Oh, I'm easy to please. I need very little.'

'Well, but if you do . . .'

'You've been too good to let me come.'

Deferent and over-polite, she reminded him of something and he saw now what it was: *the Governess arrives*, as shown in old cartoons. Generations of women must have stood like this in unsatisfactory bedrooms, protesting their love of pink. Corralled off from servants and family, they would have eaten lone meals on trays, as Sister Judith was going to have to do in a little while since Michael definitely did not feel up to dining with her *en tête à tête*. There was no point overestimating your forces. He felt weepy already, might weep, would certainly get drunk. Out, out. The house had depressed him before but with this voice from the siren past there would be no getting through the evening. He must leave before he disgraced himself. Without hurting her, if that could be managed. A governess. Yes. Hers was the governess generation. Ireland had peopled the world with them: nannies, governesses, mother's helps. Catholic and English-speaking, they'd been in demand all over Catholic Europe and had travelled in their thousands: decent spinsters for whom there was nothing at home. At least the Granddad's failed social revolution had got rid of that deference. Had it? No. It was gone everywhere now. Not just here. The grandfather was not God Almighty, Michael. Beware of the personality cult, *post hoc ergo propter hoc* and other pitfalls. She was smiling sadly, shyly and with a decided shiftiness to her teeth. He couldn't stand it: the pain of the world. Grandfather, etcetera, let this chalice pass.

'Listen,' he fumbled. 'Mary here will make you comfortable. Snug. Can you bring up the TV set, Mary? On your own? You can? Ah, you're a fine strapping girl. Unfortunately I have to go out or I'd have enjoyed a chat. My wife will be coming home soon. Our son too. Then we'll make acquaintance as a family. Meanwhile I have this errand. Will you be all right? You will? Grand.'

He smiled. They smiled. He fled.

*

Rain fell in ropes and wind shuttled through them, webbing the city in its ephemeral weave. Vertical rain, horizontal wind. Vertical. Horizontal. Sister Judith concentrated her mind on the monotony of this but couldn't daze herself into sleep. Monotony was what she craved, missed and would probably not recover. In the convent, clocks, bells and timetables had been reliable. Holy Offices, the sounds from the school – breaks for prayer or hockey, elevenses or singing – had been as cosy as the functions of her own body. More predictable. Reassuring.

It was extraordinary being without them. Like a loss of gravity or the proper alternation of night and day. Some science-fiction thing she'd seen on TV had taken its characters to a place where these were lacking and psychic disturbances had been set up. Sister Judith understood completely. You needed your routines. You needed them more as you grew older. She would have liked to explain this to the girl but felt she wouldn't be interested. The girl was kind but scatty.

'Need anything, Ma'am?' she'd asked. 'I'm dashing out for an hour or so. Can I take you to the lavatory now?'

'Not now, thank you,' said Sister Judith, who needed to be able to count on having someone there at given times. She could arrange her needs but only if she had a schedule.

'Like a cup of tea before I go?'

The girl was some sort of maid, a bit like their own maid, Bridie, at home long ago. Long, *long* ago. Bridie, if she was alive at all, would be ninety.

'Tea?'

'Ah no, thanks.'

Tea would make a trip to the lavatory more necessary and if Bridie was going out, better not. This house was a desperate rookyrawky of a place. Nothing was on the same floor as anything else. Sometimes Sister Judith could manage stairs very well. Sometimes she felt quite spry. But she couldn't count on being spry in an hour's time. When your body was not predictable, other things had to be. Sister Gilchrist had helped her in the past. She was getting on herself and understood. Now she'd gone to Birmingham to stay with a married sister. Later, she would come back and teach Latin in the slums. It surprised Sister Judith that they should want to learn Latin in the slums but Sister Gilchrist said there was a big enrolment and the nun teaching it now wanted to be released for more active work. So Sister Gilchrist could still be of use, unlike Sister Judith who was a burden to poor Bridie. 'No thanks, Bridie,' she said.

'My name's Mary,' said Bridie.

'Ha ha,' said Sister Judith a bit nervously, the way you did when you didn't see the joke.

GRAINNE

'No point travelling First,' the man at the Euston ticket office had advised and Grainne took him at his word. If he was wrong, Cormac and she could pay the difference on the boat. They bagged seats on the top deck in what seemed to be the prow and she was just as glad she had decided against taking the plane. Returning to one's husband from an escapade should not be done too extravagantly on family money.

Shopkeeper's ethics, she jibed at herself, then thought, why not? Hadn't her great-grandfather kept a pub? She laughed at the way the wind was ruffling Cormac's hair. It was the colour of kelp and some shades lighter than her own. Freckles the same colour saddled the bridge of his nose. Apart from them, his skin, like her own, was bluish white: skim-milk colour. 'Like a corpse warmed over,' his mates liked to tease but in fact he'd be smashing-looking once he got out of the awkward stage.

'Oh Mummy, we're turning,' he wailed. 'The boat is turning.'

She too felt stricken by the omen for now they would be travelling at the back. Engines thudded. Fixtures creaked and a sudden turbulence of wind whipped women's hair into their eyes.

'Want to change to First then?'

'The best seats will be taken now. Let's stay here.'

'Righto.'

A man near them leaned over the deck rail, holding a schooner of beer. Drinking at 9 a.m. She noted this with the trained eye of a woman married to an alcoholic. The man waved and foam from his beer flew sideways then alighted on the foam below. People on the departure jetty waved. On the deck, four small children, each with a miraculous medal safety-pinned to its sweater, waved too at the last of the green Welsh coast, then turned to their mother to ask for food. Their carnival greed had something moving about it. Maybe it had its origins in some memory of the famine days?

'Wotcha got there, Mammy, eh?'

Toppled, the mother's shopping bag disgorged mince pies, Mars bars, Jacobs' Club-Milk biscuits, potato crisps, apples and bottles of sticky lemonade. Grainne turned to nudge Cormac, then remembered that her amusement might be taken to be snobby and that she was on duty as a Mum. Cormac was only fourteen.

She had a brief, forlorn yearning for adult company and reproached herself for this. Lots of women *liked* being with children. It made them feel fulfilled. It made Grainne feel useless and used up like a ruff of old blossom drying in the dimple of an apple.

In the seat next to her, a teenage boy and his girl, dressed in motorcycling gear, sucked lollipops and a small child practised with consistent ineptitude on a toy flute. The boat had begun to heave. Sooner or later, some of these people would be sick.

'Sure you can stand it here?' she asked Cormac.

'I don't care about anything except that we're going home.'

That was a reproach. Or it might be forgiveness now that she was taking him back. Don't inquire. Don't confront. Cormac had some legitimate gripes.

'I'll see how far forward we're allowed to go,' he said, and left her with a quick, apologetic grin. Wanted to be alone? All right. She watched him pick his way between orange and blue-bag blue backpacks. A girl smiled at him and Grainne felt a nip of sorrow and excitement, a thrill as tart and mouth-puckering as a first bite into unripe fruit. Her own sensations were always taking her by surprise. Cormac would be a tall man, taller maybe than his father. He was already as tall as herself: five feet eight. His wrists stuck out from his school blazer. Poor Cormac, what a mistake the English sojourn had been for him. Well, if she left again she wouldn't take him. She didn't suppose that she would leave again.

'Remember you're always welcome,' Jane had said. She'd have to say that, wouldn't she? Grainne laughed aloud, then, embarrassed, pretended to be choking a sneeze. She'd been thinking of a joke about two old biddies discussing the hospitality of a third. 'Did she offer ye a cup of tea, same?' the first one asks. 'Ah, she did,' the other tells her, 'she asked me but she didn't press me.' A towny's joke, it was an affectionate and nostalgic mocking of old-time country rituals whereby you were meant to refuse once from politeness and so the first offer didn't count. Grainne had seen the same thing happen in Italy when she was there as a girl. People sitting in a train would never eat without asking you to have a bit, but you were expected to say no. She sighed, remembering. Italy was where she'd really got to know Michael. Fifteen golden years ago. Ah well. She and Michael had been apart five months now and the separation had resolved nothing. He was drinking – she had her sources – as much as ever.

'You can't carry him,' Jane had said. 'Leave him. Take a job. The longer you hang on the worse it will get. You're thirty-three. You're not getting younger.'

This was disturbing advice to get from someone as good and concerned for others as Jane. It boiled down to saying: put yourself first, and this, besides running counter to tradition, was risky. Supposing you took the advice and then messed up your life? You'd have neither sympathy nor the rewards of virtue. Jane was unmarried, had never, Grainne guessed, had a man at all; her counsels sprang from an amputated logic which left out most of the things which swayed Grainne.

'What things?' Jane had asked, and Grainne had been unable to say.

'Look,' she'd tried, 'I don't mean sex.' Because people who had never had any gave *that* the wrong weight and Jane, who had taken courses in psychology, saw it everywhere.

'My whole adult self grew up with Michael. Oh, I know people like me divorce, but then people lose their minds and memories too and are cured and function. They *must* be diminished. They'd have to be. They'd be emotional amputees remade with false bits and hollows in their heads. Horrid. Sad.' She was stopped by Jane's face which said, plain as a pikestaff: sex, habit, inertia.

Michael, at good moments, though, was still the best company Grainne knew. He wasn't only part of her; a partner in a shared past, he justified her, needed her – they were fond of each other, damn it. Those who did understand were the women at Jane's Halfway House for Battered Wives, where Grainne had spent the last five months. Jane had been begging her to come since she'd started the place. There was no therapy, she claimed, like helping others and it would give Grainne a new perspective on marriage.

Michael had found one of these letters and read it. 'That cow!' he'd shouted. 'She's in her element. The fox who lost his tail put it about that tails were an excrescence. She'll never get a close perspective on marriage anyhow.'

Men and Jane had never seen eye to eye. Listening to her on Michael or Michael on her would drive you into the arms of the one under attack. Grainne felt like a bone between dogs. The other women at the Halfway House said they knew just what she meant.

'Of course, she's a very *decent* person,' they would start out cautiously and Grainne would know that they wanted to gossip. 'Buts' were implicit.

'Yes,' she'd say.

'God help us, though, she doesn't know much about life! I suppose she's as well off the way she is.' Their laugh was pure subversion.

Most of the women were Irish and Grainne understood them. They wanted to gossip because, in the Home, Jane was boss. She was in the position of the men they had fled and one of their consolations had always been complaining about these men. Analysing and cutting them down to size restored pride. Anyone in authority must expect the same treatment.

Grainne, Jane's assistant and a refugee from marriage, had a foot on each side of the fence and found that this made her look harder than was comfortable at divisions within herself.

Her coming here had been an impulse: a light-hearted i
exasperated bolt from Michael, who needed shaking up. Let':
see how he manages. A spell on his own should teach him a
thing or two. Only slowly did it strike her that it might also
teach *her*. She resisted the doubts which comparison with the
other refugees aroused. Their predicaments were unmanage-
able; hers was not. She had taken French leave from her
husband on the assumption that everyone would tell her to go
back. Surely that was the safe advice to give? Grainne had been
prepared to reject it but never got a chance. Mores, it seemed,
had changed and she was shaken to find how fashionable it
was to attack marriage and how little resistance the institution
seemed to have. She had recently heard women pull it apart
as they might unravel a knit shawl and say: 'See, all there was
to it was some crinkly wool, a few warped impulses.' 'Let's
break down the argument,' someone was always saying at the
group meetings where the battered women were encouraged
to take a cold look at their problems. Grainne didn't want to
look coldly at hers, and breaking things down began to fill her
with indignation. She wanted to warm up, solder and stick
things together. She preferred fights to analyses and missed
the nesty vigour of family life. What did it matter if her concern for Michael was 'really' cover for her fear of independence? It was still concern. She didn't care to find out whether
her move here had been theatrical or neurotic, directed against
Michael or herself. She was just glad that it was here she had
come and nowhere else. Precisely because this was a 'halfway'
oasis, return home from here would not look like the capitu-
lation it would have seemed if she had taken a job or signed
up to work for some diploma or degree. Maddening though
Michael might be, she didn't, she began to see, really want to
break up her comfortably unsuccessful marriage in which the
worst fights had long ago been fought, the sourest words
spoken, and bad memories begun to mellow into jokes.

When the time came to go home, she felt some shame at
leaving the other women behind. But one felt *that*, she
remembered, even on leaving a hospital. It just showed how
you could get sucked into a group, especially when the common denominator was pain. Oh dear – might that apply to

marriage too? Nonsense! Pull yourself together, Grainne!

She thanked Jane sincerely, saying that the experience had indeed given her a new perspective on marriage and that she hoped Jane would not regard her as one of her failures. It was the wrong note to sound and Jane did not smile. The real failures of the Halfway House were the women who went back to violent husbands and, worse, came back again with blacked eyes, broken ribs or punctured kidneys. Each time this happened Jane got very upset.

'I can understand them going back,' she told Grainne 'because they've nowhere to go. This isn't a permanent home for them. How could it be? But they *could* get jobs. Not good jobs but jobs. Something to tide them over. They don't go back from need. They go back because they're addicted.'

Grainne began to laugh. 'Addicted to men?'

'To violence. It's addictive. I've learned that. There's an excitement . . .' Jane looked knowing and Grainne had an insight into the women's dislike of her. Her experience was unearned and her advice clinical. Yet she was no doctor – just a woman like themselves. She never laughed, probably from respect for the unhappiness all around her. The battered women, though, laughed at the drop of a hat.

'Ah well, strife's better than a lonely bed,' said one of them when she heard that Grainne was going back to her husband.

'Cormac will be pleased anyway,' Jane conceded. 'This trip hasn't worked out for him. Will you be sending him back to his Irish school?'

'Oh, I think so. He hates the English one.'

'You're not afraid that he may fall under bad influences again? His great-uncle's?'

One reason for taking Cormac to England had been Grainne's anxiety when, some weeks before leaving Dublin, she found a stack of IRA papers under his bed and subsequently discovered that he had been attending meetings of a junior club affiliated with Sinn Féin. Michael's uncle was to blame.

Where was Cormac now anyway?

She stood up, leaving her beauty-case to hold her seat, and walked around the deck, then down a gangway into a room full of juke-boxes and slot machines. No sign of Cormac. She tried a cafeteria and TV room where a few teenagers lounged. Further on, people were queueing to buy duty-free cigarettes and beyond them was the bar. Cormac could hardly be there, could he? He was under age. She walked in anyway, deciding to have a tonic water to help swallow some aspirins. Ten-thirty a.m. The boat had been at sea no more than an hour and a half but the place was already awash with beer, the counter sticky with it and half-drunk glasses on every table. She took her tonic to an empty one, counting four men asleep before their tankards as she passed. Probably they had been up all night, travelling from London, Manchester, or Birmingham to meet this early boat. They were recognizably Irish navvies. She had seen their like doing roadwork all over London. Blowzy, chubby, and the worse for wear, like angels fallen from some baroque ceiling, stripped to the waist in warm weather and stunned by the vibrations of their pneumatic drills, theirs was the fate with which recalcitrant Irish students had been threatened from time out of mind. 'Work,' she remembered teachers warning young boys, 'eat your books, pass your exams or you'll end up digging the streets of London.' Girls might be expected to end up *on* the streets but the less delicate threat was rarely voiced. Rocked by the boat's movement, one of the sleepers' heads twitched across the table until his hair was soaking, like sedge, in a ring of beer.

On her other side, four young labourers were telling jokes. They leaned pink heads together to whisper, then, in unison, like the opening petals of a flower, leaned outwards to guffaw.

'A queer wan, wha?'

'Fuckin', fuckin', fuckin', fuckin' . . .'

'Dja get it, though? Didja?'

Three were on Guinness. The fourth wore a pioneer pin – badge of total abstinence. Extremes, thought Grainne, we go to extremes. Were these the sort whose wives ended up in Halfway Houses?

'Caught you!' Hands over her eyes.

'Cormac! Where have you been?'

'Looking for you. All over. I came here last because I didn't think you'd taken to the bottle.' He grinned. 'What's in that? Gin?' He tasted it. 'Tonic! How boring. Buy me a coke?'

Air which could have been coming from a deep-freeze chopped at James's ankles and a blink of sudden sleep made him dream he was walking through a supermarket with Therese past the frozen pies and dinners. He was jet-lagged, hungry, and in doubt as to where he was. A nose blew in the darkness and he remembered O'Malley. O'Malley had been offering to sell James his grandaunt.

'To a Hollywood tycoon like yourself,' O'Malley had kept urging, 'it's small change. She's priceless. One of a kind.' The aunt, he assured, was a live source for which any historian should be ready to give his eye teeth.

'Shit!' James's feet slid on something slippy. 'I need a taxi.'

'You won't get one round here. Come home with me and you can phone for one. I'd give you a lift,' said O'Malley, 'but I'm grounded.'

Larry had warned James about falling foul of the locals. Clearly he practised what he preached. Everyone James had met this evening seemed to be a friend of his. They were hearty fellows with faces out of cartoons by Grosz or Gillray who kept promising to take him to the best, oldest, or most typical Dublin restaurant as soon as they'd tanked up with enough drink to prepare them for the road. At various points James had piled into cars with them in pursuit of this quest only to disembark at the door of yet another pub. Hunger and jet-lag kept gaining on him until he felt ready to faint.

'I need food,' he said finally. 'Now.'

'We'll fix that.' O'Malley, into whose keeping he had fallen by then, coaxed a saucer of olives from the barman. 'Eat up those,' he told James. 'They're full of nourishment. Then we'll go back to my place for a snack. I'll just have another quick one. A bird never flew on wan wing. Am I right?' he asked the barman.

But the man's good fellowship had run out.

'He never flew on twenty neither,' he told O'Malley. 'It's closing time and some of us have homes to go to.'

The next James knew they were in the street, while the pub door closed them off from all amenities.

'Here we go then!' O'Malley, as though put in gear, collided with a lamp-post and, rubbing his jaw, set off in the opposite direction. 'A hard man,' he said, 'a hard man!'

'Are you sure you know your way?'

'Ridiculoush!' was the haughty reply. 'Know thish shitty like the back of my . . .'

'OK, take it easy.'

'Short cut!' O'Malley darted into traffic.

James caught his elbow and together they negotiated a rainslick road. O'Malley, a time-waster he might have shunned elsewhere, had recommended himself in the first place as an exhibit. Later, he had taken charge. Now he was losing authority. But James held to his elbow. At worst, the man was a native guide to his own moist, subdued and saddish city.

Images of this, or rather of its pubs, in which James had put in the equivalent of a short working day, washed through his mind like clothes through a washer. Plush, mottled like marked-down meat, rotated with stretches of linoleum, brass and a light bulb stuck behind a bottle of Crème de Menthe. A greyhound-racing calendar whirled slim dogs nose-to-tail in a pulsing circle.

'When I got him,' a voice connected with this, 'he was no bigger than a snipe and I raised him on babyfood. But the bugger hadn't the urge to win.'

'They're too intelligent,' said another. 'Sure a dog could nearly ride a horse for you. Would *you* knock yourself out chasing a mechanical hare?'

'Jesus, I might, but.'

'This place has great character,' glossed a voice which James, in memory, assigned to Corny Kinlen, the man responsible for his present plight. Kinlen, a director of Radio Telefís Éireann, RTE, was to give advice on Larry's film. RTE, Kinlen told James, hoped to serialize it if it wasn't too blatantly Republican.

'Tricky ground,' Kinlen expounded. 'We're all Republicans, but it would take a fine instrument to assess the degrees of commitment. I'm delighted to see you. How's Larry?'

There had been a note at James's hotel when he checked in, asking him to ring RTE and an hour later Kinlen was drinking with him in the hotel bar. He quickly put forth the notion that a foray into the city was the thing needed to get James into condition to work.

'We'll have a few jars,' said Kinlen, 'a dekko at the citizenry, take the local pulse.' As Kinlen leaned against the counter, the flap of his jacket was nudged up, neat as piecrust, by the thrust of his ass. Clothes and body fell into place with the ease of habit. Barmen knew who he was.

'I'm interested in your project,' he told James. 'Recording oral history before the old men die off. Why not? Well, there *are* reasons why not. Here. Now. In the minds of some.' His eyes moved restlessly. 'That's why outsiders can do it and we can't. I speak,' said he, 'as one stuck with imposing self-censorship if I am not to draw the governmental sword of Emergency Powers down on all our heads.' Kinlen's head had a semi-deflated look, as though it had set out to be eighteenth-century, rubicund and spherical, then shrunk. He had sandy hair, pale eyes, a small moustache.

'The terrorists,' he told James, 'have appropriated the past.'

'I'm just doing these interviews . . .'

'Memory can be subversive.'

'Well, if you're opposed to the project . . .'

'Me? I oppose nothing. God help me, I don't know *what* I oppose. Self-censorship,' said Kinlen, 'means you let the Inquisition inside your head and it paralyses you. You're damned if you publish and damned if you don't. Memory,' he nailed James with his eye, 'is the opposite of thought. What the hell, maybe that's no harm? What I do know is that the thinking man keeps his mind open while the remembering fellow narrows and simplifies until the memory becomes as crude and bald as a Hallowe'en lantern. You'll come up against this when you start interviewing your old-timers.'

'Well, if memory is as you describe it,' said James, 'it can't be *very* subversive.'

'Wrong!' groaned Kinlen. 'You're forgetting that other citizen of our land, the activist revolutionary. You've had these chappies in your own state, so you'll know that to them myths are ammunition and the past is the future. Myths are motor power. The turnip-lantern blows up like a bomb. Padraig Pearse was a prime example for he died hamming to his script which then became unassailable. *De mortuis nil nisi bonum*. He was inspired by the mass, a daily sacrifice, as every Irishman knows. A corrosive example. Cyclic. "One man can free a people," wrote P.P., "as one Man redeemed the world . . . I will go into battle with bare hands. I will stand before the Gall as Christ hung before men on the tree." Hubristic? Mad? But his death in 1916 did rouse an apathetic country. "Gall" means "foreigner", by the way, and Pearse's father was a foreigner and a maker of funerary monuments. The son made his best speeches by the sides of graves: speeches, I may say, unsafe to put out today on our national wavelengths. Have another?'

James said he thought it was time to eat.

'Coupla chaps you should meet,' said Kinlen. 'Haven't shown yet. Give them another few minutes.' Waiting for refills, he flashed cheery false teeth around the room. Toothwork, James noted, was primitive in this pub. All around him were Draculas, Bugs Bunnies and hay-rake grins. A surprising number of drinkers seemed to talk fast and *sotto voce* out of the corners of their mouths. As intrigued by secrets as the next man, he tried listening but all he managed to make out could have been safely roared by microphone. Maybe self-censorship was a local game?

'I'm talking,' he heard a voice whisper, 'of the man in the street.'

'Which man,' came the conspiratorial rebuttal, 'in which street?'

James wondered whether this might be a Republican pub. Maybe Kinlen had his eye out for veterans for him to interview. Larry had specified that these were to come from the ranks of the obscure and anonymous.

'There's no such thing,' was Kinlen's response to that. 'In his own village no man is obscure, and, in the city, one half of the population poses for the other. This is the green-room of Europe,' he instructed James. 'Why? Because we lack the social indicators with which Englishmen are kitted out at birth. We lack them and we want them, as we want everything the old enemy ever had, good or bad, including social identity. Here, however, the criteria are easily rigged.'

James guessed that the guy got verbal diarrhoea in pubs to make up for all that self-censorship from which he suffered on the job. He was coming back from the counter now with fresh drinks.

Corny greeted a man some tables away who wore a pin-stripe suit of Chaplinesque slovenliness and had a pale, sad, handsome face topped by a bristle of angry-looking hair. 'That's Michael O'Malley,' he told James. 'You'll have heard of his grandfather, Owen? Michael's a lush but great value when he's not footless, which means he's usually OK until about 7 p.m.'

'Well, I'd be interested to meet him.'

'Drink up and we'll go over,' said Kinlen. 'To get back to the problem about getting the old hams to forget their learned lines, think,' he invited, 'how you'd sound yourself if someone from the media asked you to give your opinion on some current issue for "News At Ten". You'd mumble, you'd be unsure. Most people *are* unsure. Revolutionaries aren't. But these old buggers you'll be talking to haven't been revolutionaries for fifty years. If you get them sounding doubtful, you've got past the piety. I drink to doubt,' said Corny, 'and stutters and ums and ahs. Beware of the smooth-speaker and the loyal man. Loyalty,' he dipped his lip in the well of his glass, 'is one reason for the popularity here of the pun. The pun's a verbal equivalent of the gun: a device unamenable to argument. De Valera's opponents called his term in office "the devil era". They called his party, Fianna Fail, "the Fianna failures" which, since *fáil* is the Gaelic for "destiny" – it rhymes with boil – is a bitter joke. Have you finished? Come and meet Michael O'Malley then.' Kinlen stood up but was waylaid.

'Howaya, Corny, me aul codger, whose ear do I catch ya bending?'

A cut-watermelon face danced close and the shout decreased in volume. 'Do you know Enda McHugh?' Cut Watermelon nodded at a second, fattish face, pallid and simmering like a milk pudding over a slow flame. The second man seemed in the grip of uncontainable rage. A tic leaped in his cheek. His mouth retracted. It was the first time James had seen someone do the opposite of smile.

'He knows you,' said Cut Watermelon.

'The whitener of the government sepulchre,' raged Milk Pudding. 'Who doesn't?'

James, embarrassed, stared beyond the pair to where O'Malley was intoning something about classical Greece.

'Talking about puns he was,' commented Cut Watermelon. 'I heard! Puns and guns! Nearly got one off himself. Fella's getting creative!'

'Have to be creative,' said Milk Pudding, 'how else could they run the news department they have at RTE?'

'The male next-of-kin,' O'Malley was saying, 'was responsible for unmarried females till the day they died.'

'You refused,' Milk Pudding challenged Kinlen, 'to let "The Late Late Show" interview Sinn Féin spokesmen!' Milk Pudding looked on the point of flying apart. Words erupted up his throat in spurts. 'Free speech,' he managed, 'how are ye?'

'Sinn Féin,' said Kinlen, 'are a front for the Provos, i.e. for terrorists. We make no apology for refusing to give them publicity.'

'Shit-scared, aren't you? Of the government? Of Sinn Féin? Of your own shadow? Pissing in your cavalry-twill West-Briton's pants? Why not admit it, Kinlen? Tell the truth and shame the devil?'

James wondered whether there would be a fight. He was in better shape than the men baiting Kinlen. On the other hand, might they be armed?

'Christ,' said O'Malley, 'has just repudiated his bride in the person of my aged aunt whom I, as next-of-kin, am obliged to take in. This country hasn't advanced beyond the social welfare system of ancient Greece.'

'What's that gurrier saying about the country?'

Milk Pudding turned on his side-kick. 'Stop distracting me. I want to ask this fellow about the RTE evening news. Did you see it tonight?' he asked Kinlen, and shook like a vibrator inside the stiff sheath of his suit. 'Did you?'

'The Church, which used to run the loony bins, is lying down on the job.'

'I'm hungry,' said James. 'I think I should go and eat.'

'No Northern news,' said Milk Pudding. 'People can die up there . . .'

'. . . between two stools,' declaimed O'Malley, 'with a cold wind blowing up our collective arse.'

'Are you listening? They can commit mayhem and murder and all RTE will show is the football scores for Manchester United.'

'I've had enough.' Kinlen beckoned James towards O'Malley's table. 'Silence is golden,' he remarked to Cut Watermelon.

'So is horse manure.'

'Wasting your breath,' came in a fierce hiss from behind their backs.

James had to exercise restraint on himself to keep from glancing around.

Kinlen introduced him to a large, energetic-looking woman who was intent in argument with O'Malley, then to O'Malley himself who had become intent on his drink.

'We'll go and have a meal in a little while,' Kinlen promised James, and turned his back on his tormentors who had followed him almost to the table and were now standing some feet away, glowering. 'We might go to the Yacht Club.'

'Bourgeois crapology,' shouted Milk Pudding, waving an evening paper about. He held it rolled like a club.

'A working class divided down the middle,' said the woman, looking up at him suddenly, 'is not the same as one that isn't. Will you grant that, Enda?'

'Who divided it?' Milk Pudding demanded. 'Who? Who?' He used words like missiles and his accent, James recognized, having heard the same one on television in America, was from Northern Ireland. His mouth was tensile in the midst of his boiling face. 'In whose interests is it to pit worker against worker, Catholic against Protestant? The fucking, boot-licking lackeys of capitalism, that's who. The media. Bastards like Kinlen and other establishment journalists in this place.

Ah fuck,' he said furiously, and putting his newspaper weapon into his pocket, he strode out of the pub.

'Who is he?' James asked the woman.

'Teaches at Queen's University in Belfast,' she told him.

James was startled to find the man a colleague. 'I thought he was a gunman.'

The woman laughed. 'Him? No, they're much less bellicose. Here's a chap escaped from Long Kesh Internment Camp.' She swivelled her chair backwards towards the next table where a small, nutty-faced leprechaun of a fellow was drinking Guinness. The leprechaun acknowledged the woman's introduction by slipping his hand into her blouse.

'California,' he said to James, 'is that where you're from? That's a place I'd love to go, now. They tell me it's a grand, warm, comfortable class of a place entirely.' His hand travelled across the woman's breast.

'You're far gone,' she told him, taking the hand and slapping it like a child's.

'Not half as far as I'd like to be.' The leprechaun winked at James. 'How do you like our colleens?' He put a hand on the woman's bottom. 'Isn't she a fine hault? Mind, she doesn't take me seriously. But she's making a mistake. Oh aye, she is. There's big goods in small parcels, as they say.' Another wink. 'Big surprises.'

Delicately, James switched his attention to O'Malley, whom Kinlen had supplied with a fresh drink. O'Malley's was a Tudor face, James thought: lean and long with a burst of hair rising above it like a bird's crest. The lower lip surprised. Normal in repose, it grew prehensile in action, shooting forward like an anteater's proboscis to scoop up prey. What the lip was geared to scoop were stray drops of liquor which it promptly funnelled back inside itself. Mobile as a second tongue, it looked as though it might be equipped with taste buds. O'Malley drained his drink, squinted at the empty glass for some seconds, then turned to James.

'Corny's been telling me about your film,' he said gravely, 'and I have a proposal to make. I would like to hire out the services to you of my great-aunt Judith.'

4

In the mornings, long ago, remembered Sister Judith, you'd be loath to put your foot out of the bedclothes for fear of the cold. Bridie used to come round the bedrooms with baskets full of kippeens for kindling and candle ends and bits of bacon rind to help coax the wet fuel to take. Downstairs, the fire in the kitchen was always banked for the night and had not been out since their father had moved into this house. He had lit it first with a few embers brought from *his* father's house, so it was a very old fire, maybe a hundred years old. For all that, the kitchen could be freezing in the mornings and flooded when the rain was heavy. Bridie bailed out water with the help of Seamus and a couple of brooms. Upstairs, skirts flapping and boots unlaced, she raced to get the fires lit before the cold had her paralytic. It would freeze a snipe, she'd say and blow with puffed cheeks like a trumpet-playing angel. 'God blosht the wet turf,' she whispered and blasted it herself with spittly breath.

Window panes were fogged and sometimes frozen with sunbursts of ice into which you could read signs and weapons. Swords. Monstrances. The water in the ewer was frozen as often as not. Judith boiled a saucepanful and tipped it in to take the edge off the rest. Cold water made her skin peel.

Porridge for breakfast was followed by bread and tea. Her father complained if there were lumps. He was given to looking backward and kept remembering how poor Eamonn had complained of the tea he'd had to drink while on the run. The country people shared what they had with him but had no notion how to make tea. They kept it stewing in a teapot laid for warmth on a few pieces of glowing turf. Imagine the ignorance. Sure it would be pure tannin. Take the stomach off ye. That was the way they liked it though. Bitter. So strong a mouse could dance on it. Knownothings! Eamonn had complained of the difficulty of dealing with them. They'd never show what they were thinking to an outsider, only lead him on, polite and restrained, then go their own way. Couldn't get it through their skulls that now the outsiders were their own people. That was what oppression did: created suspicion. Obstinacy. Eamonn used to curse their carelessness. They'd leave guns to rust and turn up late for a drill or even an ambush. Farmers had no knowledge of clocks. They went by the sun. Lloyd George had been reported as saying that giving self-government to Poles was like giving a clock to a monkey.

'Maybe it was that same slackness got poor Eamonn killed?'

He'd been killed fighting in the mountains. In an ambush. Mountainy men were a race apart.

'Lloyd George feels the very same about the rest of us,' Kathleen lit into their father. 'What do you want quoting him for? That's the slave mind: always ready to condemn our own. Eamonn wouldn't be proud of you.'

'Oh faith, I don't know which of the two of ye, Owen or yourself, will be the slave,' said their Da, 'you've a tongue so sharp it would cut rope. That poor man, for all the Greek and Hebrew he studied, will be no match for it. A sharp tongue in a woman is a match for all the ancient tongues, ha ha!'

His jokes were pathetic but a way of making peace. He was proud of Owen's learning. Uselessness gave it price. Owen had been in a Jesuit seminary for a few years but had thrown it up to join the fighting.

'You're not going out?' the Da asked Judith who had put on her hat and coat.

'The First Friday.'

'In that rain?'

'It's only a step.'

'You'll catch your death, Miss. Listen to me. You've got the weakness in your chest whether it's shown itself or not. Didn't your mother die of it? To hell with your Nine Fridays. What do you need making novenas for anyway, tormenting Almighty God? Don't you think he has better things to do than to listen to the ulagoanings of females? What are you praying for anyway? What is it you lack?'

He really wanted to know. Applying over his head to God showed lack of confidence. 'Well?'

'Ah, leave her go,' said Kathleen, and nodded firmly to Judith who was hovering, upset by their father's tone. He had grown pettish since Eamonn's death, feeling that in one way or another they were all fixing to leave him.

'I'll take the umbrella,' Judith conciliated and ran out into the rain. Her boots squelched and the bike skidded. The umbrella was useless so she hid it by the gate.

The next trouble was the red setter, Bran, who ran after the bike.

'Go home outa that. Bad dog! Home.'

He wagged his tail, paused but then raced forward. Turning to roar back at him, she felt the bike skidding and gave up. She'd tie him to a tethering stone by the church. He'd be drenched but whose fault was that? Twice before he had followed her up the nave, cool as you please, and given scandal by walking inquisitively up to the altar to where the priest was saying mass. Horrified titters unnerved the congregation as the red-plumed animal, scandalous in his innocence, poked a damp snout under the celebrant's skirts. An altar boy had grabbed and walked him in custody down the nave, demanding in a piercing whisper that his owner should come forward. Judith had been ready to sink through the floor.

'So you can stay there now. Sit.'

The soft resignation in his eyes reminded her of the Da.

Coats steamed in the warm church. Judith had no precise intention to pray for. She was making the Nine Fridays for the same reason as Eamonn had joined the Volunteers and Owen the Jesuits: to stretch herself, to find a discipline. She had divined these aims from hints they let drop. The church smelled of wet tweed, leather, bad breath, the guttering candles which sank into molten pools in the sockets of their brass containers. She put a coin in the box and lit a fresh taper before deciding why, then remembered her father and decided it was for him. Let it ward off all evils threatening their house and protect its weakest inmate, the Da.

Eamonn's death had brought his loneness home to him. He felt – said he felt – superfluous, left over stupidly when the boy he had been working for was dead. What was the good of his success, the pub and custom he'd been building up, if there was nobody to take it over? Owen and Kathleen didn't want it. Seamus was going to go back to medical school if the fighting ever finished. Maybe, he hoped, Judith might marry some steady fellow who wouldn't mind standing behind a counter?

'For God's sake, can't you sell it when you're too old to run it?' Eamonn had demanded.

The Da had been outraged. Eamonn and himself had had terrible fights. The Da remembered them now, going over them uselessly while he sat looking into the fire or having little nips in the pub. That was his latest habit and everyone knew that a publican who took his own medicine didn't last long.

The worst was the time he discovered that Eamonn was with the Volunteers. Dirty Fleming let it out. It had been a Hallowe'en. Young fellows kept coming to the door dressed up as ghosts. Then Dirty Fleming came by for his supper. He was a tramp but a steady one. He had his regular days when people fed him. Nobody knew where he slept.

Eamonn was blacking his face with burnt cork intending to go out himself and call at the house of a girl he liked. Dirty Fleming, who was said to have been a Fenian in his day, and could be any age from seventy to a hundred and ten, said he wouldn't like to meet a black face like that of a dark night.

'Though there's plenty driving up and down the country in their Crossley Tenders with their faces blacked and tisn't for sport either, God blasht them!' He spat into the fire. Curfew might well be a problem to an old man like him of no fixed abode. He had no teeth and his words were hard to follow. Kathleen cut the crusts off bread for him and he soaked it in tea, sucking this between his gums and feeding himself from a saucer. 'Ah well,' he said to Eamonn, 'I hope yous give them buggers a run for their money. Yous'll need better fighting weapons than the yokes I seen yez drilling with beyond in the West field.' He laughed gently to himself, gleeful at having seen what he had. 'I seen yez,' he grinned, 'sabre-charging with broom handles.' His grin was as ramshackle as their weapons.

Eamonn said 'goodnight all', and was out of the door before his father could say a word. The girls tried to divert Fleming to memories of the distant conspiracies he'd known himself: hopes which had come to nothing, a litany of ineffectual planning, betrayal, imprisonment. While he mused over them, mashing soda bread between his gums, their father was silent: maybe he'd guessed all along? Eamonn had used his courtship of the girl he'd just gone to see to cover too many absences. It was happening in half the families around. Parents were like ostriches, willing away knowledge.

Kathleen gave the old man a cup of beef tea. Between slurps, the dates of defeats dropped from his lips like the sorrowful mysteries of the rosary: 1848, 1867 . . . the Phoenix Park Murders . . . the Manchester Martyrs . . .

Suddenly their father lit into him: 'How fair ye never managed to do any good for the country! How fair ye were such bunglers that the young fellows today have to start from scratch, risking their necks all over again! What good were ye but a lot of cods? Idle lasthers! Windy!'

The old man stopped chewing. Embarrassment paralysed them all. Kathleen pressed her hand on the shoulder of the insulted old Fleming, who was trying to mobilize his bones to depart in dudgeon.

She whispered. 'He didn't know about Eamonn. Pay no attention. He'll be mortified in the morning.'

Judith couldn't help enjoying the drama. Awful, really, but how not to be excited by the shock pulsing in her father's cheek and in the aghast, bloodshot roll of the two men's eyes? They refused to meet each other but, rambling in different directions, settled on things like saucepans as though they planned burning holes in them.

The Da was out of step. Always had been, she suddenly saw. What he'd done and could never be made to see he'd done was insult a notion which was the cornerstone of Republicanism. It was – she groped her way towards seeing it herself – part of an argument which ran like this: the English had no right being here and never had had. This was proven by the fact that the Irish – Dirty Fleming among them – had always and always struggled against them. Their presence was therefore an interim, doomed, haphazard thing, no more disgracing to the native Irish than the presence of a cow who broke into your garden or of a neighbour who made a habit of walking through it. You had to stop cow and neighbour and assert your rights from time to time to prevent them establishing a right of way. That was the value of the old struggles. They kept us from being slaves who assent to their servitude. But the Da couldn't see that. Didn't want to. Pieties, he said, annoyed him. Hot air. He'd gone to America to make money and had convinced himself that you were what you had and the rest was blather. Now, twitching his shoulders inside his jacket and feeling at odds with the rest of them, he mumbled about how words never hurt anyone, so why not shake hands? They sidled towards a truce. Fleming accepted his usual sup of porter to warm him against the elements and Kathleen produced a pair of old boots with wear in them yet. He accepted these too. He couldn't afford to stand on dignity.

When he'd said good night, they heard him in the yard cursing a gang of Hallowe'eners who were singing their rhyme and baiting him. His voice broke in hoarse, spittly barks. 'Ye have no respect . . . for age and infirmity . . . Domn and blosht! Give me back my stick. Where is it? Damn yez. I can't see. Let go . . .'

Bran began to bark and set off an answering chorus of barks and curses up and down the hill.

Judith, pierced by the imperfections of the world, imagined the rheumaticky old Fleming, spittle-threads escaping from his wobbly mouth, trudging into the wind. Where would he sleep? She felt pity for his fragile bones and imagined taking him in her arms and warming him in her own well-covered bed. But the too-vivid notion disgusted her. She had insufficient charity, pushing him away in fancy, despite her nobler strivings. He'd end in the workhouse and after that in a pauper's grave. The inevitability of the thing choked her.

'What's up with you, Miss?' Her father was still on the boil. 'Weeping for the sins of your father, is it? And for what,' he roared at Kathleen, 'did you want giving away my second-best boots? Nobody in this family thinks anything of property, only how to get rid of it hand over fist. Saint Francis of Assisi isn't in it with ye. Yez have him bet. He divested himself of what was his but ye're so charitable ye have to give handouts of what doesn't belong to ye at all. It's easy seen no one of ye ever worked for a day's wages in yeer lives. There's Eamonn off playing soldiers with a broom handle. God help us! Soldiers. Make a cat laugh. But work? Oh no. They've no respect for it or what it earns. Is it out drilling he is this minute?' he wanted to know. 'In the wet? It would be the price of him, and him with a weak chest.'

'He's over at Eileen Cronin's,' Kathleen told him. She was making porridge for the morning and letting him have his say. He might as well get it all out now that old Fleming was gone and Eamonn not yet back. Judith could read her thoughts.

'Eileen Cronin has a broad back,' said their father sarcastically. 'I thought he was leppin' mad with the love for her he was there so often. But now it seems he wasn't there at all. Tell me,' he asked in sudden anxiety. 'Does he only drill or has he been out doing real fighting? Taking risks?'

'You'd better ask him that yourself.' Kathleen kept stirring away.

The Da poured himself another drink. He had clearly no intention of going to bed before Eamonn got home and Eamonn would of course stay out late in the hope of dodging him.

'Bloody heroes!' he said contemptuously and rattled the poker against the hearth. 'A coupla years back they were fighting so as not to have to fight! Out demonstrating against the conscription. Yelling neither King nor Kaiser and throwing stones at the peelers. And now look at them. Broom handles! Shouting the day after the fair. Codology.' He was working himself up.

Kathleen took the whiskey bottle. 'You've had enough of that,' she said. But this was a mistake. The quiet man's wrath was up. The worm had turned.

'Give me that!' He seized it, his hand trembling. 'Your poor mother, God rest her, is dead and there's nobody to say whether I can drink myself into the grave to join her.'

'Ah wisha aren't you full of pity for yourself!' Kathleen was as cold as ice. 'You're terrible mawkish!' she said, using her brogue for derision.

The brogue was something you could thin or thicken, put off and take on. It was part of them but not an essential part. Judith and Kathleen had been taught elocution in the convent and the Da had lived for ten years in America where he had learned to talk like a Yank, a Wop or a Polack. When they were little he had done turns for them, acting out jokes about these funny foreigners, describing their antics in a saga which they ended by knowing as well as he did. A lone adult in a house of children, he had been closer to them than was usual in families. This made Eamonn's betrayal hard to take. For it was a betrayal in this house that it might not have been in others up or down the street. Joining the Volunteers was to turn your back on the Da's ideal of personal prowess which he had spelled out for them time and again. It was a dream which haunted him because he had been unfaithful to it. He had settled for too little, turning away from the vast, uncertain lure of America to bring home the small prizes which he had won too easily: a pretty wife and the money to buy a tidy pub by the age of thirty. It was not by quitting so soon that the Rockefellers had made their fortune nor the Fords. Dissatisfaction gnawed at him and his children knew he was dreaming old, obsolete dreams when he sat warming his toes at the fire and staring into its red, uncompromising gullet. If he hadn't sold his share in a Boston grocery store, might he own a chain of stores today?

'Maybe we shoulda stayed,' he wondered often. 'Your mother might not have died. They have grand doctors over there.'

'We'd be Yanks now,' Seamus and Eamonn used to shout in amusement. 'Ballpark,' they repeated like parrots. 'Soda-pop, candy.' They might have been talking about China or the moon. There had been slitty-eyed Chinks in Boston too. Running laundries. The Da pulled his eyes sideways to show how they looked. He swore he'd eaten sharks' fins in a place called One Hung Low. Judith couldn't see why that was funny.

78

America was a myth and the myth had a moral. Any man who worked there could get ahead. Any man smart enough. There was the place where the sheep got sorted quickly from the goats. You betja. Their mother's uncle had gone out ahead of them and earned enough to buy a partnership in a grocery store. When he died she'd come into it and with what their father had earned himself the couple had been able to get married and come home to buy this pub.

'That's independence,' he said pugnaciously. 'Working. Making something of yourself by your own efforts.'

Joining up with a throng of corner boys and idlers to shoot policemen and burn down property ran counter to the code he'd learned in America. Or so he'd said that night after old Fleming's departure. Other nights he spoke differently. He wasn't consistent. He understood dreams too well not to half-sympathize with Eamonn. Half only though, for their dreams conflicted and, besides, he was coming to see dreams as a weakness, like drink. They could corrode a man. Hollow him out. Especially political dreams. Look at that poor bugger Fleming how he was ending up. Though in Boston, mind, politics were something else. A different kettle of fish. No moonlight drilling for them, only hard bargaining, ganging together to wangle what could be wangled and get the best you could for your own people. It was hard-headed and business-like and had nothing to do with moaning and ulagoaning about defeat. Jesus, but they hugged defeat to their bosoms here as if it were a sacrament, a sign of being too good for this world. Losers! Derisive, he parodied the old songs in a snivelling voice, chanting like a sexton with a cold in his nose:

> 'Who fears to speak of '98?
> Who blushes at the name?'

Begob and they should blush, we all should if we had any sense!

> 'When cowards mock the patriots' fate
> Who hangs his head for shame?'

His lips twirled in a fury of contempt.

'The men that's going now,' Kathleen told him, 'aren't

looking for defeat any more than you were. *And* they have the full and enthusiastic support of your friends, the Irish Americans. They've already achieved more than any other generation before . . .'

'*My* generation . . .' He took everything personally. His generation had looked to constitutional reform, and he began talking of Gladstone's promises of Home Rule. But soon he was back in America in Murphy's Irish saloon singing comeall-lyes about going back to Erin. He closed his eyes to concentrate on the words and his voice throbbed with a nostalgia which showed him so sunk in memory that he was longing to return to where he bodily was. His spirit was lost back in Boston in the days when he was courting the young girl who wanted to be brought home across the ocean wide and wild and had died a few years after he had brought her back, while still young and red-cheeked with the glow of consumption, but otherwise looking, from the testimony of the photograph album, very like Judith.

Eamonn's cork-blackened face appeared like a ghost's at the window and Kathleen motioned to Judith to go on up to bed. She'd stay below herself to fulfil the peacemaker's role which would allow each man to feel he had not backed down.

Judith lit her candle and carried it upstairs. Behind her, the syrupy song stopped and there was a crash of furniture, a shatter of glass, and her father's shouting. Kathleen came backing up the stairs. Peacemaking wasn't wanted. She hadn't had time to get herself a candle.

She drew Judith into her room. 'They're having it out.'

'What happened?'

'The Da threw his glass at the wall. He's drunk but Eamonn isn't and Eamonn's stronger. They'll be all right.' She looked sad though, perhaps at the discovery their father was going to make if he tried wrestling with Eamonn.

There was another crash.

'Jesus, what's he broken now?'

Kathleen worried for the clock and some Staffordshire figures. No question in their minds but that it was the man who put his pride in property who was throwing it about. Eamonn would be trying to reason with his father, patiently and sensibly, having time and history on his side and probably entirely forgetful of his sinisterly blackened face.

Their father's voice came raised in lamentation: 'Riffraff!'

Something else fell, making a lesser, muted noise and Kathleen shook her head.

'Maybe it's only a saucepan?' Judith hoped.

'A good thing your mother didn't live to see . . .'

Eamonn's answer didn't reach up the stairs.

'And suppose you get killed?'

After that the talk became subdued and went on so long that Judith went to bed and left her candle to Kathleen. Some sort of peace was made that night, although their father was distant and drank heavily all the following week and Eamonn could not be pumped about the terms.

'I'll bet the pair of ye wept like babbies and threw yeer arms around each other!' Judith threw the provocation out as bait but it wasn't taken up.

Some months later Eamonn was killed and Seamus, his younger brother, was out training fellows to charge. He'd learned himself from a fellow who'd been with the British in India and he gave Judith lessons on afternoons when their father was busy in the pub. They rigged up a sort of scarecrow with a bed-bolster for a belly and had it in flitters after a few training sessions. Judith had insisted on using a hay-fork. She attacked the bolster with such vigour that Seamus said he'd let her have a try with a real bayonet as soon as he could get his hands on one. It was a pity women weren't being armed, he said. It might calm them down to do a bit of real fighting. As it was, they had no outlet and were a sight more blood-thirsty than the lads.

She should not have come back. Jane had been right. Though how could you live your life in a Halfway House? After a glass of Michael's whiskey, Grainne was on the point of deciding that there was no better metaphor for life.

She'd got home to find chaos. No Michael. Only a new maid some agency had palmed off on him who was fresh from the Aran Islands and as unhousebroken as a new kitten. She'd probably have nits and be confused by a flush lavatory. Then there was the aunt. Sweet Jesus! If even Doris, the char, had been there! But it wasn't her day and there was just this new maid, Mary, and the incontinent aunt. Why had nobody told Grainne she was incontinent?

'How long have you been here?' Grainne asked Mary.

'A week.' Sullenly. The place was filthy. Shit on the floor. Maybe Doris would give notice?

'If Sister Judith can't get to the bathroom then other arrangements should be made. Didn't my husband tell you?'

'Nobody said nothin'.'

'Has he been upstairs?'

'She only come the other night.'

'Has Doris been in?'

'Not since she come.'

So that was all right. Grainne cleaned up the unfortunate aunt, got Mary to clean the mess in the corridor and unpacked her own suitcase. While she was busy, depression stayed at bay.

The old woman looked at her with shuffling eyes and mumbled about Owen and being found out. She was either *non compos* or unsure of her surroundings, which needn't be the same thing. Grainne had a bath in some scented oil bought in London and got herself up prettily to seduce herself back to life. By then it was seven and Michael, if he had been coming back for dinner, should have been in. She had been planning a surprise but it had misfired. Quickly she fried up some food and took a tray up to her aunt.

'God bless ye, girl! Listen here to me.' The cunning, frightened eye fixed her and a hand grasped her skirt. 'I want to go back. I never came here of my own accord. You be my witness now. I never wanted to leave the convent. He said he'd commit me, have me committed if ever I left. That or gaoled.'

'Who?'

'Owen.'

'Why gaoled?'

The old mouth closed like a zip. Chewing, it moved sideways, left, right, left, right, like a grazing animal's. The fear in the face too was animal.

Grainne sat down. 'Aunt Judith.'

The mouth stopped its motion. The eyes dodged.

'*Sister* Judith,' Grainne corrected herself. 'Has Michael explained to you who we are? His grandmother was your sister, Kathleen. Remember? She died.'

'Ha! They keep saying that. Died. Died. They even say Owen died. Maybe some day someone will be born?' There was a charge of derision in the voice.

'Don't you believe me?' Grainne wondered. 'Owen is dead.'

'Maybe so.'

And maybe that was what depressed her? The news – it appeared to be sudden – of her contemporaries' deaths, mass deaths they must seem to her, could hardly be cheering. Michael seemed to have done a poor job of welcoming her.

'We're having a commode put in your room,' Grainne told her, for want of anything more positive to say. 'It will make things easier.'

No answer. The old lady popped food into her mouth. As though she had no back teeth, her mouth bulged over each morsel. Dressed in a poncho which might have been made from a punctured billiard-table cover, she had the air of a disaster-victim, one of the stunned women photographed after an earthquake in Turkey or Venezuela. The niff from her clothes was the one you got from unaired spaces affected by organic rot: a vegetable bin, or the inside of a well-worn shoe.

'Listen,' Grainne offered, 'would you like me to take you shopping tomorrow? We could buy you some clothes.'

'Clothes? What would I want with clothes? I'm going back to the convent.'

'All right.' There was a pause. 'I see,' Grainne noted, 'that you've got the TV here. Do you watch it?'

The face relaxed.

'What's your favourite programme?'

'It varies,' said the nun with composure. 'There was a series on India which I liked. Bayonetting. I think I must have witnessed a bayonet charge.'

'Really?'

'It came to me as I watched them. Ghurkas? Not clearly. I just had a feeling . . .' She kneaded the air, closing her eyes in exasperation. 'My old brain,' she remonstrated with it.

'A feeling of having been there before?'

'That's it.'

'Did you ever see people killed? Ambushes?'

'Me?' Suspicion was back. The mouth twitched like a spider worriedly patrolling its web. 'Ambushes? How would that be?' Left, right, left rushed the mouth. 'Who gave you that idea?'

'You yourself, just now.'

'You misunderstood.'

'I see.' Grainne stood up. 'Perhaps you're sleepy?' she hoped. 'Ready for bed?'

'Now?'

'Or you could watch television.' Grainne was tense with the need to get out of the room. The sight of the old woman's ruined flesh had given her a pressing desire to use her own, to refresh it in sex with Michael whom she was going to assault with a demand for conjugal rights the minute he got in the door. 'Here,' she told the aunt, 'I've put on the box. I'll be up later to get you to bed.' A feature film came on. It would fill up the time until close-down. 'There now, Aunt Judith, you'll enjoy that.'

Grainne left the old lady watching and fled down the stairs. She closed the drawing-room door behind her on an attenuated rollicking of cowboy music. Rescue, rescue jounced the music as she poured herself a drink. The whiskey tasted tinny. The truth was she liked it only in company. Lone drinking had morose implications and the room looked down-at-heel.

She poked the fire, stirring up sparks which curled like wind-bent barley then drifted back down into the maw of turf. *Look* at this room! And she knew he wouldn't have kept his dental appointments. Self-neglect was slow suicide and he'd commit it in the end if she didn't keep after him. He shoved her into the role of the awful, manipulative wife. But if she didn't manipulate he flopped like one of those life-size Japanese puppets which have to be held up by black-clothed puppeteers.

Grainne had a flashing image of herself cutting a hole in Michael's chest and shoving a battery inside it to make him go.

She thrust the poker through a turf sod and twisted it like the key in a doll's back. Like that, Mikey, sod you!

'You don't give a hoot about Daddy,' Cormac had yelled an hour ago. They'd been having a row because he wanted to go out.

'You haven't seen your father for months,' she accused, 'and you want to go out without even waiting for him to come home.'

'And why haven't I?' Cormac threw back. 'Whose fault is that? You don't give two hoots for Daddy, and don't think he doesn't know it. Why do you think he drinks?'

His mother was astounded by the accusation.

'You're no wiser than I am,' Cormac went on. 'I'm going to see Granduncle Owen Roe. You can't stop me.'

This was true.

'Why can't I see him?' he asked.

'He's a bad influence. He could get you into trouble. And himself.'

Probably she, in her time, had been told the same thing about Michael. The phrases came automatically to her lips but she was unsure of them. For her own parents there had been right and wrong and no doubt about it. Cormac was the same. Michael and she, a peace-time generation, were like children before this assertive son of fourteen and a half. They turned words round in their heads until they grew porous and weightless. For Cormac words were as solid as bricks. This had become clear last summer when she discovered a gun in his sock drawer and demanded an explanation. It was not, it turned out, a lethal sort of gun, just the sort a boy could get without a licence. However, he had hidden it from her and had used it to do target practice with his great-uncle. She had roped in Michael and the two clamped down on Cormac. No more guns. Why? Because they disliked violence and one thing led to another. The boy had cut through this with contemptuous clarity. The government, he said, was violent itself. It was interning and torturing men who were the salt of the earth.

'I suppose you'll tell us next that the felon's cap is the noblest crown an Irish head can wear!'

'Just because you say it in a funny voice, Mummy, doesn't make it less true. People of your generation make jokes because you never want to have to take sides on anything.'

Grainne had been stricken. 'Is that your granduncle's opinion?' she had asked.

'Oh I know you think I can't work anything out for myself. But I can and I've got to be given the right.'

'You don't work things out,' Michael told him. 'You parrot slogans. Do you think you've said one original thing?'

'Why should it be original if it's true?'

Some of the lines Cormac got off were better than those which seemed to go with his parents' roles. Style was on the side of subversion and could look like truth. So could anything put to ballad music. Great-uncle Owen Roe sponsored a youth club which had ballad-singing sessions. Ostensibly harmless, the place was a recruiting centre for activist Republicans.

'Well, we can't stop Cormac going to ballad-singing sessions.'

'I suppose not.'

The dilemma had drawn Michael and her together. Briefly. Sadly. It was dispiriting to be found woolly and tentative when faced with bundles of energy like Owen Roe who was Michael's uncle, Grainne's cousin, and a political opportunist who had been forced out of his party some years before for intriguing with the IRA. Now he hoped to turn his downfall to advantage by appearing more Republican than the Republic. Knowing that the Northern conundrum would not solve itself overnight, he dallied in the wilderness, pleased to let the men in office compromise their reputations. Later, his chance might come to catapult himself into power. His personal standing, enhanced by the almost mythic reputation of his dead father, would probably be increased several notches if younger members of the family – Cormac – were to get into trouble for Republican activities.

Mother's paranoia? Maybe? Maybe not. Owen Roe was bad luck. After all, he had inherited the woollen mills which should by rights have come to Michael and that wasn't all she had against him.

'Cormac, I'm not going to argue with you about your great-uncle. Some matters are too complex . . .'

She saw his smile and knew what was behind it. Lovers of the *status quo* always said that things were complex. Be on your watch for that word: a Quisling's word, a Pétainiste word, a word for the politically cowardly. She knew the argument, had heard Owen Roe produce it. Cormac was primed.

Bright indignant eyes judging her.

'You are not to go out without your father's permission.'

'My father's drinking his head off in some pub.'

'I forbid you to talk about him that way.'

'You? You don't give two hoots about Daddy.'

And out he'd gone, either to Owen Roe's or the Youth Club. She phoned there and got Patsy Flynn on the phone.

'Oh, you're back, Mrs O'Malley? Well that's great news. Looking for young Cormac? Ah no, sure I didn't even know yez were back, either of yez. Not a sign of him. What? Send him home if he shows up? I'll do that. Yes. You can rely on me, Mrs O'Malley.'

She could just imagine the contortions of Patsy as he winked at Cormac, covered the receiver and played the conversation up for laughs. He was childish as a result of having been beaten round the head in a British gaol, where he had spent a number of years for planting bombs in Britain during the IRA campaign of the 1950s. He now worked for the Grateful Patriots' Youth Club and was mindlessly devoted to Owen Roe.

'I hear your grandaunt is out?' he remarked. 'The Captain' – he called Owen Roe 'the Captain', giving him a title he had earned in a youth corps to which he had once belonged – 'the Captain says she should be put away in the national interest.' Patsy laughed his ricocheting, idiot's laugh.

'I don't know what he means,' said Grainne coldly. 'You'll remember what I said to tell Cormac?'

'Oh, don't have a worry on that score, Mrs O'Malley, now. You can trust me.'

And he must have delivered the message, after all, for Cormac came home shortly afterwards and sneaked upstairs.

She caught a glimpse of him through the bannisters, dodging upwards with a stack of papers under his arm.

He must have got something to eat while out. Michael too. The skipped meal left her feeling that the family structure had collapsed. Meals were the pivot of a housewife's function. Now Cormac was getting his from the likes of Patsy Flynn, a bad influence in anybody's book. She had heard him last year indoctrinating Cormac. '*Be* Irish,' he had kept begging in his whining, nasal voice. 'Ah, now Cormac, for yer grandfather's sake, *be* Irish.' Patsy's mental make-up was as simple as his shape which was like that of a man in a child's sketch. His face could be drawn with a compass; there were two red spots on his cheeks and his hands were like hunks of steak. There was no question as to what Patsy meant by being Irish. His prison sentence had been for placing bombs in British pillar-boxes. Grainne had seen him singing in the club, his face a sweaty glitter of fervour.

> 'Whether on the gallows high,
> Or on battlefield we die,'

he had sung,

> 'What matter if for Erin dear we fall?'

If anyone should be put away in the national interest it was Patsy Flynn.

After half an hour, she slipped up to Cormac's room and found him asleep. She tucked him in, half eager to kiss his unprotected face, half repelled by the unfinished awkwardness of it and the knowledge that he would have turned from her if awake.

Beside the bed were the papers he had brought home. The top one was a comic paper. Cheaply printed, with sooty photographs, it featured a hero, Super Mick, who outfought a bowler-hatted robot standing for British Capitalism. The paper was called *Focalín*, Gaelic, she remembered, for Little Word. Whose? The distributing address was in London and the thing so illiterate, it could have been a product of the British Special Branch aimed at undermining the Irish psyche.

It mocked hard and knowingly. A letter signed 'Turd Police-man' made literary reference to a distinguished Irish novel and jokes of no distinction at all about IRA detainees' alleged habit of torturing themselves in their cells so as to discredit the Royal Ulster Constabulary. The passion for self-abuse, complained the purportedly hard-conned constable, was forcing the force to forego tea breaks and watch at all times lest suspects damage themselves under cover of sleep. The half-clever, half-infantile humour struck Grainne as perfectly attuned to the likes of Patsy Flynn. Looked at another way, the paper, if Irish, was itself a form of self-abuse.

Bereft, she stared at the turf sod which was going whitish-grey like the muzzle of an old dog. Why wasn't Michael home? She had a physical illusion that she would be whole again only when she held him in her arms. Did that merely mean that he was to her as routine was to laboratory mice and institutions to inmates who grew addicted to them?

But Michael *could* come alive and blaze with a gaiety which was the more thrilling for the long wait between times. He could be iconoclastic, insightful, funny, perhaps a tiny bit mad? She had hoped that her coming back would spark him off. She had, with equally forlorn logic, reasoned that her leaving, five months ago, would jerk him from his apathy.

'Forget it. Just quit tormenting yerself with hoping. There's not a single thing you can do that'll make a pick of difference.' This, the verdict of the O'Malleys' char, Doris, had been delivered shortly before Grainne left. 'Get it into yer head,' Doris had advised, 'that you and yer hubby are goin' to have to jog along the way yez are doing for the rest of yeer mortal lives. Mark my words. Miracles don't happen.'

It had been this prophecy which had sent Grainne hurtling from the house and across the Irish Sea.

'Yiz aren't the first,' Doris put the matter in a stern per-spective, 'and I doubt yiz'll be the last. Annywan taking to the drink the way your hubby has . . .'

'Are we walking in circles?' James couldn't be sure, for the roads seemed to wind and a spiral might be the only way to advance. The ground was filmed with grease.

'City's built on a bog,' said O'Malley. 'Founded by Norsemen. Seafarers. Lovers of wet. Cellars flooded all winter. Here we are.'

James, who had begun to despair, saw that they had turned in the gate of a driveway. Gravel was gritty underfoot. An early-Victorian house stood away from them like a theatre backdrop. Steps rose to its front door which was surmounted by a fanlight. On either side were high-pedimented windows screened by blinds. Abruptly one knifed upwards, revealing a lit room which hung like a suspended stage half-way up the dark façade. A woman silhouetted in the foreground swung what James took to be a pole.

'May I come in?' Limp-necked, like a faded daisy, a head of white hair hung just in the door. Aunt Judith swung from the handle, pulling and leaning on it so that the door hinges creaked.

Grainne opened it wide. 'Come in,' she invited. 'Is anything wrong?'

'No, girl, no, don't worry yourself!' The old lady advanced in a tremor of hesitancy. 'It's just the TV. They say it's dangerous to leave it on after close-down and it's different from the set I'm used to. I didn't want to turn the wrong knob, break it maybe?' She was all uncertainty. 'I know how intrusive I must be. A stranger in the house,' she commiserated. 'Burdensome.'

'Not at all.'

'Oh yes.' Her accent was old-fashioned genteel. Grainne tried to recall when she'd heard it last, a Dublin specialty but of a period long gone. 'People have their ways. But, you see . . .' The electric blanket on her bed was turned on too. One read warnings. 'Electrocution.'

She smiled, deprecated, might have been charged with the current already. Doubts steamed from her, hissed – something about her teeth or palate? – and she shifted from foot to foot as though about to levitate. She looked ungrounded, frail.

Grainne was ashamed. 'I shouldn't have left you alone. I'm sorry. Look, why don't you sit down. We can have a chat.'

About what, though?

The two perched, doubtfully, across from each other.

'Would you,' Grainne hoped, 'care for some warm milk? Tea?'

But the old lady wouldn't. She swooped to the floor, retrieving what looked like a scrap of felt. Her clothes seemed to be moulting. Yes, she had enjoyed the show. Her supper too. 'You're too good to me. I've disrupted your lives.'

'No.'

'Oh, I have.'

'Michael,' Grainne hoped, 'will soon be back.'

'Who?'

She refused to go into this again. But into what could they usefully probe? The aunt's nunnish status embarrassed Grainne who feared she might expect visits from priests, and religious statues in her room. Probably she would. Grainne, who had rid the house of any she'd inherited, would have to go to some shop which sold illuminated images of the Infant of Prague or perhaps the Sacred Heart drawing aside his robe to reveal an organ bleeding solid pigment for our sins. Of omission and commission. All this was only if the old thing was staying on, which as a long-term proposition would have to be thought about hard.

Smile at her. Shuttle of vigilance in the old face. Wonders why she's here and where next. *The Times* had a piece the other day about how the mad can fake sanity. She's looking at me. Perhaps *I* look mad? Contagion. Say something.

'I'm afraid,' Grainne looked around the room, 'you'll think I'm a dreadful housekeeper. I've been away, you see. To-morrow, Doris will clear things up.'

Reaching behind herself to illustrate, she retrieved a hockey-stick from deep in the recess of the couch in which she was sitting. Must have been there for months. Pencils, coins, crumbs and hair-grips disappeared in that maw. Now this.

The old lady held out her hand for the stick.

'May I?'

Her fingers felt frail as chicken bones. They tried to clench around the handle. Had she arthritis? No, she'd managed to make two fists. A twitch of humour flicked for the first time around her mouth. 'I'm seeking a memory,' she told Grainne in a social voice. 'Very old.'

'Oh. Did you play hockey?'

But the old woman was not holding the stick like a hockey-stick. She had it upside down and was thrusting forward as though making hay. 'You said,' she surprised Grainne by remembering, 'that my brother, Seamus, was your grandfather. He used to teach recruits to charge with bayonets. Drilling for the Volunteers.' She laughed, jabbed. 'I'd forgotten. They gave me shock treatment, you know. It impairs the memory. Also, I sometimes doubt whether I want to recover the things they buried. Memories? It might be as well not to dig them up? One can get nasty surprises. Not everything buried is treasure.'

'Indeed.'

Grainne stared in fascination. A sensuous apathy had come over her. She watched the old woman's fledgling movements. Jab, went the old thing at a cushion, jab at the air. Was some tapestry of remembered images being built up in Aunt Judith's mind by these embryo movements? Her gestures were unmartial. She reminded Grainne of pictures of Victorian women playing tennis with those tear-shaped bats. They had always served under-arm, hadn't they? Probably the tight sleeves they wore wouldn't permit them to raise their arms. Scoop, they went with their rackets and scoop, jab, went prim Aunt Judith.

'From below up,' she informed Grainne. 'Into the guts. Oh, you may think of it as brutal, and wounds in the intestine *are* terrible, but if you're going to have war then there's no room for sentimentality. Seamus used to say that. Owen, too, and our poor brother, Eamonn, before he died. Our lads had no ammunition. That was why they had to use ambushes and hand-to-hand combat. They'd jump out from behind some-thing. Like that. Close up. See. Pow!' Aunt Judith manoeuvred delicately around the sofa. 'Then quick into the guts! They couldn't waste bullets. Seamus used to say that you had to be several jumps ahead of the other fellow. Ready. Determined. Not panicky. Wait till you see the whites of their eyes and then POW! Who's that?' cried Aunt Judith, tremulous and

breaking her own rules. 'Who?' she panicked, her weapon at
the ready as the drawing-room door opened. 'You trapped
me!' she accused Grainne, who was by now ready to behold
a ghost.

It was merely Michael. Teetering, he interrogated: 'Grainne?
Back, eh? Dint say you were coming or . . .' Daunted, he
trailed off, 'Wha . . .?'

Aunt Judith's voice rose an octave. 'A man? *Here?* I should
have known!' She tilted her hockey-stick into his stomach.

Michael could have been fighting bees. Drunk Grainne
saw, and saw in the same moment one of his bee-flailing
hands catch Great-aunt Judith on the side of the head.

The aunt crumpled. Michael, steadying himself, collapsed
in safety on the sofa. 'Bugger,' he declared. 'Think I'm going
to be . . . sick.'

Oh vo, vo, vo!' came from the floor. 'The girl's a stool
pigeon. You won't catch me that easily. I deny it all! Violence,'
she cried. 'I never thought I'd see the day! You'd hit an
old . . .'

'Are you all right, Aunt Judith?' Grainne tried to haul her
up but the poncho had slid down over her aunt's elbows and
was pinioning her like a strait-jacket. Grainne wrestled with
wool. Michael retched into the coal scuttle.

'A conspiracy,' cried the benighted creature on the floor.
'You're Owen's cat's paw! Who are you anyway?'

Smells were thick in the room. And, Oh Lord! A man stood
in the doorway. A stranger. Respectable, Grainne judged. He
wore nondescript clothes but they were clean. Thank God for
that. You never knew with what class of customer Michael
would hitch up in his cups.

'Can I help?' he asked, and put his arms around Aunt
Judith, lifting her bodily. He was a big man. Fair-haired. 'I
don't think she's hurt,' he said. 'She was just caught off
balance. Maybe we should get her to bed? I'll carry her if
you'll show me where.'

'It's upstairs.' Grainne was mortified, but led the way.

Noises came from the fireplace as she went out of the
door: 'Grainne, m'dear, mush introdushe . . . friend. Oh
God, I think she has punctured my shtomach!'

'Don't be idiotic, Michael! She couldn't puncture a cushion. Do try not to be sick on the carpet, will you? I'll be back in a minute.' Shrewish, but what could he expect, welcoming her home like that after all his solicitations?

The man followed her up the stairs carrying Aunt Judith in his arms like a baby. The old thing was croaking. 'Destiny,' said she, and added several bird calls. Then she started to sing an old song that Grainne hadn't heard in decades and the aunt must surely not have heard in many more:

> 'But the boys of Kilmichael were ready,
> And met them with powder and shot,
> And the Irish Republican Army
> Made bits of the whole shaggin' lot!'

The man laid her on the bed and helped pull off the poncho. She had some sort of shift on underneath it which Grainne decided not to bother removing.

'My name's Grainne O'Malley.'

'James Duffy.'

He was an American, she saw now, paying attention to him. He was examining the photographs laid out on the bedside table.

'The background could be Boston,' he observed.

'Maybe it is. Aunt Judith's father was a returned Yank.' Oh dear, he was a Yank himself. 'You've been a great help,' she told him. 'I'll manage the rest. Why don't you go down and get yourself a drink?'

He left and she finished getting her grandaunt to bed.

'That was him, wasn't it?' said the aunt in a shrill, childish voice. 'Sparky? The Yank?'

'Who? No, don't worry,' said Grainne, deciding that the old thing was still delirious. 'Relax, Aunt Judith. You're among friends.'

'He's sweet on you,' said the little girl's voice. 'I can tell. I watched him watch you.'

'Good night now, Aunt Judith.' Grainne summoned a ward sister's authoritative manner. Better bully her for her own good. What would they *do* if she was really mad? Would their GP be able to cope? Would he even come, she wondered? It was getting on to midnight. 'I'm leaving the nightlight on,' she said. 'Sleep well. See you in the morning.'

Like a child seeking protection from night-time fears, the old lady had scooted under the clothes. Grainne, turning in the doorway, saw nothing but a nose rising from a turbulence of pillows and noted that her aunt looked more like one of the phantoms from which a child might be hiding.

5

In the drawing room the American was not drinking, which led her to hope that he might now leave.

'Your husband asked me to help him to bed. He's resting.'
That meant out cold.

'You've been kind,' she told him. Her hand jumped to her face. 'Have I a smudge?'

'Sorry, I was noting the resemblance to your aunt's photograph. She was beautiful, wasn't she?' There was a charge of attention coming at her, as though he had concentrated his energies into that steady stare. He must think he'd fallen into a stage-Irish household. Probably he'd dine out on this.

Interrogative echoes hung and she realized that he had been asking questions. About what? Taxis, was it? Telephones? Damn, she thought. Michael had let her down again. Let himself down. Cut an idiotic figure in front of this stranger and upset the aunt whom *he* had landed them with. The unfairness of it! He'd conked out conveniently too, leaving *her* to feel embarrassed. A flurry of rage hit her and she thought simultaneously of waking him up, throwing out this embarrassing witness and smoothing the thing over. Oh God, she'd probably been making faces.

'I'm afraid I'm between worlds,' she apologized. 'It's not Hallowe'en, is it? The souls of the dead seem to be about.'

The eccentricity of this struck her and she was obliged to explain about Sister Judith's fear of being committed by Owen and how the poncho had turned into a strait-jacket. For a moment she thought of telling him how the aunt had mixed *him* up with someone called Sparky. Then she decided not to.

'As though the dead generations were weaving spells.'

He asked whether the Owen she had mentioned was *the*

Owen O'Malley and she said 'No less!' But the irony missed him. 'Usually,' she said, 'the old bastard stays tidily in the grave and the subconscious, and impinges less . . .' Remembering afterwards, it seemed that the guest had said nothing, just politely listened to her laborious efforts to make her family seem sane. At some stage it got through to her that the man was impressed rather than shocked and then, of course, her excuses began to sound like boasts. Being Owen O'Malley's grandson, she heard herself say of Michael, must be in some ways as trying as being George Washington's might be in the States.

'God,' she interrupted herself, mortified by the pretentiousness of this, 'one shouldn't try humour with strangers. It never works.'

'Don't worry about it. Say, I've been nerving myself to ask. You wouldn't have some food around, would you? Anything would do. I've been trying to get to a restaurant all evening and . . .'

So that was all that was wrong with him: hunger! She laughed. 'With Michael one never gets to a restaurant. I'm starving myself,' she realized. 'There's ham in the kitchen, also some hock. Come on then. Between one thing and another I forgot to eat.' Her hand, she noticed now, was doing a jig. That was hunger but looked like Parkinson's disease.

The American patted it. 'Relax.'

'It's not drink.'

'I didn't think it was. You've been shaken up.'

The understanding was insidious. She could have wept or thrown her arms around him. Controlling these midnight impulses, she led him to the kitchen. 'Sandwich?'

'Great.'

Like herself, the fridge was febrile. Leaning her elbows on the deal table, she bit into a sausage and said, 'This is the first time I've relaxed all day.' She sloshed whiskey into her glass – the guest chose the hock, but she needed a quicker fix – and felt its ease flow into her fingers until they slowed, then ceased their tattoo. 'People seem to be flinging themselves into history's embrace,' she said. 'I had a row with my son. He's fourteen and consorts with bombers.' She was talking too much. Nerves. Anger twitched in her as she saw that unjudging look in the man's eyes and diagnosed it as medical. Of course, finding her in this madhouse, he must doubt her sanity. Silence was an easy trick. Priests and doctors cultivated it, nodding behind confessionals and desks and wrapping themselves in an air of sagacity. Grainne, an ex-Catholic, had transferred the odium she might have felt for priests on to medical men. False prophets she thought them – her mother had died of cancer – sanctimonious, raking in the money, intruding into people's lives and bodies. Terrified of her heredity, she had to go regularly to a gynaecologist who poked lubrified fingers inside her vagina to take a smear test, exactly as her confessors, before she left the Church, had poked spiritual probes into her head. Often doctors were clumsy, catching some of her soft inner tissues in their metal specula and tearing out pubic hair. If she made a grimace, they looked at her with the mild condescension she saw on this man's face. He was eating her food and being placidly polite and superior in his silence. She vowed to try silence herself, then heard her voice carrying on regardless.

'The people who need bombs,' said that brittle voice, 'are not the fourteen-year-olds. They'll escape the family trap in the next few years.'

'You mean they're free?' he asked. 'But that's awful too. Each choice diminishes the freedom. Surely you remember?'

She didn't. At Cormac's age she had been intent on her inner life which was unfree, fanatical, and flung itself about like some creature afflicted by unassuageable desires. Her thoughts then were perverse, her aspirations disincarnate. After an acute crisis of religiosity, she had given up the Church. There had been no logical progression to this. The movement had been like that of a tennis ball which, smashed back and forth, finally spins off course and leaves the court through a gap in the fence.

'But Cormac,' she cried, horrified by memory, 'isn't under the sort of pressure my generation was.'

'There are always pressures.'

'You think history is more like tennis than, oh, what? Golf? That things bounce back and forth?'

She didn't hear his answer, having just had one from her own body: a surge of lust. Absurd, familiar, forgotten: it was what she had often felt when she went to confession for the man invisible behind the dark grating who talked to her of the spirit and made her mouth parch, her breasts burn, her womb heat and melt. Why? Perversity. Tennis. Too much of one thing drove her to its opposite. She had never felt such a thing for a gynaecologist. She hadn't felt it for years. Surprised but gratified – for *now* what the old, once-loathed, sensation meant was a resurgence of youth – she stuffed her mouth with bread.

'Have some,' she pushed the breadboard his way. 'Brown bread. Home-made, I've been missing it in London.'

Had she been away then? he asked and she said she had. Mechanically, her mind sent out conversational signals, like some sleepy, all-night, disc jockey, while she focused her main attention on the bread. When had he arrived himself, she asked? Oh? And for how long? Of course you don't want to go to bed with this fellow. It's a reflex, knee-jerk. Means nothing. Think of bread. And he'd met Michael in a pub? With Corny Kinlen. I see. She visualized her teeth sliding in and out of the boggy texture, soft crust, damp pith spiked with bits of rough husk. Brown soda-bread was her mnemonic, her madeleine; its turfy substance told her that she was home. You ate it with smoked salmon or oysters, marmalade or egg. It reminded her of childhood, picnics, smokey cottages and the Shelbourne Rooms. It was the substance of Ireland. She was taking communion under two species: brown bread and whiskey.

The guest – what was this his name was? Duffy? – said he had come from the States to interview people with memories of the Troubles. 'I gather that your aunt . . .'

That fixed her attention. 'Aunt Judith? Oh, indeed, she's the ghost patrolling the battlements without hope of deliverance or revenge.' What luck, she thought, that someone should value what the poor thing had. 'She's a touch gaga,' she warned. 'From what I can make out, she seems to have had an appalling life.'

'Why? Because she was a nun? But mustn't that have been a free choice?'

'*You* just said that choices are cages.'

'Did I?'

'Something like that. However, it wasn't her having gone *into* the convent I meant but the fact that she then had to come out. Imagine: after fifty-five years! The monastic alternative was never gay but used to be reliable. Repudiation was never in the contract when you became a bride of Christ. If Jesus is a Judas,' she shrugged, 'then . . .'

'Anything goes?'

'Doesn't it?'

'There's always the highway code,' said the American. 'Civic virtue works quite well when religion dries up. But why do you suppose your aunt had a poor life? The life of the body isn't everything.'

Grainne laughed, then, realizing that he *hadn't* meant sex, blushed her furious redhead's blush. He was looking tranquilly at her. Had he meant something spiritual? she wondered. People had funny religions now in America. You saw them on television. Moonies. Hare Krishnas. Even in London, by the Goodge Street Underground, disciples tried to lure you into the lair of Ron Hubbard. It made her angry to think that after all the centuries it had taken people to escape the yoke of traditional religion, these eejits were sticking their necks under freak ones.

Under this official line of thought, she could feel rogue notions skittering. One was continuing embarrassment at her blush. Relax, she told herself. What does it matter what this fellow thinks. He's a ship that'll pass in the night. Sharp as a pincer came the knowledge that she didn't want him to. She wanted him to stay where he was, beaming attentiveness at her. When had she last felt its glow?

She laughed again. He joined with her. Laughing was something he did easily, she noticed. She felt joined in its medium with him as though they had been both immersed in some liquid. It was not a humorous – not an Irish – laugh.

'Why are we laughing?'

It struck her that she knew nothing about him. At the same time she remembered when she had last been looked at this way. It had been in Italy and she had hated it. She had been eighteen and social considerations were of vital importance. Men defined you then. Men talked. Other men listened and what was said could decide a girl's future. Then.

'An individual came asking for your address,' a secretary at the embassy had told Grainne on some occasion that year. 'He hoped we might have a list of our resident citizens. Naturally, I refused,' said the man, and looked with disfavour on the girl who attracted the attention of brazen individuals. Definitions then were the name of the game. Not only was Ireland a small community but, in those days, the Irish carried their signalling network wherever they went. Grainne's mother used to sing a song whose refrain went:

> 'What has a poor girl but her name to defend her?
> Oh Barney go home, I will not let you in.'

Clearly, Barney, whoever he was, lacked social credentials. He was also probably – though Grainne saw the fallacy of assuming the asocial to be always thrilling – someone the girl would have *liked* to let in, if only because his proper place, like a yard cat's or a mountain lion's, was out. He was not husband material and Grainne, at eighteen, had been in search of nothing less. She was not proud of this. The rules had changed and young women nowadays could afford to be adventurous. The yardstick for judging them was less harsh – but you reckoned with the one in use in your time. Anyway, *now* she was not seeking definition any more. What a man could do for her now would be to help her forget herself. Provisionally. Grainne had ties and duties. The tide of permissiveness which lapped the shores of Ireland, like an oil slick riding the warm Gulf Stream, was safely navigable only as long as you kept off the coastal rocks. Laws here had not changed, nor people's attitudes underneath. Not for women. Like a group riding the last steps of an escalator, Ireland moved with the times but stayed in the rear. Women could now live openly with lovers but legal protection lagged. There was no divorce. Alimony – if you obtained one abroad – was hard to collect. Moreover, thrifty husbands had been known to fall back on an old trick of the livestock trade and sue a wife's lover for sizable compensatory damages. Caught between canons, you could go wrong. The old said: 'Thou shalt not be promiscuous nor basely sensual.' The new: 'Thou shalt have orgasms and enjoy God's good gifts to the full.' The old, being old, had been eroded by custom. An ill-married woman might, it conceded, have a discreet fling if nobody got hurt in the process. The new was rigid: be honest, it bullied, be frank. Speaking most recently through Jane's mouth, it demanded that women be true to themselves and break up a bad marriage instead of trying, hypocritically, to smooth things over. Unsatisfactory mates should be replaced.

Honesty and mate-jettisoning horrified Grainne. Yet she felt prepared to believe the part of the message which said that good sex made you a healthier and better-balanced person. Her balance was bad. She didn't need anyone to tell her that. But you had to decide how you were going to play things. As this fellow had said, choice caged you and the best choice, she felt, was a charitable hypocrisy. It was easier on families, more exciting for the hypocrite. She had seen the new, frank mode in operation among foreign friends. Married or not, according to this formula, you brought your bed companion to dinner and acknowledged him. This revived the matter of social definitions and table manners and the discredit he might reflect on you if he didn't have them. But where then was the romance of finding a creature uniquely appropriate to night, intimacy and bed? Someone as anonymous as a merman or satyr with furry, frondy thighs. Asocial and outside time. She had seen paintings of these lewd creatures of old fantasy when she was in Italy and they had taken her breath away. Right in the museums, framed in ornate gilt: a publicly acknowledged ancient dream of pastoral bliss and folly. Naked girls in forests, minotaurs and goatmen licking at them. Frondy wetnesses, clear streams, pink nipples, mouths open down to their tonsils. She forgot the names of the painters, remembering only Raphael who painted virgins, God help us, with prim little mouths. She hadn't profited from that year at all. It had been the wrong time for her and the men were terrifying. She remembered their eyes X-raying her clothes. She had been innocent but had understood. You couldn't fail to. Their thighs pressed against the cloth of their trousers and so did their genitals. Was it all an act, you wondered, or were they really that mad for it? That great at it? You'd like to know. To have tried just once. Instead, she'd married Michael and after a while she'd given up wanting it. Maybe an emotional duct dried up on you. Like religion: use it or lose it. Of course there *had* been – no, don't think of *him*! That had been a case, if ever there was one, of falling between the old and the new. 'Make yourself cheap,' warned the old ethic, 'and men will take you lightly.' She had and he had. Very. But with a stranger, an anonymous man of the night, you didn't care about being taken lightly. You *wanted* to be wanton like witches who, in nocturnal orgies, did the opposite of everything they did by day. It would purge and renew you. Surely it would.

She had been reminded of her ancient female dream by this man's electric look. Was she counting her chickens before they were hatched? Was she even sure that she had a hold of an egg? Maybe this fellow didn't even know he was looking? Had a cast in his eye? Dare she ask: 'Sir, is yours an anthropologist's or a tourist's scrutiny? Are your intentions reliably dishonourable? Do you realize that you've shaken a decent wife and mother out of her ethical corsettings? Do you know the responsibilities that that entails? She needs a new shape: needs the surround of a new presence, like a cuckoo's egg, in the nesty warmth of some unknown bird.'

Mad, she thought. Fool. He's not thinking of you at all. They're just not taught manners and not to stare. Cultural divide. Mixed signals. Forget it. You'd better take up jogging or something. Get rid of your appetites. Assault your husband. That was the thing, really: she had been primed for bloody Michael and the pulsings of her body had nothing to do with this man at all. The bastard was good-looking though. Too good-looking? A queer? Oh, what did it matter? She wished he'd leave.

Frightening her – for if he could read her thoughts how appalling that would be – he said, 'I should go. It's late. Could I use your phone to call a taxi?'

Possessions were vital to Cormac's well-being. In his English boarding-school there had been pain – no, there had been panic in the way his sense of himself failed when he was obliged to undress in an open dormitory, with only one drawer to call his own at the foot of his bed and a few hooks in the cloakroom for shirts, jackets, mac and coats. There had been other small areas reserved for him in the school: shoe-holes, a shelf in a games cupboard for his sports kit, and another in study hall for books. At night, sleepless, feeling like a martyr whose bones lay scattered on Alpine mountains cold, he would inventory the places where his belongings were, going over them, as a dog might be imagined to console itself by remembering sites where it had buried bones. The martyr image was closer. Cormac had felt dismembered. Mid-terms spent with his mother at the Halfway House had been unspeakably worse. He never ever wanted to think of them again.

Back home tonight, the relief was so acute he could hardly get used to it. His glee was near-lunatic each time he awoke to awareness of being surrounded by a wardrobe, chest-of-drawers, cupboard, trunk and tuck-box, all stuffed with his own things and all fitted with keys which he kept on a ring under his pillow and touched from time to time with utter satisfaction.

Outside, in the garden, was the patch which he had marked off as his when he was five. He had planted several old Christmas trees there after they had served their time indoors and had buried a defunct pet rabbit called Mopsy and a dog killed by a car. Most of the plants he had put there during a brief craze for market-gardening – he had sold baby marrows to his mother that season – were long dead, but the trees throve, grew and pursued their vegetable lives steadily, unhampered and on his behalf. They were his trees. The comfort he drew from this astonished him. Experimentally, he tried to feel sympathy with the sap rising through the branches of *his* trees and found that he actually did experience a coursing tingle in his limbs. He hoped he wasn't mad or too materialistic and wondered what it would be like to have a family – live humans, sons perhaps, products of your own body, breathing and sleeping in surrounding rooms? He thought he'd love it, although his imagination couldn't quite make the leap. Did his parents feel that way about him? No, they'd have had more children if they had and wouldn't have sent *him* to bloody boarding-school. It didn't surprise him, really, that they weren't patriotic. How could you feel for a whole country if you couldn't even keep a family going properly?

He hoped they hadn't let anything happen to his trees while he was away. Cut them down even? His father was capable of it. He didn't respect mine and thine and had been complaining last year that one tree was blocking a window. Shit, Cormac should have checked before rushing out to the club. He would have done but for the row with his mother. Where were his slippers? Bother. And his electric torch? No good trying to sleep now until he'd at least counted his trees. Then in the morning he'd make a proper inspection.

James had been caught up in something to which he couldn't put a name. Was he merely drunk? Outside time? He was certainly between times, for here it was the small hours, and at home – he saw from his digital watch which would have to be taken to a store for adjustment – it was late enough to be at work. Whatever the source of his headiness, he liked it. In part it must be this odd old house, canting as though undermined by some subsidence of the soil – or perhaps by some defect in his own eye? It was like a house painted by Soutine, with verticals out of true, bruised shadows, surfaces fuzzy with the bloom of use. Even the silver cutlery, laid out for the scratch meal, had a soft-edged look. Its pattern was half-eroded and its elegance spoiled by the careless mixing in of some stained, pewter spoons. Quite possibly poisonous, these disturbed like black teeth in a mouth. James, whose native city was the capital of cosmetic dentistry, had seen teeth like this in the pubs tonight for the first time ever and experienced unease. The sight of other deformities stepped this up. Mangled features, worthy of a gallery of grotesques, blazing red skin, rheumy eyes – in one case the unmasked absence of an eye – tics and an innocence of orthodontia registered like so many reminders of mortality. James had been shaken. At the same time, his own healthy flesh had begun rampantly and defiantly to make his appetites felt. He was out of true himself, exhilarated, keyed up and, oddly enough, his hostess seemed to be at a similar pitch.

Their hunger went some way to explaining this. His had been compounded by jet-lag. Hers, apparently, was acute. She explained that she had to eat frequently and got migraines and tremors if she didn't. Normally, she made sure this didn't happen but tonight, he gathered, had been trying. Family situations . . . He apologized but was delighted to have intruded. One relished other people's dramas and how regret stumbling into one so promising with historical echoings? He got little from her about the aunt but determined to do some research. Owen O'Malley's sister-in-law? A mad nun? Splendid stuff. He'd hit the jackpot there.

Mrs O struck him as a familiar type. Thanks to Therese. She was not like his wife but there were traits he recognized. He was like a dog-breeder encountering a specimen of his breed. A raiser, say, of Salukis. Both Mrs O'Malley and Therese had that abundant, flouncing hair and willowy backbone. Like a yashmak, the hair provided cover and probably affected their characters. Therese fought her tendency to vagueness, goading herself as the Irishwoman almost certainly did not. There was about them both a hesitant, unfinished area: bruise and bite, doubt and coquetry.

Therese had matt skin. Mrs O'Malley's was transparent, green where veins showed through. Vulnerable. Like a water nymph. Changeable too. Slightly watery eyes. Too big for reliable beauty, they could look like raw eggs or, with a twitch of the head, remind you of certain formal styles in painting or sculpture – old Mesopotamian, Etruscan – in which the immense eye cavity probably figured receptivity and submission. He was moved by the alternations of beauty and homeliness and tempted to tell her how to paint her lids.

It wasn't the woman *qua* woman who appealed to him, but the glimpse she was giving him of alien lives. He was the demon in an old story – which came suddenly to mind – who lifts the roofs of houses and looks inside. Asmodeus?

Reminded of his intrusiveness, he said he ought to be calling a taxi. Better not wear his welcome out at one sitting. *He* was coming alive, feeling full of beans but that was jet-lag and she must be bushed.

She showed him the phone. No dice with taxis. Most of the people he rang seemed resentful at being woken up. Between calls he heard her talk to the drunken husband. Her tone surprised him for, he suddenly saw, he had misread his feelings completely. Also hers.

'*Darling!*' he heard her cry, 'whatever's wrong? I thought you were asleep. Feeling all right? *Sure?* ... Listen, did you get any dinner? ... Oh, I was but I've got over it ... Yes, promise. Listen, you'll catch your death ... There is, but he's leaving now. He's ringing a taxi. I'll be up in a ... Oh, sweetie, stop being so silly. Really, why should anyone have cut down your trees? ... What? ... Well, no, I didn't but it's dark now and it's pouring with rain. Can't you leave it till the morning? Mmm? *Please.*'

The cajoling tone annoyed him. He was jealous of the drunken sot. What was that about *trees*? His own intrusiveness confirmed, he was now anxious to get a taxi and leave but could find none. Humiliated to find he had been dallying in his mind with a woman so thoroughly bespoke – surely she had indicated that she wasn't? – he was now doubly so at having to throw himself on her mercy for a ride.

'I'll walk,' he suggested, 'if it's at all possible. But you'll have to tell me the way.'

'Which hotel are you at?'

'The Shelbourne.'

'Too far,' she told him. Worse: she couldn't, she explained, take him there in her car. She was tired, had drunk too much, and would never pass a breathalyzer test if stopped. 'Michael's already barred, which means I've got to be extra careful if the household is not to be driverless.'

'I'll walk.'

'No, no. It's miles and it's raining. Listen, why don't you spend the night? It's the easiest thing. This happens quite often so we keep the spare-room bed made up.'

'I hate to ...'

'You're not. Come. I'll show you the way. I'll get you some towels just as soon as I check that my son's gone back to bed. He's gone slightly dotty tonight. There must be a full moon.'

'Was that your son you were talking to just now?'

'Yes. Cormac. Here's your room. I'll be back in a jiffy with the towels.'

She forgot to come back to show him the bathroom. Minutes after she had left him, he came out into darkness and began slapping walls in search of a light switch. When he located and got one on, he found all the doors on the landing closed. He proceeded to examine them with some stealth, thinking that it might be embarrassing if he were to burst in on the nutty aunt.

Bending, he laid an ear to the keyholes of the first and then the second door. Nothing. Listening for breathing, he screwed his ear into the third door aperture then, exchanging it for an eye, became aware that he must look like a Peeping Tom caught redhanded to the boy who – he knew in afterthought – had been watching him for some minutes from the upper landing.

James stood up. The boy leaned over the bannister. Silently. The ball was in James's court.

'Hullo,' James attempted to sound off-hand. 'I'm looking for the bathroom. Didn't want to disturb anyone. My name is James.'

The face above him did not adjust to accommodate this. James reflected that the boy himself was an unwinning figure: nervous-looking with wrists and ankles protruding from outgrown pyjamas. Gas-jet blue eyes blazed with hostility.

'Did one of them ask you to stay the night?'

'Yes. Can you show me the bathroom?'

The boy gave a minimal sideways nod at one of the doors. 'Which?'

'Your father. Is he expected to clear things with you?' James was sorry when he'd said this but could see no way to soften its impact.

Surprisingly, the boy looked a shade friendlier. 'Thought you might be one of my mother's cases,' he said.

Can of worms, thought James. 'You're Cormac?' he supposed.

'Yes. Go and use the bog,' the boy told him. 'I'll wait.'

James went into the bathroom. It was the right sort for the house: high-ceilinged, draughty, cold, with a claw-footed bath, plaster roses on the dado, a flowered porcelain wash-basin and towels which had the impermeable texture of old suede. He had his pee, washed his hands in medicinal-smelling soap, threw water on his face and came out. The boy was still there.

'If I show you my collector's badge will you cough up a donation for the IRA Prisoners' Defence Fund?' he asked.

'No, I'm afraid I won't.'

'May I ask why not? Don't you believe the money is going to be used for peaceful purposes? Are you opposed to their aims or their methods?'

'What's this? A survey?'

'Sort of. I'm doing it for a group I belong to. You're the twentieth person I've asked. Each of us is to ask twenty then pool our results.'

'What are the results so far?'

'Anti-IRA. Some of the others will have a different cross-section. What's your answer?'

'Don't know. Unsure. Suspect there are better causes.'

'It's got to be for, against, or indifferent. Are you an indifferent?'

'I guess so.'

'Those who are neither hot nor cold I spit them out of my mouth.'

'The Bible,' James acknowledged. 'But I've got company it seems.'

'Oh, this is the Age of Indifference,' said Cormac. 'The only one who said "yes" was my Grandaunt Judith but then she's daft. Hasn't got the money for a donation anyway.'

'Well, what about you?' James asked with curiosity. 'Are you for or against?'

'For,' said the boy, and gave him a suddenly good-humoured grin and a clenched-fist salute. 'Good night,' he said.

James slept dreamlessly and awoke at what his digital watch

claimed was twelve o'clock. That would make it about eight a.m. local time. He heard the boy argue with his mother in the hall down the stairs from James's room.

'Got your sandwiches?'

'Stop pretending to be a good mother. You're not. You took me to live with daft zombies. Everyone knows about it around here. I'll never hear the end of it. You know what they think, don't you?'

'They can think what they like.'

'Do you know what it's like to be me? Do you? They say we only went there because Daddy battered you. Do you know why they say he battered you?'

'Cormac, they don't bother me.'

'You must be mad. You live in the world, don't you? I had a fight with a fellow at the club. He said you'd have to be a nut-and-fruitcake case to have gone there for no reason. He asked did you like a bit now and then on the side. And he was bloody big, a big moron. They think the same thing at school. I want to leave that school.'

'You said you wanted to come back. You didn't like it in England.'

'I didn't like being with yobbos. I don't want people here knowing we went there. It's all part of the same thing.'

'Rise above it. We're back now.'

'I can't rise. I'd have to be a karate black belt. I don't want to have a mad mother. Can't you settle down?'

'It was social work, Cormac.'

'Nobody believes that.'

'Doesn't the truth matter?'

'No, *no*. What matters is what they believe. Besides, you did desert Daddy, leaving him on his own. Why do you think he's drinking?'

'Listen, you're only fourteen, Cormac. There are things you don't understand . . .'

'And you?' The boy's voice wheezed hoarsely, broke, wheezed: 'Are you sure you understand?'

James heard the door slam and the mother's footsteps retreat.

*

Sister Judith's memory had been shaken up. She'd had some sort of shock.

'It's better now,' she told the girl who had asked how she felt. 'It's sifting back.'

Judith pictured her memory as a library. At the moment it was a library put to the sack. Feet stamped behind her eyeballs. Who was this girl?

'You're the principal girl now, aren't you?' she said, and waited cunningly for clarification. None came.

A headache flamed through her skull and she had to let it simmer down before trying to rebuild her retrieval systems.

'I'm a bit moidered,' she apologized, in case she had been making a bad impression. It was best to show you knew you'd slipped up. Stole their thunder. 'My poor head!' She scrutinized the girl. Another sly Miss.

There were definite losses. Volumes were smoke-blackened. A shelf of books gave way and, in spite of her efforts, crumbled.

She hoped she wasn't making a bad impression on that girl who might report her to the Reverend Mother. She would give them no excuse for further action.

When a newer, gentler girl came to wash her, Judith thought she might as well complain about the last one.

'Very rough,' she said, 'she pulled out handfuls of my hair.'

'There was nobody else here,' the girl said. 'It was me. Grainne. I'm sorry if I hurt you.'

'She was not at all like you,' said Judith, making a stand. 'She was rough.'

'Well, she won't come back then.'

'There was a boy here too,' Judith said. 'He must have come to repair the television. Men are not permitted in the community rooms except for such purposes. He was inquisitive. You should be careful about people like that. They might be casing the joint for a burglary.'

Later she asked, 'Where is Sister Gilchrist?'

'She's staying with her sister in England.'

'Who are you?'

'Grainne. Your niece.'

'Are you a nun or a lay teacher?'

'Neither. You're living in our house now. The convent is closed down.'

Sister Judith did not believe this. She probably hadn't heard it at all. It was her brain playing tricks on her and she mustn't let them think she was thinking such silly things or they might take the kindergarten teaching away from her, as she knew they were scheming to do. They said it was because she hadn't a diploma in education but she guessed that what they really thought was that she was going soft in the head. Maybe they were testing her?

'Where are the children today?' she asked, trying to sound alert and capable. 'I'd like to tell them a story.' She had done Trojan work with the kindergarten, nobody could deny her that. With or without a diploma.

'There are no children here,' the girl told her. 'Only Cormac who's fourteen.'

But there were no male fourteen-year-olds in the convent. She knew then that they were laying traps for her.

'Where are my clothes?' she asked. 'My habit. Where is it? Who produced these rags? I can't leave my cell in these.'

'These are the clothes you came in. I'll buy you some dresses if you'd like me to.'

'I don't want dresses. I want my habit. I can't teach the kindergarten wearing these things.'

'There are no habits any more,' the girl told her. Sister Judith had a feeling that she'd heard that before. Maybe it was true then?

Later the TV repair man came back. 'Are you for the IRA?' he wanted to know. 'Would you give money to the IRA Prisoners' Defence Fund?'

'We take vows of poverty here. We're not even allowed to handle money except in exceptional cases,' she said carefully, 'such as when one is in charge of the children's lunches.'

'But you support the IRA?'

'Yes.'

'Aren't you worried by their methods? The Church condemns wars which cannot be won since they expose people to needless suffering. Now, the IRA can't win by arms since they are a minority.'

'Are you here to repair the T V ?'

'I'm Cormac. I'm conducting a survey for our citizenship class.'

'You're a spy!' she shrieked, her terrors confirmed. 'Go away.'

When the girl came back she refused to answer her questions or say why she was crying. She thought now that taking the kindergarten teaching away from her might be the thin end of the wedge. Owen might have heard that she had stopped wearing the habit. He would protect himself. Woe to her by whom scandal cometh.

'Please, can't I have my habit back?' she wheedled. 'What is it you're after?'

'Aunt Judith, calm down. We're on your side. We're family.'

'Who?'

'Me. I'm your niece.'

'Ha!' shouted Judith, seeing it all. 'Owen sent you. You've been trying to drive me mad. You,' she remembered with a horrid lucidity, 'made me bayonet – what did I do with a bayonet?'

'It was a hockey-stick.'

'Stool pigeon,' shrieked Judith. 'Blood tells. Owen's daughter. Blood!' she screamed.

The girl went away and came back later with a man who asked: 'Are we feeling better?'

'You're a doctor!' Doctors called you 'we'.

'Clever girl. I'm Doctor Doherty.'

Doctors who called an old woman 'girl' had something up their sleeve. Judith felt exhilarated by visible danger. 'I want you to know,' she took a deep breath and gripped the arms of her chair, 'that I am in command of my faculties. I never had any intention of throwing off the veil and if I am wearing these odd garments it is because *she*,' pointing at the intriguing, bold-faced slip of a thing, 'hid my habit.' She remembered then that habits had perhaps been abolished. Had they or hadn't they? Memory refused to yield up the vital fact. 'Clothes,' said Judith with supreme craftiness, 'are unimportant. Saint Francis gave his to the birds.' There was something wrong with that. 'I am content to wear poor garb,' she added hastily. Silence after all might be best.

'It has been a tiring week, hasn't it?' said the doctor. 'We need a little rest. What about a little injection?'

Here Sister Judith's television knowledge came to her aid. He could have *anything* in that hypodermic needle: drugs, poison, something which might make her truly mad. There had been a case in 'Colombo' unless it was 'The FBI'. One or the other. 'Little' was a sinister adjective.

'Owen's arm is long, isn't it?' she said, trying to sound as casual as she could. 'I suppose a Cabinet Minister can buy a doctor any day.' That was unwise. The man must not be made angry. 'Forgive me,' she said. 'I have been threatened in the past, you see. There is nothing personal in this,' Sister Judith pleaded. She was at the end of her resources. 'I don't *know* you, after all. Try to see how it is for me,' she begged.

'Who threatened you?' the doctor asked.

'My brother-in-law.'

'He's dead,' the girl said, then added surprisingly: 'He might have though. He was quite capable of it. Let's forget the injection, doctor. A nice glass of warm punch would probably do as well. Would you like that, Aunt Judith? I'll share it with you since you're so suspicious.'

Later she came back with two glasses of whiskey-and-lemon punch. They drank them while watching some programme on social questions. Sister Judith was bored but she saw the girl wanted to watch and, as she was beginning to feel guilty for having been so distrustful, she pretended to enjoy it.

'That,' said Doris, the O'Malley's char, 'will put lead in your pencil. Eat up.'

She was feeding Cormac who had stayed home from school, saying he was sick. 'Yer terrible jumpy for a kid your age,' she said. 'You should be on tranquillizers. Now stop talking and eat and I'll tell ye about the film I seen last night at the Regal. I went with my girl friends because Ted's after joining a men's club. Off out every night of the week. Playing darts and the like, and in the weekends now it's golf. Golf for the working man, if you don't mind, and drinking fancy drinks.'

Cormac, who knew all there was to know about Ted, was not listening. He was worried about his own family and wondering was it time he took a hand. At first he had thought his mother was the flighty one. Certainly it was she who had started people gossiping, and Cormac had had to put up with fellows too big to fight asking him had she had it off with English fellows on the q.t. and would he maybe be having a little English half-brother one of these days. On the other hand, it had to be admitted that his father drank and didn't have a real job. Cormac had only recently come to realize that his father's was a joke job and that his father, and in time Cormac himself, would have owned the family woollen mills if the grandfather hadn't disinherited them in favour of Great-Uncle Owen Roe. That sort of news made you wonder about the old man. Feeble.

'Coming home stocious five nights a week,' said Doris, but was talking about Ted.

Cormac had learned a lot in the last year about family life. What shocked him were not the things people did to each other in secret. Nothing he'd heard in the Halfway House had been new. Though it was upsetting to hear stories from people they'd happened to, the stories themselves were no worse than the ones Doris told about what went on in her street, where houses were small and the walls too thin for anything to be kept hidden. So it wasn't hearing about someone's Dad bashing their Mum so that she had to have ten stitches that was so bad. It was the way families covered up for the bullies and the shame they felt. When you came from a family like that, people thought the badness rubbed off on you. Kids in the Halfway House had known that and picked on Cormac who wasn't one of them and might feel superior. Now that he'd got home, the shoe was on the other foot. People here thought he was tainted. They'd seen a TV programme on the Halfway House and had pumped Cormac with questions. Then, they turned on him because the things he'd told them had made them sick. Their own families, they let him know, were disciplined, religious and nice to each other. They drew strict pictures of their homes. Cormac was annoyed and envious of the ordered perfection in which they claimed to live.

'My father,' one boy had said, 'wouldn't ever let my mother live in a place like that. He'd have been over after her on the next plane.'

'Why'd he let her take *you*?'

'People in those places are all from the slums.'

'No,' Cormac was an expert on his sad subject. 'There was a vicar's wife, even.' But he was sorry he had given them ammunition to use against him. What sort of parents let their children lodge with the children of mad vicars? Now there was a loony right here in the house and his mother spent hours at a stretch talking to her. This morning he had heard the two planning to take a trip. He could hardly believe it. His mother was in need of a firm hand but who was to supply it? He had considered asking the parish priest but knew a fourteen-year-old would not be listened to and, besides, his mother wouldn't listen to the priest. She was forever giving out about priests. She was out of control, and what his school mates would think of this new move he couldn't think. For the moment, at school, nobody knew of his mad aunt. Cormac wanted to keep it that way. But his mother's plan – it was hard to believe even of her – was to get the aunt on television. He'd heard them discussing it and it was hard to say which of the two sounded more spastic.

'Do you remember the American who was here last week?' his mother had asked. 'He carried you upstairs.'

'Sparky Driscoll?'

'No, but he's interested in Sparky Driscoll. He makes television films. He could put you in one, like an actress. Would you like that? Would you tell him your memories, Aunt Judith?'

'But what about Owen?'

'He's dead; there's only you left to tell us the story.'

'Would they put me in prison?'

'Not prison, Aunt Judith, television.'

'Don't breathe a word, girl,' said the old loony. 'Especially to an American. There was money involved. Millions. The money de Valera raised in America. So he was important to both sides, do you see.'

'Sides of what?' asked his mother.

He wondered did she think the aunt meant sides of bacon? One was as daft as the other. They'd turn the family into laughing stocks if they appeared on RTE.

'Are you listening?' Doris wanted to know. She'd been telling him about the film she'd seen. 'Or are you on the moon?' She was cleaning the windows. Insides only. Time was when window-cleaning was a char's job but, as Doris regularly reminded Cormac's mother, 'Them days is gone!' She demanded extra pay even for insides. Making extra was Doris's passion. She hoarded it. It was hers: a secret from Ted, her useless husband, and she could do exactly what she wanted with it. Sometimes she had given Cormac some when he was smaller, saying 'Go buy yerself sweeties,' with a queenliness which, even at the age of eight, he had recognized as touching. He liked Doris. She had always been there and he knew how to deal with her changeable humours. Sometimes she was his friend, united against his parents, when she helped him break some rule of the house or when he connived with her against his mother. 'No need to tell yer Ma I'm borrowing this,' she'd said one time and slipped a dress of his mother's inside her coat as she was leaving. 'I'll have it back on Monda.' Cormac had been shocked for a moment, but had quickly seen that there was indeed neither need nor advantage to tale-telling. That was in the days when Doris still went to dances and liked to cut a dash. She could also gang up with his mother against himself, or she might remind them both that her real friends were the neighbours in her little back street, the working people who were at last coming into their own now that they had free medical care and other benefits. 'It's about time too,' said Doris ungratefully, and gave out about doctors who paid less attention to her ailments than she suspected they did to their paying patients' ones. She was spending time with a psychologist once a fortnight. 'Time was,' said Doris, getting angry with the past, 'when you'd have to be dying for them to pay attention to you in them dispensaries. But them days is gone.' They were indeed. Cormac's mother said *she* couldn't afford a psychologist. He wondered did she need one?

Doris was still talking about the film.

'He had a son.' She sprayed a window-pane with a great generous sweep of Windolene. 'And the only joy in his heart was this little son.' She spoke in time to her window-cleaning movements which were broad and swishy. 'And he was very cruel to his wife. Very unfair and the money was running low.' Doris took a breath and moved her cloth in an arc across the hazy glass. 'Their fortunes were going into a decline. Then the stepson decided to wreak vengeance.'

Cormac tended to listen to Doris's film-stories with half an ear. It was soothing to know that the thing had a perfectly accessible pattern which he needn't consider. There it was: contained and remote and unlikely to spill out of its limits and bother him. But his attention had just been caught.

'The mother's heart was broken.' Doris attacked the next freshly fogged pane with wastes of paper towel. She deliberately used too much of everything. This made it easier to pinch stuff for her own household: perks. 'But she deserved all she got for bringing in an outsider to squander her son's inheritance. Even the son's kindness was gall to her for he chased away her beloved Barry and she' – squeak went the paper on glass – 'had to spend her days in shame and loneliness' – squeak – 'watching her wronged boy rebuild his ruined estates.'

Doris became noble and sad when she talked about movies. Cormac felt stimulated by this story.

'How long's it on for?' he asked. 'I might like to see it.'

'Too late,' Doris told him. 'It's left. I'm going now.' She took off her overall and took a pair of high-heeled shoes out of her shopping bag. 'Have to go and clean up my own place. No rest for the wicked. Listen, I forgot to make a note of it so will you tell yer Ma a gentleman called? A Mr Duffy. Don't forget now.'

'No,' said Cormac. 'I won't.' One way to deal with his mother would be to complain about her to Uncle Owen Roe. If Daddy's job depended on him, that meant he was boss, didn't it? They'd both have to listen to him and, after all, Cormac would only be doing it for their own good. 'I won't forget,' he promised Doris.

6

James wrote to his wife and to Larry on postcards showing spinach-green countryside and villages where cement-fronted houses were aligned with the austerity of tombstones. The air here, he told them, was metallic and effervescent. The people were a disappointment. They reminded him of Middle America, that sector of the US psyche which Californians despise. He had driven with a taxi-man who favoured cutting off the hands of bank robbers.

'There isn't a week goes by without a hold-up,' he told James. 'They have the economy destroyed.'

'Are they raising funds for the IRA?'

The man snorted. 'Maybe ten per cent of the robberies. The rest have jumped on the band-wagon, learned the tricks, profited from the situation, don't you know. The police are at their wits' end and when they rough up a suspect the papers start yelling "torture" and "human rights". I'd give those yobbos rights. I'd cut off their right hands. It's in the Bible.' said the taxi-man.

'Are you sure?' It wasn't a book James had read much, but he was surprised.

'Tis,' said the man, 'and tis what those layabouts need: discipline. Sure you can't walk down O'Connell Street after dark now without being mugged. I'd bring back the cat o' nine tails and the birch. They have that in the Isle of Man. The government there tried to ban it but the people wouldn't let them. *They* know what's good for Law and Order. Give power to the ordinary men in the street and they'd settle the disorderly elements in no time. You'd see. Settle their hash for them in two shakes.'

The taxi-driver's brother-in-law, he told James, was a

money-lender who had been obliged to take the law into his own hands.

'People wouldn't pay up,' he explained. 'Nothing but hard-luck stories. You could predict them: husband out of work, father got a heart-attack and nyanyanya, crying this year for next year. The police wouldn't help.'

'Why? How high was the interest?'

'Why? How do I know? Anyway, the brother-in-law wasn't standing for that. He hired a few fellows who knew their own minds. Got them to give his debtors a pasting. Men *and* women. The brother-in-law believes in equal rights, ha ha. A right pasting his lads gave them and *then* they paid up. They had it all the time you see. The money. Might is right,' said the taxi-man and proceeded to overcharge James, who only realized this later.

'So you'd support the IRA?' James asked, mindful of his assignment to take the country's pulse.

'Support *them*? I'd support *them* on to a gallows, and pull away the stool.'

'Driscoll?' said Great-aunt Judith, her eyes bright with whiskey punch, 'Is it Sparky Driscoll? Sure the chap practically moved in with us in the summer of 1921. I remember as if it were yesterday coming home from school in June and finding him ensconced like a long-lost relative. He was always dropping in to chat with my Da about Boston and Philadelphia. The Da had been to those places as a young man and didn't often get a chance to have a bit of crack with someone who knew what he was talking about, so he was forever pressing Sparky to stay for supper. I didn't take to him as much as the others did. Well, that was pique at finding him settled in like one of the family without my having had a say in the matter. It put my nose out of joint. But the other thing I had against him was more serious. You see, to my mind it wasn't the Da he came for at all but Kathleen, and Kathleen was engaged to Owen who was in prison. People took a poor view of girls who played around when their men were behind bars, doing their bit for the country. And we had no mother. Seamus was away a lot and our father had no sense. Or so I thought. What was it you wanted to know about Sparky? Politics? Ah, I'd be no help to you there. No, I was young for my age, the last of the brood, don't you know. The others could never believe I'd grown. They kept me in the dark. I'd be no help to you about politics. What was he like? Giddy. Light-headed. Always skitting and laughing and playing silly jokes. He used to tell Kathleen that she should assert herself more and that women in America were freer. Well, what use was that sort of talk, I ask you, when she was engaged to a fellow like Owen, a spoilt priest, set in his ways and hard to get on with? If the same Sparky Driscoll had had it in mind to marry her and take her off to America, there might have been some sense in it, but not at all. One time I heard him telling her that she should emigrate.

'Is it on my own?' says she, giving him a chance to say that maybe he'd look after her, but he didn't take it up.

'Owen must have heard something because when he came home from gaol he never liked the Yank. One time Kathleen and myself took him to the Devereux Estate to show him where the dance had been that the Tans had raided. You'll have heard of that? Yes? Well, Timmy, the caretaker, played his accordion and Sparky and myself did a few turns on the ballroom floor for a lark. Afterwards, Owen got to hear of it and got it into his head that it was with Kathleen that Sparky had danced. Nothing would persuade him of the contrary. Sparky didn't like Owen either. They were like cat and dog. Politics? Oh, I suppose it came into it. What didn't it come into in those days? But no, I can't remember exactly. I will. I'll try to remember so. I'll tell you if anything strikes me.'

The humidity was tangible, a membrane through which people moved with effort. Belted into raincoats, pedestrians had a look of parcels. Cornices dripped. James bought a paper and shoved it inside his jacket to keep dry. In the nearest pub he brushed drops from his hair, ordered a whiskey – he had begun to see why people here drank – and opened the paper to see what they might be reading.

Item: a small one-engine plane had flown across the city trailing a banner inscribed with a patriotic slogan. The string of the banner had got entangled in the plane's motor causing it to crash in a rugby field. The pilot had been knocked senseless by the propeller and subsequently died. Item: a girl in South Dublin had bitten into a commercially made doughnut containing a rat's leg. 'It was very disgusting,' said Miss Maire Breen, 'I shall never again eat anything but cakes baked at home by my mother.' Under *Positions Wanted* James noted several gentlewomen looking for posts as housekeepers. A lady desiring room and board in exchange for light duties, stated ingenuously – or not? – 'anything considered'. The Minister for Health had revealed that nearly half the hospital beds in the country were occupied by mental patients. This reminded James that he was to lunch again with Mrs O'Malley. She claimed to have a plan to stir the memories of her aunt, whose recollections had dried up disappointingly when confronted with a tape-recorder.

'No,' said the aunt. 'I never wanted to leave the convent. Why would I? What sense would my life make elsewhere? I believe,' said she smoothly, 'in the spiritual life. Prayer.' She closed her eyes while she said this and gabbled inaudibly. The moustache on her upper lip was like a hump of stubbly earth with a mouse rooting beneath it. The deceitful mouse was her tongue, wriggling darkly in deceptions.

'You said,' her niece tried to remind her, 'you *said* that Owen wouldn't let you out. That you wanted to come out, and he bullied you.'

'No.' The aunt closed her mouth like a trap. 'You got it wrong.'

'Sorry,' said her niece in disbelief.

A nod acknowledged this.

'More tea?' Cajolingly.

Another nod. They were at the R T E studios. Sun shone on lawns, and green lozenges of glassy reflections climbed the windows, breaking down barriers between indoors and out.

'Nice and modern,' the aunt had said when she arrived. She had been elated at this trip and chatted intriguingly. Then something roused her suspicions and she turned morose.

James tried another tack. 'Tell us about Owen?' he suggested. 'What was he like?'

'Turn off that machine.' The aunt was cagey now. 'That recorder. Policemen use that,' she said venomously. 'I've seen them in films.'

'I'm not a policeman.'

'Turn it off so.'

He turned it off.

'He came out of the seminary. Gave it up. That was a shock to his family. They moved heaven and earth to stop him but he wouldn't be stopped.'

'Because he was in love with your sister?'

The old woman picked her teeth with her nail. She had curiously foul habits. The niece's hands twitched. She wanted to stop her but didn't want to interrupt the old woman's train of thought, which had been so promising just now. Sister Judith farted. She seemed unaware of other people most of the time, then suddenly stricken to know they had been watching while she forgot about them. 'Love?' She considered the word. 'He was too gone on himself and too mad about Ireland to have time for love. They were all like that then. You wouldn't imagine. Idealistic. Cold. Stiff with righteousness. Sometimes they were gay too. Too much, you might say. It could have been nerves. They were all for horseplay and wrestling with each other and practical jokes.'

'But there was a row between you?'

'Between who?'

'You said so, Aunt Judith.'

'It's on tape. You said it just a while ago.'

'I won't talk with that machine on any more.'

Later, Mrs O'Malley had said, 'She forgets things.'

'Or lies,' James thought. 'Or loses track.'

'Does it matter?'

'Well, it undermines credibility. I'd want an interview where she said what she said in a sequential, reasonable way.'

'Why? You're telling a story?'

'Other people on the film will do that. My job is to establish facts.'

'What *did* she say?'

'I'll play it back for you,' he said.

Corny Kinlen had taken the old nun off on a tour of the building and Mrs O'Malley leaned back in her chair as James rewound the tape. Listening to its fricative lick and whirr, she said, 'She gets under my skin. I hate myself for not feeling sorrier for her, but she's like a bundle of old things I thought I'd thrown out which suddenly turn up strewn around the place to shame me: the unwanted past. Can you imagine? Poor thing, it's dreadful to strike people that way. Like old droppings. Her stale phrases, her nunny words: stuffy, niffy, lower-middle class, and dull. I hate myself for hating her style. Perhaps the whole generation was like that: the wild boys, the heroes?'

'I don't notice her saying nunny things. Which?'

'I don't even mean religious things. It's more the way she uses "refined" as a good word, whereas now it's a bad word. Hers was a revolutionary family, but it's the snobbery and resignation which strike me in her talk. The tags: "buckle down", "grit your teeth", "toe the line", be "up to the mark", "offer it up" – Jesus.'

'But it's because they did all that that you got a republic at all.'

'I suppose I'm ungrateful.'

James picked up her hand and held it.

'That's dangerous.'

'I know.' He put it down. 'Shall I grit my teeth and offer up the impulse?'

They laughed. Grainne, however, was dissatisfied. He kept making inconclusive moves more in keeping with a worshipful schoolboy than the satyr for which she had cast him. She wanted a wanton love affair and if he didn't get a move on the moment for wantonness would have passed. They'd be friends and friendship was fatal to lechery. Surely she had indicated her availability clearly enough? For a moment she thought he was about to kiss her, but instead he turned on the tape-recorder and Sister Judith's voice came on.

' "Out of failure comes success," ' said her aunt's voice. 'That's from Pearse's writings. "And from the deaths of patriot men and women come living nations." Owen twisted that. Pearse meant deaths freely risked but Owen meant murder. "Execution", he called it. There was a lot of that sort of talk. It wasn't so bad when it was ourselves against the English but things got bitter later when factions began to form in our own ranks. It was a muddled time. 1921 that was. Secretive. You couldn't trust your closest relative. Owen was windy. The split didn't come until the next year but he foresaw it and he foresaw that the money the Americans were holding for the IRA might go to the other side. "We have to take precautions," he used to say, "and keep on the good side of the Yanks." He didn't want any rumours getting back that might turn them against his side. There were stories of all sorts flying. Talk of betrayals. Gossip. Silly chatter. And the Yank, Spartacus, you know, Sparky, could have picked up too much. Owen was afraid of loose talk. "Keep your lip buttoned," he'd say. He had Kathleen under his thumb, as they were shortly to get married, but I was a worry to him.'

There was a pause on the tape, then James's voice asked: 'Did he persuade you to go into the convent?'

'I didn't take much persuasion,' said Judith's voice. 'I was sick of them all. Sick. A lot of us were. A pox on both their houses, we felt. Civil war is bitter. Divides families. Seamus was engaged to a girl whose family took the other side. Staters. There were fights at every meal. Tears. Abuse. I couldn't wait to get out of the place. There was the danger too. More than in the war with the English. Your own knew too much about you and feeling was savage. My father was half mad with the worry. He never slept a wink for months. Chronic insomnia he had and he didn't understand what the split was all about. It was beyond him. He'd never understood Republican politics, so when they split he thought they were hopeless altogether. Kathleen, of course, was all on Owen's side. I couldn't wait to get out.'

'Of the family?'

'Yes.'

'Later you wanted to get out of the convent?'

'Did I? I suppose I did. Later. That was years later. But, sure, I couldn't.'

'Why?'

'Owen threatened me.'

'And now?'

'Now I want to stay in.' The old woman's laugh skirled. 'I'm like a cantankerous cat,' she said, 'always asking to get to the other side of the door.'

The tape stopped.

'You see,' he said, 'it's full of contradictions.'

'Listen,' she said precipitously. 'There's a cottage up in the mountains which used to belong to Michael's grandfather. I have to go out there for some things I left there last spring. Would you like to come and see the place? I have a plan, besides, for stirring Aunt Judith's memories.'

'Great!' said he 'when?'

'The day after tomorrow?'

'Fine. Do you want to hear the rest? Before they come back?'

She nodded and he pressed the 'on' button.

'I was odd, you know,' said the voice. 'I could have been put away. I got some sort of a shock. Well, there were shocks every day of the week but one must have affected me. I was terrified of the asylum. I'd been there on a visit. Owen had a friend worked there and later, when he was on the run, he dressed up as an inmate. A lot of them did. It was a perfect disguise. There were jokes about that, about how it was no disguise at all. But with his connections, he could have had me put away. No question.'

'Why?'

'Security.'

'What was the secret, Sister Judith? What were they afraid you'd tell?'

'I never knew. No, really. I came over odd from some shock and the next thing was that Owen said I should try the convent. Later I was given electroshock. I was confused. I never knew which particular thing they were worried about and, of course, they wouldn't tell me. Let sleeping dogs lie, they must have thought.'

'Did your relatives come and see you in the convent?'

'Kathleen came once early on. Well, they told me she came

twice but I remember the one time only. The second time they gave me drugs and I didn't know her. Looked at her like a zombie and she broke down crying and begging me to call her by her name. That's what they told me and after that she stayed away for years. They'd given me the treatment because of what I'd done the time before. I attacked her, they said. I don't remember. She was pregnant and she had a miscarriage after. Owen blamed me and wouldn't let her come again unless I had the treatment.'

'What do you remember about the first visit?'

'She told me all about the Civil War. I'd missed it, you see. I only remembered the start. And about her honeymoon and wedding. I'd missed those. And how Owen was out in the wilderness but Seamus's party was in power. They never met. Fraternization was forbidden. That went on for years. She had on a purple hat and a big tenty coat. Yes, she was pregnant all right. I remember. Of course she did start visiting again years later, but then we never discussed the past. I think Owen told her not to.'

'What else do you remember about the first visit?'

'I asked her about Sparky Driscoll or his name came up. I forget. Anyway, she told me about his being killed in an ambush. Hacked to pieces. By Orangemen up North. He must have gone up to see the fighting. He'd want to report back to the Clan na Gael in America. He was their observer over here, you see. She said the remains had to be shovelled into a coffin.'

'Who else visited you?'

'Oh, I forget. Owen once or twice. But there was a period when I couldn't talk to anyone. I was odd. Later I recovered but they'd lost touch with me. Maybe the doctors were against it. I never knew.'

'And you even started teaching?'

'Yes. The kindergarten. Oh, I was quite myself again. I'm all right now, you know,' said the nun's voice, sharpening aggressively. 'Who are you?' she asked. 'What's that machine for?'

'I'm a journalist. I'm interested in . . .'

'Turn it off. Turn it off.'

*

Black-plumed horses passed the pub regularly for it was, ran the local joke, on the way to the graveyard in more ways than one. Hats came off and shutters closed to show respect. Coming back, the mourners would be in for drinks. A good funeral had several horses pulling the hearse and two to each carriage behind it. The harness was black and silver and the plumes nodding above the furry foreheads were as big as busbies on the King's hussars. Black tails matched the plumed crests and when the funeral was political it was followed by contingents of slow-stepping Cumann na mBan in their green uniform skirts.

Judith dreamed of death with which all passion seemed connected and slept in the death position recommended by the nuns. There was pleasure in imagining the dark tide engulfing you, though the reality would of course be different. Almost everything thrilled her, from running a grass blade along the nape of her neck to walking down the village street where old men played pitch and toss or pulled chairs into doorways to sit squinting and spitting in the sunlight.

'A fine day, thanks be.'

'It is that.'

'Any news of Owen?' they asked. 'There's talk that the prisoners will be home by Christmas.'

'I heard that.'

''Twill please your sister.'

'Tell her we're praying for her intention.'

'I will.'

More spitting sealed the promise. Wary of consumption, she kept her distance. Further on, a crowd of corner boys leaned against a wall as if holding it up. Beyond in the hills drilling continued. The truce was on but who knew for how long? Rumours were rife.

In the shop which sold everything from nails to potatoes a number of women were waiting. Some already had filled their baskets but stood around exchanging views on the price of paraffin and the dance to be held that Saturday in the parish hall. The priest had been giving out the pay about young girls who wore the V-neck. Wouldn't anyone think they'd have something better on their minds? At a time like this?

'Ah, I dunno now, Missis. Loose morals is the cause of a lot of trouble.'

'Well they're not the cause of mine. If my Jimmy had spent more time running after girls he might be here now. Guns is worse than girls.'

'True for you, Missis, but sure some girls is what gets the young fellas to take to the gun. Some young ones aren't happy till they've sent out as many mothers' sons to die as they can coax into a Volunteers' uniform. Then the same ladies'll be dancing as happy as crickets beyond in the hall of a Saturda. Throwing their comehither on more poor innocents. Vampires! You see them marching at every funeral with knives in their eyes. The Cumann na mBan. I'd keep them lassies out of the churches if I had my say. Sure even a young fella who's going for the priesthood isn't safe with some.'

'Are you referring to my sister?' Judith asked the woman.

'Arrah, hullo Judith. I didn't see you there at all, dear. Is it hiding you were?'

'No. I wasn't hiding. Were you talking about my sister, Kathleen, and Owen O'Malley?'

'Och, we're very touchy, I must say. I was talking in a general way, Judith, but of course if the shoe fits.'

'My sister's been engaged for years to a man she hardly sees. Do you think that's fun for her?' Judith had to speak fast before the rage choked her. She got into tremendous rages and very quickly began to shake. There wasn't a thing she could do about it. She had to make her points fast, racing the access of trembling blushes which would overtake her in a moment. 'She's been in no position to put her comehither on anyone at all, so your nambypamby sons are safe from her, Mrs Kennedy.'

The woman, a great fat creature wearing a shawl which bound her bottom, bosom and basket into a bundle as comfortable and curved as a snowman or a bag of loaves, laughed with an air of surprised indifference. 'I don't know what's eating the girl,' said she with great innocence.

'They can sit tight and benefit later from what others did,' said Judith.

'Oh law, I see we have another recruiting officer in yourself!

The Countess Markiewicz isn't in it with you! Maybe you should take to the gun yourself, if you're so free with your opinions? It's too easy altogether to sit snug at home after sending out the men. Sure it's great excitement to yez! War is the breath of life to girls like you! Americans and all sorts coming to the house while yeer men are away. Yes.'

'You'd rather British soldiers, I suppose? Peace at any price means going back to where we were before all the Troubles began and then people like Mrs Foly's Jimmy will have died for nothing.'

'You'd rather send more after him!'

'Did you ever hear of a war without fighting, Mrs Kennedy? Or of the British giving away anything unless they had to? We've got something now . . .'

'What have we got? What? Tell me? Houses wrecked, families destroyed, young fellows mutilated and murdered and sent out of their minds raving – is that what you're so pleased with, you blood-thirsty bitch?'

'Ah now, Mrs Kennedy, sure the girl is only speaking her mind. Her own brother was killed. Eamonn. Remember that. And Seamus is a Volunteer. And Kathleen's taken risks. There's things you don't know, Missis. Sure the people in this country are altogether too ready to criticize the ones who do anything at all. The bulk of the people is like trained mice, windy . . .'

'That's for me, is it? Well, there's some would wreck Ireland for Ireland's sake. Commend me to the diehards. Weren't we offered Home Rule in 1914? What have we got now that we weren't promised then, once the war was over, if we'd a sat quiet and played the game?'

'Their game, is it? The English game? Aren't we sick and tired of playing their game and being fooled up to the eyes? I'm sorry for anyone would rely on English promises. The crowd up North isn't sitting quiet. They're bringing pressure all right, screaming melia murther to stop the English keeping any promises they made to us. And *they*'ll be only too pleased to say they had to give in to Craig and his Orangemen if our lads don't bring as good a pressure on our side.'

'So, it'll go on forever, is that it? Yous have me poor head addled and moidered with yer talk. I don't believe yez want peace. I think there's people in this country that's got so they need war the way some need strong drink. Yez wouldn't know what to do with yerselves if there was peace tomorrow. Look at this girl breathing fire like a salamander. My poor sons are working their fingers to the bone trying to keep a roof over our heads, but there's some have made the gun a way of life. Looting and calling it – what's that word they have now? Requisitioning, is it? Ah, that's a lovely word entirely. You steal people blind and need never do a hand's work because stealing's called "requisitioning" now.'

'That's very unpatriotic talk! I'm surprised to hear an Irishwoman talking like that.'

'I'm as good an Irishwoman as any here, but I don't like hooligans.'

'And the IRA are hooligans according to you?'

'I didn't say they were hooligans. I said there was a hooligan element . . .'

'Element, is it? You say altogether too much, Missis.'

'Do I now? Well maybe I'd better leave this patriotic company. The moral tone is puzzling me poor brain.'

She flounced out, her shawl held high over her jutting chest, the swish of its tail making the kind of fine rhetorical movement which a coat could never accommodate.

There was a moment given up to shrugs and sighs.

'What'll it be today?' the shopkeeper asked Judith, who had trouble remembering her needs.

'I'll have three pounds of back rashers,' she recalled, 'cut as thin as you can, a pound of black pudding and half a pound of white, tea, sugar, candles, oatmeal, matches, paraffin . . .'

Behind her, someone sighed. 'That poor woman, God help us, who's just gone out . . .'

'Mrs Kennedy?'

'The same. She had a brother-in-law killed by the lads.'

'Killed deliberate?'

'As a spy. He was found in a ditch with the words "All Spies Beware" on a piece of cardboard pinned to his chest. No, but that's not the whole of it. Wait till you hear. You see if he *was* a spy nobody could blame the lads for what they done.'

'And wasn't he?'

'He was not. He was a farmer living back in the hills and there was a house friendly to the Sinn Féiners nearby where they used to store their weapons and hide out when they were in that part of the country. The Flying Column. It was their headquarters and they had it fixed up with hollow walls and the guns hidden under the floorboards so that even if it was to be raided nothing could be found,' the woman paused, 'in the normal way.'

'So?'

'Well, one day didn't a couple of tenders full of Auxiliaries drive up to it and it was as clear as day that they'd had a tip-off because the one IRA fellow who was there had a story ready, false papers and everything he needed to convince them that he was an honest farmer. He was as cool as you please and had been in and out of as many tight corners as Mick Collins, so he didn't turn a hair but had all his answers pat. Only this time the Auxie officer took no notice of his story. "Tear up them floorboards," says he to his men. "Break down them walls." Well, of course, once they done that the poor fellow's goose was cooked. They whisked him off to gaol and from there he managed to get word out about how it had happened. Then the neighbouring farmer was blamed for the leak. But, don't you see, there was no proof at all that it was him, only the word of some more neighbours who, as it came out later, had an old score to settle with him, a quarrel about a boundary. Farmers is very vindictive. Six months later the lads found who the real informer was but it was too late then to bring the innocent man back to life.'

'Thin please,' reminded Judith, whose rashers were being sliced.

Haunches of bacon had a human look with the pale hairy skin. She thought sometimes of becoming a vegetarian but decided that was soft. She'd seen pigs killed. A good butcher could find the heart in one blow. Were the IRA as quick with spies? Behind her the women capped stories of mistakes the lads made and the British made and about hosts of innocent poor goms who – if you could believe this gossip – had been killed for no reason at all.

'Saving yer presence, Missis, the poor fella had to be supported between two spades the lads stuck into the ground and tied him to so he'd be upright while they were firing on him. And didn't he soil his trousers from fright and the stuff running down his leg . . .'

These were women who in peace-time would be whispering under the edge of their shawls about monstrous births and miscarriages and labour pains. She'd been hearing scraps of bloody talk since she could talk herself, always interrupted to respect her innocence and all the more troubling for that.

'God help us all.'

Judith paid for her groceries. 'Will you send that round this morning then?' she asked the shopkeeper. 'Thank you very much.'

As you left the shop you felt the lull which wouldn't be broken until you were out of earshot. Then your reputation would be sliced as neatly as the rashers.

Judith tried for charity but found only contempt. Reasons why these women were the way they were, like an insanity plea at a murder trial, left them stripped of dignity. They were ignorant. Brutalized. Only horror could rouse them. Random happenings were all they saw in the revolution. Its aim was beyond most of them. In church, doing the stations of the cross, they stared at the red streaks crudely painted on the Christ figure's plaster flesh. The redemption for which they prayed was unreal to them. Heaven, they said, and threw their eyes upwards and sighed. The crucifixion, God help us, yes. Then. Now. Sorrow. Joy. One was as unrelated to the other as two tickets in a sweep-stake. You might get the good one. More often you got the bad. There was no doing anything about it, was there? Not a thing you could do, so carry on, gabble prayers, comfort yourself by thinking how much worse, the Lord between us and all harm, things might be. Not one of them could cook.

Outside, in the sunlight, the spokes of passing bike-wheels spun like knives.

Judith asked her sister, 'Is Sparky here to bring money to the lads? Doesn't their money come from America?'

'How would I know?' Kathleen asked. 'They don't shout things like that from the roof-tops. Sparky's here as an "observer".'

'The time Owen went to America they said he'd gone to get money.'

'They go for support. Different kinds. They tried to get the Yanks to put Ireland's case before the Peace Conference in Paris. That was no go, so they tried for other kinds of help – money too. Why are you interested anyway?'

'Would they smuggle the money here in a bag or something? Or would they leave it over there in the bank?'

'What a babby you are, Judith! Can't you see that any lad blethering about that sort of business would be likely to earn a tombstone before his time?'

Grainne was taking tea with her grandaunt. A plateful of Huntley and Palmers' milk-and-honey creams lay on the table.

'Have one, Aunt Judith.'

The old lady did, absently.

Grainne was disappointed. Greed, she had reasoned, was the only appetite open to nuns and, hoping to cater to her her great-aunt's, she had gone out of her way to please.

The damask cloth had not seen the light of day since her mother had died. Ditto the Cork-silver sugar bowl which was shining unaccustomedly after being treated with Silver Dip. Grainne, if left to herself, was as apt as not to put the sugar pack on the table. Today, she had been stimulated to make worldly things look good to this exile who had been thrust so unceremoniously back into the World.

Convent-educated, Grainne knew the importance nuns placed on etiquette. It provided rituals for dealing with those who might have no knowable values.

Nothing, moreover, displeased nuns more than seeming nunnish. They preferred assessing worldlings by the World's own codes.

She remembered being quizzed when she was a senior girl about the mini-skirt in which a past pupil had turned up to a reunion. 'Is that the fashion?' asked a nun, meaning 'is it socially acceptable outside?' and Grainne, aware of the nun's predicament, since snobbery, being worldly in a sinful sense, needed careful negotiation, had given a helpfully informative reply.

Concern with form must have disappeared now that the nuns themselves had taken to wearing hybrid black and white, like old-time parlour maids. Aunt Judith, however, a victim not a promoter of this state of affairs, should surely relish the old graces?

'More tea, Aunt Judith? Another biscuit?'

The biscuit was, to Grainne's mind, more luxurious than caviar. Caviar had not appeared in her childhood and she classed it with things first come across in adult life, like driving tests, foreign travel, hysterectomies, and drink. It appealed to her moderately and did not thrill her at all. Huntley and Palmer biscuits, on the other hand, had existed in the nursery. From thrift or principle, her parents had always bought them mixed. There was only one chocolate biscuit, a few creams and a single jam-inlaid shortbread wheel, to what seemed like dozens of plain biscuits. To merit the fancy, you had to eat your way through the plain. The jammy wheel, Grainne's favourite as a child, had reminded her of the red Cellophaned window in her box of building blocks. You held it to your eye to watch the world go red. It was the most interesting brick, just as the wheel was the most interesting biscuit, and pleasure had remained tied in her mind to something red and rare and sweet and luminous. To buy a whole box of jam biscuits seemed as profligate still as it would be to buy a building-block kit containing nothing but windows: a capricious anarchic gesture which she had made this afternoon. Since her aunt seemed unmoved by the offering, she must, she felt obliged to admit, have done it for herself. With a shiver of glee, she ate a third red wheel as it struck her that now there actually were buildings constructed entirely, or apparently entirely, of coloured glass. Particularly, she remembered reading, in Southern California.

The chaplain from the Juvenile Prison had dropped in to the Grateful Patriots' Youth Club to pick up comic papers which the boys left for him when they'd read them. Patsy

Flynn saved them in a cardboard box. Sometimes Patsy slipped in a few Republican papers which the chaplain had to discard.

'Against regulations,' he told Patsy. 'My wankers wouldn't want these anyway. Cheesecake and action is my fellows' taste. Explosion and release. Same thing. They're locked up so I suppose it's natural.'

Patsy pursed his lips and took back his papers. He didn't like dirty talk and neither had he ever liked priests. The combination confused him. This roughneck in the dandruffy polo-neck sweater was hardly like a priest at all. Patsy offered him a cuppa.

'Oh, that'll be grand,' said the chaplain. 'That'll hit the spot.' He was overdoing things, thought Patsy. Priests made you feel they thought they were Christ between thieves when they gave you a bit of their time.

'Well, I'm out of a job,' said the chaplain, who wanted to be called Mick. Patsy avoided calling him anything. 'The nuns I was with have shut up shop. Said my last mass there last week and deconsecrated the chapel. *Sic transit* the glory of the other world.'

'What happened to the O'Malley aunt?' Patsy wanted to know. 'Is she staying with the Michael O'Malleys for good or what?'

'I doubt they'll be able to handle her,' said the priest, and blew on his tea. 'She's as mad as a brush. Thinks she's privy to secrets of national importance. Her own words. She was always tormenting me to help her remember them. Something to do with money and an American. Therapy she wanted which was hardly my job. I sent her off with a flea in her ear. All delusions. The poor old cow hadn't been out of the place in fifty years.'

'She might know something all the same,' Patsy remarked. 'She'd have visits.'

'Her brain's addled.'

'The government gun-runners at the time of the arms business of 1970 used a convent to hide the stuff.'

'True,' the chaplain admitted. 'That was up near the border though. In so far as could be gathered. All kept deliberately unclear, wasn't it, even at the trial? You might know though,' he remembered. 'The Captain was involved in that caper, wasn't he?'

Patsy assumed an air of discretion. 'He tells me nothing.' He hoped this sounded less true than it was. 'Close-mouthed the Captain is.'

'Well, nobody can mind your business like you can yourself,' said the chaplain. 'I'd best be getting along. Thanks for the tea.'

Patsy watched him go with some gloom. He suspected the fellow of being a Republican courier between the prisoners and their mates outside. Young Republicans had no time for Patsy, holding it against him that he sometimes took a sup too much and got excited or even wept. If the little sprats had suffered for Ireland as he had – ten years he'd done in the nick, how many of them could say as much? – they might have had more tolerance. He didn't like to see the Church going the way it was either. As a young man, he'd hated the institution, picturing it as a huge beast which sat on the country's neck and stifled its best energies. Priests then had held the place in a military grip and it was from them that Patsy had learned the importance of pomp and insignia. He'd gone to a clerical day-school and knew what it was to be regimented. Tie, cap, scarf, socks and the badge on your jacket gave you away. If you got into trouble on the other side of the county, it would be reported back to the head of your school and they'd be asking at the next jaw-session that the boy seen wearing our colours while fighting, indulging in horse-play, talking to girls or stealing from Woolworth's please stand up and give an account of himself. Through the confessional, they kept tabs on your inner life until you finally nerved yourself to damn your soul and defy them. When it came to organizational techniques the Republicans were nowhere in comparison. Patsy's hatred for the clergy had been an admiring one and now that they were disbanding, like a colonial regiment before the colony's loss, he felt depressed. He had a nasty feeling that without the old bully to keep the tension up the country might go soft. Materialism and selfishness were creeping in. A lot of the young fellows who came to the club struck him as lacking in ideals. Big, overgrown louts who'd been fed too well in their childhood, they put muddy boots on the club sofas and treated Patsy as a servant. It seemed to him that they didn't think of themselves as owing anything to anyone *but* themselves. The chaplain, whatever else about him, had ideals.

So had Patsy. He was hollow with them, tenderly thrilled by his hopes for the country and it hurt him deeply that the IRA had no use for him. He was past it, they considered, and even the Captain did not take Patsy into his confidence. The Captain, to be sure, had to watch it and move with caution. Patsy appreciated that. He wasn't the eejit some might think, even if campaigns fought in silent dignity by the faithful and the few in such battlefields as Brixton, Holloway, the Scrubs made him emotional in a way which embarrassed them. The Captain's was the political end of things and had to be kept separate from the militant. Patsy did see this. The two had come close at the time of the government arms trial, spilling dangerously towards each other like chemicals from broken vials, and the Captain was now lying low. Patsy guessed, though, that he was secretly active. He had done some snooping in the Captain's house where he sometimes did odd jobs, using the carpentry skills he had learned in gaol. He had no shame at all about this. His conscience was clear and his aim protective. The Captain could never say what he was up to. Like those politicians in America at the time of Watergate, he must preserve 'deniability'. Patsy had noted the word with approval; it applied.

Thought of America brought back what the chaplain had just said about an American. Patsy had reason to take this more seriously than the chaplain did. For one thing people often dismissed *him* as soft in the head, so he wasn't so quick himself to dimiss other people. The old nun could be bright as a bee under her eccentricity. Like himself. He was sharp enough, so he was. Whatever people might think. Sharper than that chaplain he bet. And he had certain knowledge that the Captain had American contacts which he didn't shout about. There had been a fellow called Larry, who'd been staying at the Captain's one time when Patsy was doing over the kitchen, installing new fitted cupboards and laying a floor of Italian tiles. They'd been in the front room talking about a film the Yank was making about the Troubles and Patsy had had a ringside seat. Heard every word. The Yank said he wanted photographs and memories of the Captain's father. Patsy had listened, timing his hammer blows so as to sound industrious but picking up the thread of the talk. He'd got an idea that the two were up to more than making a film. Hard to put your finger on what it was. A tone, something about their timing. When you'd been in the nick you got sensitive to things like that. Anyway he got to thinking and, when you thought of it, what better cover than a film for bringing in loads of God knew what? Hardwear. Camouflaged. Why not? To be sure, he hadn't breathed a word. What he was wondering now was whether this old woman, who had maybe got wind of what he'd got wind of himself, might be talking her head off. He'd have to get young Cormac to keep an eye on her and – wait a minute? Hadn't the lad said something about a Yank wanting to interview her on TV? *There* was something to worry about. Plenty of people would go to any lengths to discredit the Captain, whom they feared might be the man to get rid of their piddling little neo-colonialist bourgeois nationalist system and bring a bit of nerve and justice to this distressful country. Patsy hoped to God he'd see the day the Captain did.

Meanwhile who was this second Yank? A CIA agent? Someone watching the other fellow? A journalist? That would be the worst. Maybe, thought Patsy, he'd better do a spot of investigating on his own. Young Cormac could be a source of information but better not tip the boy off about his own fears. Security, decided Patsy, secrecy and a close mouth were the order of the day. That was how the old IRB had functioned, a grand organization which, so he'd been told, had been the model for all the secret societies in Europe in the nineteenth century. The Celts had contributed more to history than they were ever credited with. Was it the wine cask they'd invented too, or was it trousers? He must remember to ask one of the history teachers that sometimes came by to give a talk at the club.

*

'Long ago . . .' said Judith vaguely.

Sometimes she seemed to unravel before your eyes like an old sock.

'Tell me,' Cormac encouraged her.

'What?'

'What it was like then. During the Troubles.'

'They said we were . . . No,' she corrected herself, 'they, *they* were fighting for a new Ireland. For the future,' she told him. 'There were to be no false distinctions. Oh, they had high hopes. In fifty years' time.'

'That's now,' Cormac told her.

'It is?'

'Yes.'

'And *are* there false distinctions?' she wondered.

'I don't know what you mean.' The words were like old beetles. He saw them in his mind's eye, dead and blackish on a white window sill. Her mind was a mess. It was like a bran tub at a fair where you paid for a grope and might come up with a prize. Equally, you might come up with an old cabbage stalk. She had known heroes though. He looked in her pinkish eyes for flashes of old steel.

'You knew Sparky Driscoll, didn't you?' he insisted. The name excited him: Sparky. You thought of hooves striking sparks on a road. 'How They Brought the Good News from Ghent to Aix.' 'Paul Revere's Ride.' Sparky had been a Yank. Sparklers. Fireworks. The blue muzzle of a gun sticking from a bush. He had died in an ambush. An arms purveyor. 'Can't you remember *anything*?' he asked.

'I'm trying,' she said humbly. 'They gave me shock treatment, you know. Electric shocks. They impair the memory.'

'Why?'

'Maybe I knew some secret thing?'

This interested Cormac. 'You should do exercises,' he told her. 'Every day. I'll help you,' he offered. She was interesting: one of the dead generations. He might do a project on her for school. 'I suppose you know prayers,' he said. 'You should try something more challenging. For the memory. Mnemonics. We make them up to help us through exams.'

'Sparky,' she remarked, 'said the means justify the end.'

'It's the opposite.'

She agreed. 'Most people put it the other way round but Sparky said that to show you had a right to fight for a better life you should start leading it at once.'

'Did he mean be religious and that?'

'He meant be happy.' She giggled. 'Americans think people should. They say it's a right. Imagine.'

'You've probably got it wrong,' Cormac told her. 'Think of something else to rest your brain. Then try and remember.'

She said she would take his advice.

7

James valued clarity but clarity was lacking in this misty city. It was lacking too in what people said.

'What-t-t?' they wondered and their 't' was a whistle of air leaked between tongue-tip and palate. 'What's that-t-t you're asking?'

'About Sinn Féin, is it-t?'

'I asked if it was the same thing as the IRA?'

'It is and it-t isn't,' whistled whoever he'd asked. 'Head and hand, hand and head – how can you separate-t-te them?'

'Would you say they had much of a following?'

'It-t-t'd depend what-t you meant by "following".'

'Do people support them?'

'What would you be meaning by "support-t-t"?'

After a while, doubts seemed to steam like wet flies inside his own head and he looked regretfully back to days when he had known where he was and what about. The seasons when he had been on his college football team had, from that point of view, been the time of his life.

He missed the purposefulness which had been his as long as living for the team had conferred significance on trivial acts and virtue been measurable on the bathroom scales. Members of the IRA must, he imagined, live similarly focused lives. He would have liked to meet some of them but Larry was all against the idea. James was to keep right away from those guys. His job, Larry impressed on him, was to get in well with media people in Dublin and do his research. Look out for the equipment that would be arriving shortly. No controversial stuff, right? Right, said James, but balked at spending hours soaking up liquor with men from whom he felt deeply alien in a physical way. He described the journalists' flushed, deliquescent faces in letters to Therese, adding that he imagined them leaving a track of cholesterol in the buttery air and polluting it with their breath.

This was only half a joke. James, on an instinctive level, equated physical with spiritual health. He had, after all, spent his teen years thinking of his body. Treating it like an animal in training, he had forced it daily and beyond the point of pain to do knee-bends, sit-ups, push-ups, dives, and flips. It must suffer if it was to improve and his lust for improvement had for a long time focused on it, rather than on his mind or bank balance. It was the sort of urge which people in other times and places – here? – might channel into religious or military disciplines. For James, at his peak, his body had been his incarnate soul and when, in his reading, he came on words like 'voluptuous' or 'sensual', he knew that they did not apply to the feeling he had for his flesh. Their softer applications did not describe the feeling he had for women's flesh either. He liked this hard. Nothing thrilled him like a girl's thighs arching over him in a triumph of fitness. While she moved, his fingers would probe the muscle meshed deep and slippery in her buttocks. Later, seeing her scissor through water or leap, with tanned flourish, across a tennis court, he would re-live the blind, tactile pleasures of their bedroom. These experiences were spare and immediate. He met few sexual rebuffs.

Over the years, as he cut down his work-outs to an hour a day, he began to feel his character change. He became curious about less healthy things and about the millions of people who did not live as he did but might have some knack for living which eluded him. At this time, he was working in the Department of Theater Arts, a hybrid position since he had no artistic skills but thrilled to the theatre's sensual surprise. What he would have liked was to catch some of this in his own life. If his athletic training hadn't left its mark on him, he might have been ready to fool around with the occult or join some freak sect. Drugs, however, were unhealthy and, besides, he had been raised by a lapsed Catholic mother – *née* Maccantaggart – who sent him to parochial school for a while when he was four and occasionally thereafter took him to midnight mass on Christmas Eve. It was not a big exposure to Catholicism but sufficient to make him feel that this was the club to join if ever he were to feel it was time to stop going it alone.

With this in mind, he had at one stage taken courses in Anglo-Irish literature and been struck by the difficulties people in his ancestral island seemed to experience in living, dating, and just plain getting along together. He was nagged by a suspicion that they might perhaps feel things more? Certainly the poet, Yeats, had managed to get a remarkable high out of his failures with women and passed it on to James who, never having got the like from his own successes, went so far as to learn off the lines asking:

> Does the imagination dwell the most
> Upon a woman gained or woman lost?
> If on the lost, admit you turned aside
> From a great labyrinth out of pride . . .

or – or some such. The words which hooked him were 'great labyrinth'. He had never previously thought of a woman in such terms and, when he tried applying them, found that they slid off the smooth-skinned, willing and limited girl, whoever she was, with whom he happened to be sleeping. Now, in Ireland, the words came back to him. He turned them over in his mouth like bits of fruit and began to wonder whether *not* making it with a woman might not be a necessary preliminary to seeing her like this?

James had no disdain for men who could not or would not let themselves score sexually. He remembered from his football days that, in the clutch, an emotional high could count as much as skill. He knew about the energy which comes in the pit of exhaustion and that negatives can breed positives. He was ready to believe that a repeatedly defeated island, throttled by ancient and fermented rage, might be the place to breed passions of a transporting magnitude. He was eager to grapple with such a passion and for the apparatus of negation which must, like a trampoline, catapult him into ecstatic orbit.

He did not, at the same time, want to distress his wife.

*

The day after her visit to the RTE studios, Grainne's cousin came to call. Owen Roe was a redhead like herself, large, assured, youthful for his fifty or so years, a bit bloated about the gills, with jutting genitals which made a fold in his cavalry twill trousers – he dressed to the right – and a righteous blue eye which could, when useful, be made to glow like a gas glimmer. He wore a fancy-dress blend often sported in Dublin, especially in Horse-Show Week: half squire, half gigolo with a dash of the bookie. She knew that if she were to get close he would smell of Ho Hang and, if closer, of more personal odours. She knew this because, the year before, she had gone to bed with him on three occasions. The affair had been brief and, on his part, brutal, for he had started it with a flourish which had led her to expect something slow-moving and prolonged. She had hoped for roses and respect and been ready to understand if he should be creaky, corsetted or unable always to perform. Needing indulgence herself, she had been ready to be indulgent in return.

Instead, quite abruptly, after three surprisingly vigorous and – to her mind – satisfactory beddings, he had, on running into her one noon in Nassau Street, remarked by way of hail and farewell: 'It's over!'

They were hemmed in at the time by a crowd waiting for a traffic light and, since this was not what she had been expecting to hear, she did not take it in. Her eyes had widened, she remembered, and she had looked at him – it was mortifying to recall – with a surrendering sigh.

'Over!'

Behind and above his head, the leaves of the Trinity College trees hung, lustreless, like drying tea-dregs, against a porcelain sky.

'Sorry?' she questioned. 'I don't quite . . . ?'

'So am I.'

'What?'

'Us. Over.'

The light changed then and he left her faltering on the kerb.

She had tried to bury the memory. But, though she managed this to an extent – her path and her cousin's crossed more rarely than she might have feared – she continued to feel undermined.

It was her first affair and had taken place largely in silence since, between stealthy physical bouts, there had scarcely been time to do more than recite some verses of early Yeats.

> I would that we were, my beloved,
> White birrrds on the foam of the sea . . .

His defection left her at a loss. Doubts about her mind, body, and amorous technique had prevented her looking another man in the eye since. Until now. And now, a year later, here was Owen Roe on her doorstep.

'Gracious!' she said with feeble venom. 'To what do I owe the honour? Michael's out and so, I'm glad to say, is Cormac. I wish you'd stop seeing *him*, by the way.'

Owen Roe raised a gloved hand. 'We'll talk about Cormac later if you don't mind. You're the one I came to see.'

Her supply of ironic looks was running out.

He followed her in the door. 'This house is ramshackle!' He reached with the tip of his expensive umbrella towards a fur of dust lying below the fanlight. 'Our social model was a decaying class. The Anglo-Irish were *dirty*. They'd gone soft at the core. Morally soft.'

Grainne wondered about her morals and her core and why he had treated her as he had. The memory, having been kept suppressed, jumped up at her, fresh with implications.

'Will you come for a walk with me?' he asked.

'Walk?'

'I need to talk to you.'

'Oh?'

Owen Roe burst into an Edwardian song:

> 'Madame will you walk? Madame will you talk?
> Madame, will you walk and talk with me?'

He put a finger along the side of his nose. 'Outside.'

She shrugged, opened the hall-cupboard door, unhooked her macintosh, put it on and followed him out. He took her elbow.

'Still angry with me?'

There seemed no adequate answer to this.

'Our social model,' she supposed, 'left you unguided? You took French leave.'

He squeezed the elbow. 'You're a grand girl, Grainne. Great spirit!'

'You took your time deciding about that! A bit Scotch, aren't you? Slow?' But she had no heart for badinage. He had hurt her and the hurt had gone through her like the split in a carcass. For months last year she had felt herself morally flayed, no: it was physical. She used to wake up with the itching shame of it. Like meat. Reduced. Devalued. She shook off the policeman's hold he had on her elbow. 'What is it you want, anyhow?'

'Listen, Grainne, perhaps I should have told you at the time. Someone sent me an anonymous letter. I couldn't afford scandal. Neither could you.'

'I don't believe you.'

Cars were few in this residential district whose men were at work. It was the adultery hour she supposed, and wondered was any going on behind the blind windows pearly with reflections of sky. Her feet, held by the suction of the mud, came away with a sound like the kiss men on building-sites always threw at her. Did her need stick out a mile then? The place felt unleavened. Gardens were deep in leafmould and shrubs fastened to the ground by proliferations of saplings.

I hate this place, she thought.

She couldn't bring herself to reproach him for the *way* he had broken with her. If he can't see it himself, she thought, and shook her head to empty it of memories. To hell with him anyway.

'Social model!' She laughed.

She had hoped that Owen Roe, a relative and an older male, would have sympathy for her. She had been looking for more than sex, or more *through* sex. Perhaps she had seen him as a patriarchal figure, the head of the family, a fountainhead of strength? Perhaps he had encouraged this? The shit, she thought. He still roused strong sensual reactions in her. Yes, he *had* encouraged that line of thought. She remembered looking up the word 'endogamy' in a dictionary after one conversation they'd had. He had been talking about how women could always rely on men of their own tribe to respect and look out for them.

'My position,' he was saying, 'was delicate, Grainne. Explosive. At that particular time. I can't tell you more than that there was something in the wind which then didn't pan out. Came to nothing. But my phone *was* being tapped. I had to stop our thing fast before it got going. I was thinking of you too.'

She made a derisive noise.

'I mean it.'

'You mean what?'

'It threatened to get out of hand.'

'Would you, Owen Roe, be paying me a left-handed compliment? Implying that you took me seriously or nearly did?'

Leather-clad hands closed on hers. They looked, she thought, orthopaedic. 'What else have I been saying for the last ten minutes?'

Dark ilexes dripped. They had come close to the Botanic Gardens. Railing spikes were ranged like spears. He smelled of expensive macintosh: rubber, leather, metal, perhaps guns? He smelled like the insides of a car. She didn't listen to his talk: a retrospective wooing of her, a shameless attempt to turn a year's neglect into a plea for her gratitude. *Plámás*, she thought. Manipulation. You had to admire his gall. He'd come round soon to what he wanted. Meanwhile, she noted with distaste that he excited her physically. He aroused her so excruciatingly that she wanted to lie down right now for him in the middle of the muddy road and let him plough through her like a car. Like a car with radial tires which would sweep over and crush and kill her dead. At the same time she didn't want this at all. Did? Didn't? She hated them both: herself and him. What one had to do was to walk in a contained fashion along this slippery road, under the dripping evergreens, and answer with sharp, needling remarks to conceal the havoc he was wreaking in one's lower self. Then one must go home, get tea, run the house and attempt to be socially adequate. How many of the mild faces you met concealed this sort of inner madness? Five per cent? Ten? All? A projected very live part of herself was kneeling in the mud unbuttoning Owen Roe and rubbing its face in his huge, horrible genitals. If the American were to make love to her would she be cured? Immunized?

Owen Roe's attraction was in direct ratio to his vitality. In politics too he charmed people and was hated. His constituency gave him an enormous vote but opponents said this was because of bribery.

'Who would tap your phone?' she asked. 'You used to be in the Cabinet. You're still a TD. Surely *you* do the tapping?'

'I'm a loner. The rest are against me. Here's my car. Come for a spin?'

They had circled and were back at her house. A spin! She remembered Michael's father saying that – he had been courting her for Michael. A steady girl, he'd thought, who'd get his son back on the rails. 'Spin' was a bicycling generation's word. Cars didn't spin. Especially Owen Roe's. It was a Mercedes. Dark. Pompous. Expensive and geometric; it was like a portrait of Owen Roe himself. Like a desk or the horse part of a centaur, it clapped on to the man in charge and enlarged him.

She got in, slammed the door and smelled leather. 'In cars like this,' she remarked, 'the driver becomes a sort of appendage.'

'The driver drives,' her cousin told her and slipped into gear. 'You're an idle woman, Grainne. Don't try to absolve yourself by pretending that we're driven by currents we can't control.'

When he stopped talking, the motor seemed to be a prolongation of his voice. They were on the sea road heading through Booterstown. Beach stretched to the horizon. The tide ebbed back for what looked like a mile, leaving pools and rivulets: wet wounds in the sand and a smell of what might be fish or sewage.

'You hurt me badly,' she told him instructively. It was the sort of thing he'd have to be told. 'Women are vulnerable, after all. I have a little pride.'

'Women are as tough as old boots,' said Owen Roe with assurance. 'They outlive men, don't they? I remember my mother. If she hadn't got cancer she'd still be around, and she had a hard furrow to plough in the background, which, let me tell you, is worse than the foreground. You get none of the excitement. You just worry and eat out your liver and wait for the hero to come home from fighting, in the fighting times, and from banquets, when he's in government, and put up with his ulcers and bad breath.'

Had it been like that then, she wondered? Owen Roe was usually secretive about his father.

'We recited the rosary together every night when he was at home. She died in the end of cancer of the throat.'

'Maybe the cancer came from swallowed rage at all those Hail Marys? The French say your blood goes bad when you rage. *Ne te fais pas de mauvais sang*, they say.'

'Ah, French!' His voice was spiteful. She'd annoyed him. 'You went to a finishing school, didn't you? You're one of the small successes of our social revolution.'

'I suppose I'm being insulted?'

'No, I sympathize, really. My old man, to give him his due, didn't want our daughters turned into imitation English-women. *He* wanted a Gaelic Ireland. But economics bested him. We needed jobs for our people and to have jobs you have to have entrepreneurs, and entrepreneurs, like your Daddy, send their daughters to finishing school. So much of their lives goes in boot-licking, they have to have an outlet for their idealism: daughters. Not wives. Wives have to muck in. Where there's muck there's brass, as the North-of-Englanders say. But daughters are what it's all seen as being *for*. They're kept above the dirt. Unfitted for living.'

Tit for tat. You touch my mother and see what I'll say about your Daddy the businessman. Grainne's father had been in the building trade.

'Unfitted because they become wives who then do have to muck in? Supposing they become mistresses?'

'It's not a career,' he told her. 'Not a way of life. Not here.'

'Well, *you* like bed enough!'

'I like it. I don't spend my time thinking about it.'

'So I was the wrong partner? Too demanding?' You were meant to learn from your mistakes, weren't you? *Was* she unfit, she worried? In what way?

'Your trouble was scruples. Making mountains out of molehills.' He waved a hand. 'The wrong woman for a politician. Do you know that the Sicilians say "politics is sweeter than sex"? Yes. Well, no reason not to combine them – until one starts to threaten the other. That happens when the woman – it's always the woman – makes a big production out of going to bed. Bed's simple really.'

He talked with assurance, driving, mashing up things – love, politics – the way a garbage-disposer mashes them to unrecognizable, recyclable, grey flitters. Simple, he repeated. Whambam. Over in seconds. The idea of Almighty God watching your activities between the sheets was ludicrous. Calling it a sin! He laughed. 'The nuns ruined you, you know, Grainne. They renounce the flesh and are haunted ever more by a wondrous notion of it which they pass on to lassies like you who end up thinking you have the Holy Grail between your legs and that some knight is going to come and find it.' Owen Roe turned to look at her. He had parked the car on the Vico Road, a lovers' lane. Three blue mountains across the bay corresponded to the hill from which they watched them. 'I hear you've got a new lover,' he said, 'the little American?'

She was too surprised to be angry. Then she thought of something: 'Cormac told you?' Who else could? Now she was furious. 'What have you done to him? Listen, Michael and I want you to keep away from him.'

'I've always regarded myself as in loco parentis to Cormac.'

She screamed: 'He's not an orphan.'

'Grainne, I make myself available. That's all. He drops round. We chat. Sometimes I take him for a run up to the cottage or a ride on Calary Bog. A boy his age needs an outlet.'

In her mind's eye Owen Roe galloped, broad backside raised over the horse's broader one, as he negotiated a fence. Whack fol de diddle o! He was the embodiment of a coarse exuberance in their joint heritage.

'He talks to me,' said Owen Roe.

'Talk! There was that target practice!'

'That was last year. Anyway it was harmless. He needs to get things off his chest. It was from him I learned how loopy old Judith is. I think you'd be doing the family a disservice if you let this young man interview her.' This was said with emphasis.

'He's making a pro-IRA film. *You* are said to be the IRA's man in the Dáil. Why don't you talk to him yourself?'

Owen Roe shrugged. 'I don't want to pull rank, rouse hackles. He might turn round and sell the interview elsewhere. Journalist Johnnies are like that. I'd prefer that *you* told him Judith isn't up to it. That she's ill or something.'

'That's what you want from me?'

'Yes.'

'Does she really know some secret?'

'Delusions. What could she know? I refused to have her, you know. She's the nuns' responsibility. Michael wouldn't have had her either if he hadn't intended using her to get you to come back.' Assessing look. 'So,' smiling, 'in a way it's your fault she's here and ready to disgrace us all. Cormac minds.'

'Will you stop seeing Cormac if I agree?'

'No.'

'Why?'

'You and he are fighting, aren't you?'

'It's none of your bloody business.'

'Yes it is.'

'Oh,' she cried, 'he's a male of the blood. You want to recruit him. Do you believe even in the things you tell him? You've snared a nestling – he's fourteen – and you won't be able to keep tabs on him. That awful moron, Patsy Flynn, spends hours with him. Did you know that? My kind of romanticism – or soft-headedness, whatever, is not lethal. Yours is.'

She felt his immovability. The sheer mass of him in the seat beside her maddened her. There he was: set in his opinions, unwilling to revise them. Her own, in contrast, were like swirls of suds. She felt febrile. He seemed to be made of some collapsed and condensed matter. His unyielding face turned to her and arranged a smile across itself.

'Silly Grainne!' Boney teeth gnashed charm. A hand stripped itself of its orthopaedic black glove and reached for her breast, cupping it with authority. She caught the hand, lifted and bit it until she felt her teeth pierce the skin. Blood flowed into her mouth but she kept biting. 'Bitch! Mad harridan!' His other hand slapped at her, back and forth, again and again, even after she had released her bite. She felt the blows, felt her face burn and her skin tighten across her skull. Lights flared in front of her eyes but she was tasting his blood with a horrified glee.

Neither spoke as he drove her back. Outside the house, he said, 'What will you say about your face?'

'That we went horse-back riding and I fell. And anyway, fuck you.'

She got out and he drove off without further talk. He had a handkerchief knotted around one hand. His bulk at the wheel was adamant in its rock-like heaviness.

'Weep not for me, women of Jerusalem,' Michael intoned. 'Weep rather for yourselves and for your children. In your case that still means me, doesn't it? Michael, the eternal child. Your face is a disaster area. Tears won't help. I can't make out how you bruised so much of it.'

'A branch hit me,' she said, 'on the face. Then I fell.'

'Better stay home for a day or so,' said Michael. 'My reputation as a wife-batterer makes me nervous. Some Lib ladies might give me what for. Especially with all the crying. What was that in aid of?'

Grainne had started sniffling in front of the television which they now watched in Aunt Judith's room. A film had come on before the news, showing a Traditional Crafts Exhibit at the Royal Dublin Society. A man threw pots, a horse was shod, a roof thatched, wool spun and bread baked in a bastable. Grainne's tears had started at the pots and she had had to leave the room just as the soda-bread was emerging, baked, risen and looking like a blown-up diagram of the human brain.

'So why were you crying?'

'One never knows.'

'Rubbish,' said Michael. 'Better vent your spleen. What have I done now?'

'Why should it be you?'

'Oho! Is it the uncle again then? Or is the aunt getting you down? We could shunt her off somewhere.'

'Owen Roe says that you only took her here so as to get me back.'

'True.'

'Well she's not an inanimate object.'

'Soon will be.'

'I can't bear your fake toughness.'

'What?' said Michael. 'Prefer lies to truth? Spinning-wheels and bastable ovens? Images of yourself as Mum with apple cheeks and a big apron baking bread which her six kids will remember all their lives? I'll have to write a letter to RTE telling them to stop undermining the morale of our housewives with this sort of pap. No more spinning-wheels. Ban the bastable. I could organize a husbands' picket.'

Michael poured two stiff doses of Paddy. 'Here,' he offered. 'My own panacea. It was an awful life, you know.'

'I know.'

'Mum had no teeth. She'd had them removed by tying one end of a stout thread to the door knob and the other to the tooth, then getting someone to bang the door. Dad was a dasher. He kept his canines. You weren't weeping for the aunt, I hope? Listen, we can have her re-institutionalized and then why don't you get yourself some sort of job?'

'You know damn well that anything I'd earn would go on taxes. I don't want the sort of job Marie-Antoinette had at the dairy.'

'I don't see why not. She might have done better if she'd stuck to it. The alternative, which I do not recommend,' said Michael with what sounded like a stab of anxiety, 'is leaving me and Cormac to our own unreliable devices and going off to join the ranks of poor cows sitting in bed-sitting rooms looking for their "identity" and tapping out letters to *Spare Rib*.'

'How do you know about them?'

'I see them in the pubs,' he told her. 'They come in with their little string bags full of convenience food and pick up their male equivalents then, from reports reaching your roving correspondent, sex sometimes ensues in the dusty bed-sits of Dun Laoghaire and Rathgar, followed usually by revulsion, self-hatred and a renewal of vows to the goddess, Diana.'

'Your own patroness.'

'Is that what you think?'

'No.'

These parody-rows could turn real at any point. They were a testing of thin ice and at some point you always fell through.

'Of course not,' she lied, putting off the moment. Michael's derision of people who reached out for a little sex and warmth, maybe even passion, enraged her. Precisely because it was so predictable, it hit a nerve. Predictable. Familiar. Men in this country had been educated by clerics and, though they might react for a while against these mentors, sooner or later they could be relied on to start talking about love-making the way he just had. Whether they were passionate men like Owen Roe, or frigid ones like Michael, either way, they needed the tongs of humour to pick up the subject at all. Monastic tradition described woman as a bag of shit and it followed that sexual release into such a receptacle was a topic about as fit for sober discussion as a bowel movement.

Or was the snideness guilt? Could Michael himself have been visiting the bed-sits of Rathgar? While she was away? Getting it up for some girl he might think of as 'light' and therefore sexy? Or who was just younger or prettier or simply different? Desolated, Grainne had to brace herself to ask:

'Did you sleep with anyone while I was in London?'

'No.'

'Why not?'

'Too drunk mostly. Too depressed.'

Shit! This – surely the worst of all possible answers? – failed to flatter either of them. Unfairly, she wished he *had* slept with someone. It would have been a sign of life. 'Do you think,' she asked provocatively, 'that if we were mature we would opt for the brave solution?'

'What's that?'

'Break up a bad marriage?'

'What's so bad about our marriage?' he wanted to know. Did she imagine a flicker of panic under the hearty tone? 'I should show you "bad".' He laughed. 'Make you count your blessings. I should put on a homecrafts exhibition: beat the daylights outa you, bring a concubine under the conjugal roof, sully the nuptial bed, and bash Cormac's brains in so that he ends up more moronic than he started out.'

These examples came from the pubs, she knew: Michael's university and club. He'd heard them from lawyers. They were true.

'They call that sado-masochism,' she said, with an effort at flippancy. 'People pay for it.' Cards in London tobacconist's windows, she was thinking: discipline and bondage; severe Swedish lessons; leather; rubber; police-women's uniforms. Lonely, lonely bed-sit-land where people have nothing in common but their yearnings. He's right. I couldn't stand it. Besides, there's Cormac.

But were yearnings maybe a deep thing to have in common, after all? Discipline-and-bondage might correspond to a need of the soul.

In the Home for Battered Wives, she had heard of women who provoked their men to hit them. 'It's a form of suicide,' a social worker had told her. But maybe it was the opposite? An effort to enliven a dead situation?

'What right have you to be unhappy?' Michael was sliding towards seriousness and acrimony. 'You have leisure,' he accused. 'No kids pulling at your tits or skirts. I don't even insist on your being a good housewife. You have all the time in the world to fulfil yourself in ways of your own. Take up water-colouring. Preserve Georgian Dublin. Find your own outlets, for Christ's sake. Don't come expecting me to live your life for you. I provide a home. More or less provide it. Anyway it's there. What more am I expected to do?'

Cleave to her. Be one flesh with her. Why had she ever thought he might? Where had she even got the notion?

From the prayerbook, that was where. She'd only recently realized this. Tidying out some drawers, she had come on prayers she had said all her girlhood. They astounded her and yet, for all that time, she had taken them for granted, let them slip into her subliminal consciousness and programme her forever: requests, no, *directions* to the Divine Lover taken at the age of seven, whom no other after had managed to emulate:

> Soul of Christ sanctify me.
> Body of Christ save me.
> Blood of Christ inebriate me.
> Water from the side of Christ wash me.
> Oh Good Jesus, hear me.
> Within thy wounds hide me.
> Never let me be separated from thee . . .

She had separated herself. Gone dry in the heart. Her lovers now were blighted. Michael was forever bathing his dried-out throat in pubs. Her fault? How dare she complain? Tell him? No.

Did she believe any of this?

The submerged part of her did. The part afraid to talk or tell, or mostly even think, except now, lubrified by the Paddy, the bottled barley-juice which was anyway finished, the bottle up-ended and the conversation, too, run dry. It had been parody anyway: all in quotation marks, bracketed between their little ears, joke gossip-column, joke pub-talk, joke God-knew-what. That didn't mean that you didn't mean what you said, but it let the other person pretend they didn't realize. Talk between her and Michael always went that way. They always let each other off the hook in the end. For this was marriage, a *modus vivendi*, and who believed in final solutions anyway?

'I'm going to bed.'

'OK. I'll lock up.'

'Don't forget to put out the cat.'

'No.'

Later, they'd lie together, like a four-armed creature fearful of amputation. At some point, one or other might whisper through the darkness the old school-yard word: 'Pax?'

'Pax.'

8

The next day the doorbell rang and there was Owen Roe holding roses.

'If those are for me you can put them where the Kerryman put the sixpence.'

'I've got to talk to you.'

'Will I need police protection?'

'I'm sorry about your face.' He stretched out a bandaged hand. 'I told the doctor it was a bulldog.'

'Doctor? You went to a doctor? Did you think I had a poisoned tooth?'

'Human mouths,' he said seriously, 'are less hygienic than dogs'.'

'Come in.'

'Is Michael home?'

'No, but I have a luncheon date.'

'Going to keep it with that face?'

'Why not? It'll be a talking point. Besides, I'll wear make-up.'

By now they were in the drawing room. Owen Roe set his roses on a chair.

'Okay if I sit? I didn't get across the essential thing I wanted to say last time. Please, hear me out. You're sure Michael's not here?'

'What if he were?'

'It was because of him that I broke our thing off.'

Grainne began to laugh.

'It's true. I didn't want him hurt.'

'You've often hurt Michael.'

'What I mean is I didn't want him collapsing into a million whimpering fragments.'

'Christ, Owen Roe, whatever about your public rhetoric, your private efforts stink.'

'What I'd *like* you to get into your brain is that he could *not* take a scandal about you. Think about this, will you? Why can't you do your philandering across the water, anyway? It's traditional. I thought you knew that. I thought you were having a lezzy affair in that Battered Wives hole? With the woman who runs it? The thing *you* don't seem to realize is that people here have always managed to have their fun and heaven too by playing their cards close to their chests. You don't seem to know how to do that. That's your trouble. You've lost the inherited canniness of the peasant and haven't acquired new savvy. You're dangerous – like a mad bulldog.' Owen Roe waved his injured hand at her. 'Ask any small-town solicitor about the revelations that turn up in wills: bastards concealed, incest, life-long lovers who saw each other regularly without anyone suspecting. There's nothing *new* about adultery. What's new is the carelessness. A man in my position is a natural target for blackmail. I have to watch it. The point is that this American is rushing in in football boots where angels fear to tread.'

'So I'm a bad picker of men?'

'If it came to that, *I* could fix you up with a selection of safe friends.' Owen Roe had a trick of taking ironic statements straight: pulling the rug of humour out from under you.

Grainne looked at herself in the mirror. 'I seem to lack instinct. Do I throw the poker at you now? Ask for a list of candidates? My breath's gone the wrong way. That's a gasp, I suppose?' Her voice bobbed spurtily. 'I'm gasping in moral shock,' said the voice. 'Isn't that interesting? It means I have morals.'

'You're stiff with them,' he told her impatiently. 'You're a naive woman, Grainne. Rigid. To function effectively in society, one's got to be able to double think. That's what divides independent from old-fashioned women. It separates statesmen from heroes, which is why it is not impossible that my respected Da may have done things which it would be as well didn't come to light.'

'Aunt Judith's secret?' She pounced. 'That's what you're interested in then? Why? How could it matter? Do you know what it is? Yesterday, you denied it existed.'

It was like him to change things round. Badgering her. Yesterday it had suited him to say there was no secret. Today the opposite filled the bill.

Owen Roe spread his legs and looked judicious. Cartoonish stances increased his presence. He said he didn't know what the secret might be.

'But there *are* secrets, stories, dirt which could discredit half the party. Things get done in a Civil War that might look criminal in peace-time. No time for due process. You may imagine. But, today, because of the new terrorists, nobody wants to be seen being *too* imaginative . . .'

'Surely, time . . .'

Owen Roe shrugged. 'Politics here is very tribal, remember. Families could be discredited. Then there are the sons of victims . . .'

She had never decided whether or not this man was intelligent. He boasted suspiciously much about his own canniness and how he had put important people right about things they should have known. Owen Roe was the sort of man who tells people how to mend a puncture. 'Yes,' he would say in a satisfied voice. 'People are always surprised at *my* knowing things like that.' As if he were Moses. He talked about football as if it was commendably human of him to take an interest. This could be put down to his having never been married. A wife would have warned him about boring people – and maybe she'd have been doing him a disservice? The bore's self-love propelled Owen Roe like a motor and his animal exuberance made you forgive him. There was something disarming about such assurance. Something antique and almost gone from the world. He laid down the law as old men must have done from thrones and pulpits and earth mounds down all the centuries when the law had been seen as unchanging and reliable.

'People have long memories,' said Owen Roe. 'To this day, you can hear fellows in bars speculating about the identity of Kevin O'Higgins' murderers.'

'That was in 1927, surely? Judith had been in the convent five years.'

'I didn't mean she'd come up with *that*. Do you know what an analogy is, Grainne?'

'What I know is that *you* don't give a tinker's damn for the party. You don't give a damn for anyone except yourself.'

'*And* the country. The country for its own sake and myself because it may need me.'

'You *would* say that.'

'General de Gaulle too was blamed for his egotism and intransigence . . .'

'How did *you* earn the comparison with de Gaulle?'

'A pantomime horse, my dear, takes two men to animate it. I aspire only to be the front legs. The rear, the past, the equivalent of de Gaulle's resistance record, is provided by my illustrious Da.'

'And it's the back legs of your Pegasus that Aunt Judith might maim?'

'Congratulations. You got there.'

Owen Roe produced his cigarettes. 'Mind if I smoke?'

She shrugged.

'Funny,' he said, 'the way this brings us close. You and me.'

'You think so, do you?'

'I know so. You feel it too. Thence all the effort at irony. Your facial muscles must be stiff. It's a pity the way things fall out. We could have got along.'

'My luncheon date is early,' she told him. 'If you're through . . .'

'With Duffy?'

Grainne pressed her lips together.

'All right, all right. Your pride is up. You won't drop him on my sayso. I'm sorry for Michael's sake but the thing doesn't concern me enough for me to roll out my big guns.'

'But the Aunt-Judith angle does?' What big guns? Which?

It was true that the look which Grainne had imposed on her face felt liable to slip and that her mouth had the unconvincing feel of cardboard. It was a look of outrage and Grainne was not sure that anything could be held to be outrageous here and now. Unless perhaps everything? Starting with Owen Roe's concern for appearances.

Objectively, the man was surely madder than Aunt Judith? Unless, to be sure, the political scene was as he said it was and mad enough to justify him? Not having paid attention to it, she had no way of knowing. She had not assumed it could affect her. She had thought of it as a stale old play, trundled out by a decreasingly talented rep. company, where attitudes were struck while the audience spent its time in the bar. That such a ham lot should suddenly draw real pistols and shoot into the audience was – what? Possible? Maybe. Maybe they'd shoot each other instead?

'If your de Gaulle scenario were anything but a pipe-dream, surely you'd have been got rid of by now?'

'Nobody has any interest in getting rid of me. What harm am I doing? I'm waiting in a disciplined and patriotic manner for the moment when I may be of use.'

'What about the story that it was you, ten years ago, when you were a government minister, who funnelled funds to the hard boys in the IRA and got them to break away from the other lot and form the Provos? That, if true, leaves you with a lot of responsibility.'

'Doing nothing also entails responsibility. You might like to recall that at that time the Catholic population up North were like mice before a predator with the B Specials rampaging through their ghettos. Our people up there were a minority. Unarmed. When they started a Civil Rights campaign they were beaten up, shot at and intimidated. The government up there was partisan. The IRA was a joke. They'd handed in the gun years before – sold their last remaining ones to the Welsh. People forget that. They forget the despair of the Catholics, the graffiti on their walls showing IRA equalling "I ran away". They forget the climate of the time which had just seen the US National Guard murdering students on US campuses. *Then* the big bullies in the popular imagination were policemen. *Now*, because of things which have happened around the world since, the popular bugaboo is a terrorist. But politics isn't played for a gallery. The aim is not to be the pin-up of the season but to be effective in the long run, and, in the long run, no matter what the media are telling you right now, access to power and privilege has always been won by violence. The violence, later, has to be controlled in order to set up a new *status quo*. A conciliatory figure has to be found to head up a new government. Someone not too closely involved with the old powers or the new – or, alternatively, someone equally involved with both.'

'You?'

'Me.'

'Up North?'

'No, no. I'm envisaging a larger shake-up which will bring forth a federal Ireland.'

'You'd be High King?'

'For a while.'

'It sounds like an opera.'

'You mustn't think I'm a villain. I didn't plan all this when we were trying to help our people some years back. I just felt *then* – and, mind, the story you heard about what happened is not accurate and I'm not about to tell you the true one – I felt that when things get going they can be given a shove in what seems the right direction. A man has few chances in his life to give that shove. It's the sin of indifference to play safe when you do get your chance. Jesus Christ was very critical of the do-nothing chappies. "Behold I was in prison and ye visited me not, I was hungry and ye fed me not . . ." Etcetera. He's angry, mark, at what they did *not* do. He doesn't say "you were drunk while I was at Long Kesh", or "you were whoring or lining your pockets". A lot of pocket-liners and whore-masters have been good for their people. Men of will and energy tend to sin as well as to save. Probably JC himself, before the censors got at his life story, was less of a Holy Joe.'

'Well, nobody could say that you have a small opinion of yourself.'

He had impressed her. In spite of herself. It was true that he was better on public than on private matters, even gave the impression of not being out for himself. Grainne was reminded of being thirteen and in love with the principal boy in the Christmas panto who, of course, was not a boy but a girl. For about half a year she had agonized over her doomed and silly love. 'He' was a she, yet fought the wicked ogre with a convincing male flourish. Grainne's present feelings for Owen Roe were similarly snarled.

'You really think you're a sort of Christ figure, don't you!'

They laughed. It was odd. An intimacy *had* been established. But then, enemies are intimate too. A current bound them.

Impatient to break it, she threw out a random dig:

'So, I'm in a position, thanks to Aunt Judith, to put paid to your heroics?'

'Our interests are not divergent.'

'But I'm *sorry* for Aunt Judith. I'd like to see her recover her wits.'

It was some physical thing about her cousin, she was thinking. Something he gave off. You let yourself feel that he was appealing to your good sense, when what he'd done was to bludgeon your senses. She had already forgotten what he'd said just now but the feeling he had aroused in her – a sort of submission – was still there.

He was talking again. About Aunt Judith and how fishing in old murk risked bringing up nasty matter which would do nothing for her wits.

'Even harmless secrets,' said Owen Roe, '*because of being hidden*, breed maggots.'

She had a sensation that his words themselves were maggots.

'I've got to throw you out now, Owen Roe. It's late.'

'In history as in matter, nothing,' he said, 'is lost. It comes back in another form. You and Michael thought that the dead time in which you grew up would go on forever. You thought the Troubles were over and the curtain down. It was an intermission. Yours is a peculiarly apathetic generation.'

'Bath!' She mimed soaping gestures, washing away his words. 'I'm off to have one. You can let yourself out. Sorry.'

He picked up his roses. 'Shall I put these in water?'

They were florists' flowers: long-stemmed, tight-budded, rusty-red like old scabs or clotted wounds oozing emissions between the bandaging folds of white paper.

'I don't care,' she said ungraciously. 'I'll be dead late. Do what you like. Bye.'

She ran upstairs. She had forgotten to bring up the matter

of Cormac which she should have done if a bargain was to be struck. Never mind. There would be other opportunities. Too many, she thought, and was grateful for her luncheon date with Duffy, a mild, civil man in whom she hoped to find a knight who could deliver her from the dragon of her lower nature, which was uncreditably responsive to Owen Roe.

It was only when she was in the bath and it was too late to call him back – she'd heard his car grind down the gravel drive – that what he'd said about rolling out guns began to frighten her. What had he meant? Why hadn't she asked? She must be out of her *mind*! Dealing with Owen Roe was like walking across a bog. You never knew when the ground might give way under your feet.

'Then why did you bring me here?'

'To force myself to decide.'

'Why do you need forcing?'

'Please,' she begged, 'don't press me. I don't think I can explain.'

'Well, then, let's try.'

'But if I freeze you'll hate me.'

'How could I?'

'You'll be angry. It's humiliating for everyone. Oh, I *am* a fool!'

'Don't you want to make love?'

'I did but I don't now. I know I'm maddening. Sorry.'

'Don't *apologize*! I think you want me to rape you,' James told her. 'But I won't. Remember there are two of us involved. I do have feelings.'

'It would be so deliberate now – after all this talk. By daylight.'

'We can close the blinds.'

'There aren't any.'

James felt impatient. 'You *are* a tease!'

'I didn't want to be. It's just that it's important to me that it should work and now it won't. We'll both be selfconscious.'

'It could be worse if we don't do it,' James told her. 'Listen, do you want me to tell you how much I've been thinking about you? I have. Every day. This wasn't an impulse.'

'Please no. I'm not playing hard to get. I mean . . .'

'Well?'

'It's – I've said it: I'm afraid it would be no good. I've waited so long, you see, for long before you came. You can't imagine. And now it might disappoint me. I might disappoint *you*. That's one fear. The other is that it might be marvellous and I wouldn't be able to do without it.'

'You're being funny, aren't you? Having me on?'

'No.'

'So you propose a double bind. Like your namesake did to that poor guy she forced to run off with her. In the Celtic saga. What's his name?'

Grainne shrugged.

'It must be an Irish knack. Listen, I'd like to know. Have I bad breath or something? Men are vulnerable too. We're not made of steel.'

She stood knotting her hands, staring at him, saying nothing. Her eyes glittered with tears. James was at a loss. Maybe she'd had a mastectomy? Or some other thing? What? Was it something he'd done?

'Does sex frighten you so much?'

'No. Yes. Not the sex.'

'Have you been burned badly some time? By some guy who left you, or . . .'

She put a hand across his mouth. 'I don't want to talk about that.'

'So there was . . .'

'I'm sorry. I didn't plan this.'

'I'll recover. You haven't blighted my life.'

'I . . .'

'Why don't you collect whatever it was you had to pick up here? I'll wait,' he told her coldly.

She moved towards an inner door of the cottage. Annoyed? Disappointed? Good.

'I'll be as quick as I can,' she shouted back at him. 'Have a whiskey meanwhile. It's in the cupboard. I'm afraid there's no ice.'

He could think of quips about that. Plenty. But forebore. She'd disappeared into a back room anyway, leaving James to ponder negatives and consider the mountain view. They were miles out in the country in this uncomfortable, rustic cottage to which he had been lured on, he had every right to think, a wild goose chase in which the goose herself had taken the initiative. Well, most of it. He poured himself a whiskey and went back to the window to stare out at the empty lake and lead-coloured mountain which rose on the other side of it. What did people do in a place like this? Beat their meat probably. Goddamn place was probably soggy with onanistic sperm. He felt like running out to add his share to it. Pour it into the grass to be eaten by cows whose milk and butter could feed it back to the already demented population. The stuff was said to be high in protein. Might calm them down. Balance their diet. A paper on a nutritional solution to the problems of old Ireland, to be delivered by J. Duffy, funds supplied courtesy of the Honourable Heirs and data by the dishonourable daughters. She had done a complete about-face. Why? Where had he gone wrong?

Casting his mind back to lunch, he couldn't see any hitch. They'd had it in his hotel: roast grouse, bread sauce, good feeling – or so he'd thought. He liked her and thought she did him. What had they talked about? Trifles. This and that. Lunch had been all jokes and for what could he take such sustained hilarity but the slow-burning fuse of sex? Savouring his awareness of this, he had played things cool. *She* was the one whose teeth had flashed and whose cheeks were sema-phores. She was a vivid creature and the skin on her forehead was as translucent as a shell.

She ate, he noted, with finicky precision, keeping her elbows pasted to her body like the trussed wings of a fowl and wiping her lips on her napkin. It struck him again that the constraints of this tight little city must be propulsive.

It was their third meeting. Between times he had boiled down impressions of her. Now they dilated like Japanese flowers in water. Her face shifted to homeliness and back so that she seemed to be several women in one. She talked of her aunt, winking, weaving webs of conspiracy designed, he could see, to while away wet hours.

'If I'm right in my guess, her secret,' she said, 'concerns

Michael's grandfather. This means that those who ride his ghostly coat-tails would not like it to emerge. The ruling party,' she clarified. 'Others too.'

'The I R A ?'

James would have liked to know for whom to be cheering, if only because cheering linked you to the local scene. The long passion of Irish history mystified him, though he had opened himself to the local geography, responding to the city's moist appeal. Dublin struck him as cryptic. It was all smear and glare. Rain filtered light. Mist masked it. Water threw it slantwise with the sly trajectories of knives. He learned that cellars flooded with the tide. This made the place seem animate, as though, circulating like a blood-stream, damp must quicken stone. He saw dry rot in a Georgian building, and the frills of flesh-pink mushrooms, bizarrely breaking through walls and woodwork, reinforced his tourist's notion that the old houses contained embryos of ongoing life. The growths resembled rows of ears – swinish? human? – as though the place were keeping tabs on *him*. James found, despite the haphazard nature of his arrival here, that he was seeing Dublin as an ancestral womb. How not? His people had come from here. On the streets he kept running into deformed versions of his relatives back home: cartoon caricatures of Irish from the States, where calm apparently descended on driven immigrants or anyway on their offspring.

Studying his face in his morning mirror, James, seeing it with an Irish eye, perceived a blandness in it and a size and pallor suggesting that he had been raised on massive doses of Valium and milk. The stock he came from was around him in its unimproved strain: redder, sharper, more malicious, sometimes more baffled-looking or angrier or merrier – always *more* something, contorted by pressures, emphatic, a trifle mad. James thought of gardening and the distinctive varieties of a plant which horticulturists will blend to produce a tougher, more marketable product: like the square tomato developed at U C Davis, which can be picked by machine and easily packed for shipping. The analogy didn't quite work since the tomato-complexion was not his but blazed like scar-tissue on the primitive, distant cousins whom he scru-

tinized daily in the Dublin streets. There, but for the despair
and the get-with-it-ness of two forgotten great-grandfathers,
went James Edmund Duffy. Would he have liked to be going
there, and thus? Of course not. He preferred to be himself.
At the same time, the poetry of lost possibilities played its
light on an imaginary James whom in his mind he christened
Seamus: the Irish form of his name. Fewer choices would
have been open to Seamus and the narrowness of his society
might have made him ambitious. Feisty? Probably. Political?
Perhaps. James didn't know enough about Irish politics to
decide. Tiring of the game, he dropped it, but, like a man
carrying dice in his pocket, returned to it from time to time for
a few pensive throws.

Therese had sent a letter in which she imagined him on the
plane over being seduced by a Polish countess in an immense
fur cloak.

> As the two manoeuvred on the seats, James saw the
> fur darken and turn pale like wind-tossed wheat on the
> Polish plains.

He was more annoyed than diverted. A diversion was what
the letter was meant to be. He knew Therese. She offered
a fictional release to ridicule real ones which must, her
mockery implied, be as banal as episodes in a blue movie.
That she should have gone to the trouble showed anxiety,
and this, since she knew him, was of interest. Watching with
her clever wardress's scrutiny, she had noted his chafings at
the persona which boxed him in. The letter was a reminder of
how tolerant and mature a relationship theirs was. The trouble
was that tolerance and maturity were part of the box. To
break out of it he, like a Jack-in-the-box of childhood, would
need a powerful spring.

Fidgety with self-concern, he had spent the last few days
walking through half-gutted eighteenth-century squares whose
brick tints ranged from smoked sausage to old port.

The passionate tourist is all idle receptivity and it was in
this risky state that he had let himself think about Mrs
O'Malley. James's senses were troubled; murky underneath,
their surface was a dazzle of impressions, scattered spokes in

169

need of a hub. He knew what he wanted the hub to be, but moved cautiously.

His emotional confusions were not all of his own making. Alternating come-on looks with chilly ones, his guest reminded him of a rooky cop he had once seen getting his signals mixed and snarling up traffic at an LA intersection. She said he must call her by her first name – pronounced Grawnya. A green light surely?

'Do you hate it?' she asked. 'It's the name of one of the love heroines of pre-Christian Irish saga. She was betrothed to the ageing warrior-leader, Finn Macool, but forced one of his fighting men to run off with her. Apparently, it was an offer the chap couldn't refuse without loss of honour, but he was done for anyway because Finn's army chased the pair of them through the length and breadth of Ireland, tracking them so close that they could never pause long enough to sleep two nights in the same place.'

'Poor guy!' James's sympathies were for the lover.

' "Graw" is the Gaelic for "love".' Her smile was like the cop's white, beckoning glove. 'I never lived up to it,' she told him sadly.

The stop-sign came when she'd drunk her coffee and said that she must go but there was no need, after all, for him to come with her to the cottage. It was a domestic chore and she didn't want to impose it on him. While saying this, she began easing on a pair of suede gloves, coaxing wrinkled skin over the bulge of each knuckle then down to the finger's roots. Slowly, conscientiously, she eased, smoothed and remarked that, on the other hand, the scenery was striking and he might like the jaunt? On the drive, besides, she could unfold the plan she had conceived for getting her aunt to talk. Stop. Go. Yield. Get ready.

Wondering at his disappointment, he saw that he had moved from dallying with the prospect of a sexual quickie, such as red-blooded tourists hope to fit in between sight-seeing tours. Quite what he had moved *towards* was unclear. He guessed he must be letting himself hope for some dream of wholeness or newness, for some change in his way of being, such as old Celtic ladies had had a way of offering men who let themselves be lured on strange trips. In Celtic tales, it was the woman who rode by on a white horse and bade the man leap up behind her.

Better haul in your imagination, James Edmund, he warned himself. The Irish Church had been tight-assed about sex and Grainne O was no pagan princess.

Living in this fishbowl town with her highly visible relatives, she would not have had much chance to learn about pleasure. It struck him that the scar-tissue faces he'd seen on the streets were the result of ways of living which would have left less visible scars. You didn't learn to enjoy in one generation. Americans knew that, having watched fortunes rise like yoyos while habits lagged. He could teach her though. Ridiculous: turning his coming affair into a project. Yet why not?

'Why are you laughing?'

He told her he'd thought of some joke. No, not worth telling. Exhilarated, he looked at her with new passion. Yes, he said firmly, he wanted to come.

'I must explain about Aunt Judith,' she said.

As she drove through the outer city – grey chrysalis of walls within walls, wadded like layers in a wet wasp's nest – he let her talk about the aunt who, he must keep remembering, was not only the pretext for this jaunt but could also be a Queen Lear, a Celtic seer or one of those sly old hags whose knowledge turns out to be of use.

He had been reading the newspapers of 1921 in the National Library and realized it had been a time of chaos. Factions. Guerrilla war. He wondered how it had been for that American, Driscoll: an earlier, simpler sort of man than you got nowadays in the States. James was curious about him. What would he have been like? Streetsmart Irish? A devious politician? Did he come over here from ambition, intending to go back and use the experience with the Boston Irish? And did he find the people here as alien as James did? O'Toole's hints about sinister machinations came to mind but did not hold James's attention. The old man had stumbled late in life on the conspiracy theory of history and was as dazzled by it as people had been back in the days when underground radio stations in LA devoted six-hour programmes to the Kennedy murders. Another era: close but gone.

Grainne O unfolded her plan for reawakening her aunt's memory. It involved returning her to the scenes of her youth and most specifically to an Anglo-Irish mansion which had been requisitioned one night in the spring of 1921 for the peaceful purposes of holding a ball.

'It seems the fighting men wanted to enjoy the fruits of revolution while the revolution was still in progress.' She sounded fired by the notion. 'Tricky,' she commented, 'but worth trying when you think how quickly revolutions can turn sour.'

The story was a version of the Cinderella story in which not one but all dancers were interlopers from the world of cinders, and doom had dangled, exploding after midnight when the Black and Tans burst in with guns blazing. One of the men arrested that night was Michael's grandfather. Judith's brother-in-law. Obviously, she would remember the event.

'I got her on the subject,' said Grainne, 'and she knew details I had never heard. I asked was Sparky Driscoll there and she said no, but that she herself had taken him to visit the place some months later. Her family knew the caretaker, you see. Now the lucky thing is that that same caretaker is still alive and living in the house. Owns it, in fact, but that's another story. Talking to him would surely jerk her out of her forgetfulness. We could drive her down there on a visit, if you like.'

'We?'

'Well, you can't go off with Aunt Judith on your own, you know. I'd have to be along. I thought,' said Grainne, 'we should manage the thing in easy stages and spend a night or so in the local hotel. Timmy himself might interest you. He's the onetime caretaker who now owns the great house. He must have known Aunt Judith quite well and he has lots to say on his own account. The place is worth seeing too.'

'Could we film it?' James collected his wits. Lights green as emeralds were exploding in his head.

'Shouldn't be any problem.' She edged the car off the road on to an overgrown grass track. The bonnet nosed through meshed bramble shoots. 'Here's the cottage.'

It was rectangular like a shoebox, and looked no more connected with the landscape than debris might, which had been thrown there by long-gone picnickers and grown mossy and eroded over the wet years.

'It's a bit Spartan.' Grainne got out of the car and fumbled under stones for a key. 'It belonged to Michael's grandfather whose publicized love of frugality was quite genuine.'

James followed her into a room smelling of mould.

'Pff! Needs airing. I'll light a fire and we can have tea. He,' she said of the grandfather, 'was the bane of our diplomats when he travelled. Would eat nothing but eggs, salt bacon and boiled potatoes. You may imagine the embarrassment at dinner-parties, since, if it was good enough for him, why not for them and their guests? Also, for a long while he refused to wear a dinner-jacket, not to mention morning-trousers. That generation was more egalitarian than the Soviets.'

James noted armchairs angular as choir stalls and thorny with tweed. A fireplace had a cheap tile surround which had started to peel from the wall.

'I'd do it over if it was mine,' she said. 'It belongs to a cousin. Well, at least the fire's been laid.'

James looked round. 'I like the austerity,' he decided. 'It surprises me for a governing class, but I like it.'

'All changed now. In the Thirties times were tough. There was an economic war with England and later they probably had to be very foxy if they were to walk the tightrope between excitable elements in the country and the British threat to invade and grab back the ports. Churchill threatened to do that in, I think, 1940. Chaos was constantly threatening. "Chassis" O'Casey called it. People still quote his line: "The whole world is in a state of chassis". Wryly. "Chassis" is back, you see.'

'Not just here.'

'No, but here it's familiar.'

'Are *you* afraid of feeling?'

She gave him a sharp look. 'It needs channelling, don't you think? Like gas.'

'Romantic scenery,' James peered out of a window.

Pricking through beards of foliage, he made out the gleam

of a lake. Coot flew across it and reeds, topped by thick pods, moved in rhythm to the suck of the waters. A mountain surged upwards like a mace. His ancestors might well have fled from some barren place like this. By that move they had given him his chance and destroyed their memory – a double bonus.

This country was populated with pillars of salt. The fancy made him think of running his tongue across Grainne O'Malley's salt-white teeth.

'It's easy for you,' she was panting behind him. 'Americans,' pant, 'are the new aristocrats.'

Turning, he found her on her knees, blowing into a wet fire. Green smoke spurted and her cheeks were like drawings of the wind in the margins of old maps.

'Let me do that.'

'It's done,' she said, scrambling up. 'But the blood's gone from my head. I'm seeing black.' Groping for his steadying hand, she fell into his arms.

It was then that he made his move and was repulsed. He called her a tease, accusing her of giving off signals like a wigwag.

'You misread them!' She bolted for the protection of brogue and laughter: 'We'll have none of that now, Misther Duffy,' she clowned. 'What about a nice cuppa to settle yer fancy?'

Defeated, he let her lead him into the kitchen where, while waiting for water to boil, she showed photographs of the heroes of the Twenties looking plebeian in cloth caps. They depressed him. Upward striving, ambition, politics depressed him. He would have liked to lie on this frugal floor with her and fuck. Strain was alien to him except in sport, where the prize was immediate. Even that seemed senseless suddenly. Was he getting old? He wanted pleasure *now* and for her to have it. Her pieties saddened him and so did the laughing faces in the photos, several of which lacked teeth.

A photoportrait of Owen O'Malley poised before a *trompe-l'œil* Grecian pillar reminded James of poor immigrants' mementoes, whose formality evokes what it was intended to blot out: the decades of thrift and hope. Sexual parsimony would have been the pivot of such lives and here was this opulent granddaughter still stuck with the habit.

'Now, now, now, now!' he found himself grinding the words like nuts between his teeth, horrified for her and generations like her. If he'd been the Holy Ghost gifted with ubiquity, he'd have descended in the form of fire on every sad spinster, neglected wife and virgin in the land.

'How,' he asked, as they sat over tea and stale biscuits by the smoking fire and she worried about possible jackdaws in the chimney, 'how *does* one woo a decent married Irish-woman?'

She looked away from him, smoothing her skirt. Her eyelids trembled and he noted the scatter of freckles under each eye. Blue-veined lids. Hair the colour of a golden cocker's. Her mouth shut pursily over those sensual teeth. Thinking. He could imagine the flavour of her armpits. They'd be reddish too, grainy, the colour of young carrots crisp with earth. Immured in her fears, whatever they were. The husband, remember, was a lush. Loyalties there would be fierce. Weaklings knew how to manipulate their mates.

'I could have gone to bed with you *before*,' she said seriously. 'While you were a stranger. Like a demon lover – you know, anonymous, faceless. Now it's not so easy.'

'Another double bind!' He jeered. 'You're mistress of the game if mistress only of that.' A cheap taunt if her concern was with emotional accuracy. 'I could put a bag over my head,' he suggested.

But she had gone to collect whatever it was she'd come to get in the back room of the cottage and, left alone, he began to feel annoyed with himself for not trying to make things easier for her. She was like a trotter suddenly required to convert to a gallop. It hit him that anyway, he was not really eager to jerk her out of her puritanism. He liked the tartness which had been missing from so many of his sexual encounters. He'd had a lot since marriage. Instant intimacy was a necessity in a town like Los Angeles, if there was to be intimacy at all and, besides, there was a whole range of people who could not communicate verbally. If you wanted to know them you had to find other ways. James did. They were his antidote to the university, his safety valve – what Grainne meant, it struck him, by a demon lover. He had not bothered Therese with mention of them and she, on her own part, had been equally discreet. Her anxieties about what he might get up to here stemmed from a suspicion that women on this side of the Atlantic might play for keeps. They might too. James felt like a sportsman who, on the occasion of some commemorative jubilee, gets a chance to play a known game by primal rules.

Bam!

From the back of the house came sounds of clashing furniture. She was taking out her frustration.

Maybe he'd been a boor? You'd think he was sixteen and hard up for sex – going off half cocked because she wouldn't hit the sack with him right away. It wasn't even fair to say she'd led him on. She'd – count them – given a negative signal for every positive one. Something like this had happened to Caesar's men when, besieging a Celtic town, they saw towns-women crowd the ramparts to point bare boobs at them. Simple souls, the Romans took this for a sexual come-on, whereas the women had been beaming bad magic their way. Therese had come on the story and told it to James as a warning.

More noises in the back room.

James knocked on the dividing door.

'Can I come in?'

'Come on.'

She was standing by a large wall-cupboard whose double doors were open, showing shelves of folded white linen. Stacks more of this lay on a bed. Several sheets had been shaken from their folds and thrown about in an angular tumult.

'Sorry if you're getting fed up,' she said. 'This is taking longer than I foresaw. I'm looking for some sheets of mine which have got mixed up with other people's.'

'Can I help?'

'Would you? There's a laundry mark on mine but it's hard to find. I've found three pairs already but there should be another two with matching pillowcases.'

James began looking. 'I'm sorry for just now,' he apologized.

'Don't be,' she said. 'I led you on. The truth is I haven't tasted this sort of thing for years: being chatted up. I didn't *mean* to lead you on but I did. I see that.'

Gallantly, he denied this. She thanked him for his denial and flung a stiff, linen sheet out of its folds, waved it like a sail then ran it through her fingers, scrutinizing the hems. Yes, she said, shrugging. That was how it was here. It could drive you to drink. He expressed surprise that armies of men weren't around her. She, in her brogue, said to get along outa that and did he have her sheets picked out. He had found one and, showing its laundry mark, leaned over the edge of it and kissed her on the neck.

'Arguing is what frightens you, isn't it?' he challenged. 'Nothing binds people like a good fight. It jumps the stages, rushes them forward.'

He kissed her this time on the mouth and was kissed back. He could feel her body wanting his, responding, but she pushed him away.

'I'm an idiot,' she said. 'But I am afraid.'

'Fear's great,' James assured her. 'It's the great enhancer. Like that ball you were describing where they danced and trembled. You can imagine how that enhanced the experience of a mere dance. You don't know your luck at being a puritan.'

She laughed.

He licked his way around her ear and buried his nose in her hair which, with the window behind her, was the colour of the flames they had left burning smokily on the hearth. She smelled of what? Cake? Peat?

'It's not safe,' she whispered.

'Everything's OK.'

'You don't understand.'

'I won't do anything. Just let me hold you.' Fondling her: 'You've got a great body,' he whispered, 'different from Californian ones. More – exuberant.' He ran his hands over her hips. 'I've been wanting to do this. Jesus, it's lovely. Generous.'

'Are you calling me fat?'

'Feminine,' he said. 'Ancient. There's probably a word for it in Greek only I don't know Greek. Maybe in Gaelic?'

The sheets he had been holding slipped to the floor. 'Sorry,' he said, then realized he'd stepped on them. 'Hell!' He tried to extricate his foot but found he was winding it in the cloth. 'Shit!' He crouched to try and release himself. Grainne crouched too but only made things worse, pulling the opposite way from him. The linen was now inextricable. Hauling at it, their hands came in contact and immediately they were in a tighter, more total embrace. He felt a pulsing and was unable to tell whether it was his blood or hers. She seemed distraught.

'It's not safe,' she kept repeating, but the moves towards the bed were coming from her. Without actively fighting her off, he could hardly prevent himself plunging with her into the farrago of sheets and coverlets of tweed which pricked like brambles and smelled overpoweringly of sheep grease.

'Why not safe?' He had caught the hysteria in her. 'Might someone come? The owner – your cousin was it?'

'I don't know.' Her hands were running over James's skin under his shirt and edging south towards his waistband. He felt himself responding for maybe the third time this afternoon, his foiled and optimistic penis rising and throbbing like a greedy fish to her bait. Angry with her suddenly, a rush of desire swept through him and he began pulling off her clothes and loosening his own belt. Abruptly he felt her go rigid. Then she caught his hands.

'Stop! Listen.'

'What?'

'A car.'

'Maybe it's not coming here?'

'It has to be. This is a dead end. Hurry. He has the key. He'll just walk in. He's Michael's uncle.'

'I thought he was your cousin.'

'My cousin too. Both. Get up. We'll be sorting the linen. God, what a mess. Get *up*! James. Please!'

He had an impulse to lie where he was and mortify her.

Please!' She seemed on the point of tears. 'God, you look a sight! You've got lipstick on your collar – you've got to wash your face. Look, there's the bathroom. There. Yes. Fix yourself up. Quickly. Please. I'm sorry. Really. We'll manage some other time if you still want to. Tomorrow.'

She was arranging her own hair in front of a small mirror, then gathering the tumbled sheets, cursing.

'Bloody hell!'

The car drew up in front of the house. A door banged. Then another.

'Cormac,' she whispered. 'Cormac must be there.'

James went into the bathroom.

9

When she got home from the cottage, Grainne went to the kitchen to heat some beef tea. She arranged this on a tray and carried it up three flights, switching on lights as she climbed and routing the dusk which crouched like some malevolent, clawing thing in the folds of curtains. There was a sucking depression about the street lights gleaming through the bay tree in the garden and about the house's small, rodent-like sounds. Inside herself, though, exhilaration glowed and she imagined it showing through her flesh, like coals through the air-holes in a night-watchman's brazier. She was ashamed of having left her aunt so long alone. The beef tea was a peace-offering. Besides, she wanted to chat.

She was curious to know what precisely it was about Aunt Judith which had put the wind up Owen Roe. Curious, and eager to pin down the old lady's threat to him before he did. Unsurprisingly, he and James had fallen foul of each other at once. Owen Roe had been patronizing, and thrown his weight about, saying, 'What you, as an American, will find hard to grasp . . .' and other things of the sort. 'Please, both of you, feel free to use this place whenever you like,' he had told Grainne with such emphasis that she began to feel as though she was acting in a bedroom farce. His final unpleasantness was to refuse to let James interview him, although he claimed to know James's employer well, a man called Larry who was a grand chap, great value, said Owen Roe in a plummy voice. As they were saying goodbye, he told Grainne that he hoped she remembered their little conversation.

'How's Michael?' he asked.

'How should he be? The same.'

'Tell him I'll be dropping by his office. I've something to discuss with him.'

The crudeness of the threat enraged her and she answered her cousin short-temperedly. The American looked surprised and she saw that each man suspected her of having some understanding with the other. Their resentment gave them a comradely look, and she guessed that each was wondering whether she had deliberately manouevred this meeting.

Why would she have? It didn't suit her at all to be found here by Cormac who, come to think of it, should have been at school. He had a hangdog look when he first came in the door and saw her. Later, he was clearly wondering why she had not given him hell for mitching. Caught out by the different roles she should have played for the two men and Cormac, she became boisterous and started teasing Owen Roe.

'The dead,' she'd said, as though explaining this to James, 'are the great allies of Republicans like my cousin here. The Republic, you see, was founded "in the name of God and the dead generations" and it's hard for those sponsors to deny them. If the living turn against you,' she addressed her cousin directly, 'you say that you have the dead men's vote. Supposing you didn't? Supposing a voice from the past were to take issue with you?'

'A ghost?' Owen Roe spoke in an amused voice but there was a twitch in his lower lids. Unreliable female, said the twitch.

Her face burned where he had slapped it, but that was nothing to what he might do. The IRA had a romper room where they beat up women whose conduct was thought to reflect discredit on the cause: girls who went with soldiers or slept with married IRA men and undermined their morals, wives who got tired of waiting while their men were behind bars. That happened up North but the people involved had allies down here, including Owen Roe. There was a rumour about a kangaroo court which two years ago had condemned a man to death for treachery in this very cottage. The body had not been found.

'Why *not* a ghost?' she'd said, facing him down. She felt high with an excitement whose nature eluded her. Anger? Gambling-fever? Memory of her girlhood, when Owen Roe used to take her hacking as he took Cormac now? His mastery over large animals had impressed her then. Owen Roe tended to own big stallions and his bulky figure was usually hung about with enlargements which had a military as well as a rustic air. 'You deal with the dead,' she told him. 'You'd better be ready for those backers to deal with *you*.'

Owen Roe's face could have been a bulletin board. She read signals off it, guessing when she was getting nervously near target.

Guiltily, she told herself that she had exposed Aunt Judith to Owen Roe's anger and that she had no right to do this. Her feelings for her aunt had quickened in the last hours. From seeing the poor thing as an inconvenient relative, she had come to see her as a victim deserving special concern. Hers was an unfinished story. Stored energies were explosive in her. She held on to her youth, in her own mind still *was* young: a girl imprisoned in an aged body. It was like a nightmare and that nightmare could spill into other people's lives.

Grainne intended to question her aunt more closely than she had bothered to do until now.

It struck her that the best way to undo any harm she might have done the old woman, by threatening Owen Roe with her revelations, was to get those revelations on tape. *Then* he wouldn't think he could suppress them by having her shoved into some institution or given more shock treatment. The tape should be kept in some neutral place, perhaps by James Duffy.

*

'Let the false Saxon feel Erin's avenging steel.'

Patsy Flynn kept time with himself as he basted an egg on the frying pan, digging his spoon rhythmically into boiling oil and tossing this in brown blobs on to the transparent goo of egg white. The oil was too hot and spurted out from time to time on to Patsy's arm. 'Bugger!' he shouted, and licked the burned spot. He had invited Cormac to supper in his small flat at the back of the Grateful Patriots' Youth Club. 'How do you like it?'

'Not runny.'

'Righto.'

Patsy told Cormac that he should keep a weather eye on his

aunt. Maybe someone should give the old hairpin a bit of a fright, eh, what? Put the fear of God into her?

> 'Stand ye now for Erin's glory,'

he told the teapot which had lost one of its three legs. Cormac guessed that Patsy had got into the way of keeping up a racket when he was alone so as not to notice his solitude. He watched Patsy stick a matchbox under the pot where the third leg should have been. He'd got that pot out of a rubbish bin, he told Cormac with pride. Waste not, want not. The grandparents of the Irishmen alive today could have lived and thrived on what was thrown daily on to the municipal dump.

'Where'd you learn all that poetry, Patsy?'

'The stuff I spout, is it? Learned in gaol for the most part. Had to do something to keep sane, if you think I *am* sane, ha ha.

> I did not wring my hands as do
> Those witless men, who dare
> To try to rear the changeling Hope
> In the cave of black despair.

Dja know who wrote that? Oscar wrote that.'

'Wilde?'

'Yes. I regard him as an Irishman,' said Patsy, 'because of how the Brits treated him. I don't learn British verse.'

'No Shakespeare?'

'No,' said Patsy firmly. He set a plate of mixed fry on the table. Black pudding, white pudding, sausages, kidneys, eggs and rashers swam in a winking pond of yellow grease. 'Help yerself. Dig in. Come here to me now,' he said conspiratorially, and rubbed a fat dollop of fried bread into the yolk of his egg. The skin of the yolk swelled, erupted, and the projectile of bread slid into the yellow well. Cormac stared in fascination. There was something thrilling about the sheer awfulness of Patsy's eating habits. 'I want to hear all and everything,' said Patsy, 'about that aunt of yours. What more have you been able to find out?' Patsy stuffed his mouth with the wad of eggy bread. 'Shpeak on, MacDuff,' he spluttered, pushing the food sideways and making a traffic lane for speech with one side of his pursed lips. 'What'sh this for shartersh about her going on TV? The Captain'sh not pleashed. That'sh putting it mildly. I heard him shay shomething about her having shenshitive information. Speaking on the phone he wash. To yer Mammy.' Patsy dealt with the wad of bread and swallowed tea on top of it. 'Well, you know,' he told Cormac grimly, 'if all the men shot for shooting off their mouths and divulging sensitive information were to rise from the dead it would fill the pro-Cathedral. Then to hear of yer Mammy wanting to put a dippy old hairpin like that on TV! It ud make yer hair stand on end.'

'Oh I don't think they want to put her on TV,' Cormac told him. 'They just *said* TV to her to get her interested. They took her over to RTE to show her the studios. But they weren't filming. My mother said they just got her to talk for a bit into a tape-recorder. Reminiscing. It was a trial run.'

'Jasus!' said Patsy. 'Mother o' God! A tape-recorder, is it? Calm down now, Flynn!' he told himself with concern. 'No use spreading alarm and panic. Easy does it!' But food seemed to have caught in his throat and he began to cough. His face went red as a peony and Cormac began to feel worried. 'Sssallright!' spluttered Patsy. 'Be hunkydory in a sssecond. Here – get me a cup of water like a good lad.'

Cormac hurried to the sink and filled a glass. 'Here.'

Patsy took it, drank and wiped the back of his hand across his lips. 'The ole gullet's never been right since they force-fed me one time we were on hunger strike. What was I saying? About your aunt. Now listen, Cormac, you have a responsibility to restrain yer Mammy if you can, and, if you can't, you should keep a close eye on her. What was that you said before about yourself and the Captain coming on her and the Yank? Huh? At the Captain's cottage? Very thick they must be. What were they doing there? That cottage has been used on occasion by the lads. For very private things. Top security. People shouldn't be prowling through it. Women like your Mammy, Cormac, though I don't like saying it to yourself, are a menace. They're security leaks. Looking for attention. They've no sense.'

'Well, Uncle Owen Roe didn't seem to mind. It's his cottage, after all,' Cormac said huffily. 'He lets our family use it whenever we like. I never knew he let other people up there?'

'The Captain's too good for his own good,' said Patsy. 'They tell me he's a genius. But geniuses can be babes-in-arms when it comes to everyday life. So yer Mammy and the Yank were there when yez came in. What were they up to?'

'My mother was picking up some sheets.'

'Sheets of paper?'

'Bed sheets,' said Cormac.

Patsy blushed. 'Did the Captain say anything at all?' he asked.

'Nothing special.'

'Oh well,' said Patsy, blushing even more furiously.

> 'Ours not to reason why,
> Ours but to do and die.'

'Keep your eye on the aunt, though. Try and find out what it was she said into that recording machine. Do you think you could frighten her a bit, Cormac? Would you be up to that? Just to try to get her to keep her gob shut?'

'No,' said Cormac. 'I'd rather not try that, Patsy. She's a bit cracked as it is. It might send her right round the bend. By the way, that's an English poem.'

'What is?'

Patsy's blush was still high and he seemed glad of any subject of conversation to distract Cormac's attention from it. Cormac politely looked at his own teacup. He understood what was in Patsy's mind. He didn't blame him. How could he? Actually, it was decent of Patsy to be so embarrassed for Cormac's sake. He felt like telling him not to worry, that he'd had to put up with worse. But he couldn't without disgracing his bloody mother who should be put in a bin instead of his aunt. Or along with her. Cormac didn't want to start blushing himself. ' "The Charge of the Light Brigade", ' he said. 'You were just saying a bit of it. It's by Alfred Lord Tennyson. "Into the jaws of death," you know?

> 'Into the mouth of hell
> Rode the six hundred.'

'Do you tell me that?' said Patsy indignantly. 'And I thinking it was a Christmas-cracker motto. Yer right though. "Into the jaws of death," I remember now. Sure they colonized our thoughts and minds. Took over our heads! It's hard to get free.'

Patsy's blush was receding. 'The buggers!' he said.

'You could learn Irish,' Cormac told him, laughing. 'Then you'd be safe.'

'It's easy seen you don't know what suffering does to the brain,' said Patsy. 'Sure I tried Irish. Wore meself out struggling with it. I even took a class. But I couldn't make any headway at all. Declensions. The Future. *Is* and *tá*. *Bean*, *mna*, *mnaoi*. I was destroyed with it. And the bitch who was teaching was one of those Rathmines-and-Rathgar types with a sports car and a fancy accent in English. She looked down her nose at me till I was dreaming at night of getting my hands on her windpipe. What I wouldn't have given to tan that lady's arse for her. Holding me up as a show to the class one time because I asked some question that musta been very stupid altogether because they began to laugh. Civil servants they were. There was even an Englishman. Oh I was mortified. I got my books and walked out and never went back. What I wouldn't have given to have had some crushing answer to give that one. But I was afraid to say a word in case I'd get my cough. It comes on in emotional moments, don't you know.'

'I could give you lessons,' Cormac offered.

'You're a good lad, Cormac.' Patsy looked to be on the point of tears. 'But I've given up. It's too late for me now. Just you keep your eye on your womenfolk and we'll count that as your good deed for the cause. OK?'

'Right you are,' said Cormac.

Sister Judith could not get to sleep. The room they'd given her was too big and its windows wouldn't close. Damp had mildewed the ceiling stucco, furring its vines and fruits with grey canker. Draughts played through the room, moving curtains and valances in a continuous rustle which, mixed with the sound of rain, gave her a sense of lying on some wild heath. The cold did not bother her, for she was wrapped in bed-socks and mummying clothes which she had brought from the convent. What did was the space. She had lived for years in a cubicle, and now here was this expanse of room. It made her nervous and this was odd for, once, decades ago, she had been equally uncomfortable in the cubicle. She had suffered then from the feeling that her space was being eroded, and had thought of herself in terms of the sailor one sees in cartoons shipwrecked on an island which is being eaten away by the sea. There is a palm tree and in the final picture the island disappears and all that is left is the palm sticking up from the water with the sailor clinging to it like a monkey-on-a-stick.

'I am a monkey-on-a-stick,' Judith had said to Owen when he visited her once in 1933. 'Look,' and she had drawn a toy monkey-on-a-stick from the pocket of her habit. She pulled the string which made the monkey dance. She was teaching the kindergarten class at the time and her pockets were full of toys, for it was by such stratagems that she managed to trick the children into finding hers an enlivening presence.

'In fact,' she told Owen, 'I think I may be heading for a breakdown. I want to come out.'

'Your vow . . .' said Owen.

'Your oath!' said Sister Judith with acerbity. Owen's party, after swearing for five years that they could never take the oath of allegiance to England's King which the Free-State constitution of 1922 required of all members taking their seats in the Dáil, had suddenly decided that they could and would take it. Various excuses had been put forward: it was no oath; they had not noticed themselves taking it – a clerk had helpfully brushed the text past their distant-viewing eyes – hadn't pronounced but only signed it, without, to be sure, reading it. Besides, to abolish it they must first get into the Dáil to repeal it. This the party, on finally taking office, had now proceeded to do.

'You'll say that's a different kettle of fish, I suppose?' Sister Judith challenged her brother-in-law, who flapped a vague and irritable hand at her. 'But if you plead constraint, so can I. I never wanted to come here, Owen,' she reminded him.

There was a silence.

'Owen, are you paying attention? I regard mine as a forced vocation. Forced,' she said, 'by you.'

Owen was at this time a cabinet minister. To be fair to him, he and his party had suffered oblivion and poverty after losing the Civil War. Owen, during the years when he was refusing to take the oath, had had a child a year.

'How's Kathleen?'

'Grand. Grand,' said Owen automatically, then, as if remembering only now that Judith, a relative, could be told the truth, 'actually, she's pregnant again and feeling a bit low. I suppose we'll be able to afford nursemaids now. The last years were hard on her. Harder than on me.'

'I'm sure.'

'*You* look well,' he said.

'I'm going mad,' she told him.

Owen sighed. '*That* might prove handy,' he told her, 'if you were unwise enough to throw off the veil. Old stories can come out. Be leaked. Especially now I'm in the government. Don't imagine I'm better able to protect you now,' he warned. 'Quite the opposite. You never know who's picked up rumours. Someone could use you to get at me, embarrass the party . . .' Again he made his impatient, dismissing gesture, as though flicking away a small, physical annoyance. 'I'm talking for your own sake, Judith, and for Kathleen's of course and our children's. Not to mention the country.'

'The country has a broad back.'

'I never,' said Owen, 'took a single action in my adult life which did not seem to me at the time to be in the country's best interests.'

Judith sighed. 'What happened to the money?' she asked. 'The money the Americans had that should have gone to the party? I heard that there was litigation in the American courts. I heard that you were over there. The least you could have done was let me know the outcome. After all.'

Owen shrugged. 'Water under the bridge. Nobody got the money. Not us and not the other crowd. The Judge ruled that it be given back to the American subscribers.'

Judith laughed and felt her laugh escape her like an animal. She imagined it jumping from her mouth like some creature in a folk tale. It was an eel, a winged snake. It was her own guts transformed and venomous. She clamped a hand to her teeth.

'So many things seem to come to nothing, don't they?' She stared out of the convent window at some freshly marked playing fields: white lines on cropped, green grass. Without looking at him, she said: 'Not all the money could have been repaid. There was a bag full of cash brought over, do you remember? Money that never existed officially on our side of the ocean. That couldn't have been repaid, could it?' She kept her eyes off him, waiting for a reply. In a paddock beyond the playing fields a donkey was grazing. A crow swooped, pulled some hairs from the animal's back and flew off. '*Could* it?' she repeated, and turned to look at her brother-in-law.

He looked impatient. 'What do you suppose the party members lived on during the five years we were refusing to take our seats, Judith? There were no salaries and no jobs for us. The other crowd had the country in their pockets. We had a right to that money,' said Owen calmly. 'It was donated to the Republican cause and we were the only ones faithful to that cause.'

'Yes,' she remembered. 'You explained that to me long ago.'

'So why bring it up now?' Owen's hand moved towards his waistcoat pocket. He had never taken to wearing a wrist-watch, she remembered. The gold chain bellying across his lean front had belonged to her father, but on Owen it looked somehow official. Like a decoration.

'Owen,' she pleaded. 'I'm afraid of going mad. Really mad. I'm afraid of seeing a doctor. What can I tell one? I said a few things to the chaplain here in confession and I could see he thought I'd imagined them. He told me to take it easy, rest, see a doctor. How *can* I? Unless you corroborate what I say, they'll think I'm raving. Isn't there some version which could help me without endangering you? I could see that priest thought I was just a silly female. Imaginative.'

'He probably thinks it's sex,' said Owen. 'Half the women in here are probably suffering from suppressed sex. The priest's like a doctor in hay-fever season. He puts everything down to the one cause.'

'So you mean I should stay here because it's next door to a lunatic asylum anyway?' Judith's tongue swelled in her mouth like a gag. She had waited for this visit, had prepared and marshalled her facts, planning and redrafting a letter which must alarm him sufficiently to make him come, yet avoid turning him against her. Arguing with Owen was like fencing with a bag of wool. Points were absorbed, then rejected, unblunted but unbloodied.

'Your vocation was in no way forced,' he told her. 'You took your vows after the usual trial period.'

'I wasn't myself, Owen. I felt terrible guilt.'

'Why cease to feel it then?'

'It was because of you, Owen. I used to admire you so much and . . .'

'You choose to think so. It suits you to. I've never been sure of your motives. Whether there wasn't some sexual thing between that American and you.'

'You're obsessed with sex. Anyway, Kathleen was the one he was after.'

'That's not true.'

'Have you forgotten how jealous you were at the time? You nagged her about it. You made her cry.'

'I was wrong. I was young, unsure of myself, a silly young pup.' Owen's mouth set in a hard, erasing line. 'I know now there was never anything out of the way. He was coarse, indelicate, but there was no substance to my fears.'

'Nor with me either,' said Judith. 'Half your colleagues, by your reckoning, should be shut up in convents. Think of that.'

'Nobody shut you up.'

'You worked on my nerves.'

Owen became agitated. 'You're not thinking of presenting a case like that to Rome?' His lips curled. Weakness annoyed him. Her femininity repelled him. Women, for Owen, belonged in a domestic sphere, like Kathleen, with whom he now talked exclusively about their children. There were three or four symbolic, almost depersonalized, widows in the Dáil. Relicts of hero-husbands, they occasionally rose, like the figureheads of ships, and spoke from the back-benches with more emotion than sense. They had their uses, since one of the functions of a parliament is to protest fidelity to principle while, when need be, taking measures which run counter to it. These widows, having been deprived of home life by the revolution, did very well as reminders of that time of turmoil, which, in retrospect, filled Owen with distaste. He had lived through it, as one lives through birth and other messy experiences from which good may come but which must be put behind one. Contagious old fevers must be isolated, germs killed, the new order protected. Owen's party, which had taken the losing and extremist side in the Civil War, was plagued by an ambiguous and motley following, many of whom would have to be dealt with in the very near future. Interned. Something. Meanwhile, here was this feverish sister-in-law fussing and wasting his time. He stood up and began pacing the room.

Judith watched him, recognizing his irritation. His temper had always had a short fuse. Very fond of himself Owen. His clothes had a clerical look. The long, lean, black coat reached to his calves. He had not taken it off, for the convent was unheated.

'What is the worst thing which could happen to me, Owen? If I tried to come out?'

'You could end up in a lunatic asylum. I'm telling you this frankly, Judith. You could be found insane.'

'I mightn't be.'

'No. But you might. And you would harm your family, Kathleen . . .'

'The country?' Ironically.

'I believe that.'

'Do you distinguish what is good for Owen from what is good for Ireland?'

'I risked my life for the country many times.'

'Oh,' she shrugged, 'that was in another era. Owen, tell me the truth. Do you really think it right that I should be buried alive here? All my life?'

Owen looked around him. They were in the convent parlour. It had been the library of the Anglo-Irish mansion which the nuns had bought some years before. They had cut trees, cleared the shrubbery and thinned out furniture, turning the place into a sparse, graceful skeleton of itself. Statues from Lourdes and Lisieux stood on console tables whose curved, callipygian limbs jarred with the Virgin's machine-modelled robes. Traces of rococo frivolity lingered in the panelling.

'What's wrong with being here?' Owen wanted to know. 'You should see poor Kathleen struggling with the kids. She looks ten years older than you do.'

'She *is* older and she's living her life. She deserves to look older.'

Distaste was back on Owen's face. He was the one who should have stayed in a monastery. In the days of great, intriguing abbots, he could have reconciled his passions. Now he was stuck with matrimony which he clearly suffered in a Pauline spirit.

'If it's children you want,' he said, 'you're teaching the kindergarten here, aren't you? I should have thought you'd have everything here you'd want.'

Owen's face had grown more ascetic with the years. His hair had receded. His eyes, behind thickened glasses, looked larger. His mouth had thinned. Sensuality had been eroded from his face, nibbled away, as the sea nibbles traces of meat from a shell.

'It's funny,' she said. 'When the fighting was on, even during the Civil War, we felt the future was ours. If the past was as bad as ours was, then we had to own the future. It was our due, inevitable, do you remember, Owen? Ours!' She let her eyes shine out at him with irony. Judith was twenty-eight that year. She had recovered from years of almost catatonic silence. '*You got your future!*' She faced him down, emphasizing her point.

'I never wanted anything for myself.'

'Power?'

He made his impatient gesture.

'You're naive,' he said. 'We have no power. The economy is in an appalling state. We entered the Dáil in a spirit of sacrifice, to see what help we could provide. We've been called every name: "pitiless idealists", "turn-coats" . . .'

'Well, you did turn your coats!'

'We couldn't leave the country to rot. We had to be practical, get our hands on the helm and steer it out of the doldrums.'

'How I hate politics!'

'You can afford to. That's your luxury.'

The convent, he implied, was a self-indulgent place in which he, if he had been free to follow his inclination, would have lived happily.

'What was done,' he told her, 'had to be done. We *said* that we would have to wade through Irish blood. But this does not mean that we should not try to atone.'

She saw that in his mind the atonement was being done by him. Cute as a pet fox, Owen saw himself instead as the noble stag at bay. He was a menagerie of men and in the old clandestine days this had reinforced his appeal, since each one saw in him what he wanted to see.

'There are young fellows still out in the wilderness,' she reminded him, 'because they believed what you told them a few years back and are so unsupple that they still do – the "new" IRA. Your crowd gaol them now.'

He didn't even pretend to be listening. He had never listened. Stubbornness – she'd seen it described in the newspapers as 'a lofty sense of purpose' – made him immune to logic. He made you feel it was cavilling. His virtue spoke for him more than the virtue of his arguments. He was Jesus and you, if you disagreed with him, were a Pharisee.

'I know what's best for the country,' he told her in a mournful tone. 'I trust my own deep instincts as an Irishman. I find the answers in my heart.'

Oh, she thought, spare me the soft soap. You're not campaigning now.

'Is Kathleen still pretty? She hasn't been to see me this long time.'

It was Owen, she was sure of it, who kept her sister away.

'Kathleen,' he told her, 'is the mother of six children with another on the way.'

She laughed. 'Look at her when you go home, Owen. Look at her for me and notice her. Is her hair still red?'

'More or less,' he told her and then, astounding her, looked ashamed. 'You know, Judith,' he shuffled, 'with a big family, we don't have much time for each other – and I do keep busy, you know!' Impish suddenly: the great man fishing for flattery. He laughed, guying himself, and she remembered reading in the newspapers that Owen O'Malley was a favourite with electors, had great personal charm. The sudden change threw her and she thought: yes, in here, maybe we do get a bit stuck in our rut. People put on a special face when they talk to us. Our social instinct dwindles. I suppose I'm like a child to him.

'Oh, I'm sure you have a lot on your mind,' she agreed.

A lay-sister brought in a tea-tray and Judith watched her brother-in-law eat two fairy cakes and a slice of barm brack. Nuns did not eat publicly in those days, so she sat, with her hands folded, watching and marvelling at how this man's appetites could make him seem more rather than less self-denying. He had sired six children and just now eaten three cakes, but neither greed nor pleasure was revealed by his face. He drained his teacup and wiped his thin mouth with a napkin.

'Owen,' she asked, 'are you happy?'

She was remembering the nightmares he used to have.

His eyes, swimming in the blurr behind his glasses, gave her a hard, magnified glance.

'The word means nothing to me,' he said. 'I have purposes, duties, people who depend on me, I . . .'

'Is Kathleen,' she asked, 'happy?'

'She has her children. She knows she is useful.'

'Do you still get nightmares?'

The glassed-in eyes looked at her blankly. Shortly after that, he left in a chauffeur-driven car which had waited for him during the visit. Judith gave up thinking of leaving the convent and settled to her life there. She had indeed got the kinder-garten to keep her busy and felt that she was probably, in her way, as useful as Kathleen. Besides, in those days, she used to pray. Later, after the electric-shock treatment, she found she no longer could. Compartments within her mind seemed to have collapsed, so that she could only with difficulty keep things separate. She sometimes confused everyday reality with what was only to be considered real in a spiritual sense. Prayer became a temptation and a risk, something from which return might prove difficult. So she gave it up except in a limited, leashed way, keeping to set, rote-learned prayers which were useful as exercises for the memory and could never be taken to be actual experiences in the way that spontaneous effusions or meditations might. She didn't know whether Owen had arranged for her to have the shock treatment. People told her lies now, she had noticed.

This afternoon, she had had a strange telephone call from someone who refused to give his name but had very distinctly threatened her.

'No need for you to know who I am,' said the strange, uneducated voice.

'Are you sure you wanted to speak to *me*?' Sister Judith had not been telephoned in years. But the girl, Bridie, had assured her she was wanted on the phone. She had even brought the instrument up and plugged it in on Sister Judith's floor so that she need not face the stairs.

'Are you Sister Judith Clancy, sister-in-law to Owen O'Malley?'

'That's right.' She waited and heard breathing. Was this going to be one of those dirty calls you heard about? Some corner boys maybe had got hold of her address and dared each other to phone the nunny sister-in-law of the famous statesman? The sort who burgled churches and stole the altar wine. She'd heard about that. The cleaning woman in the convent had had a store of such information that would keep you going for weeks if you let her get started. 'Who is it?' she asked again, intending to hang up if she didn't get an answer quickly.

'Sister Judith?'

'I'm still here.'

'This is a warning,' said the voice, speaking very slowly now. 'I don't want you to think it's a joke. It's a serious warning and you'd better heed it. You don't know me but I know you and I've information that you intend talking on the TV about sensitive matters. Sensitive, do you understand that, Sister Judith? Do you know what I'm referring to?'

'I do not,' said Sister Judith angrily, 'and I'd like you to know that you could be prosecuted for making calls like this. Nuisance calls.' She'd seen cases on television. The person being called was supposed to hang on as long as they could so that the police could put a trace on the caller. But there were no police to do that here and she was on the point of hanging up when it struck her that she might be hearing things. 'Are you there?' she asked, wishing she had the Yank's tape-recorder. That was a wonderful instrument. It would prove once and for all what was a delusion and what was not.

'I'm here all right,' said the voice, 'and I want you to know that you should keep your gob shut if you know what's good for you and divulge no information whatsoever to yon Yank. Or to anyone else. If you know what's good for you. I'll know,' said the voice. 'I know every move you make. You are under surveillance, Sister Judith.'

'Bridie,' screamed Sister Judith.

'Bridie! Tell me,' she asked her, calming down and forcing herself to speak quietly, 'who was that on the phone just now?'

'I dunno, Sister Judith.'

'Now Bridie, think. You called me to the phone, didn't you? You took the call. There *was* a man on the phone, wasn't there?'

'Of course there was someone on the phone,' said the girl. 'I don't know who he was.'

'But there *was* someone?'

'Yes.'

'Well, thank God for that,' said Sister Judith.

*

Dear Therese,

This is not going to be an easy letter to read.

The prospect of *writing* it has been tormenting me, but I feel it would be unfair not to tell you the truth – if I can get hold of it. Here, then, is an interim report on the emotional cyclone which has hit me: I think I may have fallen in love with someone here.

Please believe that it is from concern for you that I am forcing myself to tell you before I am really sure of my feelings – so as to go on deserving your trust. I am desperately anxious about you – about *us*, Therese. I wonder will you believe this? It's true. I care. I worry. I lie awake and wonder how you will take this and whether it – this, what I'm telling you – is an insane delusion, some sort of erotic fever which affects people when they travel. Is it unfair to bother you with something which may blow over? I don't know. I've found myself weeping with indecision. Maybe I shouldn't mail this? Yet, I feel I must. I don't want you deceived even for a few days about what *may* be serious. I can't tell. I don't know. You won't want details.

I'll write again in my next moment of sanity.

I send many – maybe all? – kinds of love.

James

James, naked and busy with his tape-recorder, talked of a telephone conversation he'd had with a Miss Lefanu-Lynch, aged eighty, who had agreed to speak to him only after he had assured her that Larry's film was committed to raising money for guns. She belonged to a political splinter group which refused to acknowledge the maimed but actual Irish Republic. Eyes fixed on the ideal, thirty-two-county one declared by the heroes of 1916, she lived in a world without flesh or geography, said James, displaying the geography of his own flesh in tigered light which fell slantwise through a Venetian blind.

'When I said that,' he let the tape rewind, 'about guns, it hit me that that might be only half the truth.' He paused, waiting for Grainne's question, then went on without it. 'The guy I work for,' he explained, 'wouldn't have scruples about playing with real people, real bombs.'

'Mm?'

'They've done studies,' he shuffled through his tapes, 'of TV-watching generations. They're so inured to violence on the screen that when they see it in the streets it hardly affects them. Seeing is no longer believing when you watch too many movies.'

'Lefanu-Lynch wouldn't need movies,' Grainne told him. 'Her crowd would eat you before breakfast.' She spoke lazily, her mind on the muscled body poised in sliced light. She too was unable to quite believe and eager to pinch like Thomas Didimus. James had astounded her by pulling off his clumsy, mass-produced American clothes to show flesh as fluidly perfect as Bernini's Apollo's. As a banquet can defeat and even sicken the starving, she had felt her lust retreat before this surprise. It annoyed her that he should be unaware of her awe. To him, he was obviously still the same person; to her he was the frog turned prince.

A while ago, he had compounded her discomfort, asking her, 'Did you come?'

She hadn't. She felt mocked and grubby-fingered. Her fingers *were* rough. At the Halfway House, she had let them go, doing odd jobs and not bothering to use cream. Just now, she had run them like sandpaper down his limbs. It was an unsettling experience. The men she knew wore well-cut clothes over age-damaged bodies. Their pride was in what showed: cashmere, poplin, fine tweed. These stripped off, their imperfections gave intimacy an extra tingle. They had to trust her not to mind or mock or tell, and *she* was the desirable one to whom *they* were beholden. The reversal of positions upset her and she kept wanting to clutch an eiderdown around herself – was, in fact, doing this on the pretence of feeling cold. In bed with Michael and Owen Roe, as on beach trips with men she liked, Grainne had taken pride in overlooking the inadequacy of the bodily envelope in which these spirits were forced to reside. Now, she was suffering the tortures of those damned for vanity.

'Do you think me irresponsible for taking this job?'

'Me? Why?'

'You were giving me an odd look.'

She laughed. 'I was looking at you in wonder. I'd thought all gorgeous men were stupid or queer.'

'Fatally flawed?'

'Yes.'

He preened without embarrassment. This was the fruit of hard work-outs, he explained. 'See. No flab. Pinch.' She did and saw that he was made, as he had said, not by Bernini but by exercise. This home-made, hard-earned quality made his body seem cosier and she had begun to relax in her enjoyment of it when he again brought up the IRA. He couldn't make out where people stood on the issue, he complained.

Remembering Owen Roe's remark, she said: 'We double think. In practical terms we're dead against them, but in some shady, boggish area of our minds there's an unregenerate ghost groaning "up the rebels". Most of us keep the ghost well suppressed, but children, drunks, unemployable men, and emotional misfits can become possessed by it. Does that answer your question?'

He looked at her. 'It raises a more personal one.'

'What?'

'Why are *you* so afraid of feeling?'

'Am I?'

'You resist *me* all the way.'

'Perhaps it's dependence I'm wary of?'

'You can have one without the other.'

That was news. Unreliable, to be sure. Shutting him up, she explored, as a blind creature might have done, sniffing and tasting, listening and stroking, then letting him do the same. That was the reassuring part and she must have needed more of it, because he felt strange to her when they began to make love: his shoulders covering her like a coffin lid, his rhythms unfamiliar, the angle of approach not good. She was too wet when he slid in so that she could hardly feel him and, though she wanted to grind her pelvic bones against his to focus the sensation or have him take her from behind, she felt shy about asking for this and fearful of seeming whorish.

'Tell me what you like,' he said.

She couldn't. She wanted him to experiment, not *ask*.

'Did you come?'

'No.' Baldly. Apologies were for marriage.

'We'll learn each other. No hurry.'

'How *nice* you are!'

'Well, I'm not a macho.'

No. He was a light-footed invader. He had slipped through her defences in no time flat. How? What had he done? Nothing she could put her finger on. It was his making the thing seem ordinary, instead of being – as it was – a double adultery in one of the better bedrooms of Dublin's best hotel.

Sister Judith felt she was living behind a sheet of glass. A shroud. Some insulating chemical. She was cut off and had no rights. No place of her own. No privacy. Words dripped away, rolled, disappeared, like beads from a broken rosary. She was getting too tired to try and find the right ones for what she felt.

Felt?

Yesterday she couldn't find her darning kit, her little quilted box that she'd had since she was a girl. With the silver bodkin and the scissors in the shape of a swan's wings. She'd looked high and low and panic had caught in her throat as if someone had a hand on it. Stolen? Hidden? The scissors had been her mother's.

She'd got into a tizzy, tossing through drawers, injured and angry at their *daring* to make off with it. Her thing. She had so little. So few things of her own and nothing else from the old days. She was panting and the floor was littered with the rubbish they'd given her: stuff she couldn't wear in man-made fibres that irritated her skin. Then she'd come on the little kit, *not* where she'd put it and, stupidly, had begun to cry.

It was their interfering, going through her few poor things, putting *their* order on them. She felt like a child again. Reduced.

That was petty, of course. She was being silly. Weepy. Silly. The way she'd been years back at the Change, but she'd got over that long ago. Now she didn't know what was the matter with her. Chin up, Judith, she told herself but it didn't work. Her mind was like her drawers: all confused.

Her will was faltering.

It hardly seemed worth while making a stand. If you didn't though, the few certainties you had got gnawed away. But her energy flagged easily these days.

It was partly the food. They brought her things she couldn't digest and she didn't like always to be complaining. She was unwell all the time now. Nauseous.

Were those phone calls real? You had to have something

to compare 'real' with. In the convent there had been known people, places, things. She'd been sure of them. Here the whole place could be imaginary.

And they were always badgering her about the past. You'd think they wanted to mix her up. What interest was the past to them, whoever they were?

Them.

Take Bridie and the Principal Girl. Who *were* they? Bridie, she knew right well, could not be her Bridie from long ago. That Bridie would be ninety now if she was a day, and this girl was in her twenties. She was sorry now she'd called her that. The other one, at least, she wouldn't name. She did impinge though. Thrust herself forward. Yesterday – was it? – she'd come into the room when Sister Judith was on the commode. Without a by your leave or a word of warning. No knock. Sister Judith had been outraged. You could have knocked her down with a feather. The intrusion! Oh, she knew the girl meant no harm but it was so reducing! She'd felt exposed. On show. Treated like a senile old animal.

Truth hurt, to be sure. There was truth in that. That was what made it so unbearable. But you'd *better* bear it, Judith, face the truth if you want to hold on to your wits. Face it. You did soil yourself once – twice. Twice now. You're losing control.

Well, if she was, there was the more need for dignity. If she was to take hold of herself, she needed support. Not to be treated as a – a what? Child? Thing? Something not house-broken. Oh *God*.

Not that she'd managed to think all this right off. No. What she'd done was to throw her shoe at the Principal Girl. Right smack at her face and then she'd slipped sideways off the commode and soiled herself after all.

Later, they'd had to wash her and she'd wept right through her bath.

'What's the matter?' the Principal Girl kept asking. 'Tell me, please, Aunt Judith?'

What was there to tell?

She was a thing now, a child, an old animal. Smelly.

'Tell me about Owen,' the girl asked.

What did the girl care about Owen? He was dead. Sister
Judith wished she was dead herself. She nearly was. Diminished. Isolated. Glassed in. Glassed out.

'Do you remember Owen?'

'Owen,' said Sister Judith venomously, 'is responsible for a
lot. He'll be paying for it in Purgatory. Oh, he'll have a long
spell there, I'm telling you. You'd better be saying masses for
his soul. And for mine too,' she added. 'God help me, I'm an
uncharitable old thing. *And* proud.' It struck her that she was
paying for her pride now, doing her Purgatory on earth.

Telegrams, wistful and cryptic, kept coming from the elder
O'Toole. James mentioned them to Larry, who had phoned
about shipments which would not be arriving as scheduled.
Some delay.

'I can't just ignore his requests,' James pointed out. 'What
do you expect me to do?'

'What does he want?'

'Shit, Larry, he uses a code. Football terms.' James tried to
remember. 'A quarterback sneak. A double reversal? Stuff
like that.'

'Have you no idea what he's up to?'

'Something about our having the wrong end of the stick
about Driscoll's death. He wants me to do some investigating.'

Larry got skittish and James guessed he didn't want him
to talk freely on the Irish phones. So why ask questions then?
James felt impatient with both O'Tooles. Surely, the old man's
plots were harmless anyway? 'Security' could only be a joke
word in such a connection – though, remembering the first
Customs Officer's reaction to the letter, maybe not? The
trouble was 'First Customs Officer' sounded like a character
from Gilbert and Sullivan. A cable from Larry followed up
the telephone conversation and reminded James about not
making waves. The O'Tooles were metaphor addicts. 'Do
not,' Larry repeated, 'not pursue Driscoll quest.' OK, OK.

Probably some old O'Edipal game was being played out
between son and father and now James had got the older and
weaker sparring partner into trouble. He felt bad about this
and, deciding at least to do something about getting the old

man his Coat of Arms, dropped into the Heraldry Commission to ask Michael O'Malley's advice. He wanted to see O'Malley anyway. James had a bad conscience about having hurt him, though Grainne said he shouldn't worry.

'He just likes the *idea* of having me around,' she assured him. 'He doesn't notice what I do. Honestly. Michael's a very abstract person. He lives in his head.'

James discounted what she said, since, obviously, it suited her to say it. Liking Michael, he felt himself to be unlikeably predatory. He wished there were something he could do for the man – a sort of payment – and, vulnerable with guilt, entered Michael's office in some anxiety lest the injuries done him should have taken visible effect.

The office was reassuring. James had expected something poky and dark, but it was pleasantly proportioned and lit by broad shafts of light pouring through Georgian windows from a roof-propped sky. Michael, looking in better fettle than at their first meeting, greeted James with delight.

'Grand to see you,' he said heartily, 'what can I do for you?'

James was amused to note his own concerned relief. Your cuckold, it became clear to him, was related to you like a sporting opponent – or sponsor. Feeling a warm gush of friendliness – almost gratitude – towards Michael, who was bearing up so commendably, he wished there were some way to implement it. Put a hand on Michael's? Hug or give him a pally tap on the butt? Not possible. James had a focused insight into the solaces of duelling. In jealousy cases, he'd lay money, the duel must often have superseded the love affair. He could imagine himself and this amiable, fuzzy-looking man putting up their pistols and repairing for cheerful refreshments after settling their quarrel. Meanwhile, it remained unacknowledged.

He handed Michael a page of squared paper with drawings of weapons: pikes, battle-axes, a bristle of cutting edges on a red field. It was O'Toole's sketch for his Coat of Arms.

'Ah Jayzuz, the O'Tooles!' Michael laughed indulgently as he examined the specifications. 'Yer man,' he told James, 'has been reading O'Hart's *Irish Pedigrees*. First edition, Dublin,

1876. Most recent reprinting, Baltimore, 1976. A piece of fiction as fanciful as any, it traces subscribers' genealogies to Adam via Noah, Japhet, Magog and their descendant, Milesius. What did I tell you!' Michael slapped his thigh, ejaculating a whinny of wild glee. He had a look of a friendly centaur, thought James, or a lateral connection of one of Darwin's apes. The nap on his tweed jacket, perhaps as a result of frequent wettings and dryings out, had begun to grow and curl. Surely, such an easy, outgoing guy would not suffer if a man who cared for her had a friendly little thing going with his wife?

'The O'Tooles,' read Michael from the paper he had received from James, 'are a Milesian family. Tell me now,' he looked squarely at James whose guilty heart jumped, 'why does a hard-nosed American with lolly in the bank go in for this? I can see why he might have a hundred years ago. The Irish-American ego *then* needed a boost the way the black American one does now. The blacks – I've heard them – will tell you Saint Augustine was black. They can have the old fart for all I care. The Irish were less modest. O'Hart, in his day, argued with exhausting ingenuity that Gaelic was the language spoken by our first parents in Paradise. Ah well,' said Michael, 'old strategies recur. New dogs play old tricks, what?' He was smiling at James who thought: what does he mean 'trick'? Am I the 'new dog'? How should I respond? Larry had warned him about the devious way the Irish communicated their thoughts.

'Womanish tricks too,' said Michael, pointing at the O'Toole armorial bearings. 'Look at the fripperies: laurels, a crest, a crown. I say "womanish" because women are bred to masquerade, being ashamed of their essential function.'

James smiled carefully at Michael, whose fuzzy look, he noticed now, was not amiable at all. He just hadn't shaved.

'*My* ego is wobbly,' said Michael, 'so naturally I look back to my Grandda and say with Emerson that man is the sum of his ancestors – but why should a success artist like O'Toole?'

'Why what?' asked James, wondering did the guy know or not know and whether he himself was paranoid. Was he, James, the 'success artist' and tool who'd screwed Grainne less than twenty hours before? Cool it, James. Smile and be a villain. Doesn't the Bible say the wicked shall prosper like the green bay tree? 'Surely it's an innocent urge,' he asked guardedly, 'to know your forbears, I mean?'

'Ego,' said Michael, 'self-promotion is what it is. People come in here from all over: Florida, Canada, Canberra. You don't think they want me to turn up ancestors for them who were hanged for sheep-stealing or poor tenant farmers who took their landlord's name, as many did?'

'O'Toole's not asking about his genealogy. He just wants a copy of his armorial bearings.'

'There you are! He simply assumes he has a right to them. Does it cross his mind that his claim may be no better than that of some black man whose slave ancestor was given the slave-owner's name? Less good,' said Michael, 'if one considers that the owners fucked the women and so the bloodline *could* be there. They did, didn't they? It's not a calumny?'

'What?'

'Fuck the black women?'

'Sometimes,' said James, 'probably. I don't know if studies have been done.' Eager to get off the subject, he said that O'Toole wasn't too worried about accuracy. 'It's just a whim,' he explained. 'He's an O'Toole fan as he might be a Dodger fan.'

'Ah, the fickle rich,' said Michael, but was writing out the names of heraldic artists to whom James could apply. The conversation was probably innocent of innuendo, after all. Yet the subject seemed inescapably booby-trapped. Michael, foraging through heraldic lore, kept dropping toothed words like 'honour', 'wife' and 'family'.

It seemed to James that their glances kept bouncing off each other.

Duffy, said Michael, meant 'black-a-vised', 'dark-featured', just as Clancy and Flynn – related to each other through the nominative and genitive of the word for 'blood' – meant 'red-complexioned'. 'Let's go for a jar,' said Michael, suddenly beset by thirst. 'Nice pub down the street. Unless you want to ask me something else? On your own account perhaps?'

'I've been discouraged.'

'God, I'm terrible at my job – still, I'm sure you'd bear disappointment lightly.'

James preceded Michael down a curving stair. The genial voice behind him was still, with or without intent, delivering ambiguous barbs. Cupid was blind and so might jealousy be. Justice too. Michael almost certainly. Grainne was convinced he *didn't* know. But what about instinct? Suddenly, at a turn of the high, spiral stair, James thought: suppose he were to push me now? Over that bannister? Splat! A flattened James would turn the floor three storeys below into a field charged with a strange device: azure-trousered, vulned, gules. But he had rounded the turn and Michael, once more in his line of vision, was a grudgeless man lost in clutters of information so coherently rounded that surely no novelty could impinge? Michael, thought James with amusement, was impervious to the unexpected. On a surge of affection, he squeezed the tweedy knob of the other man's shoulder as they walked out of the door into the bright safety of the mid-day street.

10

Sounds from the North Wall.

Sleep cradled Grainne, ebbing then flowing in again, like mud tides around a mollusc. Fog horns mourned through humid air. Hooves rang on the asphalt outside her window. That would be some civil servant headed, in mac and hacking-jacket, for his morning canter on Booterstown strand. Sthurrand, sthurrand. Receding, the sound was absorbed into opaque returns of dream which charged it with associations: prancing of dressage horses in Vienna, of carriage horses in films of Paris in the Nineties, glitter, dust, ducks, an exuberance of leaves and of ladies whose life was a narrow dedication to pomp. Limited objectives: their achievement must have provided focused satisfaction.

So did Grainne's waking memory that she had a lover.

Revelling, she lay and felt the shape of his absence in her bodily cavities. His penis had been everywhere. The dart of his tongue had astounded, then driven her half-mad with nervous pleasure. Yesterday, after making love a first time, she had begun, playfully, to cavort with him on the bed while his tape-recorder played through interviews he had made earlier in the week. Thawed out, no longer taut, she had been as relaxed as he. A pair of albino dolphins, they nuzzled and bussed each other in imitation of childhood's imitation of sex and, before she knew it, he was doing something to her which she had not even imagined, awakening sensations where no sensation had been, livening areas of her secret flesh, causing a whirr and cascade, an unravelling, dissolving thrill so that she was moaning and he had to pause to tell her to stuff her mouth with a pillow. He couldn't reach it himself, being down between her thighs, his pale, stubbly hair incongruously sticking up like a wheatsheaf through which she kept running startled hands.

Afterwards, she felt tender towards him and grateful. The recorder was playing and his formal voice came on the tape, politely coaxing the old-timers.

'Tell me, sir,' said the stiff, Yankee voice, 'what it was like at the time. Was there great bitterness?'

She glanced at the tongue which had just now been sliding in her vulva, like a neat, tail-flirting fish.

'Tell me, sir,' she mimicked, 'I hope it wasn't bitter down there?'

'Bland,' he told her, 'a bit like home-made bread.'

'Bitter enough,' rasped the voice on the tape. 'When de scrap was over – we called it de scrap, don't ye know, de scrap with de English . . .' The old man's throat groaned like tired plumbing. 'We hoped,' he gurgled rustily, 'for better times but twas worse times we had to face. Tin time worse . . .' This man, Grainne judged, was from Ireland's Deep South, County Cork, where the bulk of the fighting had gone on in what would have been his heyday. 'Dere were no jobs and any dere were went to de boys who'd accepted de Traty. De rest of us could whistle for dem. De country was destroyed: roads up, bridges down and de blame all put on us . . .'

'Turn it off,' she'd groaned. 'Ulagoaning. Moaning. Misery. How can you listen?'

'History is full of things like that.'

'I don't think of it as history. It's fate: something that will go on and on.'

'*You*'re not living on the breadline.'

'No. But give me credit for imagination. Others are. Besides the thing ricochets up. In other countries people sometimes come to grips with something new. Here the old bogy returns. You start to laugh and then, Jesus, the damn thing turns out to be real.'

'Was there no help for veterans?' James's voice asked on the tape.

'For de Staters dere was. And tin years later our day came. Yis. When our lads went into de Dáil, dey helped dere friends. But a lot of preferment had been given out by den. Many had emigrated. Gone. I had a butty was given work smuggling sweepstake tickets into America. He was on de pig's back but many's de lad was left widout a tosser.'

'Pitch and toss,' said Grainne. 'You needed coins.'

'I'll need you to translate this stuff. I should give you a salary.'

'You don't think I'd collaborate on your hawkish film.'

'Do you disapprove of it?'

'You said yourself it's propaganda to get Americans to pay over money for guns.'

'No, I don't think our producer is committed to guns. I mean I've no reason to think so except paranoia, which I've been breathing in here with every breath. From what I learn from the old vets I've been talking to, I should be cautious too about listening to lassies like yourself who belong, they tell me, to a well-heeled, sycophantic class who now run this country and have sold out to an international conspiracy of the Right which includes my own country, Japan, the IMF and multi-national enterprises generally.'

'You've been talking to hallucinating Trotskyites?'

'I've been talking to whoever would talk. I have the tower of Babel on that tape-recorder. None of them agree except on one point which they put pithily: Brits out.'

'What does your international conspiracy want?'

'To keep wages low and plunder your natural resources. We want you as an economic colony.'

'And American self-distrust makes you wonder if it's true?'

'Well, I'm plundering one natural resource, right?'

'I'd better get dressed. I've got to fly. My neglected son will wonder where I am. He's suspicious of you. He's keeping an eye on his unreliable Mum.'

'The other thing my interviewees agree on is that the younger generation will make up for the corruption of their elders.'

'Typical Ireland! They get the youth cult ten years late.'

'Can I phone you at home?'

'God no. The place is full of extensions and Cormac is nosy.'

'I can ask about your aunt? We could have a code.'

'He disapproves of your interest in her. So does Michael since Owen Roe has been leaning on him. No. *I*'ll phone you.'

'When?'

'This evening.'

'What about the extensions?'

'I'll go out to a phone-box.'

'Maybe I should interview Cormac. Would he like that?'

'No. He's mad about privacy. That's what he has against you. You're the media.'

'Maybe I can brainwash him? Would he take me to visit his Youth Club?'

'I wouldn't count on it.'

He caught her arm, reaching over her shoulder with his other hand to close the door. 'Hey! Kiss me.'

They kissed. She closed her eyes, opened them. 'Listen,' she pleaded. 'Don't play with me. You'd undo me.'

'I thought you were a tough lady.'

'I am. I'm like a snail with a tough shell. But you could lure me out and then I'd be vulnerable.'

'Do you want to be lured out?'

'Only if it's safe.'

'I'll tell you,' he promised. 'I'll let you know when.'

*

Therese,

No letter from you and that's a relief. I couldn't bear to read the kind of letter you might have written *before* getting mine – and I dread your reaction to *that*. Besides, why should you write? I have left things dangling. I suppose this seems selfish? It is an attempt to say no more than is honest.

I feel that as I have begun by telling you what is happening, I must go on doing so, and what is happening is that I am possessed. I can see that this is how my condition might strike an observer. Reading this must be painful to you. I am not sure that it is only from honesty that I am telling it. Perhaps there is a cry for help in this impulse to confide? Perhaps I am trying to steady my nerves. After all, I have no friends here, though already acquainted with half the city in a boozy way. The hotel, like all big hotels, is anonymous.

Facts: the woman is married. She is my age. I don't

know how much she cares for me. Yes, as you are surely thinking, it may be 'just sex'. I am certainly hot for that all the time. When I am not with her I think of her and of you and the two of you fuse in my consciousness. In my dreams you are one person and all is resolved. I wake up to agony. No need to write a gloss on that. Yes: she is quite beautiful and, I think, intelligent though not an intellectual. Not like you.

I feel shame at my animal greed and at the same time panic that here may be a chance of happiness which may never come again if I don't seize it ruthlessly – like in fairy tales where alternative values are suddenly invoked and the victor is the one who can learn and play by new, surprising rules. People here are saturated by folk memory freighted with messages which probably tempt and frighten them. This may explain their puritanism. The temptation to break loose is surely insidious – unless I project?

I should add that the part of myself which I prefer and esteem is the part loyal to you. But she, I think, is more vulnerable.

Forgive me,
James

*

Sparky Driscoll dropped by one day while Judith was alone and accepted a cup of tea.

'Are you enjoying your stay?' she asked politely.

'Well, I'm not here for pleasure,' he said, 'but yes, I am. Though I'm not sure everyone approves of me.' He laughed to take the barb out of this.

There had been arguments. Some were afraid that certain people might be preparing to sell the country short. The British were negotiating but who'd trust them? Divide and conquer was their old strategy and there were always bad eggs on our own side: funks and windy lads who might be all too ready to hand in the gun. If a division did come it was important that American help go to the right people – and important that Driscoll send home a true account of the way things were in Ireland.

'I have to form my own opinion,' he told Judith. 'I know a lot of you think I may be taken in. Listen to the wrong people?'

'Well, there have always been traitors.' Judith thought of the dance where Kathleen had been waltzing in her pink satin when the Tans broke in. Tipped off by whom? 'It must be strange for you here,' she supposed.

'I like it,' he told her. 'I'd always heard about it – heard those songs your sister sings.'

'You like *her*, don't you?' It was part of his openness, the fact that he showed it. Last time he'd been over, Kathleen had told the story about how she and some other Cumann na mBan girls had spirited their dead brother Eamonn's body from where the police had left it, so that his comrades could give it a soldier's funeral. They'd done it at night and held the ceremony in a place where the volley fired could not alert authorities. Kathleen had told the story in a whisper, looking over her shoulder lest their father hear and be reminded of his grief. Judith had seen Driscoll savour secrecy and watch Kathleen with dog's eyes.

'She's pretty,' he acknowledged now, 'but you're more beautiful. Will be.'

She didn't believe she'd heard him right. *Her*?

'Didn't you know?'

She blushed and hated him.

'I'm sorry.'

'What for?' She had to ask.

'Dragging you out of childhood.'

'You have no small opinion of yourself!' There was a supply of such remarks.

'You see, it's happened,' he teased, 'you're flirting.'

The impudence! But she wouldn't believe him. Redheads were rarely beautiful. 'How old are you?' she challenged his authority.

'Twenty-seven,' he said, which was ten years older than herself. It made him more reliable for public but less for private matters. Fellows her age might feel differently about freckles and her hair.

'The fellows who'll be running the country now,' she said,

'are no older than that. Kathleen's fellow, Owen, will be in the Dáil for sure. It'll be a country run by young men.'

'What about the women? They'll have a say now too, won't they?'

She shrugged. 'The men in this country would never let women have a say.'

She imagined the women he'd know. Americans. Did he have sisters?

'Have you a girl in America?'

'Several.' He laughed. 'Which means no serious one.

'So you could marry a girl from here so?' This was banter and not to be taken seriously. If he didn't see this she'd give up on him entirely.

He said he wasn't ready yet to settle down. 'I want,' he told her, 'to travel.'

'Have you seen Ireland?' she challenged.

He had been to Dublin. Someone had taken him to the Abbey Theatre. Then he'd been to Cork to talk to the IRA on the spot. His friends in Boston and Philadelphia were interested in knowing how the spirits of the ordinary fighting-men were. They were leery of politicians.

'It's an old story now,' he said, 'that they come to us looking for money and tell us what they think we want to hear: blarney. Then after promising us they'll do so and so, they go back and do the opposite.'

He began to question her about Owen, saying what a shame it was he was in gaol. What had Owen thought about the people he met when he was in America? Had Judith heard of the bad blood between Irish leaders over there and some of the delegates from here? Money was at the bottom of the row, Sparky admitted.

'Am I boring you?' he asked suddenly.

She was offended. 'Too much for my pretty little head?'

'I didn't mean that.'

What kind of a man was Owen? he asked again, and Judith began to wonder whether it was this fellow's interest in Kathleen that made him so curious. Owen, she assured him, was manly, upright and straight. She admired him, she said, and the family was proud that he should be marrying Kathleen.

'Does that answer your question?'

Sparky backed off a bit then and talked more generally about the tensions between the Yanks and the Irish. His business, he said, was to promote a better understanding. Some of the men back home were a bit old, maybe out of touch with today's Ireland. This was why they'd sent a man as young as Sparky to represent them. 'Things change,' he admitted, 'and my countrymen are more ready to see this than most. However, we don't like being taken for a ride. We like to know the score. Shareholders in a business have a right to know what's being done with their money.'

It struck her that she was talking to someone who was himself to have a say in the way things would go. Could such a man be moved by a person as ignorant and unimportant as herself? Robert Bruce had been influenced by the sight of a spider making and remaking its web. But the spider, to be sure, had not known its own importance. It had given its lesson in persistence by just being a spider. She wished passionately that there were some persuasive thing she could do or say, and, mind filled with the wish, became incapable of saying anything at all. What an idiot she was. Owen might have persuaded Sparky if he'd been here, but he wasn't.

History, she thought, looking at the ordinary young man with surprise. It came, like the Blessed Virgin's apparitions, to touch the most unexpected people. At least in republics it did and maybe that was the best argument in their favour. Realizing that she had been staring at her guest with intent excitement – it was a way she had, which the nuns had described to her as 'pop-eyed' and also 'owlish' – she tried to remember what they'd been talking of before he got on to politics. Her looks? No, not that. Oh, seeing Ireland. Yes.

'Have you been to New Grange?' she asked.

'No. What's there?'

'A pagan site where the Druids may have spilled human blood to renew the energies of the soil.'

'Like now,' he said. 'Isn't that Pearse's notion?'

'Oh we're bloody enough. Is that what you want to promote with your money?'

'I'm not here to take sides,' he said. 'Only to see what's happening. Thanks for the tea.' He stood up. He'd be back another time, he said, to chat with her father.

Afterwards, she began to wonder why he'd been so curious about Owen. Too curious? Had he come to pry? And had she said anything indiscreet? She went over their conversation in her mind, worrying and trying to imagine the uses to which any information she had given out could possibly be put. She decided in the end that, though the bold Sparky had definitely been fishing, she had given nothing away.

'Was the Yank in?' Seamus asked Judith.

She said he'd been around.

'You know what he's after? Why he's over here?'

'Observing us, isn't he? Reporting back to New York on our spirits and whether we'll fight to the death or cave in to Lloyd George.'

'There's that,' Seamus agreed. 'He's looking for some lost funds too. The Yanks are touchy buckos when it comes to money and Clan na Gael in New York is making ructions over sums they say were fecked in New York.'

'And why would he look for it here?'

'They think it was spirited over. There's great distrust between some of the leaders here and the ones over there. Wigs on the green, I believe. You see our crowd found that the Clan had raised big sums among the American Irish for the cause of Irish freedom, only, when it came time to cough up, didn't they use it for their own local politics. Well, a lot of our lads felt that that was theft. You can see why they might feel justified in taking any they could lay their hands on. It would be easy enough to get it back here, as our delegates were always smuggled in and out of America anyway. They could spirit it back as easy as pie.'

'Who?'

'I don't know who. One of the fellows from here who was over.'

'But they wouldn't keep it for personal gain, surely?' Judith was shocked. 'Wouldn't it be turned over to the ministers of the Dáil?'

'Well, there's a rumour that there might be a split in the IRA any day and one half of the lads may well be knocking the lard out of the other. If that happened, a secret hoard would be useful to the side that didn't agree with the Dáil leaders. *Also* it would put the ministers in a tricky position to be handed fecked dollars. Whoever has it is likely to sit tight for a while.'

'Are you making this up?'

'No.'

Again Judith wondered about the money in the yard. Seamus couldn't have put it there. He hadn't been to America. Owen had. Did Seamus know and was he sounding her out or tipping her off about keeping a closed mouth? Or just gossiping? If he knew he wouldn't dare gossip, so that meant only she did. But what about Kathleen who was sweet on Sparky? She was unreliable. On the other hand, Kathleen would never go lifting the flagstones on the back path and neither would Sparky. If everyone kept their mouths shut no trouble was likely. It turned her against the Yank, though, to know he was a spy.

*

Therese,

I don't know whether or not to write. You will want to be kept informed – or, if you don't, then you have the option of tearing this up unread. So I write. But there is little new to tell except about my own narcissistic anxiety: fear that I am using you by confiding.

If I could make a choice, reach a resolution, I suppose I would find calm. Instead, I am like a dog barking at a door behind which he smells a bitch on heat: glaze-eyed, hot-tongued, maddened, unassuaged. I saw a gang of just such canine males yesterday which is why the image comes to me. One sees things like that here: manifestations of nature which don't seem to occur in LA. Two days ago it was the screams of a pig being butchered which suddenly spoiled a walk through the heather on a Wicklow mountain. Yes, I was with her and awareness of blood-letting behind the farmyard wall both excited and revolted me. Nature here is unwashed and unimproved. The place is full of mongolian idiots which families keep and send out to play with other children. They look like cloth dolls with their button-nosed, puffed faces and little beady eyes. People say they are very affectionate.

People here talk and I listen. I don't speak much – even to her. It is part of my role as an observer to project a bland image, but anyway I have little to say. *They* are noisy like clever children: sly, devious in an obvious way, often parodying themselves and each other. They think highly of their own tricks and imagine that foreigners are perplexed by them. Judging by myself, the foreigners are entertained, but not inclined to join in. The histrionic note is hard for a sober adult to sustain. Do I sound smug?

I see, rereading this, that, by implication, I have described her as a child. I hadn't thought about it but suppose that I do think this.

Also: I can't be sure that this sense of having stepped into a theatre hasn't set off a glandular reaction in me. Here are social norms whose violation resounds on the sensibility. Here is guilt, shock, a tight-assed little world. I excite her greatly, trouble her in her flesh. I give you this as ammunition. You have a right to know. And, yes, *I* am out of control. As they taught us in parochial school, it was the first step that counted and that I *could* have avoided. Looking back, it was more of a stumble than a step.

Am I being exhibitionistic? Sorry.

James

*

Patsy Flynn put on his best clothes. They were not very good. His shoes particularly were not good and he saw, looking himself over in the mirror with the borrowed eye of the bouncer in the Shelbourne Hotel, that he might not pass muster and might be asked to leave. Not wanting this to happen, he slipped into the cloakroom of the Grateful Patriots' Club and collected a gaberdine raincoat which someone had left there and a Belvedere School scarf. He put them on, brushed his hair and surveyed himself again. There was a goatish look to his face and a mad roll to his eye which did not escape his own scrutiny and would probably not please a bouncer, but he counted on its being outweighed by the scarf. Life had punished him, he thought. Life had toughened him and he looked the outsider that he was: a fellow who did not aspire to sit in plushy hotels but was more likely to stand outside them with a one-legged companion, playing some musical instrument, begging and tipping his cap, thanking the plutocratic bastards for their shame and their sixpence. 'Help an old veteran, sir, fought in the wars.' Not *your* bleeding wars but ours, and up yours, which is where I'd like to shove your mangy charity.

However, he walked into the lobby and asked for Mr James Duffy's room number. Mr Duffy, said the clerk, had just gone into the bar. I'd say you'd catch him, sir, if you hurry. Sir, thought Patsy to himself, sir, begob. It didn't take much to impress the lackeys, did it? He walked through to the bar and saw that it was populated by men no different from himself. This depressed Patsy Flynn, who had somehow imagined that the sycophantic capitalist class who were mis-using the country would bear their guilt with a difference. He had supposed they would look grander and more obviously pampered. There was something unsettling about the dis-covery that he could pass for one of them. It made him feel that he could, despite himself perhaps, *become* one, slip cravenly into their ranks and, succumbing to the argument from Original Sin, decide that justice being impossible, inequality inevitable and jungle-law irrevocable, a fellow might as well spend his brief span here beneath chandeliers, swigging twelve-year-old Jameson's, as struggle for a cause doomed to corruption. What did that make of Patsy's past? The years in gaol? The proud, lonely refusal to bow the knee? Sent it up in smoke, begob. Yes? No.

The place was full of fancy mirrors and Patsy, giving himself a shifty glare in one, had the impression – distinct, unmanning – that the eye looking back out at him was a shade less honest than the last time he'd seen it and the jaw less set. Jasus, but these places got to you quick. Contamination was the order of the day. Bad apples rotted the good. Luxury subverted. No question but that people living in these sorts of surroundings lost touch. You'd have to forgive them or kill them for they knew not what they did. String 'em up, thought Patsy, and fiddled with the knot of his tie beneath the old Belvedere scarf which was not, of course, his. Up against the wall! He'd have been a different man if his parents had had the spondulicks to send him to Belvedere. Would he though? Might he not have seen the light for himself even in such cossetted surroundings? Another glare at the smokey mirror told him he would not. Probably. Hard to tell. No, he bloody would. You'd have to be deaf and blind to fail to see through the hypocrisy of the crowd running the country today. Wilfully ignorant you'd have to be, thought Patsy, with a renewal of rage and a desire to shout insults to the deaf whisperers around him. They were muttering and tittering into their drinks, keeping their voices low to show their gentility. They'd call the bouncer if he did anything like that and where would that get him? The thought reminded him that he was here for a purpose and he began looking round for Duffy, the American. Paid minions they used. Bouncers, police, the Special Branch, the Heavy Gang who tortured Republicans now as a regular thing. These fine fellows tittering into their ladies' ears need never give a thought to the like. They delegated dirty work. Forgot about it. That was how they carried on. The right hand censored what the left never knew about. Some of these buggers might have started out with ideals. Their fathers before them might. Yes. Hadn't the state been founded on a promise to give Ireland back to the working people of Ireland? And to whom had it been given instead? An elite. Look at them. Tossing back the short drinks. Taking to the good life with as much gusto as the Brits ever did. Faces like Patsy's own. Accents like his own. Buggers who'd climbed over the corpses of their comrades or whose fathers had, then turned into mirror-images of the old oppressors.

'What can I do for you, sir?'

'What's that?'

'Can I get you a drink?' asked the barman. 'Or are you

looking for someone perhaps? We could have them paged if you like.'

'I'll have a small Jameson,' said Patsy. 'I'm looking for a Mr Duffy, a Mr James Duffy, an American.'

The price of the drink was sinful, thought Patsy, counting it out to the minion who scooped up the coins with the deferent caution of a man who has a good job where jobs are scarce.

'The American gentleman, is it?' he asked. 'That's him over there.' The lackey flashed Patsy a grin radiant with false consciousness.

Patsy squared his shoulders and bore down on the Yank.

'Mr Duffy?' The man seated next to James had a face like a russet potato and prawn-pink fingers which he kept unclasping and reclasping around his glass.

'Yes?' James could see the waiter eyeing the man from the other end of the bar. Queer customer, said the waiter's eye. The man had not removed his tweed cap. He smelled.

'I have a message for you.'

'You have?' James smiled to reassure the waiter. The smelly man could be from one of the Republican organizations with which Corny Kinlen had promised to put him in touch.

'It's from certain parties,' said the man in a low, excited voice, 'who want to issue a warning to you, a foreigner, who may not realize the standards of morality we aim for in this country. They're being patient on that account. But they'll only warn you the once.'

'I see.' James too was being patient. He was also puzzled.

'The said parties,' gabbled the man, 'do not approve of adultery, consorting with married women or poking your nose into private concerns. They told me to get a message to you which is this: knock it off. I hope you take their meaning. They're referring to your interest in the old nun and in the wedded wife. Leave the two alone and no harm will come to you. Is that clear?' The little man spoke breathlessly. 'I was told to make sure you understood.'

'Well I don't,' said James. 'Not a word. Are you sure I'm the man you were told to talk to?'

'Are you James Duffy, a US citizen?' asked the little man, with nervous formality.

'Yes.'

'You are acquainted with Sister Judith Clancy and her niece, Mrs Michael O'Malley?'

'Yes.'

'Well, you're to stop seeing them,' said the man. 'Pronto. No publishing anything the old one told you and keep your gob shut about this conversation.'

'Is this a joke?'

'It's no joke, Mr Duffy. The people I represent have no time for humour. There's a war on, though the likes of you may not know it. Do you get it now?' The voice was suddenly vicious with spite. 'No publication and keep a tight lip.'

'Did Corny Kinlen send you?'

'I don't know who you're talking about.'

The small man slid off his bar stool, tossed back the dregs of his whiskey and made for the door.

James came after him. 'Hey,' he caught his arm, 'who are you anyway?'

The man did not blench. 'I'm only a messenger,' he said. 'It's no good assaulting me.'

'A messenger from whom?'

The man wrenched his arm free. 'Use your loaf,' he said. 'The Republican Movement.'

'It's a joke,' said Grainne. 'What else could it be? What did you say he looked like? And you just let him go?'

'Well, I'd have looked silly reporting him to a policeman, wouldn't I?' said James. 'My word against his. It's not a pleasant joke,' he remarked, wondering if anyone from her family could be involved. He didn't like to raise the question. 'He wore a cloth cap,' he said, 'and a football-fan's scarf. He wasn't very tall.'

'Nobody in the movement is tall. I went to a demo once and it was like being among dwarves. They're undernourished. Except for Owen Roe.'

'He had a queer smell,' James remarked, 'sweetish: a mixture of sweat and eucalyptus. And he had red spots on his cheeks. Like a clown.'

Ha, she thought: Patsy Flynn. He chewed cough-drops all winter and rarely washed for fear of catching cold. Was he working on Owen Roe's account? Yes, he would be. She felt relief and anger: relief because if Owen Roe had done this it meant he was not about to do worse, and anger at his continuous interference in her life.

'So you think they're behind it?' James asked. 'The IRA?'

'Of course not. No. It's a stupid, disagreeable joke. That's all. Ignore it.'

'Shall we?'

'Yes.'

FIRST TREATY BETWEEN SOUTHERN IRISH AND ENGLISH GOVERNMENTS SINCE 1172 SIGNED ON EQUAL FOOTING * TREATY CONFERS STATUS OF DOMINION ON SOUTHERN IRELAND * NEW FREE STATE TO HAVE FULL FISCAL CONTROL * BRITAIN TO RETAIN NAVAL BASES * BOUNDARY COMMISSION TO DETERMINE FRONTIER IF PROTESTANT NORTH EAST REFUSES TO JOIN FREE STATE * SOVEREIGNTY OF CROWN ACKNOWLEDGED * ALL PRISONERS TO BE RELEASED * RUMOURS DENIED THAT CERTAIN IRA COMMANDANTS PLAN TO ARREST RETURNING IRISH DELEGATES AS TRAITORS * DELEGATES ARGUE TREATY WAS BEST BARGAIN AVAILABLE * DÁIL DIVIDED * MR DE VALERA REJECTS TREATY * MR COLLINS ARGUES FOR REALISM * MR CHILDERS ALLEGES TREATY PLACES IRELAND IRREVOCABLY UNDER BRITISH AUTHORITY * BITTER ABUSE OF DELEGATES BY WOMEN DEPUTIES WHO STAND FIRM ON ROCK OF REPUBLIC AT WHATEVER COST * CHRISTMAS ADJOURNMENT OF DÁIL ÉIREANN *

December. Rain fell like pickets, fencing people in. Fires smouldered and cooled in shaggy embers as hollow as the corpses of winter animals. Peace looked to have firmed up now that the Treaty had been signed in London. Journalists were jubilant. People cheered and laughed with relief. Some wept and others went to their churches to give thanks. Crowds of Irish Catholics had been photographed kneeling on the pavements of London, praying.

Three days later half the Dáil Cabinet repudiated the Treaty.

They did what? Which ministers? Oh. And why so?

The country was in limbo, suddenly unsure what toasts to drink in this pre-Christmas season. Debate raged in every pub, drawing room and kitchen. Peace? War? Compromise? Principle? The swish of hot pokers, plunging into mulled stout, amplified the dazed hiss of toothless pensioners who had nothing to do but wonder what the lads could be up to at all, at all? The leaders were at each others' throats. What could anyone make of that? And, the divil blast it, were we forever to be giving the world a spectacle of Irishman turning on Irishman? Heh?

Judith's father had taken on new authority. He'd always said, hadn't he, that politicians here were amateurs? This clinched it. This put the kibosh on it. By Jay, they should be sent to Boston for a spell of studying ward politics. Maybe they'd learn something. One evening in the front room, when a dreamy young man stood up to recite a poem, the Da told him to shut up outa that. Enough ulagoaning. It was what had us the way we were. The young man didn't hear. His eyes were glazed. Once or twice he shut them and a cloud of dim hair floated low on his forehead.

> 'Oh! there was lightning in my blood,'

he intoned, swaying in time to the rhythm.

> 'Red lightning lightened through my blood,
>   My Dark Rosaleen!'

Rosaleen was Ireland: chronically sorrowing, chronically in need of help.

The Da laughed, mimicking and mocking the youth.

> 'All day long in unrest,'

crooned the boy, who might have been shy of saying anything

like this in his own words and probably outraged if he'd seen the fat, older man clowning behind him.

> 'To and fro do I move
> The very soul within my breast
> Is wasted for your love.'

Judith wondered whether he had a girl and whether he mixed his patriotism with feeling for her. In the last verses, the softer sentiment disappeared and menace pounded on alone.

> 'Oh the Erne shall run red
> With redundance of blood.
> The earth shall rock beneath our tread,
> And flames wrap hill and wood
> And gun-peal and slogan-cry
> Wake many a glen serene,
> Ere you shall fade, ere you shall die,
> My Dark Rosaleen.'

By the time he finished, the boy had caught the mockers in his cadences. Rapt, they nodded to his beat and even the Da applauded.

Judith did not want the Treaty to hold. This was wrong of her for war was a means and not an end. To want it to go on was wicked – but she did want it to. She had grown up in the expectation that it would be her adulthood, her confirmation as a person. And now, when she was ready to join in it, it had stopped.

Arguments raged and dissipated. She could not concentrate her mind on the reasons given. Blood-lusting demons were in charge of her waking and sleeping dreams.

They were at work in the country at large as well. The Dáil itself was split into those who accepted the new Free State – 'Staters' – and diehard Republicans who could not renounce the dream for which they had been fighting: an All-Ireland Republic independent from the exploitative and haughty old oppressor. For them, the delegates had sold the pass. The Treaty should never have been signed and must not be ratified.

Judith's brother, Seamus, who was training men against the

day when fighting might take up again, said that, for all he knew, he might be teaching lads to shoot who would turn their guns on himself in a few months' time. The army itself could split, he warned. There were blowhards in it and mad idealists who had fought their war with a gun in one hand and rosary beads in the other, and no authority over them but their local commandant and God. The Irish people, said Seamus, would take a while understanding the contradiction between those two weapons. Religion promised everything later on and somewhere else. Politics aimed at getting something now. But try explaining about politics to the tearaways! Throughout the fighting they'd had little back-up from headquarters, and discipline was a thing whereof they had no conception.

None. He was destroyed trying to instil sense into them. Moonstruck men, as cold as spring water, blood-crazed, they might never be normal again, he warned. This kind of a war could destroy men for life. *They* were the danger, and theorists sitting in newspaper offices and pubs should be wary of putting a match to such straw.

'The politicians,' he said, 'debating beyond in the Mansion House about this clause and that in the Treaty, think they're settling the fate of the country. But the fighting men don't give tuppence for politicians.'

In the evenings now there was always a small crowd drifting between the pub, the kitchen and the good front room at the Clancys', where they sat in front of the embers and argued the toss. Idleness had descended on the men, for there was no fighting and no jobs. To hear them, every last mother's son of them would have made a better fist of haggling with Lloyd George, the wily Welsh Wizard, who had fooled the delegates up to their eyes. Mick Collins was conceited, said the diehards.

'The gouger's got a swelled head. All the bloody politicians have.'

'It's the gunmen have the swelled heads. Every little commandant in the country is so used to having power of life, death and requisitioning over the unfortunate people that he thinks he's God. Those fellows can't get it through their skulls that their usefulness is at an end.'

'Why should it be at an end? Why? So that the politicians can sign away what the fighting men won for them? The delegates weren't long showing the white feather when they sat down to negotiate with the English. Not long kowtowing to them. Didn't they sign away the Republic? And in favour of what? A Free State that owes allegiance to England's King and doesn't extend to the North! Listen here to me: why should we follow the politicians now? They were ministers of the Republic and they destroyed their own authority when they destroyed *it*. Answer that conundrum.'

Already, men who had been strained up towards a bright, unbounded future found themselves talking of the past. A new order had begun. The whirling wheel of fortune had jammed.

But many young men could not accept that no more could have been got from the British. Change was addictive and anyway there were no jobs.

Grainne and James were picnicking in his hotel suite: oysters, Sancerre, brown bread. Outside, branches were glazed. Pavements oozed. Gutters were torrents. Now and again a banana-coloured leaf zigzagged through damp-choked air before being caught in the sludge. Grainne, if asked, was planning to say that she had lunched alone in the Kilkenny Design Centre. The napery, wine bucket and flowers, familiar from screen fictions, made the occasion seem illusory.

'You,' James accused, 'have a Manichaean view: pleasure is a trick of the sense. Doomed. Let me offer another pair of glasses. You can get to work on your sexual techniques. Therapy teaches us to live with ourselves. Gym improves the God-given body. Love helps us live with others. Now sex, combining all three, must be the healthiest activity.'

'Is that the word from California?'

'Yes.'

'And what about your wife?'

James looked sombre. 'I find myself turning against her, which is obviously unfair. I've started resenting her claims and seeing her worst sides. You can do that to anyone.'

'Yes.'

'She's older than me.'

Silence.

'A bit possessive. Domineering even.'

Grainne said nothing.

'If I don't say it, it festers. I'm beginning to hate her.'

'Not "hanging loose" then?'

'The formulae can let you down.'

'Have more Sancerre?'

'That's the Irish route, right? Get drunk?'

She looked annoyed.

'Sorry.' He held out his glass. 'Listen, what if I were to ask you to choose between your husband and me?'

'You'd be horrified if I took you seriously.'

'Oh, I don't know. Old instincts rise in me. They're probably connected with reproducing the species. They tell me to build a nest around you.'

Grainne twisted a sheet. 'Here's the nest. How long do your signals want me to stay in it? Nine months? Or till laundry time? What's wrong with my sexual techniques?'

They kidded, but the rationed meetings – an hour or two a day – were driving James into a fume and fret such as he had never known. It was his role to be the cool and heartening one when he was with Grainne, but he began to see that she was more mistress of herself than of him. He was off his ground, unsure where he stood. She did not seem to mind her own unsureness. The seesaw of sexual play suited the indolent, non-linear way she lived her life. Her trouble had been with the first step. Having taken it, she was ready to dance it again and again, like the participants in the set figures of an Irish dance who cover the same ground over and over, weaving back and forth, getting nowhere.

'But where *should* we get?' she asked in surprise. 'Eternity is here. Now. Don't you feel it?'

He did. He also wanted to freeze it. Fix and pin it down.

'We're great together, you know.'

'I know.'

'So shouldn't we?'

'No.'

'What?'

'Anything.'

'*You've* got what you want,' he said. 'I'm your demon lover. To whom you owe nothing. Invisible. Asocial. You come to my room as men used to go to brothels. All *I* am is a fuck.' He struck away her hand.

'*Now* who's the puritan!'

'*You* are! You divide yourself into the decent and the improper. Sex – me – kept out of sight. The bourgeois ideal!'

'You're married too! It suits you.'

'It doesn't!'

'It did.'

'I didn't see the hypocrisy. I'm being treated like a goddamn nineteenth-century whore. You won't be seen in the street with me. I'm a penis. That's what I am for you: a promenading penis!'

'A lovely penis! Shall I recite Rabelais' litany to the penis? I know quite a bit of it.'

'You would!'

'Why would I?'

'Because you're a product of this butcher-shop morality.'

'Look, do *you* think sex is obscene? Because if you do . . .'

'It's you who do.'

'You told me you had lots of little quickies with girls in California and never told your wife. What was so different about that? The word is awful anyway: quickies. Like a throwaway product. Like do-it yourself sex kits. Then you say *I*'m insensitive. Words give you away . . .'

'Words! The Irish are great with words!' he exclaimed. 'But they don't *mean* anything,' he roared. 'They obfuscate. They play about with. They lie and deny. They skirmish and ambush. All your whole goddamn literature is about evasion. The exile who had to go away. The lover who lost his lass. I bought a book of popular love songs to fill my empty hours – I told you I'm like a kept woman. I have to fill the time. And I see now what you meant by negatives. Renunciation. Dig my grave both deep and wide. Laments. Goodbyes. No commitment to anything but giving up. The system is the way it is and ochone and mavrone and leave me alone and I'll sing a song about it.'

She laughed.

'Don't laugh.'

'You were funny! You're learning a way with the words.'

'I don't want words. I want you.'

'The word made flesh.'

'To take away with me.'

> 'The sunlight in the garden
> Hardens and grows cold,
> You cannot cage the minute
> Within its nets of gold . . .'

'I suppose an Irishman wrote that.'

'Does that make it less true?'

'There are different truths. They're tied to time and place.'

'Well, so am I tied to time and place.'

'Are you?'

'I think so. So are you. That's why you're getting angry at your wife. Poor woman. You've turned her into a bogy: the embodiment of everything that stops this going on forever. This: the Sancerre, and the furtiveness, and the electricity our bodies make, impalpables, newness, hope, even our anger, even our guilt. It's part of the fireworks. You can't prolong that.'

'That's *not* what I want to prolong. I want you and me together, able to walk down the street and have a drink in the lounge.'

'We can have a drink in the lounge now. I could say . . .'

'I want to have a drink in the lounge whenever I like without your having to *say* anything.'

'You don't. You want the glow of guilt and at the same time you want public absolution. They don't go together.'

'Your language is obsolete, my love. It's what you learned in catechism class. People start new lives nowadays every day of the week. Don't you read the papers?'

'I think they're deceived. They might as well never have bothered to try putting their name tag on each new love or bottling the genie. It can't be done.'

'Well, it suits you to say that. British hypocrisy – which *they*'ve shed, by the way – got dumped here as part of their colonial cast-offs and you preen in their old cast-offs and think you've liberated yourselves.'

'Darling, you're being boring and, besides, it's time I left. I have to do the shopping and . . .'

'Can I come shopping with you?'

'You know you can't. Jesus, if we were seen pushing the same supermarket trolley, it would be like being seen pushing a pram. It would be like putting a notice in the papers. Now, don't scold. This is my town. Not yours. I'm the one who runs the risks and . . .'

'And I'm the secret sex object. What will I *do* all afternoon?'

'Go and interview your old-timers.'

'Do you realize I'll soon be finished? Then what? I'm stringing it out.'

'I've got to fly. Help me with this zip. Lovers haven't time to argue. You should get adjusted to that.'

'That's why I want to marry you.'

'To argue?'

'To win.'

'You've won already. I'm woozey with pleasure with all the goals you scored. Or *was* until you started in carping. Bye.'

11

Sparky Driscoll brought round a copy of the *New York Times* in which American Irish leaders called the Treaty 'an insult to the dead who died fighting for an independent Irish Republic'.

'Hell's cure to the Yanks!' Seamus was disgusted. 'Let them think of the living and forget the dead.' The country was in a shambles. What was needed now was peace and a chance to get the new state on its feet.

'And what about the Republic?' someone asked. 'The IRA took an oath of allegiance to it and . . .'

Oaths, said Seamus, gave him a pain in the craw. They belonged to the days of secret societies. 'Forget all that,' he instructed. 'We'll have our own state now and manage our affairs in broad daylight . . .'

'Starting off with a betrayal!'

'Ah, for Christ's sake!' He struck his forehead in mimicry of a man worn down by the folly surrounding him. The Republic had been a symbol, he explained, a rallying cry. Were they all so literal-minded that they couldn't see that? Anyway the Free State would be a stepping-stone. They'd get the Republic itself in time.

As for the North, he said, didn't the world know that those buggers up there were descended from small, land-hungry planters brought over in the seventeenth century. He'd been up there and seen them himself, an embattled crowd: thrifty, with eyes like bullets and snarling voices which they used sparely. When they talked at all, said Seamus, it was through teeth clamped as though in fright that somebody might steal their tongues. There was no forcing the likes of them into an Irish Free State, much less into an Irish Republic. They'd been Protestant bigots since the days of King Billy – pronounced

'King Bully' – and to their mind such a state could only be a sink of Papist iniquity dedicated to ending their privileges. Seamus tightened his lips into a piggy-bank slot and imitated the Ulster accent: 'Aye,' said he, 'Ulster would fate and Ulster would be rate!'

Sparky Driscoll showed glistening teeth in a laugh. He was living up to his name, thought Judith: vivid in spanking new togs he'd had tailored for himself in Dublin. A masher. Kathleen seemed to be always finding reasons to fill his cup or catch his eye. Owen was expected home from gaol any day.

'Owen will agree with me,' said Seamus. 'You'll see. He's a man who understands politics. Not a gunman.'

Judith was certain that Owen would disagree completely. He would see through the paltry and expedient reasoning of her brother, Seamus. The Treaty was a horrible thing if it was making young men who had been ready to die for Ireland three weeks ago talk in this mealy-mouthed way about a betrayal no better than those of the men who had been found shot with notices pinned around their necks saying 'All traitors beware'.

The lad who'd recited 'Dark Rosaleen' the week before asked Seamus, 'What about the Catholic minority up North?' He had a sad, brooding, Celtic face, elongated and unfleshed. 'Our suffering people,' he mused.

Seamus said that the Boundary Commission would narrow down the Northern territory until it would be economically unviable. 'Lloyd George himself told Collins.'

'Lloyd George . . .'

'He who sups with the devil needs a long spoon.'

'Later,' said Seamus, 'when the Free State is working and on its feet will be the time to think of the North.'

He and Sparky began punching each other, wrestling playfully over something Judith hadn't caught. Some double meaning. Fellows were forever making remarks not meant to be picked up by girls. As in the secret societies derided by Seamus, half the relish came from someone not being in the know. Judith didn't want to be. Not in the least. She carefully kept herself from knowing about soppy things like love and courting. Sparky and her brother yelped like puppies and held each other in a clinch. They were big-wristed lads with too much energy. You could just picture one of them leaving a girl in the lurch to sing:

> 'My bonny lies over the ocean,
> My bonny lies over the say.
> My bonny lies over the ocean,
> And he's left me in the family way.'

She blushed for the impropriety of the song and wondered how she had come to think of it? Secrets and treachery had reminded her. That was what.

*

Therese,

I have been unfair; for all my efforts not to be – I have been unfair to *her*. I have not kept copies of my letters to you but I know I have given the impression that my relationship with her was purely physical. This makes her seem like some piece of animal bait with which Ireland trapped me. Maybe it excited me to think so. It's not true. She's a fine person and one has no right to turn people into playthings, even in one's fantasy.

Maybe you'd rather not know. It's just that, having misled you, I now feel I've got to put the record straight. I don't want to tell more lies than I have to. Obviously, around here, we're having to tell a few. She has to be discreet because of her family and I don't want word of what's happening getting back either to Larry or to Los Angeles. The Irish gossip. God, do they.

Yes, the furtiveness did excite me at first. I admit it. I may have told you so. The need to keep up a front, touch as if by chance, grope beneath tables and behind doors – all that cooks up excitement. It's part of the drill that never made it West of the Rockies. Playing with what might be fire. Might. Might not. This country is between worlds. 'Strong' farmers in the provinces get sued for having alienated the affections of the wives of lesser ones. We've been following a case in the *Irish Times* with a mixture of hilarity and fear. Cynics say the lesser farmer sets his wife up to entice the strong (i.e.

rich) one, who then has to pay the 'outraged' husband restitution. Cases like these are rare in England now but, like I say, this is Ireland battling with imported and dumped legislation. It hots up the atmosphere. *I admit*.

What I want to say – in my defence – is that this was an adjunct, the parsley round the roast – shit, forgive the imagery. I'm whacked, writing this at two in the morning after a tough day. I don't want to tear it up and start again because I haven't the stamina. And however dumbly or raggedly I write, I do want to keep those envelopes coming. I want us in touch.

What I set out to say is that she's a decent person, worth while, someone *you* would like – in other circumstances. And I've intruded in her life. I'm responsible for setting it back now on to an even keel. Somehow.

Therese, forgive me if I'm a selfish and insensitive bastard. I'm at a loss. I'll write more consecutively next time. Please be of good cheer. I love you – in my fashion.

James

*

James said Aunt Judith could borrow his cassette-recorder – he had two – to record the phone-calls she claimed to be receiving. That way she'd be sure that they weren't coming from inside her own head.

Grainne hoped that would calm her down. 'She's excitable,' she said. 'She told Cormac that nothing was worth living for which wasn't worth dying for. He was impressed.'

'I'm impressed.'

'*He* takes it literally.'

'Great.'

'What's great about it?' She was indignant. 'The culture is full of pious adages it would be demented to take seriously. Fourteen-year-olds do though. Cormac could do something cretinous.'

'I take them seriously. I love you. I take that seriously.'

This annoyed her. He was putting himself forward. Cormac and Aunt Judith were capable of dangerous insanity. Was he? Exhibitionism was in poor taste.

'What might Cormac do?'

'How do I know? Children are *used*. Everything innocent is: shopping bags, coffins. It was in the evening papers that a car stopped at the border two days ago had explosives under the back seat. The driver's three toddlers were sitting on it.'

'That's how you fight a guerilla war.'

She guessed him to be thinking of films by Boris Ivens and Gino Pontecorvo. She had seen them too. Also of pub chat. But *she* was thinking of Cormac, a real person, a bundle of intractable adolescent impulse and generosity. *Her* Cormac, the loose skin of whose testicles she had caught one day in a zip when she was undressing him on the beach. He had been four years old and had screamed his head off while Michael began trembling, unnerving her and yelling that females brought up in convents were unfit to be let near male children and did she know how much she had hurt the boy? She didn't. The two had kept up their clamour while she extricated the tiny sliver of skin from the zip. Later, she bought Cormac an ice-cream and worried that she might have maimed him for life. Later again, when he was five or maybe six, she had told him stories of patriot heroes and sung him ballads which had seemed sage, being defused by the decades-old peace which had looked like lasting forever. Nobody in those days gave a thought to the North except to pop up there to buy contraceptives. Well, maybe those very tales were bearing their fruit now. How could you tell?

'It's not *our* war,' she told James.

'Pontius Pilate.'

'I have every sympathy with the man. You wouldn't be so indulgent about the fighting men if you knew them. They shoot bullets through the kneecaps of their own men for sexual offences.'

'Wartime has its own morality.'

'Maybe. But bystanders have no right to approve of it. How come you didn't go to Vietnam if you're so war-minded?'

'I managed . . .'

'You managed. You chose the peaceful values. They come easily to you. Not to me. I'm struggling out of a dour tradition. No, don't start kissing me. I'm angry now.'

'The fighting spirit finds its own outlets.'

'That's the thing. We need time to breed it out and there's Cormac cultivating it in himself. I could cry. I'd try beating peace into him.' She laughed. 'Did I tell you about the Battered Wives' Home in London and how most of them had been battered by Irish husbands? What does that tell you about our fighting spirit?'

'That your government should introduce bull-fighting to channel off spleen. Why not get your politician-cousin to propose it?'

She didn't want to talk about Owen Roe. 'That bastard is lepping with nostalgia for the days of all-out gun-fighting.'

'What about you?'

'I'm a character from *Moby Dick* trying to live in *Cranford*. It's not even a quiet Cranford. Old phantoms stalk the privet hedges. Cormac dreams of being a gunman.'

'It doesn't sound workable. Why don't you come away with me? Come to California. Bring Cormac. I'll teach him to surf. That'll deviate his dare-devil drives. Or to hang-glide.'

'Are you planning to get a divorce?'

'I don't know. We'd have to see. You might even like my wife.'

'Oh. Do you have polygamy over there?'

'No. But situations can be fluid.'

'Mmm.'

*

Cormac had written:

Dear Dom Patrick,

I am asking you to excuse Cormac from the excursion to St Michan's crypt. He has been there before and as he is suffering from varicose veins in his legs the doctor has suggested that he walk as little as possible. For the same reason, we hope that you will excuse him from taking part in sports for the rest of term. The scholastic part of his curriculum should benefit from this enforced rest. Yours sincerely, Michael O'Malley.

Cormac was expert at forging his father's signature and had been writing notes like this for years. He didn't think the old man would blow the gaff if he were to find out. Daddy hated trouble – which, in a way, *was* his trouble. Cormac sometimes had the feeling that he had stolen something of his father's self by impersonating him so regularly.

It was as if they were both plugged into the same current and Cormac was using up too much. Certainly the old man was getting dimmer, while Cormac felt charges inside him curdling his blood and brains. Probably it was adolescence and would pass. Or he could be a touch mad? His heredity wasn't too reliable, so he'd better hope it was just puberty. Other fellows in school didn't seem to suffer from it though. Maybe they were sublimating?

Dom Patrick had explained to the senior boys that the thing to do with sexual drives was to sublimate them on the sports field. He'd read out bits from some book on psychology. Cormac thought the old twit was spastic. Since listening to him he couldn't look at a ball or stick.

Anyway, sexual drives weren't what troubled Cormac at all. What was boiling up in him was more a kind of total disgust. Many things revolted him, especially having to touch anything which was less than clean. That was just about everything these days, for in school the monks were filthy and at home his mother had become a sloven. It was having the aunt in the house, he supposed. *She* was niffy and Mary, the maid, also had a pong. Cormac wished he didn't feel that way about them, but he did. The other day he had found a long red hair in his mouth while eating a pie. He had pulled it out with difficulty because it had got tangled up in the food he was chewing and it was all he could do to stop himself being sick. He'd managed to refrain from complaining, partly because mentioning the thing would have made him even more disgusted. Also, he was having trouble keeping his mother from kissing him and he didn't want to be always hurting her feelings.

The rolling about in tangles of arms and legs on a mucky playing field, which seemed so healthy to Dom Patrick, was especially nauseating to Cormac. Actually, Dom Patrick himself was icky. He had dandruff all over his black, clerical clothes. A barber had told Cormac that dandruff came from nerves and nerves from unsatisfied desire. Cormac wasn't sure that the chap mightn't have been pulling his leg but anyway the stuff revolted him. He couldn't keep his eyes off the grey flakes scattered like the scales of small, moulting beetles all over Dom Patrick's cassock. The monk's hands were grey too, like the hands of the skeletons you were meant to shake for luck when you visited St Michan's crypt. These had great flaps of leather over their chests. They released brown dust like old puff-balls when you moved them. They were supposed to be the miraculously preserved bodies of old crusaders but the preservation was so poor that you could hardly be impressed by the miracle and anyway, according to the guide book, the crypt wasn't old enough for them to be crusaders at all. So where was the point of the excursion? Piety? Lies? A typical Dom Patrick move. He'd make them all walk through town in a crocodile wearing their blazers to give the school some free publicity. Dom Patrick himself would be swanning along in front with his dandruff shining in the sun like castor sugar.

Anyway Cormac had got off the outing and rung Great-uncle Owen Roe to ask could he come riding with him up on Calary.

'Haven't you got school?' his uncle wanted to know.

'There's an excursion. I'm not going.'

Great-uncle Owen Roe had been unusually pernickety. 'I'm not going to fight your battles with your mother for you,' he'd warned. 'I won't try to stop your coming to visit me but I won't square it with her either. It's up to you.'

Cormac guessed that his great-uncle didn't want to seem to be horning in on Cormac's father's place.

'Been seeing the uncle, have you?' Daddy sometimes asked. He always called Great-uncle Owen Roe 'the uncle', as if he were a character in a comic. 'How's the uncle?' he'd ask. 'Still plotting to take over the country? Getting too big for his boots, eh?' Cormac had the feeling that what Daddy meant was 'plotting to take over my family'. There was always the notion around that Great-uncle Owen Roe was 'up to some-thing'.

'So you want to come for a bit of a canter on Calary Bog?' his uncle asked.

'Yes.' Riding was the one sport Cormac loved. It was just risky enough to take all his attention. By the time he'd galloped over a few miles of bogland and jumped a few fences, he felt his mind combed clean of the messy half-thoughts which usually cluttered it and his body felt purged. It was as though he had shucked off inessential parts of himself. The friction of the air, the bath in milky sky, the razoring wind cleansed him. He came back smelling of sedge and horse. It did for him what confession and communion were supposed to do but didn't.

'You haven't been coming to confession, Cormac?' Dom Patrick had remarked. If he thought Cormac was going to insert himself into a smelly confessional, breathing the same bad air as Dom Patrick, to tell him his sins, then he had another think coming.

'I go with my mother to the parish church,' Cormac lied. He stared at the scaling skin on the monk's eyelids. It was a trick he'd learned which made the person you were talking to think you were looking them in the eye. Dom Patrick was very keen on being looked in the eye. Man to man. Straight. He couldn't distinguish a look at his eyelid, though, from a look into his pale, jellyfish eyeball, and looking at the lid left Cormac feeling coldly superior and in control. He knew that Dom Patrick was aiming a hard look at him, but it missed him. The monk didn't believe that either mother or son went to confession but he couldn't say that. Having the sort of parents Cormac had did have advantages. At the same time he felt furious with the old twit for daring to think badly of his mother.

'They have minds like sewers,' Patsy Flynn had told Cormac. 'Monks. They learn about sexual positions,' Patsy added surprisingly, 'by using pennies.' He went on to say how Republicans in the past had been the only ones who wouldn't bow the knee to them, and Cormac didn't get a chance to ask *how* pennies could teach you about sex. Pennies? Penis? *Penis angelicus*? That was a joke from *Focalín*. Cormac wished he hadn't brought the paper home. His mother had seen it. She'd come to kiss him good night and, trying to avoid *that*, he'd pretended to be asleep and she'd looked at it.

Embarrassing. His mother was sexy-looking. Fellows had remarked on it. Cormac would have liked to cover her up in some old sack, though he knew that this was probably immature of him. You had to take the world as it was, the natural world anyway. Cormac's trouble was he didn't know the meaning of life or why he was alive. If you rejected what people like Dom Patrick taught you, you found yourself at a loss. You had to start from scratch and be suspicious of every single tiny thing you'd ever been told. It was daunting. Of course, if you decided to go in for politics, which Cormac thought he might, then you didn't have to start so far back. Action would take your mind off the vaguer questions. A bit like horse-riding really.

'So can I come?' Cormac had asked Uncle Owen Roe. 'Riding? On Calary?'

'Only if your mother rings me to say it's OK.'

That put paid to it. He couldn't even *ask* his mother since she'd know he was meant to be at school.

'I'm sorry, Cormac,' said his uncle. 'Your mother is getting touchy about our outings.'

It was late in the day for her to be coming all over the responsible mother but, all right, Cormac had to admit that he'd wished she'd pull her socks up about this in the past and so now he had no right to complain. It was his old trouble: not knowing whether he wanted revolution, independence, and to break the idols, or an ordered, properly run, stable world. He must really make his mind up before he could complain about anything at all. Meanwhile, when Excursion Day came, he'd have to skulk around the house if he didn't want to be caught mitching from school. He'd have to sneak food from the kitchen for his lunch and maybe spend good money in the afternoon to see some wretched movie he didn't even want to see. Anyway, he'd have to keep out of sight. It was a bore.

So their cauldron bubbled behind closed curtains in his hotel bedroom. Toil and trouble might be the sediment but they tried not to stir it up.

'I want to eat pineapple chunks out of your cunt,' he said.

240

It was the season for play, but she began armouring herself against reality which sooner or later must erupt. She was worried about Michael, who was hardly ever home.

Fearful at first of hurting him, she began after a while to dread that he already *was* hurt but would never let her know. She imagined the knowledge of her betrayal, secret as a cancer, corrupting his health, and longed, selfishly, to have things out. He must guess something? Why didn't he ask her? But no. He moved through the house like a new butler unsure of his duties, pausing in doorways, coughing at the turns of corridors, whistling as he came in the gate. What did he imagine he'd find if he just walked in on her?

'Are you all right, Michael?'

'Me? Yes. Why?'

'You look peaky.'

It was an opening but he didn't take it.

'Odd?' she suggested.

'Odd compared to whom?' he could have quipped, or: 'Where were you all afternoon?'

She could have explained then about how this was just a sensual release which at her age he could hardly deny her. *He* had never wanted to eat pineapple from between her legs, had he? So, if she wanted to play such games while he played his in the pub, what harm was anyone doing anyone? He wouldn't deny her the sex he didn't enjoy himself, would he? *Would* he? Or the explanation she needed in order to feel absolved – it wasn't for her sake that she wanted the show-down. She wanted to be able to tell him that the best part of her loved him. The mind and heart, Michael. Please. Really. Didn't all that count? Didn't he *want* to know he had it still? He didn't. He slid in and out the front door like a barely tolerated cat. His clothes looked shabbier. She couldn't think where he got them. Maybe from the Salvation Army? He was promenading around in rags so as to punish her, so as to show her up to all Dublin as a neglectful wife. In the evenings, she cooked remorseful meals for him and got herself up seductively, brimming with excess sex. But he didn't come home or, if he did, gobbled a few mouthfuls then rushed back out to meet some man in a pub. What? No, he couldn't take her. A men-only occasion. Sorry. It would bore her anyway. He had his key. Don't wait up.

He eluded her. He always had.

'He's a casualty,' she told her lover, 'of our family.'

'People,' she said, 'thought I'd made a great catch when I married him. I remember a man at our wedding telling me that any lassie who could put salt on the tail of a young fellow like that knew on which side her bread was buttered.'

'What an oaf!' James was shocked.

'Oh, he was drunk. But he said what they all thought. Michael was fetching and he was expected to inherit his father's mills. Later he was disinherited after he took to the drink.'

She was remembering Michael's wide-spaced eyes floating like sea-slivers above his cheek bones. Nowadays they were bloodshot and surrounded by swollen flesh. He was losing his eyelashes.

'Unless I destroyed him myself?' she wondered.

'Alcoholics,' James told her, 'are the destroyers.'

That, like a lot of things people said, was only half true. James, Grainne noticed, chose the workable halves of truths. It was perhaps unfair to fault him for this but she did. It implied, didn't it, that *she* should choose the workable half of her life: James's and cut Michael's out? This made a sort of harsh, pragmatic sense and was maybe honester than the solution she *had* chosen which was to rush, like a tight-rope performer, from one man to the other, changing her face *en route*. The rope was not strung between the two males but between their emotional territories. One night recently, she had found herself lunging sleepily for the cock beside her and even for the mouth which, while silent, was only flesh. When Michael *said* something, he at once became his quirky, easily hurt self and woke Grainne up to awareness that she was committing two-way treachery in her marriage bed. Seeing things partly with James's and partly with Michael's eyes, she felt herself turn into a hybrid, double-visioned creature who had to keep sorting herself out.

'I've never done anything useful with my life,' she tried to explain to herself and James. 'I feel that being a private person – unlike, say, Owen Roe – it's up to me to do good in my private life and that means to Michael. You're trouble-free, so I don't feel I deserve you.'

James gave her the answers she wanted: reassuring, sensible. American answers which – she saw as soon as he gave them – she had been shamelessly soliciting. Overtaxing your powers, he said, made things worse all round, worse for *him*, for Cormac even for Michael. Yes, she was being a bore. She saw that. It was these brief meetings that did it. All they had time for was to eat and fuck and talk in an excited, unnatural way. There were no pauses. No dead times. That made you take yourself a lot too seriously. She must arrange to spend a day with James, well, anyway, a long afternoon. Cook up some excuse.

She did this and found that after the food and the fucking, she was talking lengthily about Michael. Well, why not? He was in her mind. Better bring him out front, as James would say. She was constantly having to remember not to use American turns of speech when talking to Michael.

The connection was a deep one, she explained. Deep and old. Being cousins, she and Michael had always known each other, although she hadn't got to know him well until she was in her late teens in Rome, where she had persuaded her parents to send her to finishing school. Michael was already in the city, studying to be a singer, sowing wild oats and sparking off rumours which filtered home through priestly connections at the Vatican.

'I'd had a crush on him,' she confessed, 'since I was six.'

That was why she'd wanted to go to the convent on the top of the Spanish Steps. She used to walk down these with other girls to have tea at Babbingtons' English teashop. Local boys sat on the steps, spied up their skirts and hissed at them in various languages. The girls ignored the boys, but later, when they met marriageable young men, remembered the lewd suggestions and guessed that the polite ones must be thinking similar thoughts.

'I'd like to lick you all over,' was one of the urchins' remarks.

Ice-creams were bought in chrome-bright bars in the

piazza and tongues, licking the coloured cones, were reflected in all the surfaces. The girls were as demure as statues, but the hiss of espresso machines set off sensations along the surface of their skin. Grainne had loathed and been fired by the overt sensuality of Italy. Michael, much later, was to admit he'd felt the same thing. They were both embarked on a pilgrimage away from the dull puritanism of their parents but had too much of it in them to accept the easy delights on offer all around. They needed some custom-made ecstasy tailored to their own hot, fastidious needs. Now, thought Grainne sadly, she had run out on her old partner and found what she wanted with someone else. It made her feel mean. Perhaps if she stated this in Western-film terms, James might understand? Though, what was the use of his understanding? She didn't want him empathizing so perfectly that he felt obliged to bow out of her life. Perhaps she was only sharing her past with him so that, if she did decide to go away with him, she would not have to leave it all behind? Love me, love my past. Anyway, at the time she'd been telling him about, she'd seen very little of Michael, she explained. He was sometimes in the tearooms but always got up to go when he saw her come in, looking as if he'd have hidden if he could, but looming head and shoulders above the squat Roman men. The girls from Grainne's group called him '*il cervo*' because, as she told James, he was forever stumbling into chairs as he rushed off, like a stag enmeshing its antlers in forest boughs. Grainne had heard that he was living with some woman and fearful lest anyone from home should know. There had been a row in the family when he chose to become a singer; further indiscretion could lead to his allowance being cut off. The romance of this appealed to her finishing-school mates, whose unique concern was matchmaking.

These girls spent hours at a stretch discussing the money a suitor must have before he could be taken seriously, and mapping on each others' bodies areas which such a man might explore on first and subsequent dates. No dates at all were permitted by the convent but, even so, to Grainne, coming from a country intoxicated by centuries of hope and disorder, the girls' expectations were repellent. She must have let them see this for they stopped inviting her to their houses. This, since there was no going out unchaperoned, meant that she remained coralled within the convent for months. Having no opportunity of losing anything else, she spent the time losing her religion. She teased God in the same spirit as the girls planned to tease suitors. 'Take me,' she defied impatiently. 'I'm giving you every chance. Let me feel ecstasy.' Nothing came of this and, in an access of boredom, she made a sacrilegious communion. 'Strike me then,' she challenged. 'Give me eczema, polio, something.' God took no more notice of Grainne than she had taken of the boys on the Spanish Steps, and her emotions remained ravening and unemployed. Finally it was spring. The city, after months of muddy inertia, began to bloom. Bird cages were put out on windowsills and clothes-lines heavy with underwear strung, like gonfalons, across courtyards. Wisteria blossomed and grew pale, shedding its flowers in a preliminary typifying of grapes and autumn wine.

An invitation arrived from the Irish Embassy. Michael was to sing in an oratorio in a church. Since the occasion was cousinly, cultural and religious, the nuns stretched their rules and Grainne was let out alone.

She took her tremulous self down past the hissing youths into the streets off the Corso, where she found a shaky filobus to carry her to the Piazza Navona. She was late and Michael, already singing, as she reached the nave, struck her as a creature apart. Grainne was unmusical. The nuns had said so in a report to her family. Not only, they complained, was she musically uncultured – 'pas cultivée du tout' – but perhaps beyond culturing. Her relatives, associating the words with the soil which they were eager to put behind them – her mother's people had been farmers – were unperturbed. This was the first concert Grainne had attended in months. The impact of the music was the more total. It wrung her nerves. The singer seemed disembodied and sustained by it and held her mesmerized like a snake.

At the concert's end a girl moved through gauzy twilight towards the singer. She wore a mantilla and the dusk knitted her contours into the church's baroque exuberance. Grainne observed singer and girl exchanging looks. Separated by a small congratulatory crowd pressed around Michael, their faces achieved a symmetry, like matched statues flanking an altar. Grainne, alert for the tense and illicit, intuited a current of passion and wanted it to touch her.

'I think,' she told James, 'I was afraid of not being able to generate anything like it myself. I didn't want to take anything from them, you understand. Just to be part of it.'

This happened. She became their confidante. The girl was English, a lovely, ivory-skinned slut in whose room Grainne was able to smell the fumes of sex at no cost to her own purity – smell them physically from Theo's chronically unmade bed and stained turbulence of sheets. Grainne would sit for hours on a smoothed-out stretch of this while Theo – Theodora Smith – waxed hair off her legs, painted her nails, chain smoked and interrogated her about Michael.

'Will he marry me?' she asked. 'You must know. You're his cousin. I can't make out these Catholic boys at all.' She laughed and the misplaced, inconsequential laughter seemed to Grainne to pinpoint the bravura of blighted love. The blight rescued Theo from banality and was clear to Grainne from the start. It was Theo's readiness to adapt which would put Michael's family off. Theo, Grainne guessed, could have got away with any one of her *personae* but could hardly hope to put across the lot. She was a rag-doll made up of scraps which told a tale. Her accent, as she freely admitted, had been learned from a lover who had found her working in a Kilburn pub and planned to launch her as an actress. Her name came from another lover. Her clothes were remnants of a trousseau supplied by the man she had ditched for Michael and in these – until she opened her unbridled mouth – she looked like a duchess. Better than many duchesses. Grainne had seen several at the convent, and Theo, at her best, outshone them. At her best, she could look like a saint. The man who had wanted her to act had been on to something, for she could imitate anyone. It was the substance behind appearances which escaped her.

'I know he's weak,' she told Grainne. 'I've been warned. He says he'll marry me but his friends say I shouldn't count on it. *You* tell me,' she flattered. 'How can I win round his parents? What should I do?' It was a tall order.

'Be yourself,' said Grainne inadequately. The advice was useless. Which self? The Kilburn self? Even that might have been acceptable if Theo had stuck to it. Michael's – and Grainne's – family, though avid for gentility, could not forget their revolutionary background. They felt unease about snobbery. If Theo had managed to look like someone who had risen by force of grit and virtue, they would have been uncomfortable about rejecting her. Grainne sensed this but, unable to put it in words, fell back on the nice-girl's rule of thumb: be sincere and with luck your sincerity will be reciprocated. For marrying one's own kind this was sure-fire and anyway the only strategy open to the young and ignorant like herself. For Theo, she began to see, it would not do. Theo could only afford small doses of sincerity.

'It's all so bloody two-faced and old-hat,' Theo complained. 'People pretend matchmaking and dowries went out with the Flood. Don't you believe it. Some milky little deb can slip in and marry the man you've been living with and maybe supporting for years. I've seen it happen.' Her face hardened suddenly and Grainne saw an older, embittered Theo with no flies on her, a brassy, disillusioned shopgirl, a Kilburn char.

Some of Theo's friends had managed to marry up. Peers two had got. A third had got her hooks into a Greek movie director and another married a playboy who owned a racecourse in Atlantic City. Compared to them, what was Michael?

'I thought he was wild Irish,' she complained. 'Now they tell me the wild Irish are all Protestant. How's a girl to know?'

Her ditched lover had written to Michael's father.

'A foul, filthy, libellous letter! I never knew he was such a shit.'

The father cut funds and the two pawned things – Michael's violin, their skis – while waiting for something to turn up. Michael did some numbers in a cabaret and borrowed small sums from Grainne who imagined one or both of the lovers dying, like Chatterton, on that stained bed. She also had sessions with Michael.

'I wish you'd talk sense into that girl,' he complained, as though Grainne had been an understanding grandmother. 'She doesn't understand,' he intoned, 'that I've got to play ball with my bloody father. I'm an *artist*. I need time to develop my voice. And I wish she'd tone herself down. We were in a trattoria the other night and I said, "look, love, that booze hound with the red nose over there happens to be the *chargé d'affaires* representing our sanctified island. So do me a favour: sit tight." Well, nothing would do her when the musicians came round but to jump up and start singing with them. Making up for her lack of the lingo with mime and cabaret humour. Knickers humour if you don't mind. And the old bastard had his eyes out on sticks.'

'He may have liked it.'

'Oh don't worry! He liked it. He'll be doing the act for my old man the next time they meet.'

Grainne's association with the lovers fired and aged her. Michael and Theo interviewed and managed to impress the nuns with their suitability as chaperones. Theo had worn gloves and a hat for the occasion and now the trio dined together almost nightly. They ran up bills in small eating-places and had a decidedly ambiguous air.

'Isn't he smashing?' Theo would croon. 'Everyone's admiring my songbird. *L'uccellone mio*.'

'They're admiring you!'

'Maybe it's Grainne they like? She's the local type. The *ragazza per bene*: the nice girl.'

'Don't be horrid, Theo. That makes me think of all those bloody girls at the school.'

'But you *are* like them, darling: a virginal voyeur. What better definition of a nice girl?'

'Grainne's all right,' said Michael. 'Leave her alone.'

The look she got from Theo was Grainne's first intimation that she might be being backed into the role of predatory little deb who swipes the heroine's man.

Years after Grainne and Michael had married, Theo turned up in Dublin for Horse-Show Week with a rich Colombian in tow. She bore no grudges. In the end it was she who had called quits, leaving Michael and Grainne to find that their meetings to talk about her were turning into talks about themselves.

'Which could have been foreseen with half an eye,' said Theo the-wordly-wise, who had dyed her hair and was wearing sables. She claimed to have a soft corner for Michael still.

'Which one?' Grainne asked tartly and was pleased that Michael happened to be away.

Theo laughed, unruffled. 'I called him my songbird,' she told the Colombian. 'Ah well, he's Grainne's now. How is he?' she asked Grainne.

'He lost his voice,' Grainne warned. 'Don't mention it if you see him. He hates to be reminded.'

By then Michael had tried working in the woollen mills and their retail outlets but had been fired for drunkenness by his father.

'*Had* to drink,' Michael had groaned humorously. 'There I was, working as a bloody counter-jumper, selling lengths of ribbon and woollen combs to farmers. "This'll keep your backside warm, sir, just the thing to wear for the spring sowing." '

'But darling,' screamed Theo. 'I didn't call him songbird because of his *voice*! What a laugh! Don't you know the slang meaning of *uccello* in Italian? Penis! You see, Michael, in that department, was memorable.'

Her Colombian lover laughed with zest. He was a short, reddish, Indian-looking man with quick, excited eyes. The year was one when group sex had become fashionable in England, and Grainne had a panicked fear that the two might suggest something. The notion froze her. Voyeurism no longer appealed to her in the least and sex had been of such minimal importance in her marriage that she had come to think it must have been Michael's lack of potency which had led to the final break with Theo. This latest news was humiliating. If true. Theo might be getting a delayed revenge. Amusing herself perhaps? Grainne shot glances at her but didn't dare pursue the matter. Questions festered however: was Michael simply not aroused by *her*? Had she somehow unmanned him? Had he married her simply so as to go on talking about Theo?

They no longer did this, but who could have foreseen the cooling of the heart?

'Do you find me sexy?' she asked James.

'Very.'

'Truly?'

'Can't you tell?'

'No. You might have a kink for frigid women.'

'You frigid! You must be crazy!'

Possibly, as in Theo's joke, sex and singing had been psychically connected for Michael. It was just before Theo took off and he got drunk in a Roman café, quarrelling first with her, then with some bystanders, that he got himself knocked down and kicked, among other places, in the throat. Theo had been demanding that he marry her and face his parents with a *fait accompli*. She wasn't getting younger, she assured him, and could not afford to wait. A girl had to give some thought to number one.

'They'd come round,' she told him. 'Parents always do.'

'Theo, I need *peace*. There would be a God-Almighty row. If I haven't got peace I can't develop my art. It's precisely because I hate that old shit of a tinker, my father, that businessman – crass, snobbish – because I hate his values that I need my art. You *can't* ask me to give it up.'

Michael had drunk a half-bottle of *grappa*. He was red in the face and his diction was thick.

'All I'm asking is that you marry me.'

'He'd cut me off. We've got to move warily. Be gentle as doves and wishe, wise ash . . .'

'You've *been* cut off. Michael, I gave up Maurice for you and I was on to a good thing there. You never mentioned wariness *then*, did you? It was all for love and share my crust under the moon. Damn it, Michael, I'm not complaining, but . . .'

'But what? What *are* you doing?'

'I'm asking you to marry me. I can't waste any more time and you can stop pretending to be so drunk. You're sober enough to understand. I know you by now. Your father would have to come round. Wouldn't he, Grainne? You're an objective outsider, I suppose? What do you say?'

Grainne tried to be fair. 'Well, the old man could disinherit Michael,' she said cautiously. 'You see, there's his younger brother, Michael's uncle, who's been working in the business and . . .'

'Another crass businessman. I spit on their business. My grandfather was a bloody hero,' Michael shouted. 'Hero. I'm going to drink to his ashes. *Cameriere*, more *grappa*. A gunman! He fought *your* bloody tribe,' he told Theo. 'He never cared for money.'

'Well *you* certainly care enough for it.'

'They should be proud to pay it. I'm the pride of their bloody escutcheon. I sing. I'm the only honour they've got since the Granddad died. They sold their own for a mess of underwear. Combs. Jockey shorts. They can put my golden throat on their Coat of Arms. Mine. All *they* can contribute to it is a pair of woollen underpants.'

'Golden *uccello*!' launched Theo in a loud voice and added a number of comments which must, given the punning possibilities, have been filthy. Grainne saw this in retrospect. The whole café became intent on the quarrel. *Passera*, the Italian word for a female sparrow, had a second meaning – vagina. That too was bandied. So were *fica, cazzo, bischero, mona, stronzo*. Theo had learned her scraps of Italian from graffiti on the Roman walls. Her virtuoso performance as a dubbed-in wife of Bath swept over Grainne's innocent head. One of the bystanders, a man who had brought his daughters to the café for ice-cream, complained to the management. A foreign whore was corrupting his children's innocence. She should be put out.

'Are you a businessman?' Michael, high on guilt and *grappa*, interrogated the father of daughters, 'a man of *affaires*?'

The Italian decided that the blonde barbarian was insulting him and that anyway the woman was a whore. '*La donna* . . .' he shouted at the waiter, '*è una sgualdrina*.'

'*La donn'è mobile*,' sang Michael with drunken zest.

The two squared up to each other. Theo yelled. Michael sang Rigoletto's aria, interrupting himself to explain, then interrupting his explanations to sing.

'*Com' pium al vento* . . . I'm an artist,' he roared, 'a bloody singer. Not a tinker or a crass businessman like my old man. *Padre!*' he roared and made a face of savage derision. He had learned no Italian, although he had been in Rome for three years. Just enough to order drinks and pronounce the words in his singing repertoire. He struck his chest in a parody of Italianate pride and went back to the aria.

The father of daughters construed this as an insult. One knew, after all, what had been the fate of Rigoletto's daughter and the civic status of Rigoletto. A pimp. He was being called a pimp. *Un ruffiano!* Him! A respected citizen. Bystanders took the insult to be aimed at the whole of Italian culture: *oltraggio alla patria*, a punishable offence. Someone went for the police but before they arrived Michael had been knocked down or had fallen over, and been kicked in his private parts and throat. Theo leaped at the men aiming the kicks. There were several but her Kilburn heritage came in useful. She fought with such vim and expertise, that by the time the police came two had claw marks etched deep in their faces. A man was hiding his eye. Another, bending over, moaned about his balls. Three men and Michael were transported with all speed to the Pronto Soccorso and Theo to the police station.

'The old fighting spirit!' James, amused by the tale, ruffled the soft hair at the back of Grainne's neck. 'Does this tickle? Or please? It's where your nerves converge. Supposed to be very sensitive.'

Grainne moved her head away. 'Not in Michael,' she said. 'He put up no fight at all. Never knew what hit him. Too sozzled. It was Theo who fought with her bare hands.'

'*O piccola manina!*'

'Yes. *I* just sat frozen. Couldn't stir. She was ejected from the country while Michael was in hospital. Or left. We never quite knew. I was shut up in the convent at the time. All outings forbidden. Then Michael's father turned up and started matchmaking. He thought Michael and I would be good for each other. My side of the family were furious.'

James put his tongue in Grainne's ear. She wriggled.

'I was in love with him,' she said defensively. 'I always had been and I thought he needed me. He'd lost his voice after the fight. If you could call it a fight. He kept talking about his father having the last laugh, but the old man wasn't laughing at all. He kept saying that Michael needed a strong woman.

'You?'

'Yes. He wanted Michael to settle down and there I was to hand and in love with him. Everyone knew I'd always been in love with him. It was a family joke. When I was a child the maids used to sing:

> 'The rain, rain falls;
> The wind blows high;
> The leaves come clattering from the sky.
> Grainne O'Malley said she'd die
> If she didn't get Michael of the roving eye.'

'Oh Jesus!,' said Grainne and began to cry. 'It's still true. I'm in bed with you and I'm in love with Michael.'

'You're a Proustian.' James stroked her thigh. 'Proust could only enjoy things in anticipation or in retrospect. Or at least that was true of his main character. You've got a magnificent thigh. Does Michael appreciate it?'

'I don't think he's seen it in years. Maybe he never saw it.'

'Do you like it when I do this?'

'Yes.'

'And this way?'

'Yes. Yes. Oh God, yes.'

'But you love Michael?'

'Yes, but I'm a *sgualdrina*. Yes, yes, yes.'

'Yes what?'

'Go on doing that.'

'This?'

'Yes.'

'Do you know what you're really in love with? Your fidelity since you were four. Or whenever. Do you want me to go on?'

'Another bit . . . Yes. Oh James. Oh Jesus.' She groaned.

'You love fucking, don't you?'

'Yes. I love it.'

'You think of it all day, don't you?'

'How did you know?'

'Because I do too. It's a sort of virus. We've both got it. I can taste your cunt in my mouth. Suddenly. I'm walking down Grafton Street or sitting in the RTE studios, listening to Corny Kinlen sounding off or interviewing some old relic of the Twenties, and my mouth fills with the taste of it. Everything disappears. The old face in front of me turns into a visual mash with veins like crushed raspberries and a blue streak of eye and my body is deliquescent, juicing, magnetized, mad to get back into bed with you and be nothing but an assembly of prehensile, oozing surfaces. I have to clench myself, like a fist, to try and function until I *can* get back to you. I know you feel the same thing and I know you hate it. You fight it, and the way you do is by telling me about your son and husband and grandfather, who define you to yourself as a responsible figure: mother, wife, civic entity, and not,' said James, sticking his palm over the dripping hair of her pudenda, 'this, or,' he ran his tongue in under her armpit, 'this sweating crevice. Here,' he swished his tongue around inside her mouth, 'taste your own juices. *I*'m greedy for them. Don't you deny them'

'They're *your* juices. I can tell.'

'They're mixed.'

'We're mingling.'

'As though dying.'

'But you,' he accused, 'keep holding on to yourself. Reconstituting yourself.'

'Well, one has to, doesn't one?'

'To an extent,' James admitted, 'I suppose. Yes.'

'I mean it's not much of a basis – this isn't. For anything?'

'What sort of thing?'

'Plans.'

'You mean it's outside time?'

'Do I?'

'What?'

'Mean that?'

'Well isn't it?' James asked. 'Like that Irish myth. The one about the timeless land, *Tir na n'óg* to which the beautiful Niav lured the warrior, Ossian. He never felt time pass while he was with her but when he came away he found he had aged beyond recognition. That could be about sex. I'll bet it *is* about sex.'

'I wish you wouldn't go on about bloody fairy stories that I knew when I was three.'

'What's the matter?'

She jumped out of bed. 'I *have* to put myself together,' she said. 'I have to go home now and feed the family. I have to function. I don't just mention them to impress you. They exist. I deal with them. Daily. How do I look?' she asked, dabbing at her face. 'I haven't time to re-make up. I look a right mess, don't I?'

'You look great.'

'What's that word you used? Deliquescent? I look that? There's lipstick on my eyelid and mascara on my chin. Oh shit. I can't walk through the lobby like this. I look like a tart and a whore and a Da Kooning woman. I am a tart and a whore.'

'We can't go on meeting like this.'

'No.'

'That was a joke. Meant to be laughed at. Jokes are a mode of communication peculiar to humans.'

'That leaves me out. I'm a prehensile piece of meat.'

'Grainne, don't cry. It'll make you look worse.'

'I can't stand it,' she said, 'the rushing back and forth. The lies. I haven't even time to wash. I smell of you. I'm afraid they'll smell you off me.'

'I know. I'm sorry.'

'You can't know. It's two realities. Different. Demanding. You just stay here or go talk to Corny Kinlen who wouldn't notice if you smelled of pure jism. My lot depend on me. I can't hurt them.'

'I'm sorry.'

'I'm sorry too. I am. I'm spoiling things. I'm unravelling. Like my tights. Which are unravelled. Oh hell. Now how do I look?'

'Better than you think. It's more expression than anything else. Think of the price of bacon. Tighten your lips. Great. You look like a Reverend Mother.'

'Bye.'

'Bye.'

Outside the hotel the streets were smeared with slime. Blue mist eroded the tyres of parked cars. A parking attendant rushed forward for his tip, breathing tatters and streamers of hot breath into cold air. He smelled of tea and bad teeth and in no way deserved a tip, since the street where the cars were parked was public and his position and peaked cap entirely self-assigned.

'A wet aul' evening, Mrs O'Malley,' he said, terrifying her by his knowledge of her name and conceivably of her activities during the last two hours. 'I'll guide you out,' he promised, agitating his arms as though she had been manoeuvring a jet-plane. 'Easy does it. Yer stuck in a bit tight. Pull on the left now. Easy. Left, left, I had a good job and I left.' Could the tea have made him drunk? 'How's Mr O'Malley?' he inquired.

'Grand,' she said, unsure whether he had seen her – where? – with Michael or Owen Roe. He had an anonymous working-class face: red, bunched, prematurely old. She got out in spite of him and gave him fifty pence for conscience' sake. Unemployment in the country was rocketing. She felt herself a parasite.

12

Judith prowled through Kathleen's bedroom, sniffing at underthings scented by lavender bags. In a drawer, she came on romances about women who lingered in conservatories and were wooed by dark, rakish young men.

Kathleen hadn't a pick of sense.

A non-swimmer in the flood of life, she would only reach shore in some strong man's arms. Judith decided to sound out Sparky Driscoll. He had been paying marked attention to her sister which, *if* he knew what he was up to, was all well and good.

Her chance came one day when he brought some American papers for the Da who was busy in the pub. Judith said she was just off to give the dog a run on the beach and, as she'd known he would, he asked could he come.

Bran, the setter, coiled his spine first one way and then the other at such speed that the movements seemed to merge in a flouncing figure of eight: a double dog. He moaned with expectancy.

'Why don't you let him off the leash?'

'He'd chase sheep,' she told Sparky. 'There's method in our rules,' she explained, and frowned at his hallooing laugh.

However, when they reached the strand she released the dog.

Sparky twirled a stick and threw it out to sea. Bran jumped in after it. His bronze coat flashed like a needle ruffling lace; arrowy, his head nosed through spume. Sparky had a way with animals. Also with Kathleen. Judith took it upon herself to describe Owen's courtship of her sister. It had been serious and Sparky ought to be let know.

'I suppose you heard,' she told him, 'that Owen was going

on to be a priest? A Jesuit? He was shut in a seminary from the start of the Great War, in the middle of a bog, miles from anywhere, and completely cut off. They were expected to detach their minds from the world. They didn't even get war news. Then his mother died and he was let out to attend her funeral. He met Kathleen at the wake and it was all up with his being a priest.'

'Just like that?'

'No. He went back in but, when it came to the point, he knew he didn't want to be ordained. His father was heart-broken; it was to have been a great feather in his cap to have a son a Jesuit. Owen is brilliant,' Judith informed deliberately. 'His father blamed Kathleen, as you may imagine. But it was politics too that got him out. He began to envy the lads who were doing the fighting. He wanted to do his bit and be part of what was going on.'

'Why did he go into the seminary in the first place?'

'It was just before the Great War,' she told him. 'There was a great strike here which became a lock-out and the people were starving. A lot of people started singing the "Red Flag" and Owen turned his thoughts to heaven.'

'Is he good-looking? Handsome?'

'I couldn't say. I don't notice that sort of thing.'

'But your sister does?'

Judith shrugged with annoyance. 'She could be misled,' she conceded. 'People here,' she told the Yank, 'can judge a girl harshly for things you mightn't pay attention to. Kathleen's engaged to a prisoner.' She looked at him hard. 'It's a small place. They have nothing to do but talk.'

The sun had gone down. The dog, loping behind them, was reduced by half because of the way his damp coat clung to his body.

Sparky looked at her thoughtfully. 'What a severe creature you can be!' He didn't sound angry, perhaps a bit awed? She hoped she had made him see where his duty lay. 'You're well named. Do you know the story of your namesake, the sacrificial Judith of the Bible?'

'We don't read the Old Testament much,' she told him. 'It's not encouraged.'

'Well, read that bit,' he advised. 'It's in the Book of Kings.'

'I'm going back,' she said. 'It will be dark in no time.'

Sparky turned when she did. 'Why did you tell me all this?' he wanted to know. 'Do you think I'm in love with your sister?'

She had decided by now that he wasn't. She couldn't give Kathleen away though, by admitting that *she* seemed soft on him.

'Oh law,' she said in a jeering voice. 'In love, is it? I was only telling you that she was known as his girl from the minute he was back wearing a collar and tie. There's nothing here for a girl like Kathleen but marriage,' she added anxiously, fearing that she might have failed to make her point or perhaps made it too well. She blushed with vexation but reflected that it was too dark by now for him to see this.

'Do you think I should try and take her away from him?'

'Is it me?'

'So you say things for no reason?'

'Look, you asked to come for a walk. Owen's name came up. So I . . .'

'Warned me off?'

She could hear the humour in his voice, could imagine curls of laughter round his lips. 'Listen,' she appealed, 'I think you don't know the effect you have on people here. Life has been hard: narrow, and then *you* come in flourishing a feeling of— I don't know how to describe it, really: easiness, perhaps, and the comforts of America.'

'You make me sound like the devil.'

'It *is* like the devil tempting people. Look,' again her voice was weak with appeal. She felt ashamed of having been too harsh with him who, after all, knew not what he did. 'Let's talk about something else.'

Sparky laughed. 'What?' he teased.

'I don't know. I'm all muddled now.'

'The fighting?'

'Oh,' she shrugged it off. 'It's over now. What's the use?'

'Is that how people feel? That they'd as soon forget it?'

'*You* tell me. It's what you're here to find out, isn't it?'

Sparky picked up a piece of seaweed shaped like a cat o'

nine tails, whirled and threw it for the dog. Setter and seaweed were the same colour in the dimming light and the long droop of weed looked as though Bran were carrying a second tail in his mouth. Sparky took it back from him and threw it into the dark.

'So Kathleen's feelings could swing the other way too?' he asked. 'My way.'

'Oh the conceit!'

'Don't you think she'd be better off with a man who had some conceit than with one who bolted for a seminary because the world looked hopeless?'

'Have you no faith in spiritual values?' Judith asked seriously. 'What sort of Catholics are you in America?'

Sparky ran a finger down her spine. 'Don't worry,' he said. 'I'm not after your sister.'

'Well, so long as you don't compromise her.'

'Oh grandmother, what big words you use!' He was laughing out of the darkness. Then she felt his arm around her neck, her chin was tilted and he was rubbing his rough, male face against hers, comfortingly, as though he had been some harmless animal creature, the red setter perhaps or a horse whose furry long nose was nuzzling hers.

Judith was numbed: astounded into submission by the tongue sliding dementedly between her lips. Was he *mad*? She wanted to laugh and push him away and instead she felt her lips parting. She felt as though a warm current of water or some unknown, insidious element had taken hold of her. Her body was behaving wildly. Were they both mad? Was this concupiscence? The absurdity of what they were doing was foremost in her mind but her mind seemed to have become detached from her body, like a kite whose string snaps on a windy day. It was he who drew away.

'Never been kissed before, have you?' said his casual voice. 'Well, that's what it's like. You ought to know, you know, before you become a marriage broker.'

Patsy wouldn't believe it. Not of his boys. The cops were down on him. Lazy. He had their number and number was what they worked by: so many arrests to the working hour: so many chats with solid citizens: 'Thought I'd draw your attention, sir, to the side door's being weak, a temptation to the hooligan element. Better be sure than sorry.' – 'Oh indeed, officer!' – 'The youngsters that's going nowadays . . .' – 'Need a bit of the old discipline!' – 'Aye.'

Give Patsy a tune and he'd sing it. What were cops but running dogs for the boorjwa element which, God help us, was on the up and up.

'I've warned you before now, Flynn,' says the pink peeler, 'some of the lads you have here are next door to delinquents, and the super doesn't think you're a good influence on them. The Christian Brothers beyond in Blackrock have you down for the trick was played on them last Christmas.'

'Is it me?' Patsy had gone on doing what he'd been doing when the cop had knocked at the door: cleaning his boots. He held a boot between himself and the cop's face and spat on it with a thick, plopping gobbet of spit. Then rubbed this into the leather.

'That's what *they* say, anyway.' The cop stared past Patsy.

'Libel, calumny and detraction. Where's your proof?'

'If we had any we'd a had you summonsed.'

'So you haven't.'

'You know we haven't.'

The Christian Bros were in the process of educating half the boys in the Youth Club – if educating was what you chose to call what they did. Patsy had been to school to them himself and had their measure. But they'd got their come-uppance last Christmas and Patsy wasn't letting on even in the privacy of his mind whether he'd been in on the joke or not. In gaol, years ago, they'd tried to get him to tell on his mates and he still dreamed that he'd done it without realizing. He'd wake up in a sweat. You got so you tried to lock your thoughts up in a box inside a box inside your head. To get back to the sorting out that was done on the CBs, ha ha, didn't one of the swank restaurants in town ring them up on the twenty-fourth of December last to say the banquet for the graduating pupils was all laid on as directed by Brother Superior with roast chicken, two veg., lashings of drink, and taxis to collect the guests, all set but for a detail or two that the manager would like to discuss with Brother Superior. Well, the old monk who took the call nearly swallowed his tongue. *Banquet*, says he, spitting like fat in a fire. Graduating what? Taxis? Chicken? Brother Superior was as tight as the skin on your elbow and it was no part of the Brothers' policy to spoil their pupils, past, present or to come. The only lashings they gave out were from leather straps. Could Brother Superior be losing his grip?

'Mistake, mistake,' the old Brother Porter had barked into the phone, mad with anxiety lest he somehow get blamed.

'There's no mistake,' says the manager, beginning to think maybe there was and that the price of perishables could be docked from his Christmas bonus. 'Brother Superior in person ordered the whole thing by phone. I spoke to him myself. "Nothing but the best, Mr Doherty," he told me. "It's our centenary, you know." '

'*Who* told you, Mr Doherty?' says Brother Porter, 'a voice on the phone? I'd say *you'd* be responsible for any mistakes, impersonations or the like.' The old fellow was sharpening up under the pressure of fear that the Order might have to fork out.

Patsy's stomach pained with the laughing when he thought of the story. He'd had it from all sides. One of the boys' fathers was in the taxi-business and hadn't seen a red penny for his wasted time. Oh, you could back the monks any day against a businessman: two predators up against each other, snake and scorpion, fox *v.* crane.

'Responsibility,' says the policeman who'd been watching Patsy grin into the leather of his boot, 'that's what anyone who's given charge of the young should have. The Brothers are a fine body of men.'

'Ach,' said Patsy, polishing hard, 'what was it but a joke? Good clean fun?'

'Not this time,' said the cop. '*This* time it's no joke.' He looked around him. 'We could have this place closed down,' he remarked.

Patsy didn't believe him. The Captain had more power than the cop and the cop knew it. He let his eye slide past Patsy's. Fox *v.* crane, thought Patsy and picked up the second boot.

He could feel the copper's dislike. He was sensitive to that. Had been feeling it all his life, hardening himself against it. It was something about him, something he blamed on his childhood. He'd always been slow physically, no good on the sports field, and then there was that something – what? – about him that made people snigger behind his back and pick him last when they were making up teams.

When they were boys, Patsy's brother would complain to their Ma about having to drag Patsy around with him like a tin can tied to a dog's tail and their Ma would tell him to watch his lip and that it was God's will if poor Patsy shwish-wishwish, whispering and making faces behind Patsy's back: 'Sh!'

Even when he joined the IRA, which he did when it was at a low ebb and recruiting had fallen off, there had been some of that. He'd developed a sixth sense for it, so that he was sharper than the whisperers and knew what was in their minds before they did themselves. He'd *known* they'd give him a dangerous job because they considered him expendable. He hadn't cared. He'd been glad to show the stuff he had in him. Maybe in another era he'd have been a hero and a leader? He'd read a lot in his life and had a big vocabulary. Even the Captain remarked on it. 'Patsy's fond of jaw-breakers,' he'd say. That was his joke.

The cop read aloud the titles of books on Patsy's shelf, biding his time or pretending to bide it so as to panic Patsy.

'*Knockinagow*,' read the cop. '*Che Guevara Speaks*.' He looked amused.

'It's a free country.'

'I'm glad you agree,' said the cop. 'No need to free it so, is there, if it's free already? The priests,' he went on, 'are fit to be tied. Father Farrel rang the station twice. He says community relations with the Protestants get set back light years by this sort of thing and that it's not from the Church that the snot-nosed little hooligans get their sectarian hatred.'

Patsy was embarrassed. Two men had just walked into the club. He could see them behind the cop's head through the hatch which separated his quarters from the public premises. The hatch was open and the cop's voice had a carrying ring.

'Urinating up and down the nave,' said the cop with disgust.

One of the fellows in the rec. room was Cormac O'Malley. He was showing the other one round. The man picked up a billiard cue and turned to take a shot. Jesus, it was that Yank that Patsy had warned off in the Shelbourne Rooms. What was the boy thinking of to bring him round here? Sacred Heart, how was Patsy going to face him if Cormac brought him in? Would the Yank denounce him?

'They killed an expensive dog,' said the cop. 'Belonging to the vicar. An Alsatian.'

Patsy edged round him towards the hatch. 'Excuse me,' he said.

'Some sort of black mass,' roared the cop, budging his fat cop's arse no more than an inch. 'Strangled the dog in the church and pissed all around it. Where do they get the ideas, tell me that?'

Patsy tried to reach across the jutting navy-blue backside to close the hatch but things had been hung on it – his space was cramped – and a saucepan fell with a clatter.

'Tell me,' said the cop meaningfully, 'before I tell you.'

The Yank was staring right at Patsy.

'Good inter-community relations are . . .'

The Yank's stare was neither of recognition nor hostility. He seemed not to know Patsy at all. Patsy would deny, he decided, that he'd ever seen the fellow. Stoutly. The guards wouldn't bother him. It was his word against the Yank's. His fear was of the IRA. They didn't like people impersonating them. Men had been kneecapped for less. Patsy's stomach seemed to flop into his bowels and he had an impulse to run out of the house. Hold it, Flynn, he admonished himself. Brazen it out. His hands were clammy. *How* would the IRA hear of it? Oh, they had their ways. He watched Cormac and the Yank approach in slow motion.

The cop (whose name, it came to Patsy who was going to have to introduce him, was Guard Kirwin) remarked that the fence dividing the garden of the club from the garden of the Protestant church showed that the burglars had reached it from here. 'This,' Patsy would have to say, 'is Guard Kirwin.'

And 'this', Cormac might say, 'is Patsy Flynn.' 'Oh,' he imagined the Yank exclaiming, 'is *that* who it is!' Then, somehow, word would reach the I R A.

'Impersonation,' said Guard Kirwin, 'is one thing, but encouraging . . .'

Issuing threats in their name? They'd never stand for that.

'It's bloody negative and backward,' said the guard. 'Give the young fellows something to be *for*, can't you, instead of always something to be *against*? Form a football team. Take them mountain-climbing. Bring in girls.'

Patsy wasn't listening.

'A bit of fun,' said the cop. 'A bit of a laugh. Why do you think they go off to England? It's not only the jobs.'

He was young, Patsy noticed suddenly: a healthy lump. All pink flesh, gleaming. All appetites. Teeth like delph. How dare he come round giving jaw out of him? A chisler. What did he know? Girls? Patsy had never touched a female. Not since his mother and he had given up trusting *her* because of the way she made signs about him when she thought he didn't see. Early. When he was maybe seven.

'Well, I've said what I came to say,' said Guard Kirwin. 'I'll be pushing off.'

Behind his head two faces thrust into the hatch then bounced shyly away. The guard turned and saw them.

'Oh, hullo,' he said cheerily. 'I've been making some inquiries about what happened next door. You'll have heard?'

He walked away with the other two. Checking on Patsy, thought Patsy, but couldn't bring himself to follow. The guards had no proof that anyone from the club had done the burgling. If they had they'd be singing a different tune. Still, they were nosy, seizing the occasion to snoop. He felt feverish. A voice rang out in laughter. Then two others joined in. They were joking. They were outside in the street, laughing. Patsy was shocked.

Suddenly he forgot his fear of the young louts in today's I R A who had no respect for men like him. He forgot that he had been afraid that the American might denounce him. How could he? A Yank. A tourist. Patsy's anger rose at not being recognized. Anger and hurt. It was unfair. After all he'd done. To be ignored, denied, told to bring in *girls*. Trivialization, he thought. Sex. The threat to him was dark. He felt as though the laughter in the street were wiping him out. The three young men were indifferent, self-absorbed, together. Even the young guard.

Picking up his boot which he had over-polished, he began to wonder who *had* committed the odd, angry crime in the church next door. Pissing in the nave, he thought. Murdering a dog? The thought began to excite him in a queer, disgusted way.

Larry phoned from the States to say that he would be in Dublin the day after tomorrow and wanted James to dine with him. Eight p.m. in the Shelbourne, OK? He wanted to hear the best of the tapes. As soon as James had picked out the likeliest interviewees, a camera crew would be coming to film them. Larry himself would be *en route* to Amsterdam. He rang off at a speed which reminded James that time was money and sent him back to a symphony of coughs taped two days before in a home for veteran patriots. Even the voices unafflicted with catarrh were next to impossible to understand. A tape made in a Cork pub was no better. Unsteady laughs racked at it. James hoped the excitement hadn't given any of those old guys a stroke. Re-running the interviews, he managed to make out a couple of phrases: 'Yish, I rimimbir. Chrish, yish.' James had made the mistake of filling the old-timers with drink to loosen their tongues. 'Oh dim were de days!' Dim was right. A frieze of rheumy eyes rose in his memory. Trick noses. Faces reduced to caricature by pressures now forgotten. Limbs like sticks inside the limp flap of their trousers: these, assured the local guide, were indeed the Joe O'Does whom Larry wanted to commemorate, unknown soldiers who had fought with Commandant Tom Barry and known Mick Collins.

'You remember Mick, do you not,' the guide had rallied an old-timer.

Heavy lids blinked. The old man might have been fished out after days spent under water.

'Were you not working with him in England,' the guide encouraged, 'before the Great War? Jimsy Doyle says you were. The Great War, remember?'

Troubled by so much attention, the man reached into a muddied memory and came up with an offering. In a cracked, heart-breaking voice, he began to sing something martial but, so thin was his pipe, that it was moments before the mortified guide recognized 'The British Grenadiers'. He had brought James a veteran of the wrong army. Titters. Claps. The tape fizzed with hilarity.

'Remember the Munster Fusiliers?'

'Towrowrow Alexander or even Hercules,
    Ulysses or Lysander . . .'

'Yiz have tin ears!'
'Mons, Wipers . . .'

    'Goodbye, don't cry . . .'

'Sing "The Lily of Killarney" for us, there's a good man.'
'Sure where did Giniral Barry learn to fight but wid de Tommies!'

The next tape featured Miss Lefanu-Lynch.

She could have stepped out of *Gone with the Wind* or *Great Expectations*. Swathed in lace, she came on like a TV ad, explaining, lest James not know, that her lace was from Limerick and made by hand. It was the colour of boiled potatoes and so was her face: a mashed affair. She was eighty-one.

'Limerick is noted for its lace,' she said instructively, 'for the verse-form improperly associated with the town and for the last stand made there by the Irish aristocracy. That was in 1691. James Shit-on-himself had let them down the year before. I refer to James II whom the Irish, on that account, called James Shit-on-himself, *Séamus an chaca*.'

If the Joe O'Does were inarticulate, Miss Lefanu-Lynch spoke like a book. She was used to interviews and started this one by handing James her album of press-cuttings. Memories,' she told him, 'culled in the garden of yesteryear.'

There were photographs of herself unveiling plaques, addressing rallies, attending funerals and marching in parades. From the Twenties to the Sixties she had marched, then taken to the bed from which she was conducting this interview. Though protected by Cellophane, the browned edges of her cuttings crumbled like cornflakes over James's lap.

Miss Lefanu-Lynch was the purest of the pure. 'I am mindful, Mr Duffy, of the many who went before, unsung heroines like my poor sisters, Kitty and Bridge, who heeded the clarion call of destiny and laboured in obscurity till the end.' Though all had suffered for the cause, no relative of hers would ever accept a pension from the successive Irish governments which had offered them. They would neither deal with compromisers nor hearken to the siren call of comfort.

James's recoiling eye was held by her scorched yellow ones. She hitched her shawl on to elbows sharp as knitting needles, then asked what he wanted of her. Why was he wasting her diminished stock of time?

Nervously, he said he had hoped for something more personal.

'Oh, human interest? Gossip? I'm afraid, Mr Duffy, you've come to the wrong person. People do not fight revolutions to exalt the commonplace but to make the worthwhile available to ordinary people.'

James fancied he could smell the clay of the cemeteries where she had so often dished out such sentiments. There were chrysanthemums in a bowl. Perhaps the rank odour came from them?

On impulse and because she had annoyed him, he asked, 'I wonder if you ever ran across a woman called Judith Clancy who became a nun? I believe she knows some story connected with an American fund-raiser, Sparky Driscoll, who was killed over here in 1922. I'm interested in the details of the affair.'

'Mary. My specs.' Miss Lefanu-Lynch took a pair of thick-lensed glasses from the maid who had stood in attendance on her through the interview. When she put them on, James realized that, without them, she must be near blind. Magnified, two pansy-sized orbs gazed at him with a guileless air. She looked now like a sweet old thing adrift in her own benevolence. But the lemur look must be covering her first scrutiny of him.

'What do you know of her?' she asked.

'Well, I've tried interviewing her. But it's a little difficult. She's . . .'

'Senile?' suggested his hostess. 'Say it if you mean it. Words don't frighten me, Mr Duffy. Never have. She probably is. She was never normal, you know. I thought she'd been locked up years ago?' She threw a taunting glance at him, raising her spectacles for a moment to show inflamed, screwed-up flesh around her naked eyes. 'Anyway, Judith Clancy was never of the least importance in the National Struggle.'

'But she did *know* people, didn't she? Owen O'Malley? Sparky Driscoll? She must have known them well, known things about them?'

'Unofficial things you mean? You're muck-raking, I suppose? Don't count on me for help. God knows I had no sympathy with Owen O'Malley from the day he turned his coat and accepted the so-called "Free State" in 1927 . . .'

James sighed.

'Well, this can be of little interest to you,' said Miss Lefanu-Lynch angrily. 'We have become used to being treated as bores, Mr Duffy. Those of us who remained faithful to the last all-Ireland parliament elected in the last all-Ireland parliamentary election of 1918 are used to being denied media coverage. President Wilson, to be sure, had a prejudice against the Irish . . .'

He saw that she could not stop herself. Words in her memory were strung like necklaces. Perhaps Larry might like to use her precisely for this reason? Cut back and forth from this unfaltering fury to a changing Ireland: traffic jams, bingo games, tower blocks, then this anomaly with her timeless broad effects?

'Owen O'Malley was no ally of ours after '27, but to say that he misused American funds is a dastardly lie. If Judy Clancy is giving credence to that old canard, she is mad. I always thought she was sexually unstable. Yes, sexually unstable. There was an imbalance there. She may have had a crush on Owen or on the American. I never listen to gossip, so I can't tell you.'

'Might she have been put into a convent to hush some scandal up?'

'Piffle! Misguided Owen O'Malley may have been but he was straight as a die. Do you expect me to malign the dead?' Miss Lefanu-Lynch removed her glasses, shrank her eyes and blotted James out. 'Ask me about something else if you want to,' she invited. 'Then it will be time for my nap.'

James asked her opinion of the current IRA campaign.

Miss Lefanu-Lynch slid down in the bed and closed her eyes. 'I may not live to see it,' she said, 'but the British will have left this island e'er long. History will uphold us, Mr Duffy. The present generation is one of the finest our people have produced.'

The maid moved towards the door, her hand expectant on the knob. James had a last look at the mausoleum of a room where infusions of dust were gathering. The old woman kept her eyes shut, simultaneously dismissing and treating him to the full-dress death-bed rehearsal towards which, he supposed, she must have been manoeuvring throughout the interview.

'Well, thank you,' he told the blue-veined or blue-painted eyelids. 'Most grateful,' he blurted, unnerved by the convincing deadness of the face, 'for . . . your help.'

The corpse-face opened its mouth and snored. The maid showed James out and left him at the top of a flight of granite steps equipped with a shoe-scraper but no porch. Rain dripped from the house's eaves and gathered in pools in the drive. Evergreens, as big as tents, offered oases of shelter along the length of this but in the spaces between them he saw that he would ruin his shoes and coat. He should have rung for a taxi, but the door had closed and he lacked the nerve to ring and ask to be readmitted. Instead, he darted and squelched down the drive, pausing under trees but deliberately not looking back to the house, through one window of which, he suspected, his plight might be being watched with satisfaction.

However, Miss Lefanu-Lynch was not wasting her time at

the window. As soon as she heard the front door slam, she hauled herself up in the bed, wriggling backwards into a position in which she was propped and haloed by a nimbus of lace-edged pillows.

'Mary?' She waited until the maid appeared at her door. 'Gone?'

'He is.' The maid wore a livery, as few did nowadays: black dress and stockings, lacey white cuffs and apron and a scrap of lace, like a diadem, in her hair. She was young, in her twenties, but of a Republican family and her mother and grandmother had both worked for Miss Lefanu-Lynch.

'Telephone,' requested her mistress.

Mary took an ivory-coloured one from a drawer and laid it on the bed. Miss Lefanu-Lynch dialled a number.

'Hullo,' she spoke into the instrument. 'Liadán here. You hadn't forgotten that you'd let me have this number, had you? It *is* urgent, or I wouldn't have presumed to use it. More delicate perhaps than urgent, though that will be for you to determine. I won't take much of your time. No, no need to flatter me. I know my place. I'm an old has-been but eager to serve and, as you thought, our interests do sometimes coincide, even if . . . Yes, yes, all right, all right, I'm glad to hear you say so. No, indeed, *real-politik* has not been my sphere, any more than consistency has been yours. You might say we complement each other. Yes. Well, I'm ringing about a muck-raker, an American working, I'm not clear for whom, on a film about 1921. He's particularly interested in Owen O'Malley. You don't? You do? Well, of course I supposed he was or I wouldn't have seen him, would I? But he may have got out of hand, got a swelled head. You know how irresponsible such people can be. Well indeed! From all our points of view. When he rang me first, he told me the film was designed to promote our cause in the US, raise money, counter the Peace-Ladies' efforts, etc. Now, instead, it seems he's thrilled with himself at having scented the bone of a buried skeleton which . . . I'm coming to that. You have to be patient with the old. We're slow-witted, you know, and a touch suspicious. I never know where you people put your loyalties. No, not bitter. Just unsure. Owen O'Malley. Does *his* reputation still count with the party? It does? I'm reassured. To be sure, he was a weathercock himself and this is the point . . . Yes, you've guessed it . . . yes . . . exactly. No. No good at all if it should come to light. I'm glad you agree. Who? Judy Clancy, his sister-in-law. Well, so did I, but it seems that not at all. Alive and kicking and running at the mouth like a leaky tap. What's more she is, for some reason, out of the convent. Don't ask me. Probably *non compos mentis* and liable to say *anything*. Very sensitive, I should have thought . . . As you say, above party interests, but then *I* am in no position to do anything. The graveyard guardian I think one of your people called me not long ago in your party organ. Did you think I wouldn't? Oh, my poor man, if I was sensitive to such snubs I'd be dead long ago. God knows I have one foot *in* the grave already. What keeps me back is the hope that what we've waited for so long may be at hand. Well, we won't argue. I'm glad to have helped. Do let me know what transpires. Any time. Yes. You'd be welcome. I'm always here and will be until I go to the other place, which can't be long now. One of these days then. Goodbye till then. God bless.'

Cormac's father had invited him to lunch.

'Like a drink?'

They were in a goodish place, Cormac thought. The menu was in French and there was a waiter just for drinks. Cormac considered his father's question with care.

'I'll have some wine from your bottle. I'm twenty months under age, though.'

'They don't care,' his father told him. 'You're tall enough to be sixteen.'

'Have you something important to tell me?'

Cormac had meant this to come out funny, the way they did it in movies. But his father looked squashed. Cormac tried to scoop up the good humour which was leaking out of the situation. He waved at a trolley loaded with crab, olives and poached eggs decorated to look like children's paintings. 'Well, this is a bit unusual,' he said, 'for you and me, I mean? Oh,' he heard his embarrassed voice mumble: 'Forget it.'

His father gave him a hurt look. 'Don't you think we *should* see each other this way sometimes? You and I? Your mother takes over when we're at home – which is grand, but . . . then there's the aunt . . . house seems in a constant . . .' As though wearied by the topics looming like traffic signs along the road of this particular conversation – getting to be a man; should talk; get to know each other; the future; subjects you'll be taking for Matric; College, etcetera, etcetera – the Dad let his breath out in a vagabond little puff: 'Peugh!' he said, 'well, you know what I mean?' He raised his glass. 'Cheers!'

'Cheers!'

They drank. Then ordered. Then, again, it was time to talk. Cormac ate a bread roll and tried the wine. It was OK. Nothing special. He wondered if he was destined to become an alcoholic? Ran in families, didn't they say? Of course, there was will-power. Interested, he drank some more. What he was tasting, it struck him, was not the stuff in this particular glass but possible destiny. A thrill ran through him but right away he felt ashamed of letting himself play-act when poor Daddy was a victim. The next sip tasted foul but had maybe gone to his head for he seemed to have finished the glass.

'More?'

'No, thanks.'

'Well, I'm glad you like it. Got to go easy though. It's treacherous.'

Cormac could have wept. Luckily, the first course came then. It too was foul: cold poached eggs and spinach. The sort of thing his mother might dish up for Sunday lunch: refrigerator scrapings. Here, though, it had announced itself as *oeufs florentines. Oeuf* meant 'egg'. Gaelic '*uv*'. There was a tongue-twister: *dih dov duv uv ov ar nav.* Meant 'a black ox ate a raw egg in heaven'. Try it on the Dad. Don't be daft. Probably he's the one taught it to you. Probably has a stock of them. Tongue-twisters were sobriety-tests, weren't they? Say British Constitution – Brishish Conshtipation. – Sorry, sir. Have to take away your driving licence. You're ploothered and a menace to the community when behind a wheel. – Offisher, I inshish on my rish. I'm a Gaelic speaker. Conshtitutional rish . . . –Oh, you're a clever Dick, are you? Say this then: *Dih dov duv uv ov ar nav.*

Cormac cupped his hands, blew into them and inhaled his own winey breath. It had a pleasantly adult smell: worldly, not sour as his father's often was. His father's – Cormac hated admitting the fact to himself – smelled sometimes like really grotty old plumbing.

'Well,' said the said father, 'we don't seem to have much to say for ourselves, do we?' He said he knew how Cormac must be feeling. 'How's the grub?'

'Good.'

'Good!'

There was a silence while they ate it. Then Cormac's father said that the reason he knew how fellows felt about being brought to restaurants like this was because he'd felt that way himself when *his* father used to get him a few hours' leave from the concentration-camp of a school in which the old man had stuck him for personal ends.

'He'd take me for a big tuck-in to salve his conscience then lob me back.'

Saint Finbar's had been the worst, grimmest and most repressive school in Ireland, but Cormac's father's father hadn't cared. He'd hoped to curry favour with the monks who ran it so as to sell them wool from his woollen mills.

'I was offered up like Esau by Abraham, except that in my case there was no reprieve. The monks were sadists,' said Daddy. 'Maniacs!' He knocked a knife off the table and said: 'Leave it. The waiter will bring another.'

Cormac had heard all this many times. Poor Daddy's childhood had been like Oliver Twist's. The sacrifice had worked, though. For decades, the schools of the Order had made their uniforms from the grandfather's wool. From pyjamas and underpants to blazers and socks, generations of pupils had been rigged out in the thorny products of the O'Malley looms. O'Malley blankets were on all the monastery beds. The monks' trousers were tailored from O'Malley 'priest's cloth' and their overcoats from O'Malley hopsack.

'Conformist sheep clad in sheep-shearings,' said Daddy. 'My father was an underpants maker: a businessman. All my life I've hated businessmen. Your grandfather was an old fart. Between ourselves, that's what he was: an old fart.'

Cormac looked anxiously around at other tables to see if anyone was listening. His father confided that he did not expect Cormac to respect *him* just because he was his father. No: if he were to behave like an old fart then Cormac had licence to think that that was what he was.

'Left his mills to your great-uncle,' said Daddy angrily. 'Owen Roe wormed his way into his confidence. Cared as little about the business as I did but knew how to curry favour. Oh yes. Politic. Slimey. Now he clips coupons.'

A waiter hurried over to pour the last of the wine.

'We'll have another bottle,' said Cormac's father. 'Have you ordered your second course yet?' he asked Cormac. 'Are we all set? Oh God,' he exclaimed, 'I sound like *him*! Like the old fart. I can't stand that. Food was all he could give me. Food and money. He was always pushing them at me. Like the witch in *Hansel and Gretel*. Used to press fivers into my pockets. The school matron was always fishing them out of the wash. Well, I hope I'm *not* like him. Not sure how to *be* a father, really. You'll have to help if I go wrong, Cormac. Blow the whistle. *Tell* me. I never had a model, you see. Except that I learned what *not* to do – not to send you to boarding school, for instance. I didn't do that – so maybe you'll be normal?'

'Daddy!' Cormac couldn't take this any more. 'Lower your voice. You'll be *heard*.'

Again his father looked squashed and Cormac wished he hadn't spoken. When the food came, he saw his father brighten, then droop.

'It's *good*,' Cormac reassured him. He had chosen pheasant because he'd never had it. The meal was educational, whatever else. Actually, he enjoyed food and was planning to have something *flambé* for dessert. 'Pudding' they'd called it in his English school. They were puddings themselves: heavy and thickish with a childish sense of humour which was both dirty-minded and embarrassed over the slightest thing.

Making conversation, he told his father how disappointing it had been on his first evening to find that the promised 'pudding' was a raw apple. But you had to watch it with the Dad. He felt reproached and begged Cormac to remember that sending him to an English school had never been his idea. Never. He was all against boarding schools after his own experience. In a day school, at the worst, a parent knew what was going on.

'I told that headmaster of yours here that if he laid a violent finger on you I'd have him before the courts in two shakes. Told him I'd send you to one of the interdenominational schools. Just you let me know, Cormac, if there's trouble of any kind. Just bring it to my attention.' The Dad looked fighting mad and suddenly Cormac noticed that he'd got a bit saggier-looking while they'd been away. This made him feel sad.

'Don't worry,' he soothed. 'School's all right. I can handle it.'

'Would you like to go to some other school?'

Cormac thought about this, then said what Doris, the char, always wound up saying when she'd been considering giving his mother notice: 'The divil you know is better than the divil you don't.'

'Divil? What divil?'

'The one you know,' Cormac explained, 'is better. It's what Doris says. Remember?'

'Oh, Doris . . .'

'Mind if I suck these bones?'

'Bones?' His father stared at him. 'Oh suck away,' he decided. 'Chew and crunch them if you like. The Italians do that. How are your teeth? Does your mother send you to the dentist regularly? That's very important, you know. Irish teeth are bad. It's genetic.'

Michael had sunk into several minutes' consideration of the matter of the boy's teeth. Ought he to know about them? Did other fathers keep abreast of such things? Had *his* father? No. But then the old fart had been saving his energies for the socially useful purpose of making money for his family and his country. Shouldn't have called him an old fart to the boy. Michael decided sadly that he was making a balls of this lunch. At your peril did you abandon the old forms, the tracks tried and true: my boy, I must pass on a few words of sure-fire wisdom. What? Neither a borrower nor a lender be. Guard your spondulicks. Oh dear, had he no sure values at all? Surely a man must? Must he? Better get the waiter to bring some water. Catching waiters' eyes was one talent which Michael had not buried but trained. Drink no more anyway. What *did* you say to a fourteen-year-old who happened to be your son? Easier if he wasn't. Probably had lots to conceal and why shouldn't he? Secrets from that half-world of when you were neither boy nor man. Probably looking for a man to model himself on and finding him in Owen Roe. Bastard had the showy virtues: rose early, kept a sharp crease in his pants. Twit! The uncle reminded Michael of his own father who'd been a workhorse and never out of harness. A sort of robot. God knew what passions he'd repressed and channelled into industry. Lashings of energy. A face like a tool. He'd been ashamed of Michael from the word go. Shoved him off to school early and told the monks to be hard on him. 'He needs a firm hand,' Michael remembered him telling them. 'For his own good. For the good of his immortal soul.'

'Water, sir?' proposed the waiter.

Had Michael ordered it? Must have. 'They've got *crêpes flambées*,' he told Cormac, recalling himself to his hostly duties. 'They're really good, made with a sauce containing three different liqueurs. A bit heady but good. It's for two. Shall I order one for us?'

Cormac said he'd rather have ice-cream. He poured water into Michael's glass. Thinks I'm drunk, does he?

'*Pêches Melba* then,' Michael told the waiter. 'And coffee. Did I tell you,' he asked Cormac, 'that at St Finbar's they'd skin the arse off any boy caught reading the *News of the World*?' Now why had he said that? Cormac looked surprised. Had they been talking about something different then? Don't falter. Confidence was worth a load of consistency. 'We used to get it smuggled in from England,' Michael explained, 'wrapped inside the *Catholic Herald*. Very primitive people monks. Don't forget to tell me if you have any trouble with them. They're good for getting exam results though,' said Michael responsibly. 'Statistics show. Good at getting boys into college. Still, one can pay too highly for anything.'

'I'm OK.'

'In the interests of keeping healthy minds in healthy bodies, our crowd made us work on the monastery farm.' Michael stopped and drank some water. The rest of this memory was unsuitable. Censor. Opportunities for discreet bestiality had been liberally available at St Finbar's farm and liberally availed of. Primitive. Primitive! Michael drank more water with a shudder. 'Luckily,' he told his son, 'I had a talent. I was the star of the choir and the choirmaster was a power in the place. Yes.'

Again he shut up, sorrowing over the loss of his singing voice and the disappointment he'd brought to the old teacher who had obtained so many favours for him. He'd got Michael off soccer, got him passes to go into the local town and, in the end, when Michael was found to have buggered and destroyed the anus of a sheep, had managed to hush up the scandal and persuade Michael's father – enraged, astounded, shamed – to send the boy to Rome to have his voice trained for Grand Opera. The old man had wept when Michael came to say goodbye: '*Un bel dì vedremo*,' he'd smiled through his tears. 'You'll pay me back. I'll see the name of a pupil of mine on a Covent Garden programme.' Now he was dead. Michael wished he'd written to him in the optimistic years when he was in Rome. He hadn't, had he? He tried to remember one small note or even card being sent by a grateful Michael back to St Finbar's. A Christmas card? Maybe. At best.

'I'm afraid,' Michael had to confess to Cormac, 'I'm not feeling up to snuff. Could you get the man to call a taxi?'

The boy looked mortified. Michael wondered could he get across the restaurant without help. The floor was rising and again rising in tidal ascent. It was the emotion. Always made him tiddly. 'Can I lean on your shoulder?' he asked, abandoning pride. It would be worse if he fell.

'Of course.'

At the door, cold air restored him. 'I'm afraid we didn't have much of a talk. I'm sorry about this,' he apologized.

'That's all right.'

'Boys change so fast at your age. I don't . . .'

'Don't worry about it.'

'There's nothing you'd . . .?'

278

'No.'

'Because if there were, I hope you would feel you could come to me with it, Cormac. No need to go bothering your great-uncle.'

'Here's the taxi!' shouted Cormac. 'Listen,' he said precipitously, 'thanks for lunch. I enjoyed it. Really. Will you be OK now, on your own? Sure? Then I'll say goodbye. I've got to go and . . .'

Michael didn't learn what he had to do. The door had slammed. Cormac, young, troubled, cheeks pink in the whipping wind, waved in what was probably relief as the taxi drove away, delivering his father and himself to the separate solace of anonymity.

13

'Sparky's after asking me to go to America,' Kathleen repeated. 'Ask him, if you don't believe me. He said there was nothing here for a girl like me, but that he'd sponsor me because I'd never be happy married to a man like Owen O'Malley.'

'What does *he* know about that?'

'He had a couple of talks with Owen.' Kathleen was like a freshly lit lamp, expanding and bright with triumph. 'And he knows *me*.'

'You're cracked!' Judith shouted. Memory of the treacherous way her own body had responded to Sparky's kiss undermined argument. No wonder they spent so much time instilling morality into girls, my goodness! And etiquette and common sense.

Luckily, Owen was once more away. He'd come back from prison and they'd all spent Christmas together. Now he was in Dublin politicking. He was to have a seat in the new parliament. The British grip was off the reins, a new era dawning and Owen all set to be an important man. What was *wrong* with Kathleen that she couldn't see this? The kiss, thought Judith, and felt a sickening in her stomach.

Kathleen tossed her foot. She was sewing something, stabbing at it with her needle as though it were alive and disagreeable. 'Oh, Owen!' She shrugged. 'He's awful. Well, you saw, didn't you?'

It was true that gaol had made Owen bad-tempered. He had taken a scunner against Sparky Driscoll and had even drawn Judith aside to ask her why the American came round so often. 'People will say it's for Kathleen,' he said, and she'd guessed that someone had been talking already. '*They*'ve no delicacy where women are concerned. They're coarse,' he warned. 'Or is it spying he is? Coming here for the pennyworth of lookabout?'

'He comes here for my father,' she'd told him. 'They talk about America.' She was trying to pour oil on troubled waters.

The truth was that Driscoll had started avoiding the old man. The Da was drinking too much and his store of anecdote had been used up. He was down now to repeating street names, like a child who gets stuck in the middle of a lesson. 'Calumet Avenue,' he would sigh. 'Calumet. Were you ever there, did you say? No? What about Dorchester Heights?' He could have been reciting a litany. There was no connecting thread and you waited for the *miserere*. 'The lights,' mused the Da vaguely, 'Oh, bedad, the lights! We used to have Thursday-morning specials in the grocery,' he'd recall and nod his head in a mixture of happiness and regret. Half the time his family had no idea what he was talking about.

Judith got the cities mixed up. Either from need or adventure, her father had been in several. When he talked of hobos who jumped trains, it had to cross your mind that he might have tried the game himself, though he wouldn't demean himself by saying so. It was clear that he had travelled poorer routes than Sparky Driscoll, who seemed to find the Da's enthusiasms puzzling. It didn't take second sight to see that the American found much of the grandeur the Da remembered poor stuff.

'Yes,' he'd say a breath late for spontaneity, 'it's lively there, I suppose. Folksy.' The condescension was the more wounding for Sparky's efforts to conceal it.

Judith decided he was a snob. How could such a man call himself a revolutionary? Or be trusted by revolutionaries?

'Did you and Owen have a tiff?' She had chosen the trivial word with care. 'He's had a bad time,' she reminded her sister. 'He's been in *gaol*.'

Kathleen stabbed and tossed. Her needle flew. Her foot twitched as though to some frivolous tune. What she was sewing, Judith saw, was a bead-bag suitable for a dance. 'I could wring Owen's neck sometimes,' said Kathleen. 'Sparky,' she added dreamily, 'thinks we put things off too much. He says hope is a disease and that we should live now for tomorrow might never come. I was telling him about the dance at the Devereux's and he said it would be a great way to go, to die dancing.' She laughed at the enormity of this. Judith saw her sister in the grip of folly. 'Under a chandelier,' Kathleen said, quivering perhaps at the reflections and memories of shots. 'Tomorrow didn't of course,' she remembered soberly, 'come for some.'

'And Owen,' her sister reminded her, 'was arrested.'

'Yes.'

'And had a right,' said Judith relentlessly, 'to suppose that you'd keep faith with him while he was locked away.'

Kathleen drooped.

'Did Sparky,' Judith pressed her advantage, 'say he'd marry you?'

'He's against pinning people down,' Kathleen stabbed a bead on to pink satin, 'or pinning himself. He wants me to come to America without obligation on either side.'

'Convenient!'

'It's from delicacy,' Kathleen defied. 'He'd want me to feel free.'

'You're not living in a penny romance.' Though maybe Kathleen was? 'Has he,' Judith produced the word with distaste, 'said that he loves you?' One must get things clear if the mad girl was to be brought to her senses. Oh, the *senses*! Judith was stricken by the double meaning.

'Not in words.' Kathleen had that girlish simper so maddening to well-wishers.

Hope, Judith saw – she saw everything; it was her curse – had turned Kathleen's head. There was a feeling of urgency in the country. Like looters when the fighting paused, people were eager to snatch at pleasure. Kathleen had a pink satin dress in her wardrobe which she hadn't worn since the Devereux dance. The bag she was sewing had been cut from a remnant of the same satin.

'He's a lovely dancer,' said the bewitched creature who needed locking up. 'I can make him love me,' she confided, 'I know I can.'

*

Memory was the Queen of Spades in the three-card trick. Some agency – God? – like a fair-ground trickster, shuffled, flashed, then whisked it out of sight.

'Why do you *want* to remember?' impatient nuns used to ask Judith when she was in the convent.

They had smelled out the worldliness of her wanting to hold on to bits of her life which she was supposed to have given to God.

Priests had wasted breath on her, preaching joy at being a bride of Christ.

But was she an abducted bride?

And what was the glisten of shame winking blackly out at her from oblivion? Something wrong? Something in need of expiation?

Ha! Armed now, she faced her confessor. This was a scruple, see, official currency in confessionals. It was not just faddy self-concern.

'I feel remorse,' she had claimed cannily. 'I need absolution. To get that I must confess. To confess, I must know.'

One young confessor took her seriously for a while, but was replaced by an elderly, domineering Jesuit.

'Have you seen a doctor?' This, he implied, was not a religious matter at all.

Now, in this place, they *wanted* her to remember. They'd even brought round this instrument, the cassette-recorder. *That* could change everything. She had always had flashes of immediate memory. But they disappeared. Went out like lights. Could not be recaptured and pieced together.

It wasn't as easy as she'd hoped, though, to trap memory on the recorder. Words were clumsy. She got excited. Images faltered as you tried to describe them. The pace of speech broke up the flow of vision.

'Do you know the story,' she asked the Principal Girl, 'of the fairy mansion that rises from the bog at night ablaze with lights and rocked by music?'

'Yes, it's an old story.'

'And the traveller who enters is in danger of never escaping. If he eats fairy food he'll sink with all the company into the bog at cock-crow and be trapped in fairyland forever.'

The girl was quick. 'You're afraid of memory?' she guessed. 'You think you'll be trapped in it? You don't want to talk about the past?'

'I do, I do, but . . .'

'What?'

'I don't know.' Judith was suddenly tired. 'My poor brain is addled.'

'Do you want me to take away the recorder?'

'Leave it, girl, leave it. I can't be worse than the way I am.'

The girl went away. Later, Judith plugged the thing in and talked to it. It was company if nothing else. One thing, she told it, that was becoming clear to her was that she had never been sure of anything. Ever. In her girlhood, people kept things from her. Lied. From the best of motives. During the Troubles, the less a young person knew the better for all concerned. Facts were in short supply but principles abounded. Great hell-raking talk. Gossip. No middle ground. Flashes of close-up vision: her dog's gay tail, waving like a blackboard duster, rubbing out – what? The flapping sole of a boot lolling like a foolish tongue; a wet coat steaming; a load of glimmering sprats, guns, milk-churns, red whorls of blood weaving together in a stream; a silver, no white, thing floating on it: a cigarette? What could you make of that? Useless. She pressed the button to erase and clear the tape.

She didn't want anyone coming on such babble.

Snatches of conversation made more sense.

'You'd want to be leery,' Owen had said, 'with Irish Americans. Why do you think de Valera fell foul of them? Personalities? My eye. It was money. The so-called Friends of Irish Freedom used the Irish cause to raise funds which they then turned round and used *in America*. For their own interests. I'm telling you. We have the figures: black and white. By the end of 1920 their so-called "Victory Fund" had contributed exactly $115,000 to the movement over here and spent $750,000 in the US.' Mutters. Whispers. Owen had always been doubtful of Sparky Driscoll. He banged the table. 'We're not their prime concern. Always remember that. They have their own interests and put them first. A lesson.'

Once, a slanderous story was printed in the *Gaelic American* which Sparky Driscoll brought to the house. According to it, de Valera 'clandestinely withdrew $20,000 from New York banks'. A lie. Even Dev's opponents agreed about this. It showed you had to watch the Yanks. Their politics were dirty.

Mistrust was the order of the day. That was the Christmas of 1921.

Lucifer, they said, had started the first civil war and put his mark on all those that followed.

A later memory was of a hospital: a big old eighteenth-century ward and herself lying in it tended by nuns. Owen bent over the bed and Kathleen sat on a chair. Peonies they'd brought. Red splotches. Top-heavy and scentless. She'd been ill, they said, and missed the wedding. Here were the photographs. The Civil War was over. What Civil War? Over, over, never mind.

'We lost.' Owen's mouth twisted in bitterness. 'The opportunists are in power. The best grow worse. It was all to be predicted.' People who'd never done a hand's turn for God, man, or Ireland had marched in the victory parade while Republicans were in internment camps.

Talk of something cheerier. Kathleen was pregnant. Yes. Smiles, kisses, congratulations. Tears.

'What was wrong with me?' Judith asked.

'Don't you remember?'

'No.'

'Our other visits?'

'No.'

Kathleen began to cry. Owen told her not to upset herself. It would be bad for the baby.

'You were ill,' he told Judith. 'Don't bother your head about the past. Rest,' he advised her. He had brought magazines. Oranges and grapes. Hot-house grapes in those days were what you got. They were firm, like sea-smoothed glass, with a bloom and a bite such as you never got on the ones going now.

Later she found herself working in the same hospital as a nun. How had that come about?

'Don't you remember?' the chaplain asked her.

'No.'

'Do you regret entering?'

'I don't know.'

Owen came back to see her and advised her to stay put. Her father was gaga. The drink. Seamus was in medical school and they'd got a man to manage the pub. No, she couldn't come out and mind him. She wasn't up to it. He threatened her. Did he? Yes. With some story. It slid round the edges of her mind, slimy with menace, what? Frightened, she stayed where she was but got nightmares, delusions and had to be given electro-shock. Now, foraging in her mind, the old images were back after lying dormant for decades. There was violence. Blood. Secrecy. She would haul out and confront it. What else had she to do now? Die? She'd die anyway. Had someone tried to murder her? Owen? She had written to Seamus years ago asking, in veiled terms – nuns' letters were read by Reverend Mother – that he come and help her get things straight. He never answered. The family behaved as though she had done some dreadful thing. Could she have betrayed someone? Whom? How?

This time she did not erase the tape. Let the rubbish pour out. Everything, silly and sensible. Later, she'd sift through and try to make sense of it.

Corny Kinlen received a phone call.

The man on the other end of the line was his immediate superior and spoke with that excessive heartiness which often means that an Irishman is finding himself obliged to be more unpleasant than he would like.

'Corny, me auld warrior, yer after stirring up a desperate hornets' nest. You'll know what I'm referring to? You don't? Well, the divil hice ye, man, you should keep your antennae better tuned. I've had higher-ups leaning on me till I'm gone two-dimensional. Yes; it *is* your fault. Listen, does the name Judith Clancy ring a bell? That's the lady. Are you beginning to get the picture? Well, it seems that you turned this American – right, right, Duffy, that's the boyo. Stinks to high heaven. Sensitive isn't the word. As much as either of our jobs are worth. No, I'm *not* exaggerating. Call him off. Well, do your best. No question of RTE touching anything he might produce? OK? The real danger would be a leak to the gutter press. What do you want to know for? It's of no interest to the world today. Yes: an old skeleton with a bone in every cupboard. Corny, it's yesterday's news but reputations could suffer. Look, I'll tell you some *other* time. Not on this phone, OK? What do you mean what do I mean? Ah, you watch too many movies. Of course I do not think your phone is tapped or mine either. Ever hear of crossed lines? Idle operators monitoring and etcetera. Discretion is the better part. *Seadh go deimhin agus na habair focal.* I don't know how you keep your job on our national media with that Liverpool accent you have in Gaelic. Let me know when you've got that settled, OK?'

'Mind your mouth,' said Judith to her brother. He had a smile which alerted her to the presence of a dirty meaning. Like the crack in a shutter, this could lead to illuminations which she preferred to avoid. In the same spirit, she had borrowed her father's old hat and put on bits of masculine gear. If people thought her a tomboy, well and good. It meant she could go out with Sparky and Seamus without embarrassment.

Seamus had been talking about Timmy Moynihan, the caretaker at the Devereux Estate who had invited the Clancys to bring Sparky to see the place. The owners were away and Timmy would show them round.

'He's a funny fellow,' Seamus had been telling Sparky. 'Was mad to come in with the IRA and at the same time is as proud of the house as if he owned it.'

Sparky was surprised that the caretaker hadn't been fired when the owners found out he'd connived with the IRA to let them use the ballroom.

'Ah well now,' Seamus looked crafty, 'they may have thought a caretaker well in with the lads was a sort of insurance, don't ye know. A lot of big houses were burned down last year in reprisal for police destruction of our people's property. Better dancing than burning, the Devereux may have thought. Anyway, Timmy is very close to the family. Queer feudal relationships you get in those big houses. The children play together when they're small and sometimes go on playing when they're big.' It was at this point that Judith told her brother to mind his mouth.

She was alert for trouble and determined not to step one hand's breadth from her sister's side. She had persuaded Seamus to join the expedition for fear that she mightn't manage the chaperoning on her own. Nature was against her. Birds sang. The ironwork of the estate gates had been gilded and the scrolled tips painted blue so that the gates seemed to have netted a stretch of sky.

Seamus led them to the house by a short cut through dense beech woods.

'We used to trespass here when we were small,' Kathleen told Sparky. 'We thought there might be man-traps.'

'It became one later,' said Judith. 'And poor Owen fell into it.' She was walking between Sparky and her sister whether they liked this or not.

'There's the house!' Seamus cupped his hands and yodelled for Timmy and also, perhaps, to defy the clothy, somehow menacing dusk. Sounds were muffled by leafmould. There was an illicit feel to their presence which set Judith's nerves on edge. They had left the beech trees and reached a walk of ornamental evergreens: magnolias, rhododendrons and great regimented hedges of Irish yew. Tufts, brown as tobacco and shaped like shuttlecocks, lay mouldering underfoot. Ahead, a river of windows mirrored milky cloud. Leading up to the house was a flight of limestone steps and, in the doorway, stood Timmy Moynihan dressed in riding breeches and a trenchcoat. He was a small man with a quick, clever, rodent's face.

'Half gunman, half gent!' yelled Seamus by way of greeting, adding that the costume suited Timmy down to the ground. 'Scratch the Republican,' roared the boisterous Seamus, 'and you'll find the old retainer.'

Timmy and he pretended to jab and box at each other for a bit. Then they started on the tour.

'Here's a Russian ikon,' said Timmy, crushing his listeners with the word they would not give him the satisfaction of admitting they didn't know. 'And this here's an Arab chest from Zanzibar.' The word buzzed like a flight of bees. Lions and sultans pranced for it so that the real chest was a bit of a disappointment. The ikon too turned out to be nothing but a holy picture.

Timmy led them to the ballroom, pointing out stucco ornamentation which was all crests and coronets, swords and sceptres, the pomp of empire manifest in every curlicue.

'The lads burned down places like this.' Judith was taking out her mood on the architecture.

'It would be a sin!' Kathleen's mood was all approbation. 'It's too lovely!'

'The new state could take it over,' said Sparky. Rich men in America, he said, left their houses for the public to enjoy.

'It wouldn't be kept up the same, though, would it?' said Timmy. 'When the family is home the gardeners supply fresh flowers for every room. They grow orchids in the conservatory here that have won prizes up in Dublin.'

'Conservatory!' Kathleen breathed.

Judith gave her a scorching look. 'I'd burn it.'

'Jesus,' said Seamus. 'The women in this country are fire-eaters. You'd be afraid to be alone with one on a dark night.'

By now the Treaty had been adopted in Dáil Éireann. De Valera had resigned as President. The IRA, as Seamus had foretold, was splitting and the anti-Treaty forces had repudiated the leadership of the Dáil.

'My family,' said Timmy of his employers, 'aren't ready yet to come back from England.' He made it sound as though they were waiting for his signal or, alternatively, as though the country should take its weather readings from the movements of the Devereux. Either way, Timmy reflected borrowed glory. He was a moon between suns.

'Yerrah why,' Kathleen's voice had an intonation of irony, 'wouldn't they?'

He grinned. 'They'll try to get the girl married over there. This is no country for her sort of woman. Besides, if mutineers go on the rampage, things could get hot again.' There was no denying his competence. He knew the old order and the new. He fetched a mouth-organ from his pocket and struck up a waltz. 'Nice and slow,' he said, winking at Seamus, 'I like to keep it coming nice and slow, as the bishop said to the chorus girl.' He put the instrument back to his mouth.

'Timmy, why don't you show us the rest of the house?' said Judith, and pulled at his elbow. She didn't want Sparky and Kathleen starting to dance.

He put his mouth-organ in his pocket and led the way past a door which was propped open by the stuffed leg of an elephant. Inside was the gun room, beneath whose ceiling a pressed python skin had been stuck as a frieze.

'This place,' said Timmy, 'is a right zoological cemetery. Demi Devereux's Da spent his youth shooting men and beasts. He shot Rooshians and Prooshians and took pot shots at local poachers. These cases never get to court. You may imagine what sympathy a winged poacher would have got from the magistrates while their crowd were still top dogs.'

Rooms led to further rooms. Mirrors, opposite mirrors, reflected flights of diminishing objects. Judith kept her eye on Kathleen to whom Sparky seemed to be paying little attention. Were they conniving to throw her off the scent? The abundance of stuffed game – salmon, deer, pheasants and the brushes of foxes – made her think of herself as a sniffing hound. In one mirror, it seemed to her that her nose had begun to twitch.

Timmy, meanwhile, was comparing himself to a mouse.

'Your big-house mouse,' said he, 'may love the place whose foundations he devours. I nibble because I love, as the cannibal said to his girl friend. Mind you, it's a two-way act. I too,' said Timmy, and postured, 'am devoured.' He brought them back to the front hall, then up a flight of stairs. 'Do yez want to see the common quarters where our own sort lives?' he interrogated. 'Behind the backdrop? Propping it up while preparing to gobble it up?' His accent was now all brogue. 'Kathleen and myself had a foretaste of the gobble on the night of yon dance, am I right, Kathleen mavourneen? All the sadder that it should have ended the way it did. But no surprise. Lady Luck has been with the landlords a fair while and she's a lethargic doxy when it comes to changing her friends.' Timmy, now two flights ahead of the others, leaned over the bannister and struck an orator's pose. 'James Connolly had the right ideas,' he shouted down at them. 'God rest him and let's hope God isn't such a crusty old patriarch as to send him below with the fallen angels. "Hold on to your rifles," said he to the Citizen Army in 1916, "as those with whom we are fighting may stop before our goal is reached. We are out for economic as well as political liberty." Do you think the jokers now getting ready to cut each others' tripes out over oaths to the Crown and other flourishes remember them? I wouldn't bet on it. I'll be round one of these evenings to have a chat with Owen O'Malley who, I'm told, will be representing us in the Dáil. I want to be sure he's representing me as I want to be represented.'

By now the other four had drawn abreast of Timmy.

'Onward,' he told them, 'to behind the green-baize door. Garrets. Attics. Demi Devereux,' he went on, 'says he's as Irish as myself and I say that in that case I'm as good a gent as himself, for all my Mammy cleans out his Mammy's chamber-pots. If he's English, then he can make much of his English gentility, but if he's trying to get into the one bed with us, he'd better shed it, because when you desert from your native army you can't expect to be let wear the old medals. That's logic,' said Timmy, 'but I've scant faith in it's winning the day. They'll manage to have it both ways. You'll see.'

'Jesus, Timmy,' said Seamus, 'you'd talk the hind leg off a donkey.'

'I'm giving you the benefit of my savvy,' Timmy told him. 'Listen, Clancy, I'm the only man you know who knows the enemy close up, close enough to see the whites of his eyes and other parts unmentionable in the presence of young girls, as well as the mindless, egotistic decency, God rot him, in his heart. The enemy is not your poor bleeding Tommy who is as fed up as ourselves with the gentry that sent him off to fight in those stinking trenches and then over here to get shot at from behind hedges.' Timmy was touring them through servants' rooms, throwing open doors and shutters, letting cobwebby light through small windows into boxy spaces. 'The enemy,' he went on, 'is Demi Devereux, as I've been telling him since I learned to talk. His father voted against Home Rule in the House of Lords. In Ireland's interests, you understand. They love us, so they'd rather kill us than give us up.

There's passion for you! We can go down the back way and I'll show you the kitchens. Mind your step, girls. They might sell this place if anyone would buy it. But I don't know. There's great fox-hunting here. Nothing like it, I'm told, on the other side. And then they have their notions about how the 'real people', which doesn't mean you, Clancy, but people like my mother, God love her, would hate to see them go. Well, it's true my mother would be out of a job if she had no chamber-pots to clean. It's not Kathleen here who's likely to give her employment. Here's the kitchen,' said Timmy, leading the way into a large, vaulted room full of giant furniture. 'The woman's imagination is limited and there's no persuading her that life is not all chamber-pots. "Ah wisha, Timmy," says she, "don't be getting above yerself and offending the gentry that give ye the bread that's in yer mouth, God bless them, where would we be without them?" She's their product. A lost cause. And it doesn't end with chamber-pots.' Timmy led them out to a courtyard surrounded by stables. 'Spiritually, they do the same thing. I, as you must know, studied with Demi until he went to Eton, which he did late because he was sickly as a chisler. Well, I remember some play we were studying one time with an old French mot that used to give us lessons. It was about Nero, the Roman Emperor, and a servant of his. Now this servant was forever suggesting the most dastardly, low villainous things to Nero and Nero would do them. But the idea always came from the servant and this, said the French mot, was because the servant was of a baser nature and so corrupting Nero who, after all, was an emperor and must have had noble instincts. Well, after that, do you know, Demi started calling me by the name of Nero's servant and what astounded me was that I could see he genuinely felt that in our games the low instincts were mine and that *he* was considerably less to blame than I was if he gave in to them. He was wiping his spiritual arse on me – no offence meant,' said Timmy to the girls who were, in fact, taking none. Talk of arses and chamber-pots was coarse but not truly shameful the way mention of sexual matters might have been.

Grainne had started having nightmares. About a funfair

ride – this went back to something in her childhood which, asleep, could harrow her still.

She'd been six and at the seaside in a house her parents rented every summer. It was in a small village where children could circulate safely and one late afternoon she had gone down with her sixpence to ask the man on the merry-go-round for a ride. Rob Redmond was the perfect funfair attendant. His nose was a strawberry and his grin like an apple slice, only brown as though the apple had been sitting about on a plate.

He took her sixpence, although he had been ready to close down, and cranked up the merry-go-round for her alone, letting her ride her painted wooden horse round and round through afternoon air thick with fermentings of the day's smells: hay, dung, petrol and quite a whiff of whiskey. The air too was whiskey-coloured and greasy. The sun had slipped down. There was a fine rain. The horse surged like a boat on a wave and when it came time to stop the attendant refused to end the ride. He laughed. His mouth, instead of being a neat slice, was like a hacked-up apple.

'You're never getting off!' he shouted, spluttering. 'I'll make you ride round for ever. Will you like that? Heh? Eh? Will you, little Grannie?'

It was an adult joke. Grainne had had to put up with the like before: from maids who said they'd tickle her to death or throw her over the sea wall. Under the joke, you knew they had started to hate you. She had been suspended over a cliff from one wrist by a girl whom her parents had hired to take her for walks. The fall below was sheer and there was madness in the girl's eyes. 'I'll drop you, I'll drop you,' she'd been singing and Grainne knew she mustn't scream lest the girl panic and really let her go. Compared to that fear, the funfair ride was manageable. Like the maids, Rob Redmond was punishing her parents through her. One day a threat would go too far and a child be found smothered in a cellar. Meanwhile, Grainne hoped to escape. She held hard on to the wooden horse's neck and hoped someone might come. The hacked-apple face laughed but she didn't scream because if she did Rob Redmond would know that she knew that the joke was not a joke. Pretence was protection. Everyone pretended and so must she. Please, she was whispering, let someone come, and the horse was slipping and the attendant roaring that he'd never let her off. Black holes tore through the whiskey sky and the horse moved queerly sideways while Grainne clutched the pole and felt terror, a strange stab of delight and a numbing urge to let herself get dizzier still. 'I think my mother will be worried,' she managed to say sensibly. 'Can you please let me off?'

'Never,' roared the mad Rob Redmond. 'Ha, ha,' he hiccupped, 'round and round you'll have to go, round and round forever. *In saecula saeculorum.*'

In the end she peed, wetting the horse and her dress, and somehow it all ended without the attendant having to dispose of her mangled body, as he might have to do with some child's if ever one of his jokes went wrong. Perhaps he would chop the child into steaks and sell them to a butcher, like the man who was caught doing this by Saint Nicholas in one of Grainne's story books?

As she grew older, Grainne hardened her pretences and ended up believing in them. Only occasionally a glimpse of people's secret, murderous hatred broke through – in IRA rallies for instance; and in dreams, from time to time, she rode that coldly perilous, ravishing wooden horse and hoped that it might take off from the merry-go-round and become a Pegasus.

She'd had the dream again recently and knew why. Sex was the merry-go-round. She did and didn't want to get off. The attendant was now inside herself. She hated her appetite, had moments of hating James and the disproportion between what you hoped for in pleasure and what came when it was over: the return to everyday. Better not rouse yourself if you had to come back. James's satisfaction astounded her. Little smiles she detected on his face made her want to sadden him. What made *him* so satisfied? Did he feel he deserved the happiness she – or so he said – had brought him? How *could* he be happy anyway? Things were so intractably finite. Yet he talked of taking her to California. The absurdity of it. California! More day-to-day ordinariness in a place she didn't even know. Why? What for?

Oh, and she did know she was wrong to think this way. Why could she not be a pleasure-lover who simply took what was offered? Or else be a true puritan and feel right about feeling wrong and regret her adultery with proper remorse. Instead, she was divided as she had been on the merry-go-round, when she half wanted the man to murder her as he and the maids would have liked to do from resentment at her white kid shoes and organdie dress, and the fact that her father's photograph was always in the papers.

'*They're* no better than us,' she had heard the charwoman tell the housemaid. 'Sure, my grandfather and hers,' raising her eyes to the ceiling above which Grainne's mother could be heard playing the piano, 'went barefoot to the same village school. *Now* look at them.'

'Money's never come by honest,' said the maid. 'Why them, not us?'

'Little pitchers!'

'Maybe one day . . .'

'Fat chance. Their kind stick together. The rich get richer.'

'*She's* sweet as honey.' Again the eyes sailed towards the ceiling.

'Gets more out of you that way. Stands to reason. Don't be taken in.'

They hated you. The I R A was only saying what had always been whispered in kitchens and sculleries. They hadn't minded working for the old stock but working for their own kind stuck in their gullets. Expected to wear livery! Well, they wouldn't. No. What was the new moneyed class but gombeen men, opportunists, the scum that rises to the surface. The charwomen whispered, spat, and would one day take kitchen knives and trim off your fat – 'fat,' they whispered, 'living off the fat of the land!' – and cook nice steaks from the flesh between your ribs.

Society was like that and so was your own body with its urges that didn't fit with everyday life. James thought that you could break up one order and found another on the basis of the body's anarchy. That she could leave Michael and marry him.

'Don't worry about your son,' he told her. 'Kids suffer less than parents think. In California it's been found that divorce is less harmful than a sick, unhappy home.'

'How do you know that our home – yours and mine – wouldn't be unhappy?'

'We're compatible,' he told her.

Well, if *that* was all he knew.

'In Italian,' she told him, 'IRA means anger. I've seen it there on walls. Just anger.'

'About what?'

'Everything maybe.'

'California . . .' said James.

'I know all about California,' she told him. 'It's in all the B movies.'

It was the sort of chat you used to fill in spaces between going to bed. He had come round to see her and talk about Aunt Judith to whose cassette he had been listening. It was eleven a.m. Michael was at work, Cormac had gone on a school excursion and Mary was upstairs cleaning Aunt Judith's room.

'Tell me,' she said, 'about our life in California.'

This was a game they had in which James strove, like an adman confronted by a resistant customer, to give his picture with a compelling realism.

'I wish you'd take this seriously.'

'What about your wife?'

'She has her career. She won't miss me.'

'A poor reference for an ex-husband.'

'You're *not* serious!'

'You'd be less so if I were.' She believed this but couldn't have been straightforward if she'd wanted. Her teasing mode, like bandiness in a jockey's child, was an adjustment to past rather than present strains. Irony and the hype which invalidates promises were her automatic responses to the male. Except with Michael – perhaps because between *them* sex had never mattered. What did was not it but an emanation of it: something like the shadow thrown by a knotted handkerchief which can be so much more evocative than cloth. The first times they'd gone to bed together he could do nothing because, he explained, of being still sexually in thrall to Theo.

'It doesn't matter,' she'd said.

'You're so good to me,' he had whispered. Sometimes he had wept.

Grainne, who had been reared on images of Christs hung on her nursery walls in the limp agony of Gethsemane, or having their feet wiped in Mary Magdalene's gorgeous whore's hair, found her response to Michael's weakness shot through by currents of an earlier arousal. Play-acting with this husband who had been put in her bed by their family, as sick children are put for comfort in an adult's bed, procured her an excitement which required little activity to fuel it. He came to her trailing the lascivious fragrances of Theo, his own misfortune, a longing on the scale of Grainne's own for things more resonant than life, and a disinclination for coping with life itself. It was a lot to have in common.

Raised to believe the world 'a vale of tears', Grainne had a sneaking sense that only the crass took satisfaction in it. Desire had been so disturbing that it had seemed sufficient in itself.

Now, with James, pleasure was delivered but finite. She enjoyed but was suspicious of her enjoyment. Reality was a wasting asset and James too urgent. She could not cope with the creature in herself whom he brought to life. Like a relative who eats offensively, she would have liked this other self kept out of sight. The wistfulness to which she had grown addicted with Michael hung, like dim light in an invalid's room, shadowing her sensibility. James was constantly shooting up the blind with the bossy cheer of a ward sister.

'Leaving Michael,' she tried to explain, 'would be a sort of amputation.'

Amputations, he retorted, were sometimes the healthy choice.

'Don't *worry* about Cormac,' he repeated. 'Kids have to snap the umbilical cord sometime.'

When, he began asking, were they taking their trip to the Devereux Estate? Two nights off Michael's ground would, she saw him think, be just the thing to shake her out of her pusillanimity. She braced herself for jollying and rallying.

'Listen,' James was saying in a confident voice. 'There's some great stuff on that cassette. Your aunt's mind is really working now. We should strike while the iron is hot. Expose her to . . .'

'*Shh!*' Grainne interrupted him. 'What's *that*?'

'I didn't . . .'

'Quiet,' she whispered, 'there's someone in the scullery.'

James stood up. 'Are you . . . ?'

She waved him away. 'Stay back.' She tiptoed to the door and threw it open. At the same moment the outer door banged. Someone was racing down the back path – someone who had been listening or anyway heard. What had they been saying? Who *was* it? She wrenched the old door open and rushed to the gate in time to see Cormac disappear around the street corner.

14

'Timmy's a card,' said Seamus turning round, as they made their way back through the woods. 'It's true he was brought up with the son of the house and now there he is between worlds.'

'He's divided in other ways too,' said Sparky, who was walking behind with Judith. It was as well to get back to a normal footing. At least it meant he wasn't with Kathleen and turning her silly head.

'What do you mean?' she asked idly.

'I imagine *that*'s why the IRA wouldn't have him.'

'What's why?'

'He's a homosexual.'

'A what?' said Judith. 'Don't tell me.'

'Why are you frightened of sex, Judith? You're a country girl, after all,' said Sparky. 'You must have seen animals.'

'Stop. I won't listen.' But he was blocking the path. A blackberry branch, pushed aside by the other two, had leaped back with a whiplash effect and barred the route. Sparky was trying to take hold of it without pricking his hand.

'Why are you so prudish?' he asked. 'A revolutionary should be able to look at things the way they are, instead of pushing your sister into the arms of a man who doesn't really like women at all. Owen may be wanting to marry Kathleen from fear.'

'What do you mean?' It was sure to be lies. He was evil. He had the look of a ferret; a streak of sun lit up his yellow hair which was just the colour of that vicious animal's pelt. His eyes looked red to her.

'Owen may be afraid of not being like other men. He may be afraid that he is really like Timmy. In the three years of their engagement, he has never . . .'

The ferret face turned and loomed. Sparky had a hold of the bramble. The touch of his flesh would appall her. His words appalled her. They had polluted her mind. She saw – from where? – two farm dogs coupling on a road. Males? A carter aimed a lash of his whip at the pair. But they seemed stuck and wheeled, like a single creature, into a ditch. The image vacated her mind. She felt a twinge of panic at what would come next. Oh, he had a way of summoning the worst, most buried filth.

'First Owen went into a seminary to escape his nature . . .'

'That's *enough*!' She pushed past him, elbowing him towards the bramble bush, not looking to see whether he had lost his balance and tipped into it. She hoped he had. It would tear his fine outfit. Good. The other two were in a clearing when she caught up with them but she didn't stop. Running, blood pounded in her head and she couldn't think. Thorns pulled at her and once she fell to her knees and got up again with a feeling of satisfaction. She would have liked to tear herself apart, to dissolve and scour out the thoughts in her fouled head. It would never be the same. Implications lurked. Owen and Timmy like those dogs children threw stones at. Naming things gave them power. Call the devil and he might appear. That, she sank exhausted on a bank, that was the meaning, her throat pained her, scraped by deep raucous panting, the meaning of the apple of knowledge. The priest had explained it to the senior girls in retreat last May. Mary's month. She couldn't, couldn't get her breath. Imagined her throat as lacerated. Could she have done the same to the inside of her head she would have. He had been a visiting priest, a sad, shell-shocked army chaplain who'd been through some of the worst stretches of the war, and Sister Benedict had warned the girls that they must behave sensibly if he broke down and wept. With decorum. Like ladies. He'd done great things, the nun explained, for the poor Catholic lads who'd joined up, God help them. Everyone knew the Irish were as brave as lions when they had the comforts of their religion and so the British army, wanting to get the best out of them, had arranged for a general absolution to be given before they went over the top. The chaplain had been with a regiment that had been wiped out twice in four years. He'd seen things, Sister B told the girls, that made him feel like Dante coming back from hell. No giggling, mind, if he wept. It was physical. He couldn't control it. A holy man. Brave. A living martyr. Then she'd left them alone with him in the chapel. Judith thought about the chapel with intensity, wishing herself back there. She was cold but wouldn't go home now until she was sure Sparky had left. She'd delivered Kathleen up to him – for Seamus wouldn't notice what was going on.

The priest had sat with his back to the altar and faced them: big lumps of girls, as they felt themselves to be, with their breasts pushing the pleats of their gym-slips out of place. They had asked to be allowed to wear something different but the nuns wouldn't hear of it; many bound bandages around themselves to flatten their busts. Their giggle was on a hair trigger and, having been warned to control it, they were on edge. The priest said nothing. They were embarrassed. The poor man had a worn cassock and no hair on his head: a pink dome with freckles the size of shamrocks and, half-way down it, a pair of demented eyes, bright blue like bits of a shattered Milk-of-Magnesia bottle. Sure enough, there were tears brimming in them. The priest must have been used to crying publicly for he just let them brim and overflow and spray all over his cheeks. When he did speak, it was a shock. He mustn't have spoken to girls – maybe to anyone? – for years. Known gigglers were glared at by companions and drove their finger-nails into the palms of their hands.

'My darling and beautiful and pure and innocent little girls,' said the priest, and a ripple of nervous hilarity ran from bench to bench. 'How can I ever tell you the joy it brings to my heart to see innocence abloom today in this ancient, holy and sacred land of ours?' Innocence, he confided, was a gift you could never appreciate until you had lost it and then you could never get it back. He could feel *their* innocence, he said, washing around him. It was restoring him. He was breathing it in. The girls, for the most part farmers' and shopkeepers' daughters, looked suspiciously at him, trying to figure out whether he was as cracked as he let on, or sly, or totally cracked but wise too in a saintly way. They were used to every kind of mental oddity in their villages, from which only the homicidally mad were ever sent away. When he finally started to sob, it was a relief. He kept it up for what seemed a long time, snuffling desperately into his handkerchief. What started him off was a story which he began to tell about a lovely and pure little girl called Eileen, who . . . But they were never to discover what had happened to Eileen or why this upset him so because, every time he reached her name, he broke down. 'Eileen . . .' he wailed and collapsed like a baby. The girls guessed that she must have died in Flanders defending her innocence. They knew a lot of stories like this. He didn't mention Flanders, though, nor poppies nor the trenches. When he gave up trying to tell about Eileen, he turned to the dangers of desiring knowledge – Eve's sin – and naming things. The girls perceived that their own peculiar virtue was one which could only be preserved by ignoring it. It was like a lamp held up to light other people but masked from the holder. Meanwhile, the priest wept and wept, tears still glistening and pouring even when his sobbing ceased. He bent over as though in pain and presented them with the bald top of his pink head. The girls were puzzled but knew that this was their proper condition.

After the session in the chapel they were skittish, commenting with amusement on the way the tears had made patterns on his cheeks, like wax trickling down a candle. They were alight with vanity at the effect their feminine virtue had seemed to have on him, a ruined creature but martial, holy, and moreover male.

This pride in the power of her own delicacy had, in Judith's case, just been crudely violated by Sparky Driscoll.

Grainne heard Cormac sneak past her bedroom door and raced to catch him before he was down the stairs and out of the front door.

'Cormac?'

He paused, not turning to look at her. He had a weekend bag in his hand.

'Where are you going?'

Still not facing her: 'Out of your hair.'

'Where? Cormac? Look at me!'

'Does it matter? Uncle Owen Roe's.'

'To stay?'

'Yes.'

'What about . . . your father?'

'He knows.'

And what else did Michael know, she wondered. Cormac's back was still turned to her. He stood, like someone playing grandmother's steps, frozen on the stairway, waiting for her to take her eyes off him before bolting from the home she had contaminated. She had confirmed his worst suspicions and his fourteen-year-old morality condemned her utterly. What could she possibly say?

Turning, she went back into her bedroom and seconds later heard the click of the front door.

Grainne looked at herself in her mirror: a bad mother, that was what she was. Years later, Cormac would explain to some girl that what he had become – drunken? impotent? a terrorist? – was all due to his mother, a lustful woman, and the shock she'd given him when he found this out at the age of fourteen. 'How awful,' the girl would say, stroking his hair and longing to help, but it would be too late for that. Only his mother could have and now where was she? An alcoholic has-been in Southern California? Deserted by her sexy second husband? Or happily married to him still, having chosen pleasure over duty?

Grainne decided to go to the hairdresser. She couldn't cry there and would be cossetted by competent hands which wanted nothing in return but her money: such easy currency. Maybe she'd have her hair cut? Dyed even? Get a new *persona*. Quick, quick – no. Michael would be hurt by it. How could she hurt him more?

Suddenly, ridiculously, she was jealous of the girl who would one day in the future hold Cormac in her arms and comfort him: a good, gentle girl with young eyes. 'I feel I can trust you,' Cormac would say to her. 'You remind me of my mother but you're more honest, more sincere.' – 'Oh, I hope so,' the girl would answer.

Grainne was crying into her powder-puff and at the same

time trying to repair her face. 'Idiot!' she told herself. 'Shut up, shut up!'

Michael woke and remembered his jealousy. His saliva tasted of vinegar.

Grainne's body felt wet. No! His palms were sweating.

Earlier, in the pub, he had had trouble getting his breath and had begun thinking of guns. Blunt instruments. Ways of registering with the careless pair who had counted without him. But he lacked conviction. Jealousy was gentle in him, oozing in like defeat.

He felt himself too unemphatic a man to hold Grainne against her will.

Grainne.

Up her back and haunches ran his fingers. They could strangle her.

He imagined – felt – the cold corpse lying there, then being taken off for burial. A death sweat on it? No. The clamminess was *his*.

He felt soothed, was even falling asleep when it struck him that only the killing part of this story was a dream. The rest was real. This came as such a surprise that he was shocked all over again.

Maybe he had always expected this? The way he expected death but managed to forget about it. He told himself that he forgot about life too, put off living it. That was why he hadn't minded her being away in London. Not really. He'd felt her safely available at the end of the telephone line. Cloistered. Still his. Now, it was as if a Siamese twin's twin had threatened to have his or her self – gender was not the point – surgically removed, taking some shared organ vital to both. That was what he felt, rubbing wet eyelids on her sleeping back. He had invested part of himself in her and here, she still was, he thought, but had no sense of contact. She was dreaming and in her dreams he was sure he didn't figure.

Owen Roe had rung him at work. 'I thought you ought to know,' he'd finished up, 'that Cormac is my source. Not that I hadn't my own suspicions. He overheard the fellow asking her to marry him. She didn't say no.'

'Cormac?'

'Yes.'

'When?'

'This morning.'

Michael had put down the phone and gone to the nearest pub. Responsibility, he thought, and had two whiskeys fast. Would she go? And would the boy suffer? Bugger the boy, he'd decided, flooded with guilt and then with panic – because if *he* felt this way, why shouldn't she? Cormac was fourteen and tough enough. Not counting on his Dad, anyway. Went to the uncle with his tale. There you were. If discounted, how did you make yourself count? Michael had no leverage. Grainne had her own bit of income. She'd have thought about Cormac already.

Decided, had she? That weeping in front of the telly made sense now. Doubts. Didn't fuck her enough, he supposed. Women wanted it. Well, couldn't she get it round here? Why did she have to go to America? Wanted it because it confirmed their sense of themselves. Women. Basic creatures, really: simple. What was her vulnerable point? Cormac? Owen Roe obviously n.b.g. or he wouldn't have been ringing up yours truly. Think of her wanting it that much, though! Convent girl when he married her: always wearing white cotton gloves. Hard on a man when women got so demanding. How fuck her now, knowing she preferred the other chap? A man had his pride. Besides, after years of marriage, *you* didn't want it that much. Maybe he should take hormones or something? Damned humiliating. Cross over to London. Visit some Harley Street chap. First have to stop her leaving. How? Couldn't face her tonight. Too drunk. She'd be sorry if she left him: a tolerant man. She should think of that. Passion wasn't always lodged in the genitals. Real love, Grainne, don't spit on it. Bloody Yanks very materialistic. Other things in life.

But he was miserable. Got into an argument with some chap about what? Pubs, when you were a young fellow, were a refuge from the smothering of home. Now had a look of refugee stations. Commuters passed through *en route* to serious living. The permanent pub population talked of fictions so large or so minute as to protect them from seeing dead-on the society in which they had failed to get a niche. Funambulists, they doddered in the stratosphere.

An ancient, titled gent, an *habitué* of bars, who had sold inherited estates thirty years back to pursue and marry a chorus girl – she'd been a Bluebell, danced across Europe before dancing circles round the fool – now a pauper but for some tiny pension, tried to tell Michael about the evils of sodium nitrite in bacon. Sounded cogent as a judge. Rapt brimming eye, rickety wrists extending from a ruff of sleeve. Spent the time he couldn't afford the pubs sitting in libraries for warmth. His chin wobbled. Cloning interested him too. Acupuncture. Cures for arthritis.

'ABC,' said Michael insolently. 'Acupuncture, Bacon, Clones! Your mind's slipping. Clones is a medieval monastery.'

'I assure you . . .'

'What happened to the Bluebell? Fuck off, did she?'

In the end, a friendly barman had to put Michael into a taxi and send him home. The price of the journey would go on the slate. Cloyne? Clones? Boyne? Clonmacnoise?

She finally decided that poor Sparky Driscoll had a deformed mind and that she should empty her own of the bilge he had poured into it. Men were unstable creatures, capable of dangerous plungings about; like stallions who injure themselves in their loose-boxes, it could be unsafe to come too close to them and this wasn't only true of the American.

Owen had been in a suspicious, snappish state when he first got home from gaol. It was no wonder that Sparky should have thought his feeling for Kathleen had blown cold, for he treated her, as he did everyone, with a gloomy imperiousness. But was that to be wondered at? The man had spent eight months in gaol and had never been easy-going. Seamus had been crazy to think Owen would be on the side of the compromisers. Owen was a man of vision. Eyes fixed on distant horizons, how could he have time for the day-to-day? Naturally, he would line up with the faction which spat the Treaty out of their mouths and were now calling themselves 'the sea-green incorruptibles'.

In spite of herself, Judith had to admit that the name suited

Owen. He was an admirable man but there was something, well, fishy about him. His small head was set high on his neck and when he wore the trenchcoat favoured by the fighting men, it stuck up from it like a turtle's from its shell. His eye-glasses gleamed in a scaly way and sometimes, in argument, spittle flew from his mouth. The word 'slimey' occurred to those who didn't like him. There were quite a few, for Owen was careless about giving offence. He had the spoilt priest's mania for self-justification and would grind opponents into the ground. '*I* have examined my conscience,' he liked to say, 'and found it clear.' Then he would stare his adversary accusingly in the eye. Kathleen had had a dose of this treatment recently. She seemed frivolous to him, took too much care with her appearance and was too gay at a time when Ireland, said Owen, was traversing a time of trial. A more tolerant man might have guessed that one reason they were all in high spirits was nervous relief over the Treaty and because they had been getting ready to welcome him home. Perhaps excitement had run away with them a bit? Owen was like a man arriving late at a party.

His return coincided with Christmas and for weeks before there had been anticipation of revelry. A pig had been slaughtered ahead of time and, for the festivities themselves, Kathleen had killed two geese. For toasting the peace and future prosperity, there was port and porter, whiskey, sherry wine, and strong tea for followers of Father Mat. Plum cakes and puddings were soaked in one or other of these fluids until they were as heavy as rained-on-peat.

Sparky had wanted to learn some Gaelic toasts, so Seamus had translated a few. The shortest was '*gob fluc*', meaning 'a wet mouth' or 'may you never lack liquor to wet your whistle'. The longest was:

> Health and long life to you,
> The woman of your choice to you,
> Land without rent to you
> And death in Erin.

Kathleen simpered in a silly way over the words 'the woman of your choice' and made doe's eyes at Sparky Driscoll, who asked whether the last lines referred to the emigrants' hope of returning before they died.

'What else would they come back to do?' asked the Da sourly. 'Isn't dying the national sport?' He recited with scorn a line from a poem he'd heard the wet-behind-the-ears patriots declaiming in the parish hall. It too was from the Gaelic:

'What can they know that we know that know the way to die?'

Verse like that would make you howl like a dog with mange, said the Da, who had a tendency to get depressed at Christmas, thinking of his dead wife, his dead son, and his own foolishness in ever leaving America for this backside of a place. Patriotic argy-bargy got on his nerves. The eejits were squabbling now over the Treaty, a piece of paper. Oh, it was the price of them. Loneliness and the dead-end of the Da's life were connected with the local mud roads, fog-smeared windows, weeping gutters. He did not want to be told that hope was here under his nose and he the only one unable to see it.

Sparky argued with him, cutting the ground from beneath the old man's feet. An American! Giving him the lie in front of people who for years had respected the Da as an expert on America! Old Clancy grew glummer as the young big-mouth declared *this* to be the promised land. Neighbours, alert to the irony, puffed their pipes and kept their faces straight. The young men in the Dáil, said the unconscious Sparky, were like the Founding Fathers.

The Da was crushed. Judith saw no way to rescue him. Silent, he broke a red coal open, letting it flare then cover over slowly with a white crust of ash.

'Ah,' he said sadly, 'you've been taken in by blowhards.'

'Heroes!' Driscoll's face had the nuzzling vigour of a young animal's. He was energetic, self-absorbed, careless.

'Ah *rameish*!' Clancy had a spurt of life. 'Mother of God!' He invoked help and patience with such rank rubbish and his hand trembled, spilling some drops of his drink. The fire glowed on them. 'Sure the wee fellows beyond in the whatcha-maycallit, the Dáil, those wee fellas couldn't run a grocery store. They'll be taking pot shots at each other in a coupla weeks. Mark my words. Sure all they know is how to handle a gun. And if they were geniuses itself. If Saints Peter and Paul were to come down from heaven to lend them a hand, how could they make a going thing of this country? Isn't it crippled with debts to England? And what other market but England have they? Ask any farmer. Ask the Trades Unions. You,' he told Sparky, 'will be off home to the US, any day, on a liner from Queenstown, and damn glad you'll be, I bet, to get back to a place where people have not only "vision", as you call it, but the greenbacks to make something of it.' The Da laughed maliciously and rubbed the tips of his fingers against his thumb, as though he was feeling money. 'Am I right?' he challenged. 'You bet I am! Your green, young fellow, is the opposite of our green! Don't forget that. Don't be taken in. Let me tell you something,' the old man leaned forward so that the fire-light threw gleams on the roughened surface of his face. They deepened the grooves alongside his mouth and shone on the stubble of his chin and on his eyeballs, so that he looked like a stained-glass image ribbed with lead. Gold flared in his mouth: a tooth fixed in America. 'When an American,' he told Sparky, 'has a vision, it's of something he intends to do. When an Irishman has one, it's something to die for or sing about, but,' he prodded the air with a black-rimmed nail, 'tis guaranteed,' prod, 'to stay visionary,' prod, 'forever. Ha! And another thing!' He seemed to be drawing sustenance from the force of his pessimism; his head reared defiantly, 'We hate work. Bowsies, over here, put more effort into figuring out how to slope off and avoid doing an honest stroke of work than Rockefeller into making his first million. You,' the Da was incandescent with spite, 'are a dangerous bugger and I'll tell you why! You're cheering on the Republicans . . .'

'I don't side with the Republicans . . .'

'The IRA then. You and your friends, safe in your own country, sent money over here to encourage young fools like my Eamonn to die.' Clancy landed a gobbet of spittle in the fire. He was trembling.

Sparky opened his mouth to argue.

'Ah, can't the pair of yez get off the subject!' Judith could have knocked their heads together. 'Tell him about America,' she whispered to Sparky.

'What do you think I've been doing?' he hissed back.

'Not like that!' She tried to explain: '*His* America. What he remembers. Baseball . . .' she pleaded. 'Remind him.'

'That's a tall order,' said Sparky.

It was, too. Clancy's dreams were perhaps dead – but whose fault was that? Judith groped for a joke which might get them going on baseball or the Boston politics of thirty years ago. But the words stuck in her mouth. His American jokes had never made much sense to her and she had begun to guess that Sparky Driscoll didn't see the point of them either. Maybe her father had got them wrong? Suddenly, she had an image of him standing on a sidewalk – she wasn't too sure what that was and so he stood suspended, levitating in her mind's eye – staring in a baffled way at some dazzling scene. Maybe he'd been a greenhorn always? On his own telling, most of the money to buy this house and the pub had come from her mother's uncle who had left it to her when he died in Philadelphia. Her father's contribution could have been very small. It could have been imaginary?

'That picture,' she said, 'where was it taken? The one of you and my mother wearing hats? She has a lace collar and . . .'

'Oh, that *hat*!' Her father grasped so gratefully at her question that she felt a spasm of pain for him. 'The women,' he chuckled, 'wore such hats! Like basins!'

'They wear them small now and close to the head.' Driscoll had finally sensed what was wanted of him.

The Da ignored him. 'Huge!' His hands sketched an imaginary hat-brim and quivered from present feeling or for old ostrich plumes. 'They could hardly get in doorways.'

His wife had been lovely. This part was true. Judith had seen the photographs. His luck at getting her overwhelmed him still. Why had she married him? She with her dowry? Because she was ill with T B? Because he agreed to come home with her? He had regretted that ever since. But his thoughts turned like homing birds to his courtship days.

'It was on Boston Common,' he said of the picture. He'd been wearing his summer straw and his wife that absurd, optimistic, fashionable hat. 'Have another drink?' he coaxed Sparky.

Driscoll said he had to go.

Judith was half glad to see the back of him, half angry at his running out on her father. When she came back from seeing the guest out of the door, the Da had his head back, staring at the black glass of an uncurtained window. 'She had a fur muff and collar,' he reminisced. 'In winter. Raccoon fur, soft as a cat's belly and warm – your mother was always warm even on a perishing day. Hot even. It was the fever. The TB. She'd let me warm my hands in the muff. Mine were always cold. They have terrible winters over there. Snow up to here. Icicles like pikes. And you'd get chilblains so bad the skin swelled and raged. "Give me your muff a minute," I'd say and get as many fingers as I could into it. You know the pain when you warm cold hands too suddenly? The skin burns. That muff had her fever in it. It was so warm it felt wet . . . Ah hell!' His eyes *were* wet. He wiped them. 'I'm an eejit,' he groaned. 'Going on this way.' He drank down the drink he'd just poured for himself: his second wind. 'We'll be dead long enough, what?' Suddenly, his mood changed. Words poured like beads off a broken string. America wasn't all it was cracked up to be either. There was prejudice there, bigotry, and corruption among our own people. Though you could see why. They'd had a hard furrow to plough. Aye. ' "No Irish need apply" they'd say when they were advertising jobs. I've seen that myself. Treated us like dirt. Snobs. Boston Brahmins. In the land of the brave and the home of the free!' He laughed, suddenly bitter. Yanks no longer justified him. The talk with Sparky Driscoll had revealed him to himself as doubly homeless, exiled also from the elected country of his dream. 'Republic,' he said, 'they say "Republic" here now and they think it's magic. They think it'll change something but the only way you get respect is by making money. I saw that in the Republic of the US. Yes. A poor man there is as poor as a poor man here. Worse, because people despise him. You wouldn't see them feeding him the way we feed Dirty

Fleming. No. I wouldn't give a thraneen for a word like Republic,' said the Da. 'Seamus is right about that.'

And so it was that Sparky Driscoll, unknowingly, converted the Da to the pro-Treaty side which was the logical side for him to be on, being the one which all the conservatives in the country were taking, along with the old loyalists who, seeing that England had let them down and ditched them, were falling over themselves, trying to get friendly with the faction likely, at a pinch, to provide stability, moderation and respect for property.

Owen came home to find the house full of Free Staters with only Judith – who wasn't revealing her opinions – a secret diehard.

It wasn't long before the fur began to fly. Seamus and Owen sat up late, battering out the argument, like a smith and his journeyman shaping some object on an anvil.

'Keep personalities out of it,' said Owen, when Seamus brought up Michael Collins.

Seamus slapped his thigh, bunched his fists, winked and threw in jokes, but Owen was unflickering, a sea-green incorruptible. Judith thought of the years he had spent learning ancient abstract things in the seminary surrounded by bog. She fancied that his eye, by a double mirror trick, had caught the immobility of flatland water flooded by the pallor of clouds. His beard was bluish in the hollow of his cheek and his hair had the black-green sheen you saw on the feathers of a rooster. She couldn't see him sitting by the stove in his braces and a collar stud, the way her father did, nor shovelling dirt from a chicken run. No, he probably *would* do those things. Deliberately. As a discipline. She admired the way he answered Seamus, whose arguments, until now, had seemed to her unanswerable.

Seamus talked of economics and of how the place was destroyed and the lads at the end of their tether.

'Economics,' said the Da, cocking an ear like a gun dog jerked from sleep by some familiar shout. 'That's the head and tail of it. Money moves mountains.'

'So,' said Owen implacably, 'can faith. The Irish people,' he told Seamus, 'will follow. They won't initiate. And don't tell me that they're tired. They're always tired. They have to be goaded for their own good.'

'Jesus, the arrogance!' Seamus was shocked. 'You should never have left the seminary, Owen. You're worse than a priest now. As a priest you'd have known your authority was borrowed from heaven. This way there's no limit to it.'

'You,' said Owen, 'say "wait, settle for less". What did waiting do for us in the past? You have the souls of shopkeepers. Don't you see?' he spoke with cold passion, 'that you've been warped by oppression?'

'Oh, I'd rather see shopkeepers run the country than lay priests, and I'll tell you another thing,' said Seamus, 'I'd rather priests than lay priests: bloody, self-appointed heroes like yourself. The anointed priest has all eternity to reach paradise and its perfections, but you want it here and now. You learned the desire for it from the Church but you lost the Church's patience. You're dangerous. Mad. Like rabid dogs . . .'

'Madness can sometimes be the only sanity.'

'Faith then, we've had our dose. Tell me, do you not think the people have a *right* to a bit of peace and normality?'

'The "people" is an abstraction. We didn't fight for one generation. When Pearse proclaimed the Republic, he wasn't thinking of the comfort of one set of people inhabiting the island at any one time. He was thinking of what each generation owes the race. A mystic continuity . . .'

Seamus held his head in mock pain. He groaned and patted his ears with remedial delicacy.

'Oh my poor ears! The codology they've got to listen to. The bad faith. Listen, it's *our own government*. What we've always wanted. Remember? We should support it if you don't want the English to think we're a crowd of trigger-happy Paddies incapable of running the country they turned over to us.'

'Still looking over your shoulder at the old governess?'

Sparky made an effort to pour oil on troubled waters.

'Surely what counts,' said he, 'is the Irish people's right to self-determination? Isn't it as simple as that? The form of government is surely secondary?'

Owen gave Sparky a cold look from his saline blue eyes. 'The "people" are clay. You can do what you like in their name but, as Aristotle said of men and women, the formative idea comes from the male and the clay is female; passive, mere potentiality. The clay here is the people who have no self and no aspiration towards determining anything at all until *we* infuse it into them. *We* are their virile soul,' said Owen. '*We* are they.'

'Hey, Kathleen!' Sparky caught her boisterously by the elbow, 'are you letting this fellow get away with this? Is this the way the Irish court their girls? Hm? My mother always told me an Irish woman could give as good as she got. Are you going to answer him or do you want us to belt him one for you? In the name of Irish womanhood?'

Owen tightened his lean lips. He was unamused. Mockery would not touch him. Jokes slid from his steaming purposefulness.

Judith felt exalted.

'What was it all for?' Owen asked, 'if we stop now?'

Outside the window, stiff, icy shirts strained at a line, swelling and flapping in tethered flight.

'The English would live up to their threats if we didn't,' Seamus reminded him. 'All-out war . . .'

'War then.'

'What for?'

'What was it ever for?'

'A better life,' said Seamus. Sparky nodded but Owen did not agree.

Judith saw that the rest of them longed to settle to the everyday and that tempestuous hopes struck them as irresponsible. She was viscerally on Owen's side. The clash of wills excited her. His vision lit up the shapelessness of life, like those blades of reflected moonlight which sometimes turn a nocturnal sea into gnashings of bright steel.

Michael looked frightened. His eyelids blinked and he passed a hand across them, palm forwards, like a child wiping away a speck or a tear. She was furious at the unskinned pain he used against her. He exposed it, like a beggar used to making a show of his sores. It was effective too: their bond. But she felt an urge to do some extreme thing, something from which there would be no backing down. How dare he expect more from her? He was responsible for the mean lines about her mouth. I could, she thought, have been *normal* married to someone else. He infected me. At the same time she saw that her rage had drained off into self-pity. She would not, now, say the final wounding thing – if such existed between her and Michael.

There was a cunning movement to his head: something infinitesimally slight; he had sensed her weakening.

He walked to the window, and leaned his forehead against the glass. 'If you want to go, you will. I can't stop you, can I?'

'No.'

If he had argued she might have produced reasons. She had strings all pat and ready. But Michael was giving her no chance to use them. He just stood there: a hulk of pain in his un-pressed tweeds which were round-legged like pyjamas and smelled of tobacco and self-neglect.

'What do you mean "go"?' she asked angrily.

His need screamed at her, silently. No other answer came and this left her standing stupidly in the middle of the kitchen, deprived of her quarrel. They had been drinking tea and were on their third cup. Green light fell through the window where she had a row of plants. It shrank the space, making Michael and probably herself look amphibious. The place actually *was* damp. Condensation had rusted the hooks from which her saucepans hung; salt in its glass container had hardened into rocks and a Victorian egg-timer had jammed so that half the sand remained in the upper globe.

'What do you want?'

'What do *you*?'

Oh this was ridiculous!

'I'm going away for the weekend with him,' she said. 'I have to.'

'Sexual fever?'

She nodded, feeling she was betraying both men. Michael's hurt registered on her nerve ends. Well, hurt was his weapon, she thought sourly, but when he turned a tormented face to her, open, exhausted and with no fight in it, her hand reached for his cheek, felt him grip it and then his head was on her shoulder. He was crying.

'Michael, please, darling, don't.'

'Owen O'Malley, you're our soul and our heart! You're the best part of us, our very selves!'

The drunk lurched, dancing, guying his own declaration, his coat-tails flying as he twirled coquettishly in Owen's path, holding up the flow of people who were trying to get in or out of the pub door.

It was Dirty Fleming in celebrative mood. 'I mean it,' he fawned, his hand held out in hesitant hope of the price of a drink. 'Your health,' he suggested.

But the new order did not dispense tips. Owen slid past him, followed by Seamus and Sparky, who were to act out the incident later, amid laughter, in the Clancys' front room.

Owen spent a fair amount of time after he got home sounding out the American and trying to bring him round to his own way of thinking.

'The fellow's a danger,' he concluded.

'More than Seamus?' Judith asked. Arguments between Owen and her brother were deadlocked.

'Seamus hasn't the power this lad has,' Owen told her. 'Our money comes from America. When he leaves he'll be playing the expert over there. The day could come when the bold Sparky will be dictating policy to us.'

'How come you didn't manage to persuade him?' Kathleen needled Owen. 'Where are your powers gone?' Owen had been out ballyragging the country, talking at fairs and meetings up and down the land.

'It does no good to persuade a weathercock,' said Owen. 'When I talk to Sparky I win him over. But for how long? He has a notion that the Irish people are boiling with patriotism. I imagine he was brought up on ballads. He has no notion of the difficulties of remobilizing an apathetic, divided population. He doesn't foresee the methods we may have to use. They'll shock him. He'll oppose us and leave us in the lurch when it comes down to it and send American funds to the other side.' Owen frowned. His breath was bad and he was sickening for an ulcer.

'As de Valera has been saying,' said Owen, 'we may have to wade through Irish blood. Wading through a dose of Yank blood,' he said savagely, 'shouldn't frighten us either.' It maddened him that the country should be dependent still on outsiders. He was leery of Sparky and had had a row with Kathleen for flaunting herself in the fellow's presence and making herself cheap. Maidenly modesty was one of the ancestral virtues which he hoped would flourish in the new, free and Gaelic Ireland to which all should be committed.

15

'*Do* you love me, Grainne?'
'Yes.'
'Well then?'
'Don't nag.'
'Christ, I . . .'
'I know. I *know*.'
'What?'
'You want me to make up my mind.'
'If *that's* nagging . . .'
'It is.'
'OK. I'll say nothing.'
Silence.
'Oh, *say* it.'
'What?'
'Nag. You might as well, James. I know what you're thinking.'
'Then I don't need to, do I?'
'I've poisoned the wells here. I should move on. That's your argument, isn't it? Cormac will be better off without a mother who embarrasses him and in a year or so we can meet on a new footing. Michael – I forgot what I'm supposed to think about Michael.'
'Don't think of him.'
'Ah!'
'You can't have a perfect conscience all the time. You've got to put up with being partly wrong. So have I.'
'We can't make our omelette without breaking hearts. Joke.'
'I've registered it.'
'I'm sorry, James.'

'So am I.'

'No, I mean I'm sorry for being sarky. Trying to suggest that I'm the sensitive one and that your advice is facile.'

'Well, it's limited. You can't expect . . .'

'I know. I *know*. Don't say it.'

'Look, tell me about the Devereux Estate and why we can't bring your aunt.'

'She fell. Mary let her slip in the bath and she put her hip out. Anyway, Owen Roe is on the warpath and if you use one word she tells you, he'll sue and he'll win. That's how the law is here. What about your boss? What did *he* say?'

James put his head in his hands. It ached. 'We had a row,' he admitted. Larry had flown into Dublin the night before and James and he, between them, had drunk a bottle of Paddy. 'His film is shameless myth-making. Lies.'

'Well, you *said* it was propaganda.'

'Yes, but mainly I think he *likes* lies. On principle. The bigger the better. Scale impresses him. He calls it "art". "Surreality", if you please. He told me I'm naive.'

Larry and he had sat up half the night arguing. Then Larry, after perhaps two hours of sleep, had taken the plane for Amsterdam, looking, James noted sourly, none the worse for wear. His own temples were hammering and he saw scoops of light when he moved his head fast.

'Did he listen to Aunt Judith's cassette?'

'Yes.' James shrugged. His own enthusiasm seemed embarrassing now. It had blinded him for the better part of the evening to Larry's lack of it. 'I know you told me not to follow up your old man's schemes,' he had started in defensively, 'and I haven't. No trying to frighten or threaten the local authorities, no making waves. I've been discretion itself. My interest in the Sparky Driscoll story is purely *as a story* for our film. The first the Irish establishment need know of our version is what they'll see on their cinema screens when it's released. By then you're home free. Right? And it's a great story, Larry. You can see,' James had rattled on, fired by the cassette, the Paddy and his own cleverness, 'that Driscoll must have fallen foul of some elements within the Sinn Féin movement, which was drifting towards Civil War in

319

the early months of '22. It broke out, you'll remember, in June. Each side would have hoped to get the Irish-American bread and whichever thought Driscoll hostile would have an interest in getting rid of him before he got in his report. What fascinates me is that I get the feeling that the guys who did him in came round later to his way of thinking. That's the only explanation for *everyone*'s wanting the truth covered up and it's an example of that Irish destiny whereby reality is so shifty that the guy who doesn't move fast enough gets left looking like a traitor. Driscoll may have moved *too* fast. He may have been right too soon. It'll make a lovely movie, Larry. The death records will have been faked but we have a chance to use oral sources before they die off. That's what you wanted . . . isn't it?'

Larry's meaty palm was lifted. 'You're off-beam, James.'

'How?'

Larry sighed. 'Jesus, man, I took you out of academe. Even if your nutty nun's got the truth, we don't want it. We're making a *film*. We don't want appendices and footnotes. Above all, we don't want material that doesn't fit.'

'Surely you can accommodate some ambiguity? Hell, Larry, if you wanted the goodies and baddies as distinct as in a Kojak episode, you could have let me know.'

Larry sighed again. 'This is a Republican film, remember? To raise funds, right? In America. We do not want to show Republicans murdering an American fund-raiser. Can you see that?'

'But you wanted to discredit the old pols and . . .'

'Listen, James, drop it, OK?' Larry poured out two tumblers of Paddy and raised his own to the light. 'We're constructing a myth,' he said, squinting at the golden liquid. 'We don't give a goddamn about truth. It does not set you free. It dissipates energies. Myths unify. They animate.' Larry waved out of the window in the general direction of Stephen's Green. 'Out there,' he said, 'there are guys fighting. They don't want an ambiguous fucking message, right?'

James gave in.

'Talking of fucking,' Larry went on, 'you'd better cool it with the O'Malley woman. There are people of importance to my backers who want you out. Maybe you should come with me to Amsterdam. You'd be safer in its Red Light district than here. Do you know what the IRA does to guys who fuck women for whose honour they feel some concern?'

Next morning a sober Larry told James that Kinlen was refusing to make RTE facilities available to Larry.

'Kinlen?' James was astonished. 'I thought we were buddies.'

'Uhuh. See you in three days,' said Larry. 'We'll talk.'

Since then, James had been unable to get hold of Corny Kinlen or anyone else he knew in RTE. 'The place has turned into something like the Kremlin.'

Grainne poured whiskey for him. 'Hair of the dog?' she offered.

'Listen, shall we go to the Devereux Estate ourselves? This weekend?'

'Without your aunt? Why? And why now when . . .'

'Why not? She was cover for me. A chaperone. It's more of a boat-burning expedition for me if I go alone. And we can investigate the place for our own satisfaction and to hell with them all.'

'You will burn your boats?'

'Slowly. Judiciously. One or two at a time.'

'Will you come away with me?'

'Maybe. What about England for a bit? Neutral ground.'

'Because you have doubts?'

'Because you may. Anyway I couldn't get a visa for the US overnight.'

'How practical you are, after all. What changed you?'

'You looked so miserable.'

'I should have known how to soften you.'

'Yes. I'd better go. I'll have to talk to Michael.'

'They won't stop you coming?'

'No. I'll phone you in the morning. We'll arrange some neutral place to meet.'

'I've made up my mind!'

Kathleen was frying bread and her hair was tied up in a cloth to protect it from the smell of grease.

'I'm telling Owen when he gets back next week. I can't

marry him and I can't stand this house, nor country nor all the palaver. It's all very fine for you,' she accused. 'We've all protected you. You never knew anything. When there were arms hidden in the house you never knew it. I've been running the place all the time you were at school and even when you were home we kept things from you. When you did guess at something it was an excitement. For you. Not for me. For me,' said Kathleen, 'it was hell. Sheer. Unrelieved. I know it's unfair to tell someone that they're young. But *you're* young, Judith, in a wilful, blind way. You don't see reality and you think you do. So don't advise me. There's no agreement between us. I'm only telling you so that when the rumpus breaks out, with Owen cursing me and saying I'm the worst in the world, you may just have some inkling of how things were for me. Me. I'm sorry to use the word so much but up to now I've used it too little.'

Kathleen was flattening the bread in the grease and had the flame too high so that bubbles leaped from the pan. Her words spattered with the same angry heat.

'No!' She held up a steaming spoon. 'Don't interrupt. Let me have my say. You don't *know*,' she insisted. 'Not really. What it was like. First we had Eamonn on the run. Then Seamus and Owen. Strange gunmen spending nights in the bedrooms above stairs and there on the settle. Sometimes half a dozen at one time. How was I to pass them off if the Tans came? As relatives? You should have seen some of them. Jesus! I didn't get a night's sleep for eighteen months before the truce. Not one. I still wake up rigid with terror of a raid. I'm not the only one. I know. I'm not complaining. Not about that. It was worse for the men and, anyway, I know it was the only way. Eamonn explained that to me. And Seamus and then Owen until the explanations are coming out my ears. I *know* this was the only sort of war that a small, unarmed people could fight against a colossus. All right. I accepted that. But *now*, I'm tired, Judith, and you've no right at all to judge me because you didn't live through it the way I did.

'Do you know one reason why we kept so much from you? Eamonn and Seamus and I? Because you're childish, Judith. You're quick at your books and, as Seamus says, people that are good at the books are often oddly stupid when it comes to practical things. They stay childish longer. They like school and they don't want to grow up. There's some of that in Owen. No, it's true. I mean it. It's one reason why you're not more frightened. Bravery is a form of stupidity. I don't want to insult you, but I want you to try and understand someone quite different from yourself: me. The war was never exciting to me, Judith. I saw too much of it.

'And another thing, you don't get braver. It's the opposite. Your nerves get ragged. I've lain there trying to get to sleep to escape my fright and when I did sleep, there it would be again waiting for me in a nightmare. You get so you're afraid to close your eyes. I know it sounds weak to you, and maybe some people are braver. Some are. But a lot of the fellows have shot nerves and one or two went mad. Raving. Had to be locked up. Ask anyone. Even Owen gets dreams. You heard him yourself. But now that we have a chance of peace, nothing will do him but to try to start things up again. Well, it's turned me against him. He's cold as ice. A machine run on will-power. He wasn't like that when I knew him first. So don't tell me that I haven't kept faith. It's him has changed. I can't stand him now. He makes my flesh creep. I'm *glad* he doesn't seem to care for me any more.'

'He does, Kathleen. It's just that he's thinking about politics, the war. He's a special man, Kathleen. You've got to . . .'

'I've got to think of myself. And I don't give two hoots if you or anyone else thinks I'm throwing myself at Sparky Driscoll. I am. I'm in love with him. Why wouldn't I be? He's gentle. He's gay. He makes me feel I exist, and the only reason he's holding back is because everyone's been telling him that I'm to be a hero's bride. Well, I don't want a hero. I want a man.'

'Kathleen . . . Listen. You mustn't . . . Please, Kathleen . . .'

'I'd forgotten what men could be like. Maybe I never knew.' Kathleen threw grease furiously on the bread, then turned round to harangue her sister. 'How could I have children with a madman like Owen O'Malley? He's arrogant, abstract, he never changes his underwear.'

'Kathleen! You're so vulgar. It's that Yank.'

'Yes. It is. He's considerate. He doesn't smell. He cares about people, not causes. God, how I hate the word "cause".'

'And if he won't have you?'

'He'll help me get to America and I'll get someone like him. An ordinary man. Even if he's not like Sparky, he won't be all mad for his own notions of himself like the lads here. I want to be ordinary, Judith. I want to settle down, marry and live my life without people pointing their fingers at me for a man-eater. I'm not a man-eater. God knows. I laugh and make jokes and dance because I can't stand to remember the last eighteen months. I think that if I got to America and had the ocean between me and this place, I'd get so easy-going and slow that I'd be as fat as an elephant in three months.'

'Well, you'd better hook your man before that happens.'

'Yes.' Kathleen began to laugh, then burst out crying. 'I'd be a good wife,' she sobbed. 'I *would*. But I'm twenty-four. I'm losing my looks. It's the nerves. My hair is falling out. It'll be too late for me soon.' Sobs shook her. 'I'm trapped,' she wailed and wiped her face in a dish-cloth. She kept it over her face while deep shudders ran through her. 'Trapped!'

'Kathleen,' Judith was both upset and frightened, 'can I help? *Why* are you crying?'

A kind of groan came from behind the dish-cloth.

'You're not . . .? Kathleen, you haven't . . .?' No. Impossible. Still . . . Girls sometimes forgot themselves. Judith couldn't even put words on the fright which had begun to nibble coldly at her, like some uncertain, clawing thing in sand-clouded water. 'Kathleen?' she interrogated.

'Of course not.' The dish-cloth came off. Kathleen's face was like more cloth: shapeless, crumpled, wet. 'Better if I had maybe,' she moaned. 'Yes, better.'

'Rubbish!' said Judith. 'You're hysterical!' She waited a moment, coldly watching her sister. 'You're sure?' she insisted with distaste.

'Of course I'm sure.'

'So what are you crying for?'

'Oh Judith, you're such a prig. You understand nothing. Nothing. You're like Owen.'

Kathleen opened the shutter of the range and threw the bread she had been frying into it. 'I'm sick of being the woman of the house!' she shouted. 'Alone! Everyone's mother and nobody's wife. Everyone depends on me and who can I depend on? The Da?' The grease left on the pan had caught fire. Flames blazed up in a sheet of greedy, brazen heat. Kathleen threw the pan on the floor. 'The house can burn down,' she yelled. 'Then none of us need worry about anything any more, need we?' She ran from the room, leaving Judith to douse the flames and clean up the mess.

Grainne had begun to clean the house. She had not looked at it with a critical eye for years and when she did she was appalled. Paint had flaked off. Skirting-boards were pitted with fissures large enough to permit the passage of a mouse. There was a furry trim of dust on every surface. Doris, the so-called cleaner, must have spent her time having pots of tea, many of them with Grainne. Mary made more dirt than she cleared. *Her* one virtue was that she was good with the aunt. She was with her now, gossiping or saying the rosary or perhaps both. The sounds drifting down from the top floor alternated a prayerful drone with squeals of laughter.

Grainne, leaving them to it, equipped herself with rubber gloves and cleansers and attacked the hall. It was a kind of therapy. She scrubbed as though she were cleaning her soul, amused that the image should occur to her – an echo of old catechism classes – yet accepting it too. She scattered Vim on the woodwork, scrubbed and found the edges crumbling into her sponge. She pressed Polyfilla into the holes but the stuff could get no purchase and disappeared, leaving them undiminished. When she did succeed in improving a stretch of wood, it made the rest look so much worse that she was tempted to dirty it all again. After an hour or so, she dumped her equipment in the box-room and decided to have a bath, then got dressed and went to Michael's office to catch him before he had time to disappear into the city's maw.

'Why don't we spend an evening drinking together?' she suggested.

It was a thing they used to do when they were first married.

Michael put on his tweed coat which was long and lean: a coat of the 1930s. In his youth he had dressed eccentrically from vanity. Now, perhaps he was not even aware of being out of fashion. Arms linked, they walked with their heads down to protect their faces from the wind. Rotting leaves flicked at their ankles and they paused to watch a swan pass on the canal. She wondered whether, like her, he was deliberately putting off the moment of reaching a pub. Once inside, he would begin to clown. She had started seeing Michael as James did and knew that the American imagined her husband to be, as he would have put it, 'insecure'. Michael was not insecure at all. Instead, he was lit internally by a cold, secret flame of arrogance. Arrogance and accidie. If Michael did not grapple with life it was because life seemed unworthy. His good opinion of himself was based on contempt for the objectives other people pursued. In the pubs, idle men like Michael and failures and would-be poets – the city was full of these; their ambitious colleagues having all emigrated – sometimes made common cause with admirers of terrorism. Theirs was a negative alliance against businessmen and professionals who would sometimes stand their detractors drinks and listen in amusement to their jibes. It was as though they paid to be scourged. Grainne could not decide whether they did this out of respect for people like Michael – 'characters' – or egged them on with the same indifference as they might have stirred up dogs or fighting cocks. Perhaps the old eighteenth-century liking for visiting lunatic asylums had lingered on in Dublin in this licence granted to the city's eccentrics?

'Let's go to some small pleb pub.' She hoped to avoid meeting anyone they knew.

'As you like.'

The wind ruffled Michael's furzy hair and froze Grainne to the bone. She felt connected to him by this punitive element. Damn, she thought, and tightened her grip on his arm.

'Put your hand in my pocket,' he offered. 'Keep you warm.'

They passed a boarded-up Georgian terrace due for destruction. The façade alone was to be kept: a sop to preservationists.

Michael peered between two planks. 'There used to be a sweet-shop here,' he remembered. 'I used to come here for a bar of Fry's cream chocolate whenever anyone gave me tuppence. I think it was tuppence. Two pennies. Or a Peggy's leg. It was a year or so after the war and sugar was still scarce. The old man who ran the shop kept his sweets for children who could ask for them in Irish. I was six.'

'And could you ask in Irish?'

'Yes. But I resented his high-handedness. When sweets got plentiful I boycotted his shop.'

'Maybe you destroyed his business?'

'If he was so pig-headed in all his business, he destroyed it himself.'

'I remember,' said Grainne, who had been born too late to remember scarcity, 'asking adults the time when I was out late and unsure whether to turn for home. Priests would always insist I ask in Irish.'

'Which half of them knew very badly.'

'I don't think anyone bothered Cormac that way.'

'A pity they didn't. He might be less of a patriot.'

'Or if we had been, he mightn't be.'

'Do you remember the joke about a chameleon on a tartan?' Michael asked. 'Our grandparents were chameleons on tartans. They were idealistic and thuggish, cunning and mad, politicians and fighting men according to need: variegated. Then came our parents who made money. Solid-coloured individuals. Green for them meant pound notes and government contracts. You and I, the chameleon grandchildren, didn't know how to react and keep our individuality. Cormac's gone back to the tartan.'

'Mmmm,' she said, shrugging at this, unwilling to go any further with it. She felt him try to web her in. Fate, he was implying, fatigue, habit, heritage, were stakes planted around her, holding her here, limiting her choices. Poor Michael, she thought, how wrong he was. She could go any time she liked. Any time at all, she told herself with exhilaration and pressed his hand in pity.

They turned into a small, wood-panelled pub where she had not been before but where Michael seemed to be known, for the bar curate greeted him and poured a small Powers unasked.

'Same for the lady?'

'Yes. The lady,' said Michael, 'is my wife.'

Is? Was?

'Good evening, Mrs O'Malley.'

It was twilight outside and the faintly mauve mist to which her eyes had adjusted made the lights here look orange. Worn plush, brass, the dimmed refractions of light from glasses and coloured alcohols evoked a hundred other evenings spent in pubs like this. The place was haunted, festive, theatrical. You looked hard at the decor and saw the flaws – old vomit marks, a whiff of staleness, cigarette burns – but with the glow of the whiskey defects merged in an overall opulence.

Michael raised his glass. 'Whistler,' he quoted ritually – she had heard him say this how many times? – 'said "I drink to make my friends seem witty".'

She raised her glass. 'And relatives.'

I am here, she thought, and not here. If I go away with James it will be a memory to save. She cast a distancing glance at a Goldflake ad and beneath it at an old man in a macintosh intent on his pint. Presumably he was relishing the mild gregariousness of this dim little pub. He had budged his chin maybe a centimetre when she and Michael came in, achieving a limited nod which neither invited conviviality nor quite precluded it.

She raised her second drink: 'Here's happiness,' she said.

'I'm not drinking to that.' Michael looked ready to commit some form of violence.

'Oh?'

The old man in the mac had his ear cocked; pleasantly alerted to drama, he bent his head as though concentrating on the foam of his pint then, unable perhaps to contain his elation, blew lightly into it. Bubbles broke, making rainbow reflections as petrol puddles used to do, she remembered, on the dark tar of country roads. Didn't cars leak petrol any more or had she not looked at the ground since growing up? Nostalgia for the acute, hallucinative boredom of childhood tingled through her, then englobed the present moment and

Michael's fierce-browed rage. I am high, she thought, it's not just whiskey, it's choice, refractions, possibilities. No matter how I choose, I shan't go on having this excitement. Choice, she thought, the moment of change: this way or that, both held in the hand briefly, briefly. I'll never have it again. Cormac will but I won't. The whiskey was glowing in her chest.

'Who said people were meant to be happy?' Michael was demanding. 'How happy? For how long? And how often? It's a bloody American fantasy. Start again and again. Break things up. Marriages. Friendships. Like bloody kids, and then if you're still not happy go on breaking. It's asinine,' he concluded. His lower lip clamped wetly on to his glass. It reminded Grainne of a squashed pink snail.

'You're right there,' said the man in the mac. 'True for you.'

'They keep looking for the initial thrill,' said Michael. 'Repeated over and over. Life isn't like that.'

'Sure they're like babbies,' the man agreed. 'Ants in their pants. Running hither and yon. Thinking faraway hills are greener. God help us.' He tittered, drank and wiped foam fastidiously from his upper lip. 'No respect for age, of course.'

'How could they have?'

'Wisdom,' said the old man sadly. 'I recall . . .'

But Michael was in no mood for recollections. 'Will you have one on me?' he asked the old man, cutting him off.

'Well thank you, thank you very much.'

'Have a short one?'

'No, no, very kind, thanks all the same, but Guinness is easier on the aul gut.' He patted his paunch with affection, as though stroking an animal coiled in his lap. 'A pint,' he said, 'will do very nicely.'

Michael ordered it. 'Happiness,' he stated, 'is a dangerous notion. It's like rights. People will murder you for their "rights".'

'Well, we're seeing a bit of that. Aye.' The recipient of the pint knew his duty.

'Now, if you put the two together and talk about the "right to happiness" . . .'

Grainne put down her whiskey glass and left the pub.

Judith was being harangued from the television. Men with sincere eyes asked her to take the margarine test and see could she honestly tell butter from Green Ribbon Marge. It was a ridiculous ad to have in a country where people were brought up on mistrust and butter. A new chap had been around asking her things. Cormac, he said his name was.

'Where's *she* then?' she'd asked. 'The Principal Girl?'

'She'll be back,' he said. He wanted to know what she'd said on the cassette. 'Anything about Sparky Driscoll?' he asked. 'How he was murdered?'

'Shovelled into the coffin,' she remembered.

'Who told *you*?'

'Kathleen.'

Then a fellow who said he was Owen's and Kathleen's son put his big face so close to hers that he was smothering her with his breath. Man's breath. Strong. All tobacco and drink and gamey food. It made her cough. 'Did my father have anything to do with it?' he asked.

She began to cry and he went away.

But now her memory was all in a state. Men on television were saying things that they couldn't be saying. They were holding up packets of margarine and squeezing them so that blood dripped from the corners of the packets. One of the men started to unfold the paper and shake it out and she saw that it was a man's shirt.

'Sparky Driscoll's shirt,' said the margarine man, smiling. 'Exhibit number one.'

He smiled at Judith. 'You ought to make a clean breast of things,' he told her. 'You'll be dead shortly. How can you make an act of perfect contrition if you're busy brushing your memories under the carpet? Pretending you don't know,' said the man and held up a small, shrunken head the size of a potato. He held it by the hair and it was unclear at first that it wasn't just a dark, root-like thing, but as it began to dilate and expand, you saw that it was a head.

Judith jiggled the TV dial and a picture came on of two children with their pet sheepdog. She went back to the first channel just to make sure that she hadn't imagined what she'd seen and there it was again, only now the head was as big as the margarine man's own head and the face on it was Sparky Driscoll's. He opened his lips to speak and Judith screamed and turned off the set.

Back in came the two stalwarts.

'What's up? Is it coming back to you?' asked the one who had said he was Owen's son. 'Can you remember what you told that American?'

'Devereux House,' said the boy. 'Does that ring a bell? Is that where they were going to take you? Why?'

'Television,' shrieked Judith.

'What?'

'Don't turn it on,' she shrieked.

'I think maybe we should get a doctor,' said the boy. 'My mother left a number. Are you OK, Aunt Judith? She looks queer to me.'

And it was as if he'd put the evil eye on her, for her heart was racing and she had a pain in her chest. A stretch of sea-green satin slid into the front of her vision. There was a gold scroll curving round it like a child's drawing of a wave. Memory, she thought with delight, and had an urge to slide into it and lay her head on the satin. It was the headrest of a sofa, she saw now. Clear, lucid memories beckoned and why should she resist them? Only she'd tell nothing to this pair. The danger with sliding into the past was that you could let things out. Babble. Tell. And there they'd be with their tape-recorders. Tricksters, shysters and offenders against the second commandment: bearers of false witness. Someone had made off with *her* cassette-recorder.

'Allegations,' she said. 'False.'

'Don't worry,' said Owen's voice. 'Plucky wee thing, isn't she? Give her a shot of brandy here. It's all for the best.'

'Brandy,' she said.

'Will I get some?' asked the boy.

'No,' said the man. 'That might finish her altogether.'

'Drink up,' said Owen. But *he* must have been imaginary for, when she opened her mouth, there was nothing there.

'That bugger had it coming if ever man did,' said he. 'We'll get the lads to have this over the border by morning.'

'She's thirsty,' said the boy. 'Here's some water, Aunt Judith. I'm calling a doctor,' he said. 'I'd say she was having a fit.'

The water was real enough, so she drank some.

'Did he attack her or what?' Owen asked.

'I wasn't there,' said Timmy.

'Feel her pulse then. Did you say she had a heart condition?'

'Call the doctor so. He can give her a sedative.'

Judith and her sister had made up their quarrel. Kathleen's face was swollen. She said she was sorry she had compared Judith to Owen. It was a terrible thing to say.

'He's inhuman,' she told her sister. 'I honestly think he's a menace to the country.'

'The menace is Sparky Driscoll,' Judith told her, but had little hope of making her sister see sense. Owen was a figure from whom weak, little egotistic people shrank back. His purposefulness would corrode their puny reasoning like acid and they feared to have the shabbiness of their calculations laid bare. 'Sparky's temptation,' she told her sister, so as not to have it on her conscience that she hadn't tried to make her face up to this. She saw now that her sister was far gone towards concupiscence. Sparky was a spoiler and a giver of bad advice. In Kathleen he had found soil only too receptive to his twaddle about self-assertion and how she should emigrate to America where, to hear him, every sort of wonder existed and people made their own destiny, each thinking only of himself. In his young day, the Da had fallen for the same tinselly bait. Mindless as the red setter, the prancing Sparky could destroy her sister.

'I love him,' said Kathleen. 'I'm in love for the first time.'

'Oh shut up. Don't be a fool.'

'What's foolish about it?' Kathleen asked. 'Even if he doesn't love me, it has already brought me more happiness than I've known in years. It's as if I'd come out from a bad spell. We've been living in a kind of hysteria, Judith, and now it's not necessary any more. I wish I could make you see that.

I'd like to rescue you before Owen sucks you into his madness. He's very powerful Owen is. Persuasive. Especially with women. I let him get me in thrall. I believed everything he said and now it's going to happen to you. When I say "physical" I don't mean he has to touch you. Quite the opposite really. It's like a power all dense inside him and you think it's reason but it's not. It works on crowds too. I've seen him sway them, even though the words he was using weren't anything special.'

'Kathleen, you're talking tripe.'

'I'm not. I'm not. If only you'd listen to me . . .'

'The one who has a spell is Sparky. He's polluted your mind,' shouted Judith. 'I honestly think you ought to go to confession and get some priest's advice.'

'Judith – what's that? Sh.'

'What?'

'It's Sparky.'

'What do you mean?'

'Out in the yard. I recognize his step.' Kathleen ran to the door. 'I can't let him see me like this. Tell him I'm out. Ask him to call round tomorrow.'

She withdrew her puffed, tear-swollen face and fled up the stairs. The sound of her footsteps had just reached the room above Judith's head when Sparky appeared at the outer door. He was all dressed up in a celluloid wing collar and ulster cape. He'd come, he said, to say goodbye. He was leaving tonight. Change of plan. Was Kathleen in? No? Where was she? Would she be back soon?

'She's gone to Dublin,' said Judith, 'to see Owen. She won't be back until tomorrow. Seamus is away too,' she added with satisfaction. 'Nobody's here but me.'

He looked, she had to admit, a touch cast down.

'I'll say goodbye for you,' she said.

'Tell them I'll write,' said Sparky. It was out of his hands, he explained. People back in the States had summoned him to return. They were curious about the rumours of splits and divisions here. They wanted him to come back and explain things.

'So now you'll be giving advice,' said Judith. 'Which side are you going to back?' She wished Owen were here.

'Well there's really only the government side, isn't there?'

'What about the Republicans? De Valera wants a fight.'

'That's not clear. Anyway the army doesn't take orders from him.'

'Did you see where he said in the papers that there are rights which a minority may justly uphold, even by arms, against a majority?' Owen had quoted the lines so often, she had them off by heart. 'What do you think of that?' she asked anxiously. The least she could do for Owen would be to find out accurately what Sparky's frame of mind was.

He laughed. 'Don't bother your head, Judith, with all that. It may never happen. I hope it doesn't for the sake of all the good friends I've made here. I'd like to think of you enjoying your own country in peace.'

'And dishonour?'

Another laugh. 'Don't let's fight on my last day. Mm?'

'Listen,' Sparky was saying, 'may I ask a favour?' He wanted her to walk over to Devereux House with him. He had intended asking Kathleen. He wanted to take some photographs as mementoes. Would Judith come? 'I want to show them back home as examples of the pretty colleens I've met.'

'And one is as good as another, I suppose? We're interchangeable?'

It occurred to her, though, that she had better get him out of the house. Kathleen might change her mind if he stayed too long. She could imagine her this minute throwing cold water on her face and wondering whether it was recovered enough to be seen.

'All right then,' she decided, and hustled him out the door.

There was a knot of men waiting for the village shop to open. Driscoll shook hands with them all. He seemed to have endless friends, she noted. His friendship meant nothing. Yes, he said. Off tonight. He'd take the boat from Queenstown in the morning. One or two of the men had been in America in their youth. They laughed toothlessly, telling him to say hello to the Statue of Liberty for them. Some mentioned the fighting that had started to break out here and there, but deviously, unsure how the American might feel and unready to show what they felt themselves.

'The Lord save us, isn't it a shame? Yes. The lads turning on each other.'

They'd say no more, not letting on which lads they were for. Maybe they didn't know? The government had only just emerged from clandestinity and keeping a tight lip was traditional. The country never knew what went on in the Dáil which, until recently, had met on the run. The Dáil never knew what the Cabinet decided and the Cabinet, said Sparky, who had been looking into this, had, during de Valera's presidency which had only just ended, been ruled autocratically by him.

'It'll take them a while to learn the ways of democracy,' said he.

Meanwhile they had reached the great golden gates of the estate. Driscoll took a photograph of Judith posed in front of them to show their size. This time they looked less splendid, for there was no sun glinting on them and in fact a storm seemed to be coming. The queer calm which precedes storms held the landscape congealed like moss specimens under glass.

'Is it true,' she asked, as they walked towards the house, 'that you offered to sponsor Kathleen to go to America?'

'Who told you that?'

'She did.'

'I told her not to.'

'Oh. Why?'

She looked at him curiously, straight in the eye as she never did look, and had been taught in the convent never to look, at men. He looked straight back and she felt a series of small shocks ripple through her. She didn't like Sparky Driscoll's interfering ways, his pushiness or his opinions, but this sensation was a binding, thrilling one. Remembering what Kathleen had said about Owen having a power all dense in himself which reached out and touched people, she suddenly saw what her sister had meant. Like sunbeams on your face, though less visible, a warmth reached out from Sparky Driscoll, a calming, exhilarating feeling which made you feel good. She was still looking at him, gauging the sensation, wondering whether the two men sensed the magnetism in each other and if that was why they had taken against each other, as powerful males did in wild herds.

'Why do you look so accusingly at me?' Sparky asked, surprising her, as she had forgotten that she had been accusing him. 'I didn't want Kathleen to tell you because you are much stronger than she is and you could make things hard for her.' They had reached the house. 'Seems all closed up,' said Sparky, breaking off to peer about. They were at a side entrance. 'Pity. I wanted to take some snapshots of that famous ballroom where people went for a snatch of happiness. Look,' he said. 'There's an open window. Are you game to go in by it? Timmy's not here.'

He had pulled the bell-pull uselessly, so this must be true.

Judith followed him into what turned out to be the gun room with the python-skin frieze. Both its doors were locked, however, and it did not look as though they were fated to reach the ballroom. Rain was starting, so they might as well wait for Timmy to turn up or, at least, for the shower to pass. Judith let herself flop on to a green silk divan while Sparky rattled uselessly at door knobs.

'Not a hope. We'll have to wait here.'

Grainne was excited. Her voice was buoyant, almost out of control. The flash of revolving glass doors punctuated what she said. Chop, chop, went the curved glass, turning like the hands of a clock. Time, she thought, choice. Am I really leaving? A woman came in with a dripping umbrella and the mercurial drip, drip was also like the motion of some instrument for measuring time.

Am I attractive, she wondered, or old and ridiculous: a raddled bit of mutton dressed as lamb? Going off for what used to be called a dirty weekend did raise such doubts.

'Tell me,' James must have said, 'about this place we're going to?' He had meant that she should give him addresses and phone-numbers to leave at the desk. He was talking to the clerk now, carefully ensuring that if Larry or someone rang they could get in touch. At first she had misunderstood him and launched into the story of the Devereux Estate. Looking back while he looked forward – was that significant? It had been over breakfast which they'd had together in the hotel restaurant: appearing as scandalous or married, as though they'd already started their weekend, though in fact she had come straight from home. Eight a.m. Michael would wake up and not find her. Never mind. There was no graceful way to run out on your husband. When she passed the corner of the Green, a woman was already selling white heather sprigs for luck. Struggle: if I believe in my luck then I needn't buy more. But if I don't, she'll resent me. I can't afford to draw any more resentment.

'Here,' she had given the woman fifty pence and taken the heather which, being bought, could be no use. You can't buy luck.

'You'll meet Timmy,' she told James. 'The one-time care-taker who now owns the place. It's a funny story. Shall I tell you? Yes? He was the bum-lover, you see, of the old Anglo-Irish owner. Well, he wasn't old, I mean no older than Timmy, but of the old stock. Demi Devereux. His father had been a general or something, but *he* did nothing except live with Timmy and go a bit native while Timmy went a bit Anglo. Then, oddly, Timmy – perhaps he wasn't all that queer? Or perhaps he wanted an heir, having gone Anglo? – anyway, Timmy married and had sons and the old landlord enjoyed Timmy's sons. There were four of them and they too married and the old man – now he *was* getting old – moved them and their wives into the house and enjoyed a third generation of boys. It was a sort of stud, you see. Stories were told about house-parties being arranged for English guests with special tastes. Who knows? That was in the Fifties, while the old man was still hale and hearty and before the place began to fall into the clutches of Timmy's tribe, who kept having children and encroaching on more and more rooms. You may imagine the result. They dug up lawns to plant potatoes, cut trees to sell the wood, bought Woolworth's ware because the wives wouldn't clean the silver, and generally adapted the place to suit their taste. It was a bit of do-it-yourself land-reform, a take-over of the sort not foreseen by politicians. Now, they say, old Devereux is afraid to move out. He is ailing and not allowed to drive. He no longer has visitors and, although he has ulcers, the women feed him on tinned beans and fried food so that he is always dyspeptic. They say Timmy and his boys have so much blackmail material on him that he is utterly in their power. He has made the place over to Timmy's family.'

'What a horrible story,' said James.

'Is it?' She was doubtful. 'I hoped you'd be amused.'

'The poor old man.'

'Well . . .'

'Being preyed on by parasites,' said James.

'Like *Volpone*, you mean? I suppose you *could* see it that way. I saw Paul Scofield in it and he made Volpone so sexy that I felt sympathy with the old rascal for the first time. But the old man in my story came of a rapacious breed who had themselves preyed on the natives, stolen the land in their time and so forth. They *deserved* to have the tables turned.'

James pretended to shiver. 'The long, venomous memory of the Celt!'

'Venomous?' she asked, 'do I sound venomous?' She touched her white heather for luck and wondered about Michael who would be awake by now. Cormac had again spent the night at his uncle's.

'Let's go,' said James, and she followed him into the lobby where he was now talking to the clerk.

She looked at herself in a mirror, checking for venom and lack of generosity, then back at the glass doors which were revolving once more. Two men walked through and up to James.

'Mr Duffy?'

'Yes.' He had finished with the clerk. He smiled past the men at Grainne.

'Could we have a private word with you, Mr Duffy?'

'Well . . .' James hesitated.

'It's important. I'll explain why – in private. I'm from the United States Embassy. If we could just . . .'

'Won't be a moment,' said James to Grainne. 'Why don't you be warming the car?' He looked perplexed.

There was some more talk with the two men, one of whom

seemed to be showing James a card or wallet. Something to do with his film, perhaps? She hoped this didn't mean that they couldn't get away for their weekend. If you screwed yourself up to burn your boats and then the wind blew the flames out or the wood was damp, it could be all up with your resolution. Picking up her beauty-case – she had bought it specially for this trip and it had an adulterous air about it: too smart and small for anything but impropriety – she smiled at James who was looking anxious and touching. Why should he be anxious, she wondered vaguely. Because of the film? It was raining, which seemed wrong for adultery. She had to put on her headscarf, which made her look like the Queen in a paddock, and push through the revolving door to the porch, then get her umbrella up, which was awkward, as the other hand was holding her beauty-case.

'Let me help.'

'Thanks – Owen Roe?' She couldn't believe it. 'Here?'

'I'm afraid so,' he said, 'and it's no coincidence. Come and sit in the car and I'll explain what's happening.'

Sparky came and sat beside her, talking about Kathleen and people's right to happiness and to live their lives. His fingers began to play on the base of her neck, curling and uncurling her short, escaping hair. She shook him off once or twice and even pointedly picked up and removed the marauding hand, but he seemed hardly to notice, intent on his speech, which that wilful hand punctuated and illustrated with its insinuating, curling gestures. Owen, he said, was an idealist. He could see that Judith, a convent girl, still tautly bent on perfections – 'which don't exist in life,' said Sparky, 'or are too expensive in terms of human unhappiness; we just have to settle for the possible' – Judith would, in the nature of things, be impressed by a man like Owen.

'He's a Savonarola,' said Sparky, 'blazing eye, curling lip, contempt for the little accommodations we all make in order to live. It's admirable. It's destructive. It leads a man to die at the stake for what he thinks is right. When that happens we applaud. When he wants a whole country to flame at the stake with him, we are appalled. Or to take a girl like Kathleen with him. At any rate, corrupt, sensible guys like myself feel that way,' said Sparky, still teasing the back of Judith's neck with maddeningly mesmeric fingers.

She jumped up, shaking her head to disperse the languor he had been inducing in her. The neck was a nerve centre. That was all it meant, she told herself, but felt spell-bound. She began walking around the room. The walls were hung with weapons and photographs of Devereux ancestors reviewing troops or embracing animals. One had his arm around the neck of a leopard. Another, bent on dentistry perhaps, was oozing back the lips of a horse. A palm cradled the ball of the snout; fingers slid along the damp, blackish gums.

'I know you resent me, an outsider, saying these things,' said Sparky, 'and I can't even say that I aspire to become a family member. I can't help noticing that your sister likes me but, really, I see my sponsoring her as a rescue operation. I don't want to marry her myself. She'll find someone . . .'

'How can you be so sure you're right? Aren't you worse than Owen?' Judith planted herself accusingly in front of him. 'You try to make people's minds up for them. In what way are you different?'

'Judith, I don't. I didn't court her. She . . .'

'And what about politics?'

The rain had begun to lash down angrily now, beating the windows like whips. The room was darkening and only occasionally lit up by lightning flashes which came immediately before the rolls of thunder. The storm must be right over their heads.

The only justification for a revolution, said Sparky, was to get rid of an unjust government and bring about a better way of life for the people of a country. Now that an Irish government had been achieved, a new revolution would lack all justification. It would cause suffering and would not bring happiness or economic stability since England, Ireland's natural market . . . She walked agitatedly away from him. Why wasn't Owen here? This man could convince anyone. He was convincing *her*. What hope had Owen's party with a man like this going back to America tonight to cut off their only source of arms? Owen had said that he reasoned like a grocer and maybe he did. Measuring. Weighing, calculating equivalents. Yes, yes. It was mean, insidious. It could convince.

There was something else, said Sparky, something confidential which he couldn't actually divulge but it was why he felt that Kathleen must be saved from marrying Owen. He happened to be privy to a secret which – well, it had to do with the reason for his going to Dublin this evening and then home, but, really, he could say no more. Only that Owen would shortly be in trouble with his own comrades. A nasty business. Better for Kathleen to be well clear of it.

'What do you mean?' Judith felt relief at having a reason to shout at him. How dare he smear an honourable man's name by hints? Oh, she cried, she had known he was envious and mean, but how *could* he hide behind such lame excuses. 'You've said too much to stop now,' she challenged.

'I'm not at liberty to say more.'

'Have you to Kathleen?'

'I can't tell you that either.'

But maybe Kathleen was his source?

'It's about money, isn't it? American dollars?' She saw at once that she was right. He stared in such surprise that for a split second she felt triumph – until she remembered how grave it was that *he* should know and how little it could avail matters that *she* did.

He began talking again, pleading with Judith to see that he, Sparky, had no choice but to do what he must. Excessively patriotic men could act, he said, from noble motives, yet, objectively, be as harmful as the basest traitors. Owen must be stopped. He, Sparky, had no choice but to denounce him. His words ran together, blurring in her ears as the garden outside the wet window dissolved in an ocean of green waves. Who must be stopped? How? It was dangerous to stand by a window in a storm, she remembered, and stepped aside. Her mind seemed to slow strangely.

'I've come to love this country,' said Sparky.

Lightning leaped along a wall and flashed on a pair of crossed bayonets with green ribbons on them: the insignia of some Irish regiment. She pointed at these.

'That's all you can do for us,' she said. 'Send us arms. Not advice. We've got too much of that right here. Words. Chat . . .'

The American walked past her and unhooked one of the weapons from the wall.

'Judith,' he said. 'Look at this thing. Just *look* at it. Do you know what you're really asking for? Have you thought about it, really forcing yourself to imagine what blood is like, death, mangled bodies? Kathleen has seen dead men. She had to help smuggle your brother's corpse out of the police morgue. That's why she's disgusted with war. *You* haven't seen anything of the war. It's all in your head. Abstract. I don't believe you would kill a rabbit.' He handed her the weapon. 'Here, feel it. Weigh it. Imagine you're driving it into the guts of a real man. You wouldn't do it. Your nerve would fail you. I know.'

She took it from him, balancing it in her hands. It was heavier, of course, than the broom handles and hurling sticks with which Seamus had taught her, but the motion would be the same. She made a lunge at a cushion, impaled it on the end of the blade.

Sparky laughed. 'Well, we'll have to hide that from Timmy,' he told her and bent down to draw the cushion off the weapon. 'Ruined, I'm afraid. It doesn't quite measure up to a rabbit. But I'll grant you have a stylish thrust.' He pulled the thing off and examined the holes she had made in it. 'Real goose-down,' he said. 'These people knew how to live. Now it's your turn. To be happy. Just let the doves settle, Judith, learn to roll with the bumps. That's the best thing I can wish you and Kathleen and the country, an ordinary, imperfect happiness and forget heroism. It . . .'

Sparky's next sound was like a cushion's when someone sits on it hard: a sudden, soft, gurgling puff of a sound. He folded on to the divan, impaled by Judith's overbalancing driving movement. She almost fell on top of him, but the handle of the bayonet steadied her. She had driven the blade up under his rib cage, through the pit of his stomach and into the woodwork on the back of the divan.

She tried to remove the thing but it was stuck in too deeply.

Putting a foot between Sparky's knees, she pushed the divan and pulled at the handle but to no avail.

'Like a specimen,' she thought. 'He's pinned to green silk like a butterfly specimen.' She felt calm and exhilarated. Something, though, had happened to her apprehension of time, for the lightning which had signalled to her to drive the bayonet into Sparky was only now being followed by its roll of thunder and the storm had not, she knew, moved from its epicentre right above this house. She wriggled the weapon gently and now it did come out so she could hang it back on its place on the wall. Right after it came a gush of blood, bubbling up in frothy curling gushes which surged down Sparky's smart tweed front, carrying goosedown feathers from the wounded pillow.

She sat on the divan opposite the one on which Sparky lay, watching his body slowly nudge its way sideways. His head flopped. The blood poured and trickled and formed a little waterfall on to the polished hardwood floor. Every now and again, lightning flashed and was followed by the growl of thunder. As the day grew darker, she found she could only see Sparky when the lightning came and, of course, she could not predict its coming. She fixed her eyes on the point where the floor would be if she could see it and, the next time the light came, saw that a rivulet had formed and run round the side of the couch, carrying feathers. The floor must be uneven, she thought. She felt tired, released as though from some appalling burden, and was ready to wait as long as necessary for Timmy's return. After some time, she fell asleep.

16

James was on a plane. 'No drinks,' the hostess told him. 'Not yet. Sorry. In a little while.'

'I can see you're as nervous as myself!'

The woman in the next seat was set to chat. Her grin trembled at him and he remembered that during take-off she had blessed herself a dozen or so times: crisscross, crisscross, her hand jolting like a mechanical toy.

Christ, he thought, oh my God!

'This is my first time up in a plane,' the voice went on. 'I'm off to Buffalo to see my married daughter. Queer names they have over there, haven't they? Buffalo? I suppose it's called after the animal?'

Her teeth might have been oystershell chippings: blackish, bashed, belonging to some persistent, earthy form of life.

'We'll be all right, you'll see.'

Her hand landed on his which had, he realized, been gripping and tightening on the arm-rest.

'The hostess is a girl from Dunmanway. She told me they'll be bringing round the tea trolley any minute now.'

Tea, think of tea: brisk whisk of perished fingers clasping the pot or cup for warmth. Beleek, Royal Worcester or Kilkenny cups raised to Grainne's lips: white against the off-white of her teeth. After the Shelbourne Rooms became tricky, they had met in rural hotels or tacky Dublin ones where one had to ring repeatedly for service. Drink was sold only in licensing hours but you could always get a cuppa.

'That'll settle the butterflies in your stomach. I seen your hands tremble. It's nothing to be ashamed of.'

James was being deported or had, anyway, been asked to leave. Told. There was no choice involved.

'We try,' the man from the embassy had said, 'to cooperate with local authorities when one of our citizens,' pursing his lips over the next bit, 'engages in illegal activity on foreign soil.'

The man's name was Berg or something. Burg? The man with him was from the Special Branch. He had held out his ID and James, leaning forward, read the name Detective-Inspector Seamus Horan.

Grainne, at the same moment, had waved and walked out of the flashing, revolving door.

'. . . somewhere more private?' the American was saying as James turned back to him. The man's face was not smiling and that was obviously not like him. He had cheeks which might have looked comfortable blowing a trumpet.

James's mind moved as though he were spaced out: slowly, repetitively, in retakes. It was the shock, he supposed. The shock.

'Private?' urged the man, and James found that he had led them into a lounge which might have been kept in readiness for just such a colloquy. Copies of the *Irish Tatler and Sketch* and the *National Geographic* were stacked on tables. Shadows hung like draperies and still all James seemed to feel was astonishment at not being astonished. Berg or Burg spoke with a robot-like diction which went badly with his cheerful face. They were having trouble, he told James, with Banned Aid. Pause for this to register.

'Yes?' said James.

'There are indications, Mr Duffy, that under cover of providing relief for the needy, the organization is smuggling in guns. It's hard to catch up with them,' said Berg or Burg, 'because they set up phony charities, phantom foundations and . . . film companies, Mr Duffy.' The embassy man raised reproachful eyebrows. 'Some of the people involved,' his shoulder jigged irritably, 'may be well-intentioned and unable to see that small-scale terrorism is going to bring neither peace nor freedom to this country. Perhaps they don't care?' The round face might have belonged to a distressed Santa Claus and James understood that the emotion which the man was keeping in check was acute dislike for himself. 'They don't have to go on living here, after all,' said the embassy man, 'and the gift of a few guns probably affords them emotional satisfaction.' The man's jaw was set. *He* himself was taking emotional satisfaction from this little `sermon, James thought, and shrugged mentally. Impotence numbed him. The man was trying to look him in the eye. 'It also prolongs an impasse, Mr Duffy, by arming people who have no popular mandate.'

Now what? James wondered, and wondered how much he cared. It would hit him later, he decided. People always said that, didn't they? Where was Grainne? Would she come back to the lobby when he delayed joining her?

The Special Branch man was looking tired. At all events, said the American, James had overstepped the law. Rash meddling in other people's lives was a thing to which some of our citizens were unfortunately prone. It gave our embassies a lot of trouble.

'In your case,' he told James, 'the Irish police have agreed not to press charges if you leave at once. Our advice is that you let Detective-Inspector Horan see you aboard a plane. This will save embarrassment all round.'

James's protests sounded untrustworthy. His indignation was larded with awareness that his innocence was of the foolish, rather than the sinless, variety. Larry had clearly involved him, intentionally or not, in a less legal side of his endeavours. 'Are you sure,' he wound up *pro forma*, 'that you haven't got the wrong end of the stick?'

Both men sighed. Then the Irishman creaked into action: 'Mr Duffy,' said he, in a sorrowful voice, 'your film was cover. There *is* no such film, is there, or, if there is, it's a subsidiary activity of the people you work for? Mm?'

A notebook was produced. James's movements, some of them furtive – those rural hotels – were well known, it appeared, to the Special Branch. His visit to the Young Patriots' Club, the trouble at Customs, even his meeting with the goat-faced man who had warned him to keep away from Grainne, his trips to IRA veterans' homes, Larry's trip to Amsterdam, calls and telegrams about tapes, equipment, camera crews – all these had been marked and noted in the judgement book. All were now decoded and all, to the minds of Berg and Horan, pointed to the one thing. They were cover; they were masks and what they were covering was not sex. That itself was a cover. His adultery with Grainne was pretence. 'A common dodge,' said Horan, shrugging. 'Old as the hills. People think the police are so thick they'll swallow anything.'

Obsessed as a pair of witch-hunters, minds zipping along their single track, they challenged him to deny any of the particulars in the Detective-Inspector's notebook. Had he or had he not, on the day in question, gone to a certain cottage in the mountains with his associate, Mrs O'Malley? Yes, and had he had an interview there with her uncle, Mr Owen Roe O'Malley, the TD?

'I want to see a lawyer.'

The embassy man cut in. 'This is no case for a lawyer. The police will not press charges if you leave at once.'

'And if I don't?'

'Your passport could be confiscated and a deportation order issued.'

And could he see Mrs O'Malley? No, he could not. She would be informed of what had happened.

'May I take it that you will cooperate with Detective-Inspector Horan?'

'I seem to have no choice.'

A chill smile: 'None at all.'

The woman's hand was on his knee. 'Here's our tea.' Smiling. Motherly. Her overtures upset him. Her sidling humility. Her Irishness. Puffs of flesh, swelling on either side of her wedding ring, made the thing look punitive: a brutal tool.

Informed? What did they mean informed? What would they tell her? And would her resolution founder now forever?

Had Larry set him up? Or should *he* have tried to tip Larry off? Was all this his own fault? How? Where had he gone wrong? Had he unconsciously – Celticly? – willed disaster on himself?

Maybe *she*'d have to get out? On whose side was her cousin?

The curse or anger poem, he had been told, was a traditional Irish genre. He felt capable of composing a stinging one extempore and phoning it to her from New York. Might it move her to come and join him? Maybe, half-way across the Atlantic, he'd stop wanting her? Disbelief in one's loss was supposed to be a prologue to grief. He'd better get to the sorrowing stage fast and get it over with.

Still over Ireland. Strips of land showed through breaks in the cloud. Green, uneven, like fallen apple-peelings, they sizzled then sank into memory's perfecting gleam. He had a letter to Therese in his pocket. Even touching it made him wince. At least he hadn't mailed it. Shit, shit, shit. He kept looking out of the window lest the woman on his other side engage him. The red sun would not sink for hours. It was buoyed up, congealed in its tracks by the plane's movement westward. Passengers had been invited to put their watches back.

Could he set himself back emotionally too? Forget Grainne and return to Therese? If she'd have him? Could he? Would she? Did he want her to? He tried to remember his letters to her and his hand scratched at the final one in his pocket. He was numb, stunned. Obviously, this deadness was a defence and not all that effective. Flicks of feeling razored through: memories of driving into the country with Grainne *en route* to some hotel, where they would pretend to rent a room for the night, keeping up a front of propriety, paying in advance, walking up the softly carpeted stairs, while manageresses pretended not to know that they'd be leaving in an hour. Then, behind the closing door, laughter, connivance, that binding euphoria of recovered childhood. It was such a proper country, so tight, so watchful – so much more so than he had supposed. *How* had anyone charted their progress down those empty mountain roads: hedged and ditched, hairy and brambly, empty but for the odd, pensive, munching donkey and the silly baaing sheep? He had more than once wanted to pull her into some hole under a hedge and pull the clothes off her freckle-flecked body which was like something spawned spontaneously by the landscape. There were lichen growths on the rocks of the same colour as the hair on her head and the secret, tousling hair on her body. James wanted to stand up and scream at the thought, must have started to do so, for the seat-belt was cutting at his thighs. 'Grainne!' A perfect name for howling in pained disbelief. Grr . . . He was talking out loud, upsetting the woman beside him, who had started up her chatter again, pushing goddamn tea-the-universal-pick-me-up and, no doubt, deprecating his peculiar manners.

Unfastening the belt, he stood up: 'Excuse me.'

'Oh, you're not feeling well. I thought you mightn't be. I'll let you out the minute I get this yoke open. You're not airsick, are you? There's a little bag in front of you, if you're short taken. Frig! I'm sorry, sorry to be holding you up.' She wrenched at the seat-belt.

'Don't apologize!'

It was that Irish thing: always saying 'sorry, sorry', some-how conveying a sense that the one who should be sorry was not them but you who had crossed some invisible, important, electrified line: 'Sorry, but do you realize that you're trespass-ing, breaking the law, charging in, committing adultery? Do you? No? Well, sorry, but you are!'

'Sorry,' said the old thing. 'Sorry.' Her grey, dishevelled head bobbed. She was flustered, clumsy and he had to lean across her to release the buckle. Her hands got in the way of his and he felt the loose, mobile slither of old skin.

Forging past her breakable knees, he crossed to the other side of the plane where he found a row of vacant seats. He sat here with a mild tremor of guilt at the snub he was delivering to the woman, who would guess that he had fled from her. He held on to this sensation. It was a screen, a thin membrane dividing off other memories and questionings which must not be let through.

Pressing the flight attendant's button, he ordered a double whiskey. He'd learned that trick in Ireland. Here's to – what? Numbness? Love? Resignation? Rage?

They'd brought him a copy of the *Irish Press*.

Not bothering to unfold it, he let his eye pause on the topmost item: a government notice fixing the retail price of bread.

In the case of batch bread and pan bread which is packed (whether sliced or not sliced) by the baker thereof in a covering or wrapping . . .

The punctilio soothed him. He imagined it coming down the centuries from Roman to Norman to British clerks who had then, with sly triumph, left it behind them in the ministries of Ireland.

> 24p. per loaf when sold in loaves of 1lb, 12oz, 3 drams, 14 grains (800 grammes), or loaves of pan bread joined together the total weight of which is 1lb, 12oz, 3 drams, 14 grains (800 grammes) . . .

He relished the dryness, the precision and the might of the pen. Grids, he thought restfully, guidelines – then shied from his approval, startled to remember that he was at this moment the victim of these old friends and props. Law-and-Order at its most arbitrary had smashed his hopes and certainties.

Outside the window, a cloud-formation made a stab at modelling Grainne's opulent ass. Then a sleeve of mist slid in along the wing and eroded his view. He ordered another drink and drank to oblivion. Love, had he not read somewhere, flourished where there were obstacles, sex where there were none? So, he drank to sex and, finding the prickly letter still crackling in his pocket, pulled it out and read it with as much irony as he could summon to dilute his pain.

Dear Therese,

I fear I have been less than sincere for all my scruples. Maybe because of them? I have led you to believe that I was not in love. I am. Hopelessly – and hopefully – and yet all the things I said are true. I *am* crazy, guilty, concerned about you, unsure how much *she* feels for me, aware of all the ingredients of this love – and yet I levitate. I feel a piercing joy. I could not, even from concern for you or for a certain idea I have sometimes cherished of myself, wish to be out of love. I would not have wanted to die without knowing this. I feel, at moments, so alive that I could stand to die on the spot.

Paradox? A sick man's delirium? Maybe I shall think so one day. Meanwhile, I am *in* it: right inside. It is the only reality of which I can conceive or in which I can at this moment believe.

A memory of what people think when they are not in the state in which I find myself makes me suspect that you may *not* rejoice with me and that I should apologize for writing to you like this. Maybe I should not tell you – now, when asking for a divorce – that I love you as I do. For I am *in* love, brimming with it and swimming with it and it colours all my feelings and relationships.

James, cheeks blazing as though he had a fever, rang for another drink. He stared a while at iridescent damp outside his window, then lifted the letter as though it weighed like lead. He sighed and read on:

When I say I am unsure what she feels I mean that I I am unsure whether she will really leave her husband for me. There is a strong bond there – just as you and I have had a strong bond – and both she and I are aware that this hurricane of emotion which has swept us up may not accommodate to time.

Even this is a lie. You see it is hard to communicate accurately since often we seem to be outside time and unable even to conceive of it. Some of the – bite my tongue – time, on occasion – how impossible these temporal adverbs are when what I want to describe is their absence – anyway, there are phases when we have no doubts and then, like a rip tide, they come roaring back. She has a son and social obligations here which means that she is returned regularly to a sense of the temporal and returns to me tainted with what she calls 'realism'.

Have I hurt you, Therese? What I wish I could do is share my joy with you. But it's impossible, isn't it? Love *is* possessive. I rebel against the impossibility and feel that if you too could climb over the barriers of everyday logic, then somehow we could all benefit from this source of warmth and happiness, as more than one or two people can share the heat of a fire. Mad? Or just unorthodox? Viable? Delirious?

At any rate, Therese, I beg you to know and believe that my impulse in writing what may be clumsy and hurtful letters is not to boast or hurt but to bring you into the orbit of this delight which I am experiencing. I know you are too generous to be resentful. I hope you feel, as I do, that *our* relationship is something too strong and fruitful to sour under the strain I am imposing on it. Love is not finite. Like energy, it is self-regenerating. Though I have given some elsewhere, I feel that now I have even more for you – though of a different kind.

So, love,
James.

Christ, thought James. What treacherous things words were! Feelings which floated, free as butterflies, could, pinned to the page, look so appalling! Could seem insincere, foolish, self-regarding. Yet, the feeling in the letter had been real. Was? Had been? It made him want to cry. It might make Therese want to cry too! Certain impulses should never be turned to words. They were of the flesh, fleshly.

Before he could let himself reflect, he began to shred his letter into his new, untouched double whiskey and water and to drink down this concoction. It stuck drily in his throat, then, slowly, with the sensation of over-large capsules of medicine being eased downwards, it did succumb to his swallow.

Across the aisle, the woman with the bad teeth looked at him in beady-eyed shock. James filled his mouth with some more of his wet letter and chewed at it furiously.

For some weeks, Patsy Flynn had been promising the Captain that he'd go over to the Michael O'Malleys' and put an appearance on the place. It was turning into an eyesore and if it was left up to the Michael O's themselves, the lawn would climb the house. Anyway, he'd finally got round to doing the chore this Saturday, and it was the divil's luck that he had for, from all appearances, there was something amiss.

The first thing to happen was that the Captain turned up with Mrs Michael. This was between nine and ten in the morning. Odd. Your woman had a small suitcase and looked as if she'd been crying. The two raced in the gate and up the front steps, leaving Patsy to wonder what *that* could be in aid of. He asked the skivvy when she brought him his bottle of Guinness at eleven: Mary. She said that the old aunt had been taken sick and that the Captain had gone off after the Missis and brought her back. Back from where? Mary wasn't saying. She didn't like Patsy, who had never had a way with women.

He decided to do a bit of weeding outside the drawing-room window. This turned out to be a good move. The old woman was inside and the Captain was asking her questions.

'Have you no recollection at all, Aunt Judith?' says he. 'Think now. About Owen. Think hard. What were you saying about him?'

'What would I be saying?' says the old hairpin. 'He's dead, isn't he? They tell me he's dead. Not that you can trust what people say.'

'What did *you* say?'

'Me? That he was dead. I'll be dead soon myself, and it's thinking of that I should be and praying for a happy death, instead of talking trash with idle-minded people.'

It was clear to Patsy that the old battle-axe had no time for the Captain. That was a rum turn when you thought that the Captain was known for being able to charm birds off trees.

'What did you say to the American?' asks the Captain.

'He's dead too, so what does it matter?'

'No, to the other one: the one with the recorder.'

'Do you mean Saint Michael?'

Patsy had to laugh, keeping his head down, stifling in the steaming flower-bed. He was getting a crick in his neck.

'Leave her alone,' says Mrs M in a cross voice. 'He's gone, isn't he? You'd think you'd be satisfied. You got rid of him.'

'He's got the tapes,' says the Captain.

'I'm surprised your men didn't take them.'

'They weren't on him. He may have given them to someone. Damn it,' says the Captain then, 'I want to know what she's been saying. It affects me. She's been spreading libels about my father.'

Oho, thought Patsy, cocking an ear. Father, was it?

'She has not,' says Mrs M. 'She said nothing. He came here for *me*, damn you, Owen Roe. For private reasons. Do you know the meaning of the word: *private* . . .' The voice creaked and strained with some strong feeling. Anger? Hysteria?

Patsy wondered where Cormac was and whether he knew what was afoot. The boy had been avoiding the club and had bolted from Patsy one time when they'd come face to face at the Captain's. Patsy's heart went out to him. It was shame. The harm women did! Mothers. His own Ma had been a cold creature, always looking at Patsy as though he were a cake that hadn't risen right.

'We were in love, Owen Roe,' shouted the mad woman inside the window.

Patsy kept well down over his weeds, pulling them out with venom. Weeds. Women. Concupiscence. Disorder. Pull. Up by the roots. Shake the earth off. Burn them in a heap. Smoke rose from the bonfire, stinging his eyes. He threw a stalk of Devil's Bread on it and the smell grew bitter. Queer how a wild plant like that could turn up in a suburban garden. The fire spurted out extra smoke. Through the drift of it he saw the Captain walk out of the door and down the path to his car. Mrs M was standing on the steps.

The Captain shouted back at her: 'It may turn out for the best.'

She was wearing a pink dressing-gown. She pulled it round her.

'I can deal with anything she may have said,' said the Captain, 'if only I know what it is before anyone else.'

Mrs M closed the door and Patsy – it was getting near lunch-time anyway – followed the Captain to his car.

'Is it the Yank?' Patsy asked, counting on surprise to breach the Captain's caginess.

'Patsy, you're nosy. A nosy Parker. What business is it of yours?'

'I'm concerned for yourself,' said Patsy. 'I'm not deaf.'

'Far from it,' agreed the Captain in a strong brogue. He threw this out like a rope thrown to bridge an abyss. Patsy had come on a lot of stories involving ropes and abysses, usually in wild and desperate parts of Africa. The Captain's efforts to bridge the gap between himself and Patsy made Patsy wonder if he thought there were wilds in *him*?

'Are things all right for you now?' he wanted to know.

'Right as rain,' assured the Captain. 'The Yank's gone. Between yourself and meself and the gatepost – and I would not want it to go further – he was given the push. More or less deported.' The Captain looked at his watch. 'He's on a plane that'll be landing in New York in a few hours' time.'

'Oh bedad,' said Patsy. 'A bad hat, was he? Trouble?'

'We can be glad to see the back of him.'

Patsy would have liked to know more but wouldn't ask. Now that the danger was gone, he couldn't pass off curiosity as a bodyguard's legitimate concern, especially as the Captain had moments of treating Patsy more as dogsbody than bodyguard. So the thing had been taken out of Patsy's hands then? Dealing with the Yank? Well, but his instincts had been proven right. The fellow was bad news. Patsy, feeling a letdown – he ached for action – made a show of silent discretion to see would this soften the Captain. But your man was preoccupied.

'I'm off,' says he, and into the car with him without slipping Patsy the price of a drink to celebrate the turn things had taken. Maybe he didn't quite believe in Patsy's devotion?

Patsy went round to Neary's pub to restore himself.

James blinked and dreamed of dolmens the colour of dolphins: streamlined, grey, suspended over Irish fields as though in flight or aswim. Blinked again and was awake and in suspense himself, wondering whether he should or could struggle with what seemed to be his fate. Reading, to take his mind off things, he got bogged down in 'Births, Marriages and Deaths', a bulky section of the *Irish Press*. Items one and two were in ample supply and there seemed to be a *cortège* of deeply regretted corpses *en route* to their resting-place in Dean's Grange Cemetery – so called, he wondered idly, after Swift, Dublin's mad Dean? There would be plenty of more recent lunatics choked on *saeva indignatio* to fertilize that ground anyway. The next column thanked donors for mass cards and seraphic certificates: religious currency on a scale unimagined by Martin Luther. Well, ashes to ashes, he was mourning to his whiskey, when he was jerked from his dirge of a mood by an announcement being garbled over the loudspeakers. He had missed the beginning. No cause for alarm, he heard now. Three engines were working perfectly but, in the interests of the passengers' safety, Captain Inaudible preferred to take every precaution. He regretted the inconvenience that this must cause to some passengers.

James waylaid a flight attendant. What was up? What was happening?

'We're turning back. There's no cause for alarm.'

'Turning . . . back?'

'Yes.'

'To Shannon?'

'No, I'm afraid there's fog over Shannon. We'll be landing in Dublin.'

'Will we be getting out of the plane?'

'Oh, I should think so. You see, the fourth engine . . .'

Fate, thought James. Now it was for him. Now he'd win. In love as in sport, being hot was everything. He'd persuade her now. He'd go right to the house, never mind who was there. She'd *have* to listen. If what had happened, fate's falter, the lucky slip that brings the cup *back* to careless lips, did not persuade her that it was her manifest destiny to run off with him, then *he* would. Quite simply, now, he knew he could.

'Could you bring me a large black coffee?' he asked the flight attendant. 'Please.' He needed to sober up.

Leaning his head back against the headrest, he occupied his mind with trying to recall in precise sequence the letter to Therese which he had swallowed with his double whiskey.

He was going to win this game in overtime.

By the time Patsy had finished his lunch-break he was depressed. An old bugger who had been standing him drinks had got him down. He turned out to have unacceptable political opinions which Patsy, having drunk three of his pints, didn't feel it would have been decent to dispute. But unvented arguments were stuck in his craw.

Morosely, he walked back to the O'Malleys' where he

began clipping the hedge. The drink had given him heartburn and he was vexed with himself for taking it on an empty stomach. If this had been any decent kind of a house, they'd have provided lunch. Irish hospitality how are ye! That bloody woman, he thought, and his rage mounted. That snake of a Yank. Deporting was too good for him. How had the Captain managed to do it? Patsy hadn't thought him that well in with the Powers-that-be. Well, there you had another case of things being kept from Patsy! Snip went the shears. Snip. He looked along the edge of the blade and there, on the other side of the road, getting out of a green Ford Cortina, was the Yank in person. Not deported at all then? Had the Captain lied? Been lied to? Maybe the Powers-that-be had laid a trap? And now here was Patsy, the Man in the Gap, unbriefed! The challenge exhilarated him. Be cool, Flynn, he directed himself. Maybe he should phone the Captain? But from where? He couldn't get into the house ahead of the Yank and the nearest phone-box was a quarter of a mile from here.

The Yank had reached the gate. Cool as you please, he passed Patsy without a nod. Snip, went the shears as Patsy folded and laid them aside. The Yank reached the front door and rang the bell. Patsy followed him up the steps.

'Can I be of assistance?'

The Yank looked down at him. 'No.'

Knew him? Didn't? Were all Irishmen as alike as potatoes to this fellow then? Micks? Paddies?

'There's nobody in,' said Patsy.

The door opened, giving him the lie. Cormac stood inside it. 'My mother's out,' he claimed. 'She doesn't want to see you.'

'Sorry, Cormac.' The Yank shoved his foot in the door. 'I'm coming in. I've got to. She doesn't know what she wants.'

Cormac attempted to slam it but the Yank's foot held. Patsy caught the fellow's elbow, trying to jerk him backwards but it was the elbow which jerked unexpectedly, catching Patsy's chin so that he staggered down two steps. By the time he had regained his footing the Yank was through the door and had slammed it behind him.

In futile protest, Patsy pressed the bell, then raced, blind with fury, round the house and into the kitchen where he nearly fell over a bucket and Mary on her knees beside it, scrubbing.

'What's up?' she goggled at him.

'The phone,' he hissed. 'Get the Captain. The Yank is back. Tell him: Duffy. Forced his way in. Used violence.'

'Duffy?' Her moron's face sought an expression. '*Misther* Duffy?' said she, the good indoor servant, stressing etiquette. 'Is it *Mister* Duffy you mean?'

Patsy grabbed the kitchen phone and rang the Captain's number, dialling three times from distrust for his own manual steadiness and for the Irish telephone system which was a shambles. There was nobody at the other end. He cast around for a weapon. That Yank was a big bruiser. Hesitating between a mallet and a meat-cleaver, he chose the cleaver, although he had a record and was squeamish. Might he have to deal with a rape? Elopement? Kidnapping? Or matters of political and public import? He rallied himself, being promoted and commissioned by the Captain's absence. Adrenalin ran high. He had been waiting for this moment for more than twenty years. Stalking his game, he slid through the hollow darkness of the basement hall. No sounds. Upstairs, a door opened. Patsy prowled upwards to ground level, then paused.

A spurty scream on the third floor located Mrs Michael and had the substance of flesh to it. Patsy *saw* it in his mind's eye, a leaping thing, quivery and perhaps clawed.

'Ohh!' She half purred, half screamed: '*Ohhh!*' As though her throat had flown out of her.

The Yank's voice was next to inaudible. 'I felt dead,' he was saying, 'numbed . . . *Would* you have given in?'

'Oh James,' she said, '*James!*' Carnal, the name became flesh in her mouth. 'Thank God,' she was moaning with an excitement which roused an odd response in Patsy, a sucker for strong feelings. His anger with her could be part-laced with sympathy. 'Oh!' she cried, 'no!' Her noises had an animal innocence which seemed to withdraw them from the strictures of the moral law. 'I couldn't have stood it,' she ululated. 'I couldn't just lose you like that.' There was a remnant of rage in her joy, he could tell, a mourning tinge which compounded his own bleak and tremulous fury.

'So we must . . .'

'Yes, yes . . .'

Their accents chinked and quivered. They sounded foreign to Patsy, like a radio play beamed in from abroad. He climbed to a small landing lavatory between the first and second floors and slipped inside. The voices came closer, ebbed, rose.

'Just that it suddenly seemed like fate.'

'But now it's reversed itself. Don't you *see*?'

Urgencies. Rummagings. A door banged.

'Shush! Aunt Judith's been in a state. Don't want to set her off.'

The interruptions were like the hops of a gramophone needle. He guessed the pair were walking in and out of doors on the floor above him, turning, descending, then retreating up the stairs.

'*Now!*'

'Oh, James, I . . .'

'. . . mentally locked into . . . In reality, you're free, don't you see? You must see.'

'I do. I do. Only we must keep our heads, think.'

'Not too much. Where's Cormac?'

'He ran out. I don't know. Owen Roe will be back though. Any minute. Listen, please, you've got to go. Hide. You'll be arrested. How did you get back?'

Patsy too would have liked to know that. He waited, fist clutched around the old-fashioned meat-cleaver. If that bugger tried to get her away, he'd pounce. Pow!, thought Patsy and, thinking, missed something.

'Has he a key? I'll bolt the front door.'

The Yank's voice was right outside the jakes where Patsy was hiding. The door handle moved. Was he coming in? Patsy raised his cleaver, but the chap must have been touching the knob idly and without intent for he had gone by. His next statement came from half a flight down. Patsy was torn between wanting to burst out and chase him and eagerness to first hear all he could. It was his duty to the Captain to find out the intruder's purposes: public or private. This, he argued with himself, was why he was waiting. But a langour gripped him too.

'I won't leave without you. Not again.'

Patsy's eye at the jakes keyhole could see nothing. He could hear though and what he heard was queer. The Yank had raced back up to the second floor from whence a chorus of stressful breathings reached Patsy in shreds and pauses. Sobs? Coughs? Sacred Heart tonight, the pair were *crying*. Their emotion locked into his own, maddeningly, like the pedal of someone's bike getting locked into yours. This upset Patsy – threw him off stroke. He was listening now – no point deceiving himself – with a kind of inquisitive frenzy. What they said was alien to him, yet comforted his ragged, unvented pain, as the hot throb of alcohol can comfort a sick body. Patsy's sickness was of the soul and chronic and here, consolingly, were a pair wrestling with something like it, clawing, like himself, after the next-to-impossible.

'I thought of death,' the Yank was saying. 'Really, I did. I thought how we waste . . . Darling, *listen*, we must be ruthless. It's now or never and . . .' More sobs. Or what were they? Could sexual congress be taking place up there this minute? For the first time in his life, Patsy felt an interest in that activity which he had thought of up to now as being irredeemably carnal. Yoked to the kind of feeling which was leaking through this house like gas, the act, Patsy had to admit, could be a way of escaping the mean limits of the self. He had heard this said, before now, but had had trouble comparing sex with prayer or song or patriotism or even alcohol, since his knowledge of it had been gleaned in farmyards and from watching stray dogs in alleys.

'. . . death . . .' the Yank said again. It was a word which always thrilled Patsy in a bleak but invigorating way. It was a gregarious word, for he thought of it not in terms of the lone grave but of the Day of Judgement which would be like a vast, exuberant political rally with all the old distinctions swept away and all mankind equal and fraternal, shoulder to shoulder, bone to bone. This picture was inspired partly by the *Dies Irae* and partly by the 'International': *Arise ye starvelings from your slumbers*. Patsy could mock his fancy while enjoying it. It thawed his ill-humour when it came to mind and could undermine stern resolution.

At the thought, wrath surged back. Why should he soften? Why? He had no business feeling sympathy with other people's yearnings. Certainly not with those of the pair above stairs. He was letting his soft heart take advantage of him and giving way to sentiment. It was intolerable: as if the beetle under your foot were to speak up with the news that it too had feelings. A beetle, a beetle! What right had that gurrier above to intrude in other people's cunts or countries? None, none. Patsy could have crowned him this minute, knocked his block off once and for all, yet durstn't show himself for the bugger was big and fit and would have to be taken by surprise. Patsy'd have to lie low another bit – and, oh Jesus, with that thought his claustrophobia started up. He could have screamed with tension, the jakes reminding him suddenly of gaol and being in solitary. Out he'd have to get. Out, out. He felt as if he'd been locked up already, nicked for the crime he hadn't yet committed: it was the story of his life. Hadn't the cops caught him red-handed the time he'd been sent to put bombs in post-boxes?

What was that? What was the pair up to now? Patsy leaned forward, ears straining but could not diagnose the noises reaching him.

Worrying the hasp of the jakes window, he wondered could he duck out that way? Someone had painted the thing closed and the wood was weak. Better not break it.

The voices up above were now like a dawn chorus. All twitters and trills. Again, he could only make out the odd scrap.

'. . . love me?'

'Yes, yes. I swear.'

There was a lot of movement. More laughs. Fornication was undoubtedly taking place.

'You see, I *can't* leave you. Not for a minute. You're not to be trusted.'

'No, no, I'll come. Really. Really, but meanwhile *you* must get out of here. Owen Roe mustn't find you.'

'But . . .'

'Really, you can trust me. I'll join you.'

'When?'

'Give me half – no, an hour to pack.'

'We'll take a plane to London, right? Now?'

'Yes, James, sh!'

More laughter. Silence. Kissing-time, guessed Patsy and wondered would the Captain be along in time to stop your woman. Surely he would, he persuaded himself. No need for violence. Best lie doggo and learn the couple's plans. Where were they meeting?

'An hour then . . . in the old place.'

And down the stairs with the fellow like a blooming yoyo. Where to? Where was their 'old place'?

'I love you.' A shout from below.

'I love you. Go, please.'

'You *will* come? No matter what? And bring your passport?'

'Yes. Yes. In an hour.'

Again the door closed, followed a minute later by the click of the garden gate. Then a car door slammed and the engine started up.

Patsy, his custodial purpose half-gone, groaned at the smelly confines of this place out of which he could not simply walk. Your woman would catch, scold and humiliate him. Envy gripped him for people who could actually walk out of their lives. Change and renew themselves. It was something so impossible for himself, that he had never till now thought to be jealous of those who could and did.

Under cover of the car's departing noise, he had, however, heaved a shoulder against the window-frame so that it shot open. Upstairs, Mrs M was running about. Doing her packing. Whore! Well, it wasn't too late to put a spoke in her wheel! It took minutes to ease his body out of the narrow window. Patsy wasn't a fat man but neither was he as agile as he had once been He had an hour. Should he have faced the Yank? He should, he should, but his stomach had failed him. It was the cleaver: a bloody instrument. Should have taken the mallet. The thing now was to get the Captain and the husband to put a stop to her gallop. Catch up with the other fellow, make up for Patsy s funk – *had* it been funk? What else? Hardly connivance, for Heaven's sake. He'd give the Captain a tinkle the minute he was out of here. There! He'd got clear of the window and was climbing down the side of the house. An espaliered pear tree which he had trained up the wall himself made a perfect ladder. Maybe his luck was on the turn? Poised to jump the last ten feet, he blinked as a flare of reflected sunset gleamed at him from the windscreen of a Ford Cortina parked on the opposite side of the canal. It had been driven right to the water's edge and was not thirty yards away. As Patsy watched, the side door opened and out came the Yank. He walked round the car to the boot, opened it and came back. He was holding a pair of binoculars which he raised to his eyes and trained on Patsy or at any rate on the house.

Watching for the other one's signal, was he? Through an open window, Patsy could hear *her* fussing about, singing a snatch of song, screeching at Mary, haranguing the old aunt. It would take her more than an hour to collect herself, he decided and jumped purposefully to the ground. His hatred of the Californicator was back in full force. While Patsy watched him, the fellow slid into the car and disappeared behind the red blaze on the windscreen.

Sister Judith was having one of her nightmares. She wished she could waken from it but, although she kept reminding herself that a nightmare was all it was, she could not break the envelope of sleep. In her dream, two men wearing suits of cloth so thick it could have been used for carpeting, were sitting on either side of her. She was in bed and they sat fencing her in. They flanked her like a bodyguard, but their intentions were not protective. One showed her his index fingers, threatening to stick them up her nose and tear her nostrils open. When she found that she could not shout, she knew that this really was a dream. However, the fear did not go away. Each man was wearing a hat and heavy boots. Everything about them was heavy and menacing. They were gangsters from some movie, she decided. She had seen them on television and now she was dreaming about them.

'Sister Judith,' said one, 'we want to ask you a few questions.'

He had an Irish accent. He had taken off his hat and his suit was less heavy than just now.

She wasn't dreaming at all, she realized, but she still couldn't scream. Then the scream came.

The girl ran in. 'What's the matter?' says she, as if butter wouldn't melt in her mouth. 'You were dreaming!' she accused. 'You dropped off.'

Sister Judith looked around her. There were no men. She wanted to ask 'Where are they?' but was wary and watched the girl slyly. This was the redhead, though they might use wigs. 'A dream,' she agreed, 'a bad one.'

'I'm sorry,' said the girl. 'Did Owen Roe upset you? He did, didn't he? He's a bully.'

Good cop, bad cop. Sister Judith knew the technique. She'd seen it on TV. 'You may think me a fool.'

'Nobody does, Aunt Judith.'

'Or mad or bad?'

'No.'

'Why were they grilling me so?' Grilling! That was the word. She was in command of her faculties, whatever some might think. She repeated it: 'Grilling!'

'I'm sorry. I'll get him to lay off.' The girl did look sorry. She looked as if she had been crying. In fact there were tears in her eyes. 'If I can,' she added.

She came over to Sister Judith's bed. 'Don't let them frighten you,' she said. 'There's really nothing they can do. Besides,' she said, 'it's all over now, anyway. Just tell Owen Roe that you said nothing.'

'Nothing?'

'Nothing.'

'About what?'

'Anything.' The girl laughed. 'Sorry, I'm light-headed,' she said. 'I'm happy.' She kissed Sister Judith quickly on the forehead. 'But it'll be all right,' she said. 'Really.'

The door-bell rang.

'Oh dear,' said the girl. 'That'll be Owen Roe. I'll try and head him off.'

She left the room and Sister Judith got out of bed. Her limbs were stiff and pictures from her dream just now were dirty in her mind. Like a stain, they oozed into the forefront of her thoughts and she had to keep rubbing her eyes and beating them back. There was that other dream too: about the chap on a couch. Shaking herself, she tried rotating her shoulders and walked towards the window. The one thing she liked about living in this place was the view. Especially at this hour. It was just after sunset. The last gleams of it were colouring the roofs on the far side of the canal. They caught on slates and skylights and trickled down the attic windows like jam. The lower parts of the houses were pale by contrast. The canal waters were paler still and on street level the long Irish twilight had an opaque, ashen melancholy to it, only faintly enlivened by the radiance around the street lamps which did not reach far, being contained by condensations of mist which clung like moth-swarms to each globe. The outer glow from one of these drew Sister Judith's attention to something happening on the opposite bank.

Patsy was approaching the Ford Cortina from the rear. The Yank – it was him all right – was sitting in the driver's seat, staring at the O'Malley house through whose front door the Captain had just been admitted.

Patsy hadn't managed to get through to *him*. He wondered whether he'd come back off his own bat or whether he'd been fetched by Cormac – unless, no – could Mrs M herself have rung him? Why would she? Whose side was that one on anyway? Like all women, she'd mix public and private. That Yank could be a blackmailer or a spy, a Special Branch or CIA man in love or pretending to be. They too must mate. What matter? The man was verminous. Hadn't Patsy himself started softening towards him back there in the house? And now look at him: on the watch, like a cat in the dusk. Had he accomplices? Where? And would he see Patsy creeping up on him through his rear-view mirror? Patsy, dodging and bent double, felt his feet slide on soft mud, and steadied himself against the car. As he did this, it lurched forward down the slope. The Yank, to get opposite the house, had driven through a gap in the chains separating road and tow-path and parked where the bank fell sheer as a chute towards the scummy waters of the canal. Patsy, almost before he knew it, had braced himself against a bollard and pushed harder.

In a side street, children were playing hopscotch under a street lamp. Sounds but not sights carried through the dusk.

'Out!'

''Tis not out.'

''Tis so.'

'Oh ya lying scut!'

With scarcely more sound than a wad of papers slithering from a shelf, the car gathered speed. The man inside heaved at his hand-brake, then tried to open the door. There was a smacking plop as the car tipped over the slick edge.

'Something's fallen into the canal. Do yez hear?'

'Stop trying to distract us. You moved her penny. Cissie seen you. It was in and you moved it. Cheat, cheat, cheat!'

Grainne was packing, throwing things into a suitcase, as she had seen people do in movies, then pulling them out again and folding them with care. What did she need? Nothing. She could just go. But Owen Roe was talking to Aunt Judith and she could not, somehow, bear to leave the house while that was going on. She had asked him to leave the old lady alone but he paid no attention to her. Just now the old thing had given one of her little screams and, when they rushed up to her room, was collapsed in her armchair, looking a bit like a beached fish. Her stomach was heaving and her face twitched on one side like a stroke victim's. However, that had righted itself and she had started in on one of her incoherent accounts of something which she claimed to have seen happen. They couldn't make out when.

'He's dead,' she said. 'Killed. I saw it.'

Owen Roe got very excited. 'Sh!' he told Grainne, his face flashing triumphant morse signs from behind Aunt Judith's back. This was it, he signalled. At last she was going to tell.

Grainne, who had been talking to her aunt earlier about nightmares, was less impressed.

'Don't torment her. Don't bully her,' she said, and went

into her own room to get on with her packing. Michael was probably out drinking and unlikely to come home before he was drunk. She wanted to be gone by then. She couldn't bear to have him see her go. But neither did she want to walk out of the door with a suitcase now, under the nose of Owen Roe. She put her passport and some money and a cheque-book into her handbag and thought that maybe that was all she need take. She went back to Aunt Judith's room. I can't protect her, she thought. I'm kidding myself. Love is egotistic. If I'm going, I'd better just go.

'He was trying to get out the window...' her aunt was saying. 'But it was sinking, you know, slowly, the way an empty bottle sinks, taking in water. And then this other fellow, on the bank, picked something up. A spade? Or an oar maybe?'

'Who? Who?' Owen Roe might have been an owl.

'I'm going out,' said Grainne. 'To look for Michael,' she lied.

But he was scarcely listening to her. 'When was this?' he kept asking Aunt Judith. 'When? Where?'

'I'll try the usual pubs.'

'He banged the hands of the chap who was trying to clamber out, you know? Banged them. Then the fellow tried to catch the oar or whatever it was but the fellow on the bank gave him a swipe on the head and that must have done for him because he sank like a stone. Car and all sank in the same minute. It was very quick at the end.'

'When? Where was it?'

'I said I'm going out,' said Grainne. 'Don't keep bothering her. Mary will be bringing her up her supper shortly.'

'It was just now,' said the old lady. 'Out by the canal.'

Owen Roe cranked his forehead. 'Bonkers!' he mouthed. 'Harmless. If Duffy got no more than that we needn't worry.'

Grainne wasn't listening. She had left her family mentally an hour before. 'Tell Cormac...' she began, but couldn't think what message to send. She caught a glimpse of her taut, feverish image glowing in a mirror. Her glance pierced back at her: the cruel face of love, she thought, and turned from it. The others had started talking again. She walked down the stairs, out of the front door and set off through the darkness, making for the nearest bridge.

Cormac had run all the way to his father's office-building and up the three flights of stairs. His great-uncle's house was too far and, besides, Uncle Owen Roe might not be there. Anyway – Cormac panted and felt his thoughts chopped at by the hatchet-catch in his breath – it was up to Daddy to see what he could do. He had to be given a chance.

'You told me to come to *you* if there was trouble,' Cormac had said, bursting into the Heraldry Commission office without knocking. 'Well . . .'

As they drove home along the canal, he smelled peppermint on his father's breath. Was this going to be any use, he wondered, and did it matter now anyway? His mother was behaving as people near *his* age were expected to behave: like young, excitable women played by actresses a couple of years older than himself. This discredited her as a mother but didn't make her feel close to him. How could it? She was just wrong, he thought furiously, wrong.

'Look!' he shouted. She had come out of the garden gate, latched it behind her and crossed the road. She hadn't got a suitcase, just her handbag. She was wearing boots and her fur coat.

'Maybe she's not going anywhere?'

'*Ask* her.'

Cormac was out of the car door before his father had turned off the engine. 'Mummy!'

She turned around.

'Daddy's here. Listen. You're not going away, are you?'

'Yes, Cormac. I am.'

'With him?' Cormac would not use the American's name. 'Yes.'

'Why?' He dared her to use the ridiculous excuse: love. To *him*! To his father. She couldn't, could she? No. It would be like trying to pay for goods at the corner shop with foreign coins. He knew she knew that and felt himself suddenly powerful. He mightn't manage to stop her but he could make her see that she was wrong. Her excuse was no excuse – and what other had she? Staring at her in a triumph of rightness, Cormac half expected her to crumple or go up in smoke like an exorcized person he'd seen in a horror film. The childish thought embarrassed him but only for a moment. Nobody knew of it and anyway it was she who had brought to mind the trashy world of cinema and silliness.

'Daddy!' Cormac nudged. His father was standing like a zombie. Why didn't he *do* something? Say something anyway? 'Ask her if she's just going to run out on us.'

'I'm sorry,' said Cormac's mother. 'Truly. But it'll be better if I go. I've messed things up here. Anyway, it is what I want.'

'What about Daddy?' Cormac's voice was embarrassingly shrill and shaky. 'What about me? And Aunt Judith? You can't just leave us.'

'You'll manage,' she said. 'Nobody's indispensable.' She looked, Cormac thought, grim and not beautiful, not justified by her beauty, as film stars were. She wasn't a star but the sort of woman who got supporting roles and should devote herself to playing them properly. Her hair was wispy.

'Daddy!'

'It's no good, Cormac. She has to go.'

'Goodbye, Michael – Cormac.'

She gave them a quiver of a smile, then turned and walked away up the tow-path towards the bridge.

They stood watching as she crossed this and started walking back towards them on the opposite side of the canal. She seemed to be looking for someone and her boots made a clumping movement through the mud.

'Come on.' Cormac's father took his arm. 'Let's go inside.'